T0359694

WESTERN

Rugged men looking for love...

The Maverick's Marriage Deal
Kaylie Newell

The Rancher's Secret Crush
Cari Lynn Webb

MILLS & BOON

Kaylie Newell is acknowledged as the author of this work
THE MAVERICK'S MARRIAGE DEAL
© 2024 by Harlequin Enterprises ULC   First Published 2024
Philippine Copyright 2024   First Australian Paperback Edition 2024
Australian Copyright 2024   ISBN 978 1 038 90577 2
New Zealand Copyright 2024

THE RANCHER'S SECRET CRUSH
© 2024 by Cari Lynn Webb   First Published 2024
Philippine Copyright 2024   First Australian Paperback Edition 2024
Australian Copyright 2024   ISBN 978 1 038 90577 2
New Zealand Copyright 2024

MIX
Paper | Supporting
responsible forestry
FSC   www.fsc.org   FSC® C001695

Published by
Harlequin Mills & Boon
An imprint of Harlequin Enterprises (Australia) Pty Limited
(ABN 47 001 180 918), a subsidiary of HarperCollins
Publishers Australia Pty Limited
(ABN 36 009 913 517)
Level 19, 201 Elizabeth Street
SYDNEY NSW 2000 AUSTRALIA

Cover art used by arrangement with Harlequin Books S.A.. All rights reserved.

Printed and bound in Australia by McPherson's Printing Group

The Maverick's Marriage Deal

Kaylie Newell

MILLS & BOON

For **Kaylie Newell**, storytelling is in the blood. Growing up the daughter of two writers, she knew eventually she'd want to follow in their footsteps. She's now the proud author of over twenty books, including the RITA® Award finalists *Christmas at the Graff* and *Tanner's Promise*.

Kaylie lives in Southern Oregon with her husband, two daughters, a blind Doberman and two indifferent cats. Visit Kaylie at Facebook.com/kaylienewell.

Dear Reader,

When my editor offered me the chance to write a Montana Mavericks book (my very first!), I was so excited that I barely slept that night. I grew up reading Harlequin books, and the Montana Mavericks continuity is a beloved classic.

I'm so honoured to be able to tell you Shep Dalton and Rylee Parker's story, which is about two childhood friends finding each other again years later. The spark they shared as kids will ignite into a romance that neither one of them can deny. But when they revisit a promise made in their teen years, it's not just their love that will hang in the balance—their future together will, too.

I hope you enjoy this trip to Montana, where the romance is as big and beautiful as the sky overhead! And for more information about me, my books and for the occasional fun giveaway, follow me at Facebook.com/kaylienewell.

Happy reading!

Kaylie Newell

DEDICATION

For Matt. Happy twenty-five years. I love you.

CHAPTER ONE

SHEP DALTON HELD the small present in his hand and glanced around. The room was packed. Actually, packed was an understatement. Everywhere he looked there were people—drinks in their hands, laughing and talking underneath balloons and streamers and two giant disco balls that tossed chaotic twinkles of light over them like confetti. Over the top, but not surprising. His old high-school classmate Janet Halstead, the birthday girl, was one of the first of his friends to turn thirty, and Janet had always leaned toward being a little extra. So, disco balls? Absolutely.

Shep didn't mind though. This party had gotten him away from the ranch in Bronco on the very same day they were worming and inoculating the cattle, which meant he was in a good mood. In fact, he was ready for a beer or two.

Adjusting his Stetson over his eyes, he scanned the room for the gift table. He needed to deposit this thing and find Janet and her husband, Frank, to say hello. He hadn't seen her since she'd moved to Wonderstone Ridge. Frank was well-off and had connections, which was why he'd been able to rent this place out for the party. The Wonderstone Ridge Indoor Theme Park and Aquarium. Quite a mouthful, but it was quite a place. It had been under construction for a while and hadn't even officially opened yet, so this event was a big deal. The entire county had been wanting to get a look inside for months. Now, thanks to Janet, her friends and family, at least, were getting their wish.

Narrowing his eyes, he spotted what looked like the gift table not too far from a floor-to-ceiling aquarium full of tropical fish. The table was overflowing, of course, and topped with a fancy-looking, three-tiered cake.

Muttering his apologies and touching the brim of his Stetson, he brushed past a group of twentysomething women drinking champagne and giggling at who knew what.

"Don't be sorry, cowboy," a pretty brunette said, giving him a wink as he walked by. "I'm not."

Shep smiled but didn't stop. She was wearing a huge rock on her ring finger that was hard to miss. In fact, most of the people here seemed to have shown up with their better halves. He guessed that was what happened when you were nearing thirty. Marriage, kids, a house with a white picket fence that was mortgaged to the hilt. Maybe that was generalizing, but it sure seemed accurate from where he stood. And all of a sudden, he felt like a damn fish out of water surrounded by all these happy couples.

"Shep Dalton? Is that you?"

Looking up, he saw Janet making her way toward him, weaving gracefully in between her guests. She wore a silver sequined dress that sparkled and flashed, and was giving the disco balls above her a run for their money.

He grinned. It was good to see her. He'd always liked Janet, who was obviously living the dream, complete with three adorable kids. At least, according to her Facebook pictures.

"I was hoping you'd come," she said, standing on her tiptoes to kiss him on the cheek. "But I know how hard it is to tear you away from that ranch."

"Happy birthday, Janet. I wouldn't have missed it."

"It's been a long time." She pulled away and smiled, rubbing her lipstick from his jaw. "Handsome as ever, I see. When are you going to settle down with some lucky lady?"

A distinctive warmth crept up his neck. *Here we go.* What was so wrong with being single, anyway? Janet sounded exactly like his mother, who couldn't wait to marry him off, just like his brothers. Still, even as he thought it, he remembered a promise he'd made years ago. And remembered the girl he'd made it to as well.

He cleared his throat. "This is a good turnout. You always knew how to throw a party."

She laughed, looking around. "Yes, well. A lot of these people are Frank's business associates, so I don't even know them that well. He saw an excuse to schmooze and took it. But some friends from high school came, so that makes me happy."

"Oh yeah?" A waiter walked by with a tray of champagne glasses, and Shep grabbed one with a nod. He'd never been much for champagne, but when in Rome… He took a sip, the bubbles fizzing on his tongue. "Who showed up from high school?"

"Oh, my old cheerleading friends. Anna Delgado from the drama club—remember her? She moved away from Tenacity about the same time I did. She lives up north and just had a baby." Janet tapped her lips with a manicured index finger. "Who else… *Oh!* Rylee Parker is here. You should be happy about that. You two were thick as thieves."

Shep had been taking another sip of champagne, but at the sound of Rylee's name, he swallowed with some difficulty.

"Rylee's here?" he managed.

"She was over by the aquarium, the last I saw her." Janet gazed up at him. "You know, I was always kind of surprised you two didn't end up together. You would've made a cute couple."

Shep's gut tightened at that. Nobody in his small hometown of Tenacity had known how he'd felt about Rylee back then. Least of all Rylee. But Janet was right about one thing—they *had* been thick as thieves. Which probably wasn't the right way to put it because the most trouble they'd ever gotten into was skipping class to go swimming in the river every now and then. And he'd had to twist her arm to do that. Rylee had always been a little shy, a great student, definitely a rule follower. Despite Shep trying to corrupt her in the best way possible.

Thinking about her now, he felt his lips stretch into a smile. He winked down at Janet, wanting to keep her guessing. Maybe this party was going to be more interesting than he'd thought.

"You never know, Janet," he said.

Her delicate eyebrows rose at that. "Well, what—"

She didn't finish her sentence because an older woman appeared out of nowhere and tapped her on the shoulder.

"Janet, honey, the caterer has a question about the crab cakes. I wasn't sure what to tell her."

"Oh, thank you, Linda. I'll be right there." She turned to Shep again and pointed to his chest. "Don't think we're done with this conversation, mister."

He nodded. Then watched her make her way toward the presumed crab cake problem as the thumping music overhead changed to something softer.

Looking down at the drink in his hand, he frowned. So, he was going to see Rylee again. With her auburn hair and those beautiful blue eyes. He imagined her on the banks of the river all those years ago, the water droplets on her shoulders sparkling like diamonds. He'd felt so protective of her back then. She was too good for him. Too good for anyone, as far as he was concerned.

Nope. Champagne wasn't going to cut it. He definitely needed a beer.

RYLEE TOOK A sip of her champagne and wrinkled her nose. She hated champagne. It always gave her heartburn. But that was Rylee in a nutshell. Not exactly super comfortable at parties like this.

Actually, scratch that. She didn't *used* to be comfortable at parties like this. But that was before. Before she'd grown into a confident, capable, educated woman with an MBA who also happened to be the recently named director of marketing for the Bronco Convention Center.

She swallowed hard. If she had to repeat it over and over again, that's exactly what she'd do. Even though her days of being the shy, studious type were long behind her now, that little girl tried to resurface sometimes, which was inconvenient at best.

Gazing at the colorful fish making circles in the aquarium, she took a deep breath. She'd stay until Janet cut her cake, and then she'd head home. Aside from a few high-school acquaintances, she really didn't know anyone here, and there was a pint of Ben & Jerry's mint chocolate-chip ice cream with her name on it back at her apartment.

She took another sip of champagne, not letting herself think too much about the fact that leaving a party to go chow down on ice cream at home was *exactly* what a shy, studious type would do.

"Well, if it isn't my old swimming buddy…"

Startled, she turned at the sound of the gravelly voice behind her.

And then she stood there, unable to say anything at all. Her heart beat like a drum as she stared up at the handsome cowboy in the red plaid shirt a few feet away. He was grinning at her. A familiar, mischievous sparkle in his blue eyes.

Shep Dalton...

She could hardly believe it. It had been so long since she'd seen him that she had to blink to make sure she wasn't imagining this. Of course, she shouldn't be surprised. He'd been friends with Janet, too. And thanks to the local grapevine, she knew he lived in Bronco as well. His family had moved a few years ago after his father had gotten lucky at the slots in Las Vegas. They now owned a sprawling ranch in Bronco Heights called Dalton's Grange.

Still, she'd never run into him in town, even though she'd expected to these last few years.

She felt her lips tilt into a smile, warmth spreading across her chest. It was the way he was looking at her. It was the same way he'd looked at her in high school—like she was different from all the other girls. At least, that was how he'd always made her feel. Not that Shep would be remotely interested in someone like her. Rylee knew that without a doubt. He was much too spirited and adventurous. He always had been.

"Shep?" she managed.

"The one and only."

He stepped forward and wrapped her in a bear hug. Then lifted her completely off the ground until she laughed breathlessly.

Setting her down again, he pushed his off-white Stetson up on his forehead and grinned down at her.

"It's been a long time, Rylee," he said. "I don't think I would've recognized you if Janet hadn't told me you were here."

She touched her hair. "Do I look that different?"

"Just more mature," he said. "That's all. But still pretty as a picture."

Her cheeks heated. She'd always nursed a terrible crush on Shep for this exact reason.

"You're still a charmer, Shep."

He leaned against the wall and put his hands in his jeans pockets. His shirt stretched over his broad shoulders, and it wasn't too hard to imagine what he looked like without it. Shep was a rancher, after all, and his body was long and lean. Muscular from working long hours outdoors.

Rylee's throat felt dry all of a sudden, and she shifted on her feet. She could still smell his scent from when he'd wrapped her in his arms a minute ago. Musky, leathery. Very, very male.

"So," he said. "Tell me everything. What have you been up to? I haven't seen you since you left for college. That's a long time to be going to the river by myself."

She smiled. "I don't believe for one second that you've been too lonely without me."

"Maybe, maybe not. But you were always my favorite swimming partner. Nobody ever came close after you left."

She leaned against the wall, too, watching him. It wasn't difficult to watch Shep Dalton. He was fairly easy on the eyes. He looked pretty much the same as the last time she'd seen him, that day she'd come to say goodbye before leaving Tenacity for college. Except his face was a little more weathered now. There were sexy crinkles around his eyes, and his skin was a deep, golden tan—another nice result of working outside all day.

"I heard you'd moved to Bronco," she said. "I've been meaning to look you up, but you know. Work, life… I'm always so busy."

"What do you do?"

"Chuck Carter recently promoted me to the marketing director for the Bronco Convention Center."

He raised his eyebrows. "Impressive."

"Well, since Geoff Burris and the Hawkins Sisters are such big rodeo stars, there are a lot more opportunities now to expand." She smiled. "What about you? Still working the ranch?"

He nodded. "Yes, ma'am, and the last of my brothers to get married or engaged. Much to my mother's dismay."

"She's trying to get you to settle down?"

"They're *all* trying to get me to settle down. I mean, is it just me, or is it some kind of law around here to be married by thirty?"

At that, her heartbeat slowed a little. Twelve years might've passed since she'd seen her old childhood friend and crush, but she remembered their promise like it had been made yesterday. *If we're not married by the time we're thirty...*

She took another sip of champagne. Either it was starting to make her dizzy or Shep was.

He smiled slowly, gazing down at her. "You remember, don't you?"

"Remember what?"

"You know what."

"I have no idea what you're talking about."

"Liar."

She laughed, unable to help it. "Shep, that was a long time ago."

"It was, but I'm not married. And I haven't heard you mention a significant other, either."

"So?"

"*So*... A promise is a promise."

She sipped her champagne again. Definitely dizzy. "Let's change the subject."

"To what?"

She looked around, desperate for something else to talk about other than their promise to marry each other by the time they turned thirty. Never mind that she was twenty-nine now. And three-quarters.

She supposed she didn't want to talk about it because it hit too close to home. When they'd made that vow, Shep might've made it lightheartedly, but she hadn't. The thought of marrying him back then had warmed her blood, and then some.

"Janet's probably getting ready to cut her cake," she said awkwardly. "And open her presents. I got her a cof-feemaker..."

He nodded, looking amused. She couldn't blame him. It wasn't exactly a smooth transition.

"What did you get her?" she asked, plowing on, feeling her face burn.

"A necklace."

"A necklace?" *Oh dear.* Her coffeemaker was going to pale in comparison. "What kind of necklace?"

"A strand of pearls. They reminded me of something Janet would wear. I picked them up at a vintage store in Bronco."

Rylee nodded, chewing her bottom lip. Something about that nagged at her, but she didn't know why. *A strand of pearls...* And then it hit her. The mayor had bought his wife a strand of pearls for their thirtieth anniversary back in January and infamously, it had disappeared right after. She remembered the description that went out locally, along with a press release begging for them to be returned. In fact, she still had a picture of the pearls on her phone.

She fished it out of her purse and pulled the photo up while Shep watched curiously.

"Do you remember that necklace of Mayor Smith's that

went missing a few months ago?" she asked. "He put an ad in the newspaper and on the radio station, asking for people to keep an eye out?"

"Vaguely. Why?"

She held the picture up and showed him. "Does the necklace you bought Janet look anything like this?" The pearls had a delicate gold clasp with a tiny rose embossed on it. A sweet touch, and something that would set it apart from other necklaces, but only if you were looking hard enough.

Frowning, he studied the enlarged image. "Actually... that looks exactly like it."

"Oh no. If it's the same one, someone could've stolen it and then pawned it."

"Great." Shep craned his neck to look across the room. "It's the same. I'm sure of it. And I just put it on the gift table. We should go snatch it back before anyone notices. I can't give her a stolen necklace."

Rylee's pulse skipped in her wrist. "Poor Janet. We have to steal her present back?"

"Before anyone notices. Are you up for it?"

Shep's eyes sparkled. She recognized that look. This was exactly the kind of thing the two of them would've done all those years ago. Dared each other on a whim. And then they'd dissolve into ridiculous fits of laughter afterward.

"Come on," he said. "The mayor will be thrilled."

"His wife will be, too."

"Janet, not so much."

"But what she doesn't know won't hurt her, so..."

"That's what I'm thinking," Shep said. "What do you say, partner?"

Rylee looked around quickly, feeling seventeen again. Apparently, this was what Shep was going to do to her.

Make her feel like a teenager again. With all the wild emotions that went along with it.

He reached out and took her hand. Heat immediately shot up her arm and into her heart. His grip was warm and solid, making her feel safe, just like it used to. Like all her insecurities were nonexistent, and it was just the two of them against the world.

"Stick close," he said. "I'll make sure nobody sees."

SHEP LED RYLEE through the crowded room, holding her hand firmly in his. It felt good holding her hand, familiar and natural. He remembered holding it years ago, when they'd jump off their favorite rock into their secret swimming hole in the river. Back then, he'd been able to talk Rylee into almost anything. But he'd never put her in jeopardy, ever. He'd cared too much about her for that.

He looked over his shoulder now, struck again by how lovely she was in her dark-wash jeans and sparkly pink sweater. She'd only gotten lovelier over the years, something he wouldn't have thought possible before. He'd found himself wanting to tell her that a few minutes ago when they'd been talking by the aquarium, but he'd stopped himself twice. He didn't know what was wrong with him. He normally wasn't so starstruck by women. In fact, they were usually the ones affected by him—or so he'd been told. But Rylee... Rylee had always been different. Special. But he didn't need to go embarrassing himself now by gushing about how good it was to see her again.

Instead, he squeezed her hand as they weaved their way toward the gift table. He could hardly believe the necklace he'd bought for Janet had ended up being stolen property. Definitely a bad look to be giving it as a present. Thank God Rylee had said something in time.

She pressed herself against him, her body warm against

his back. "Who's going to be doing the swiping?" she whisper-yelled. He could barely hear her over the music overhead. "You or me?"

He turned to her, leaning close. He could smell her perfume, something flowery and sweet. "One of us will have to swipe. The other one has to be the lookout."

"I don't want to be the swiper. I'll be the lookout."

"Fair enough."

"I think we need a backup plan in case someone sees us."

"We'll just say I forgot to put the card with it or something," he said. "That's believable."

"Talk about a mission impossible."

"Maybe not impossible. But definitely a mission awkward."

She laughed, like she might be enjoying this a little. Which wasn't so weird, because he was, too. He'd had a few beers by now, which were definitely making him less inhibited than he would've been otherwise. He rubbed his thumb along the back of her hand, struck by how soft her skin was. Like satin.

"You ready?" he asked. "I'm counting on the lights from the disco balls distracting everyone."

She laughed again. He'd been right. She was clearly enjoying this, which made his gut tighten.

"I'm ready."

"Okay," he said. "Cover me."

He made his way to the gift table, hoping he looked inconspicuous enough. If anyone did see him swiping the present, he'd have to explain, and the thought of that made him cringe.

He sneaked a glance at Rylee, and she gave a quick thumbs-up. Apparently, the coast was clear. It was now or never.

Looking back at the gift table, which was significantly fuller now than when he'd left it earlier, he spotted the little box next to a few brightly colored gift bags. Maybe this would be easier than he'd thought. All he had to do was sidle up to it and snatch it back with nobody seeing.

Slowly, he stepped up to the table and took a deep breath. But when he looked over at Rylee again, she suddenly shook her head.

"Can you believe all those presents?"

Shep turned to see an older man standing there holding a glass of wine and looking a little unsteady on his feet. The lights from the disco balls flashed on his bald head.

Shep smiled. Probably too widely. He'd almost been caught in the act.

"Right?" he said. He could feel Rylee watching from across the room. "A lot of presents, for sure."

"Once my wife gets a load of this," the other man said with a hiccup, "she'll want a party like this next year. Who can afford it? Renting out an entire aquarium?" He shook his head, as if he'd been waiting to get this off his chest since walking through the door.

Shep nodded and watched as the man finally meandered off.

He looked back at Rylee, who gave him another thumbs-up. Before he could second-guess himself, he stepped close to the gift table again, grabbed the present and shoved it behind his back. Probably looking guilty as sin, but whatever. At least he'd gotten it back.

Grinning widely, Rylee motioned him over.

"Can you put it in your purse?" he asked, walking up to her. "Otherwise, it'll have to go down the back of my jeans, and that's just wrong."

She laughed. "Sure. I'll take it back to the mayor this week. He'll be so happy."

"Mission accomplished, partner."

"We do make good partners, don't we?"

"We absolutely do."

"It makes me think of when we were kids…" She let her voice trail off and looked away, as if suddenly embarrassed.

"What's wrong?"

"Nothing. It just brings up old memories. It wasn't always easy growing up in Tenacity, was it?"

He frowned. That was the understatement of the century. Tenacity was a blue-collar town. Full of hardworking people, ranchers mostly, who barely scraped by. Shep's home life had been hard: his parents' marriage was rocky; his dad cheated… And Rylee's childhood had been difficult sometimes, too. A surprise baby and the youngest sibling of three older brothers, she'd felt lonely and isolated growing up. She'd always been close with her mom, but her dad had been strict and stubborn, and not always the easiest to get along with.

As neighbors, he and Rylee had been close because they'd had so much in common. Mainly wanting to leave Tenacity for greener pastures as soon as they could manage it. She and Shep had both gone to college, but he'd stayed local. Rylee had gone out of state, excelling in her university classes, just like she'd excelled in high school.

And now, here she was. Very grown, very beautiful, obviously a success. She'd made something of herself, just like he'd known she would. Yet he could still see traces of that girl underneath. A little shy, a little sad. It was hard shaking your past. He should know. He'd been trying to shake his for years. Trying to wiggle out from underneath his father's questionable shadow. Attempting to convince folks in Bronco that his family was more than just their "new money." But that was how everyone always treated them. They hadn't exactly been welcomed to town with open arms.

Suddenly, that sweet, vulnerable look on Rylee's face made him want to wrap her in his arms. More than that, it made him want to kiss her.

She gazed up at him, her eyes impossibly wide and dark. Maybe it was the beer, but he didn't think so. There was more going on here than just the alcohol flowing through his veins. There was a distinctive heat growing between them that was hard to deny.

Her gaze dropped to his mouth. And then, before he could think about it, he leaned down and pressed his lips to hers.

CHAPTER TWO

RYLEE THOUGHT HER knees were going to give out. Or her heart. She could hardly believe that Shep was kissing her, and more than that, she was kissing him back. Eagerly.

All thoughts of whether or not people would see (which, of course they would, since she and Shep were standing in the middle of the room) entered her mind fleetingly and then left like a sigh on the breeze. Right then, she simply didn't care. She just wanted him closer. To be kissing him longer, deeper.

He wrapped a strong arm around her waist and pulled her close. His body was solid and lean, warm against hers. His lips were soft, but insistent. His scent, that musky, leathery scent that she'd caught earlier when he'd hugged her, enveloped her senses and made her stomach curl into a tight little ball. She'd imagined kissing Shep plenty when she was a teenager, but never in her wildest dreams had she known it would be this good. That *he* would be this good.

From somewhere distant, she realized that people were clapping. And whistling.

Her eyes fluttered open at the sound.

Slowly, Shep broke the kiss. Then pulled away and looked around.

Sure enough, there was a half circle of people standing there smiling at them. Obviously happy to see a young couple in love. Or what they thought was a young couple in love.

Rylee touched her tingling lips, her face flushed.

Shep cleared his throat. "Just giving my new fiancée a kiss," he told the crowd with a wink.

Rylee gaped up at him as a collective *aww* moved through the room.

"What are you *doing*?" she whispered.

He leaned close to her ear. "Having some fun. Everyone else here seems to be married or engaged. Why shouldn't we?"

"Nobody's going to believe we're actually engaged, Shep."

"Why not?"

"For one thing, I'm not your type. Clearly."

"Isn't that the other way around?"

She stared up at him. Before she could answer that, a woman walked up and patted Rylee on the shoulder.

"Well, congratulations, you two," she said.

Shep beamed at her. "Thank you."

"Uh…thank you?" Rylee said. Shep had come up with some wild ideas when they were kids, but this took the cake. *Engaged?*

Still, even at that thought, she couldn't deny the warm feeling spreading through her body as he rested his hand on her lower back. Protectively. A little possessively, and what woman in her right mind wouldn't want to be possessed by Shep Dalton?

When they were alone again, Rylee turned to face him square on. His cowboy hat bathed his face in shadow. He looked like a rugged hero out of an old Western.

"What do you think you're doing?" she asked, planting her hands on her hips.

"I'm sorry. I should've asked before I kissed you. That would've been the gentlemanly thing to do."

"Well, I kissed you right back. But that's not what I'm talking about."

He smiled, two long dimples cutting into each scruffy cheek.

"Shep…"

"Okay," he said. "I'll admit I got caught up in the moment. This party, everyone here. All our friends and family getting married, and there's so much pressure to do the same. But honestly, what can it hurt? We just play along for the night, and we get to see what all the fuss is about."

She shook her head, but the look on his face, that playful, youthful look, was so familiar that she could feel it whittling away at all her sensible excuses.

"Aren't you just a *little* tempted to play along?" he asked.

He had to know she was. Her heart had swelled to twice its size when that nice lady had walked up to congratulate them just now. And when everyone had clapped at their kiss? She'd loved that feeling, too. Happiness. Pride. Excitement. All of it. It was *very* tempting to pretend that she was Shep's fiancée. At least for a few harmless hours.

"Maybe a little," she said, looking down at her shoes.

He touched her chin with his fingertips, until she looked up at him again.

"A little?"

"Okay. I'm tempted."

He smiled. "Fun, right?"

She smiled, too. They'd always had fun together. Climbing trees, swimming in the river, riding their bikes. And the trouble they'd gotten into? It had sustained her when she'd felt the loneliest of her whole life. Shep had a way of making her feel vibrant and colorful. Adventurous and spirited, just like he was. He'd always rubbed off on her, and he was rubbing off on her now. Not such a terrible thing, when she thought about it. There were worse things than feeling vibrant and colorful.

"Fun," she said.

And meant it.

"I GUESS I had more to drink than I thought," Rylee said, touching her temple.

They were standing in the small motel lobby, waiting for the front desk lady to run Shep's card.

"I know," he said. "Me, too. Staying the night is definitely the right call. We can't drive back to Bronco like this."

It was true, they couldn't. But he also wasn't hating the idea of spending the night with Rylee, either. Even if they'd gotten the last room available, and it only had one bed, which meant he'd be sleeping on the sofa.

That was okay. He simply wasn't ready for the night to be over with yet. Pretending to be engaged to Rylee had proven even more entertaining than he'd thought. They'd spent the rest of their time at the party dancing, laughing and getting hearty congratulations from Janet's guests. Not to mention having a few more drinks, which had eventually landed them here. The Mountain Summit Motel, which was right across the street from the aquarium. A good thing, since Shep's head was way too fuzzy to drive.

He smiled down at the lady checking them in, and she smiled back, handing him the key card and telling them where the ice machine was.

"Y'all have a good evening," she said.

Shep nodded and followed Rylee out the door into the early April night. Stars sparkled overhead, and the air was chilly against his skin. He could hear semis passing on the highway at the edge of town, but beyond that, the shadowy mountains loomed in the distance, where he knew the Montana evening would be alive with the sounds of nature.

Rylee looked up at the stars, her silky hair falling past her shoulders.

"Can you believe how many of them there are?" she said.

He looked up, too. "I know. It makes you feel small, doesn't it?"

"It really does."

"Did you miss Montana?" he asked, turning to her again. "When you left for college?"

She smiled, her lips looking soft and painfully kissable. "California is great," she said. "And it'll always have a special place in my heart, but yes. I missed Montana."

"I used to think about leaving, too," he said after a minute. "But when Dad bought the ranch in Bronco, he talked my brothers and me into coming to work it. We didn't want to. But my mom had just had a heart attack, so we wanted to make her happy…"

Rylee frowned, gazing up at him. "Oh no. Is she okay?"

"She's okay now, but it was touch and go for a while there. It forced some perspective on all of us. Especially my dad. You know how rocky their marriage was…"

"I remember."

"But they've worked things out. I think it helped that we stayed together as a family. Dalton's Grange has kept us close."

"I'm sure you're right."

He shrugged. "So, here I am. I'll probably always be a rancher, and that's okay. It's in my blood. But sometimes I wonder what it would've been like to leave. Like you did."

"But I came back…"

"That you did."

They began walking down the motel's breezeway, toward their room at the end. A peaceful silence settled between them, and Shep had to work not to put his arm around her. Despite having kissed her like a teenage boy tonight, and pretending that they were engaged to boot, they actually weren't even a couple. In fact, there was a reason why Shep hadn't settled down like his brothers. He'd never taken relationships seriously. And to be completely honest, calling them relationships was generous. Shep had flings. Flings with the same type of women over and over again—pretty women, women who were more interested in landing themselves a wealthy cowboy than anything else.

Up until this point, they were exactly his type though, because they hadn't required anything more from him than some charm on dates and some skill in bed. He'd been able to protect himself from falling for anyone, because there'd never been anyone worth falling for.

But here, now, walking with Rylee underneath the lights of the motel breezeway, there was a sudden desire for more. He had no idea what *more* meant, but the feeling was definitely there. Something that was trying to fill some kind of emptiness inside him.

Whatever this was that he and Rylee had going right now, it was delicate, and he didn't want to mess it up by kissing her again or making her feel uncomfortable whatsoever. Which meant keeping his hands to himself. And absolutely keeping his lips to himself.

"I think this is us," she said, pointing to the last door on their right.

He pulled the key card from his back pocket and unlocked the door. Flipping on the light, he looked around. The room was small, clean, simple. But just like the front-desk lady had said, there was only one bed. A queen with a print of a mountain lake over the headboard.

Rylee looked over at him.

"It's okay," he said. "I'll take the couch."

"It's too small, you'll never fit."

"I've slept on worse."

"Shep..."

"The couch it is."

She tossed her purse on the bed. "Well. You're a gentleman."

"Don't let it get around."

"I'm exhausted," she said, stifling a yawn.

"Me, too. I'm not used to dancing like that."

"I haven't danced like that *ever*. But it was fun, right?"

"It was fun."

He smiled at her, and she smiled back. For a minute, they were quiet, just looking at each other. Shep's chest tightened as his gaze dropped to her mouth. That *very* kissable mouth, and he had to force himself to look away before he said something, or did something, to embarrass himself. He was still buzzed and didn't trust his own judgment. At all.

"I don't suppose we're going to talk about that kiss," she said, sinking down on the bed and taking off her shoes. "I mean, we probably should, right?"

He walked over and sat on the couch, bouncing on it a few times to test it out. It was lumpy, but he'd live. His biggest problem was going to be not thinking about Rylee in that bed with her jeans off. He imagined her soft, milky-white legs moving underneath the crisp sheets, and his throat tightened.

He took his Stetson off and put it on the end table with a sigh. It was going to be a long night.

"I have to be honest," he said. "I don't regret it."

"Kissing me?"

"Hell no. Why would I?"

"Well…" She frowned, seeming to contemplate this. "What about the complications?"

"What complications?"

"Feelings…you know."

"I can see how that might happen. But at the moment, the only feeling I'm having is being worried I'll do it again."

She smiled.

He took off his boots and stretched out on the couch. His legs hung all the way off the end. Hooking his elbow behind his head, he eyed his feet dangling past the armrest.

She curled up on the bed and turned to face him with her pillow underneath her cheek. She looked so pretty that all of a sudden he couldn't believe she was actually single. Men had to be lining up for Rylee. Why in the world was she still on the market and pretending to be engaged to *him*?

"What?" she asked. "What are you thinking?"

"I'm just wondering how it is that you're not married. Or spoken for."

She wrinkled her nose. "Oh. Well, I was. Once upon a time. Not married, but engaged. He broke it off right before the wedding. So, I haven't exactly been lucky in love."

"I'm sorry," he said. "That couldn't have been easy."

"It wasn't. It took me a long time to get over it. And now I've got some trust issues that I'm working through. You know the drill."

He really didn't, as he'd never committed to anyone in the first place. He used to tell himself he wasn't interested in commitment, and maybe that had been true when he was younger. But lately, he had to admit there was some fear there, too. Fear of turning out just like his father, who'd been a dismal example of a husband most of his adult life.

"What about you?" she asked. "Have you ever gotten close to marriage?"

He shook his head. "Nah. I don't think I'm the marrying type."

"I doubt that. You just haven't met the right person yet. It'll happen, and when it does, you'll know."

"Never say never. I mean, I went from being single to engaged in about two minutes flat tonight, so there's that."

"Oh my God," she said, slapping a hand over her eyes. "I completely forgot about that. How did I forget about that?"

"The champagne."

She readjusted the pillow underneath her head. "Shep. What if people in Bronco find out? My parents and your parents? What if word gets around that we said we're engaged? I mean, it's bound to."

He thought about that. Actually, it was the first time he'd stopped to think about it the entire night. Which was exactly like him. He didn't usually make a habit out of looking before he leaped. But the problem was, this time he'd leaped with Rylee alongside him.

He scraped a hand through his hair. "Maybe not. I mean, Wonderstone Ridge isn't right next door to Bronco or anything."

"But what about Janet?"

"I think she's got her hands full with her own life. She might be curious... Okay, she'll be curious for sure, but we did a good job of steering clear of her after the whole engagement announcement thing. I know she was a little tipsy, just like we were. She might forget all about it by morning."

He knew this was stretching it, but he didn't want Rylee to worry. The truth was, though, that news traveled fast in towns like Bronco and Wonderstone Ridge. The chances of people hearing about this were fairly decent. He'd have to admit it was all a joke, and by then his poor mother would know about it. She was so desperate to have him settled down, it would be a shock to her system.

Across the room, Rylee was deep in thought and nibbling on her bottom lip, which wasn't doing anything for his willpower. He'd already been having a hard enough time not imagining her half naked, and now this.

"I think I'm gonna take a shower," he said. *A cold shower.* "Unless you need the bathroom first?"

"No, that's okay. I'll wash my face when you're done."

Sitting up, he rolled his head from side to side until his neck cracked. Yup. It was going to be a long night.

RYLEE COULDN'T SLEEP. She kept staring up at the motel room ceiling, listening to the soft sound of Shep's breathing a few feet away.

He'd come out of the bathroom earlier in his jeans and nothing else. When she realized she was staring, she turned into her pillow, trying to pretend she was drowsy.

He'd flopped down on the couch with a groan, and after a few minutes, she'd gotten up to use the bathroom and wash her face. But she'd been picturing him shirtless ever since.

Shep had always been blessed with good looks. When he was a teenager, all the girls in their high school had crushes on him, and Rylee, of course, had been no exception. He was a rancher, through and through, but he reminded her now of the boys she'd met in California. The ones with the sun-kissed skin and the messy blond hair. Always looking like they'd just come back from surfing or spending the day at the beach. But none of those boys could hold a candle to Shep Dalton, or his rock-hard abs.

Or those broad shoulders and thick biceps. *Or* that teasing smile that made her want to melt into a puddle on the floor.

She rolled over for what must've been the tenth time in a matter of minutes, her heart thrumming in her chest. When he'd taken his Stetson off earlier, she'd had the ridiculous urge to cross the room and run her hands through his hair, through the ring his hat left behind. It was so tempting that she'd had to bite her cheek just to distract her dumb ovaries.

He sighed, and she wondered with a pang of guilt if he was uncomfortable on the couch. He'd looked so funny earlier, with his feet hanging off the end. He'd have to be scrunched up now. How was he supposed to sleep that way?

She could hear him shifting back and forth, trying to get settled. The couch creaked and popped under his weight, and she finally sat up to face him in the dim light of the room.

"Shep," she said. "There's no way you can be comfortable on that thing."

"I'm okay...just finding the right position."

"There is no right position," she said. "Why don't you just sleep in the bed with me?"

He was quiet at that, and all of a sudden, her face warmed. He probably thought she was coming on to him. But could she blame him? It sounded like some kind of line. Some kind of cheesy way to get him into bed. Literally.

"I mean...if you want to," she said. "You don't have to. I just thought you'd be able to sleep better over here."

"Well, I'd be more comfortable for sure. But I'm not sure I'd sleep any better."

Rylee could feel her pulse skipping in her throat. This was *so* unlike her. She clearly remembered a time, back

when she and Tyler had been together, when she'd been too
shy to come out of the bathroom in a skimpy nightie that
he'd bought her. And now, here she was, inviting her old
childhood crush into bed with her. Sure, she hadn't been
planning on jumping his bones, but he didn't know that.

"Are you sure?" Shep asked.

She gave a quick nod. Then realized he couldn't see her
in the dark. "I'm sure," she said, forcing an evenness into
her voice that she didn't feel. "We'll behave ourselves."

After a minute, he pushed himself off the couch and
walked over to the bed, his muscular body dark and im-
posing in the shadowy room.

He pulled back the covers and climbed inside, and she
could immediately smell his scent. That incredibly erotic
scent from earlier tonight that gave her butterflies now.

He plumped the pillow underneath his head and turned
on his side to face her. This close, she could clearly see
him smiling. Maybe even see that teasing twinkle in his
eyes. But she could be imagining that part.

"Thanks for sharing," he said. "My legs were starting
to cramp up."

She laughed, pulling the covers up around her shoulders. The bed felt warmer with him in it. Her body *definitely* felt warmer.

"I'm surprised you lasted as long as you did," she said.
"That couch is tiny, and you're not exactly a small guy."

"I know. I went through some weird growth spurt after
high school. The good news is that most of my brothers
have to look up at me now, so that's a plus."

"How are your brothers? Other than married off?"

"They're doing pretty well. Dale is the only one who
isn't married yet, but he's engaged. He's also going to be
a stepdad. Mila is eight and adorable. Morgan's also got a
daughter, Josie, who's three."

Rylee could hardly believe the boys she remembered so well were family men now. But then again, she couldn't believe she and Shep were almost thirty, either. It seemed like just yesterday that they were sneaking to the river together.

"How about your brothers?" he asked. "How are they doing?"

She swallowed hard. Her family was a touchy subject for her these days. The truth was, her older brothers, all in their early thirties, had had a tumultuous relationship with their father for as long as she could remember. Living on the ranch hadn't been easy for them. Braden and Miles had finally left Tenacity, following in Hayes's footsteps, who'd been the first to go. He'd broken up with his girlfriend, Chrissy Hastings, crushing her heart in the process, and had left years ago, never looking back. It was still a sore spot in their family, an open wound that hadn't healed.

"They're okay," she said quietly. "They moved away. We talk, but I don't get to see them very much, which makes me sad. But living with my dad just got to be too much for them. You know how he is."

Shep nodded somberly.

She was sure he remembered her family's complicated dynamics. Her father loved his kids, but he was notorious for being hard on them. They couldn't be good at something; they had to be the best. Something that Rylee had struggled with plenty. Her brothers struggled with it, too. Maybe even more so, since they were the ones their dad expected to take over the ranch someday, and the ranch was everything to their father.

"And how are your parents?" Shep asked.

"They're doing pretty well. I keep trying to get them to come visit, but Dad doesn't like to leave the ranch very often, and Mom doesn't like to leave him. So it's this whole thing. I try to get back when I can, but honestly, it isn't enough. I feel guilty about that, but I just had to leave when I got the chance, you know?"

Shep sighed. "I know what you mean. Tenacity was a hard place to grow up. But it's full of good people. Honestly, I miss it sometimes."

She let that settle. Shep's family was well-off now. He didn't have to worry anymore about all the things that had plagued them as kids. The things that had bonded them from the beginning.

"From Tenacity to Bronco," she said softly. "And not just Bronco Valley, either. Bronco *Heights*. That's quite a change."

"It is. The Daltons are finally getting to see how the other half lives."

"I'd love to get out to your ranch someday…"

"I'd love to show it to you. Do you still ride?"

Rylee smiled against her pillow. As a kid, she'd had an old gelding named Tuff that she and Shep used to ride bareback. He was the best horse in the world. But since she'd moved from her family's ranch, she only rode periodically now.

"Not as often as I'd like," she said.

"Well, we might have to fix that. I have a pretty Appaloosa that you'd look awfully good on. Just saying."

They lay there quiet for another few seconds, just watching each other. Then suddenly, without warning, Shep reached out and brushed a lock of hair away from her eyes. His touch was so soft, so tender, that her heart just about stopped in her chest.

"I've missed you, Rylee," he said, his voice low. "I'm sorry I never kept in touch."

She swallowed hard. His fingertips left a tingling trail along her skin. She still couldn't believe she was lying here next to him. If anyone had told her this morning that this was how her evening would end up, she would've laughed at the absurdity of it. But here she was.

"I've missed you, too," she said. "You were my best friend. I'm not sure what I would've done without you all those years."

"Let's make each other a promise."

"Uh-oh. I've heard that before."

He smiled. "This one doesn't involve getting married. Or pretending that we're going to get married."

"Okay, then. I'm game."

"Let's not fall out of touch again. No matter what happens, okay?"

She smiled, too. She was finding it nearly impossible not to smile when she was this close to him. He had that effect.

"I promise," she said softly. "Cross my heart."

CHAPTER THREE

RYLEE SAT ACROSS from Shep in the little booth with the red checked tablecloth and opened her menu. The spring sunshine was out in force this morning, shining in through the diner window in long shafts of warm gold. It felt good on her shoulders, even better on her cheeks. She hadn't slept much last night and resisted another yawn as she read through the breakfast items, which looked heavenly.

"Do you still like waffles?" Shep asked. He had a way of reading her mind. An unsettling thought, since her mind had been full of nothing but him for the last sixteen hours or so.

"I *love* waffles," she said. "But they don't love my thighs, unfortunately. I'm trying to cut down on sugar."

"That's no fun. Plus, I think your thighs are perfect as is."

She smiled, lowering her lashes. He said that like she was sexy, beautiful. When she knew very well she wasn't either of those things. She was pretty enough, and that was fine. She'd always been okay with that. There was much more to life than looks, but she had to admit, it was nice feeling beautiful. In fact, she could get used to it, and that worried her a little.

"What about you?" she asked. "What sounds good?"

"I think I'm gonna have the cheese omelet with a side of bacon." He patted his nonexistent belly. "Gotta fuel up for today."

"What's happening today?"

"The rest of the cattle inoculations. I'm sure my brothers are a little pissed that I wasn't there to help yesterday."

"And that you didn't come home last night."

"None of their business. But I'm sure there will be questions. There are *always* questions."

She nodded. She got it. Sometimes it seemed like she was her brothers' favorite topic of conversation. Who she was dating, who she wasn't. What her life (or love life) looked like in general. They never let up, always wanting to insert themselves where they weren't needed. But that was the problem—they still thought she was a little girl. Overly protective and assuming they were needed constantly.

Her phone buzzed from her purse, and she pulled it out to see a text from her best friend, Gabrielle Hammond, flash across the screen.

Her stomach dropped. *Shoot.* She'd forgotten to let her know how the party was, and she never forgot to text Gabby. She'd be worried, probably thinking Rylee had ended up in a ditch somewhere. Even though they'd only known each other a relatively short amount of time (Gabby and her little girl, Bella, were fairly new in town), they'd hit it off, and were more like sisters now than anything else.

"Everything okay?" Shep asked.

"Yup. It's just my friend Gabby. I was supposed to check in last night, and I kind of went radio silent."

"Uh-oh."

"Do you mind if I answer this really quick?"

"Go for it."

Rylee sat back and opened Gabby's message.

Girl, I went for coffee this morning, and I ran into Tessa McAlister, who used to live on the second floor at BH247

(Remember her? She's got the cute little wiener dog?), and she said her brother went to Janet Halstead's birthday party last night, and that he saw you and Shep Dalton there, and that you two are ENGAGED??? Text me back, or I'm gonna have to come find you.

Rylee blinked at her phone, hardly able to believe what she'd just read. All of a sudden, the thought of food turned her stomach.

"I don't like that look," Shep said, leaning forward. "What's wrong?"

"You're not going to believe this, but Gabby wants to know why she just heard that we're engaged."

He stared at her, his blue eyes wide. "What?"

"Yeah. We thought word traveled fast in Bronco, but it's more like lightning speed. What are we going to do?"

He rubbed the back of his neck. "I'll fix it. Don't worry. I got you into this, I'll get you out."

Rylee looked back down at her phone and typed out a quick reply to Gabby. Something that would tide her over, with a little groveling thrown in for good measure. This was definitely something she'd have to explain in person.

After a minute, she tucked her phone back in her purse and set her elbows on the table.

"The easiest thing would just be to come clean, right?" she asked. "I mean, that makes the most sense."

"Right. We'll have to explain ourselves and take some ribbing, but it won't be too bad."

She chewed the inside of her cheek. She had to admit, despite everything, there was a part of her that hated to see this end. Last night was so fun, twirling around that dance floor in Shep's arms, having him hold her in front of everyone, like she was his, and he was hers. It had almost been like a dream come true. At least, for the teenage girl inside her.

Shep took a sip of his coffee and set it down with a sigh. "I have to admit though, hypothetically, it would've been nice having my mom off my case for a while. She means well, she really does, but she's been driving me nuts about getting married. Having a family. All of it."

Rylee watched him, her heart beating steadily inside her chest.

"Hmm," he said.

"Hmm, what?"

"I just had a crazy thought."

"*You?* Never."

He smiled that old mischievous Shep Dalton smile, and her belly curled.

"What if we kept it up for a while?" he asked slowly.

She stared at him.

"I mean, *technically*, we could tell people we're engaged," he continued. "We've known each other forever, so that wouldn't be too much of a stretch. Definitely fast, but nothing unheard of. Then, after a few weeks, we could fake break up." He shrugged. "That way my family would give me a relationship breather, and we wouldn't have to come right out and admit that we led everyone astray at Janet's party. Win, win."

She grew still as the words sunk in. There were all kinds of reasons to say no to this. It was wild, even by Shep's standards. But she could also see reasons to say yes, too. And yeah, okay, getting to pretend to be engaged to him was at the top of that list. But this also might be a way to get her brothers to come home again. She'd be willing to bet they might if they got news she was going to be married. And having everyone under the same roof together was almost too tempting to pass up. Of course, she'd eventually have to tell them the wedding (or fake wedding) was off, but by then maybe her family would be on their way to some kind of reconciliation. It could happen. Anything could happen.

She felt her lips tilt into a smile. "Partners in crime. I guess old habits die hard."

"There *would* be a fair amount of acting involved, though," he said. "I mean, we'd have to make it look believable. At least, when we're out in public."

He didn't have to know she was looking forward to that part. And not just a little, either. If she wasn't actually going to marry Shep Dalton, she could at least pretend she was going to marry him, and that was a close second.

"I don't have a problem with that," she said evenly, somehow managing to sound almost nonchalant about the whole thing. Who said she couldn't act? "I'm up for it if you are."

He smiled again. And there was an unmistakable twinkle in his eyes.

Rylee's pulse quickened accordingly. There was a time when that look had set her heart on fire. This morning, a whole decade later, she found that nothing much had changed. Her heart was still burning for Shep Dalton and those impossibly blue eyes.

She took a sip of her iced tea, hoping it would cool her off some. So, they were going to be engaged for a few weeks. At least as far as Bronco, Montana, was concerned.

She just hoped she and her burning heart could take the heat.

SHEP FLIPPED HIS truck's sun visor down as he made his way along the newly paved drive that led to Dalton's Grange. He could see the ranch house in the distance, a sprawling two-story log mansion that reminded him of something out of an epic western. It wasn't his taste, but his parents had loved it immediately, so he kept his mouth shut. Their ranch in Tenacity had been more his style. A smaller, lived-in home, and a one-hundred-year-old barn that sat up on the hill overlooking the pastures.

Dalton's Grange was much fancier. The fencing along the property alone was worth more than their old house. The barn was state of the art, with room for all the family's horses, plus some boarders. It was a nice spread, an expensive spread, but Shep thought it was ostentatious. He felt like people in Bronco thought the Daltons were tacky with their Las Vegas money, and this place definitely didn't help.

He rubbed the scruff on his chin. Spending last night with Rylee had him in the strangest mood. Reflecting on his childhood and all the insecurities he'd had as a teenager. Growing up in a family that was complicated at best, stormy at worst, Shep hadn't made a habit of confiding in friends back then. Rylee was the only one, and it hadn't taken long to fall right back into that old place with her. Talking into the early hours of the morning and for two more hours over breakfast, when they'd decided about how to move forward with this fake engagement.

He guessed he should probably feel like he was in over his head. Like they should come clean before the whole thing got out of hand. But he felt exactly the opposite. Calm and collected for the first time in months. For one thing, he knew his mother would be happy about this. Sure, she'd be upset when he and Rylee "broke up" in a few weeks, but for the time being, it would give him a break from the constant relationship nagging. And when the time came to break the news that they were no longer together, he'd let his mom down gently. It would be fine. She'd be fine.

But what really had Shep invested in this was the fact

that he was going to get to spend so much time with Rylee. And not just that, he'd be pretending to be her man. Childish? Maybe. But ever since they'd fleshed out the details this morning, his heart had been pounding strong and sure inside his chest. His gut had been tight, anticipating getting to hold her again. Maybe even getting to kiss her again, in front of anyone curious and watching. It was like getting to be in an amazing relationship, but bypassing all the crap leading up to it—getting to know someone, being nervous around them, worrying where it was going and how fast. With Rylee, all those things had already been addressed or didn't apply anyway. And the bonus? He was crazy attracted to her. This was just going to be fun. Period. Ever since he'd run into her last night, that was the word that kept reverberating in his head.

He pulled his truck into the big, circular drive and came to a stop next to his dad's Mustang. A fire-engine red midlife crisis that his mother had just signed off on. "As long as he doesn't drive into a tree, I'm okay with it," she'd said with a shrug. His mom was a saint.

He put the truck into Park and killed the engine, looking up to see his older brother Boone making his way down the house's front porch steps.

Shep took a deep breath and braced himself. Boone had that look on his face. That look that said Shep was in trouble. Probably for skipping out on the cattle branding and inoculating yesterday, but honestly, he'd do it all over again if he had the chance.

Opening his truck door, he climbed out as Boone stalked up to him.

"Where the hell have you been?" his brother asked, his brown Stetson pulled low over his eyes. Boone was a big guy. Thick through the shoulders and a little taller than Shep—the only brother who was.

"I told you. I had that party in Wonderstone Ridge last night. Can't help it if your memory has slipped with your old age." Shep closed the door and jingled his keys in his hand.

"You're only four years younger than me, smart-ass."

"Yeah, but apparently, much younger cognitively."

"Since when do you stay overnight at parties?"

Boone was watching him closely. The news about Rylee was going to come out sooner rather than later (in fact, Shep was surprised Boone hadn't already heard), but he didn't feel like going into it right then, so he stepped around his brother and made a beeline for the house. He was going to have to change clothes before heading out to the pasture and fielding the rest of Boone's questions. And probably his father's, too.

"I smell bacon," he said over his shoulder. "Did you save me some?"

"Go ahead," Boone called after him. "Run away. I'll find out what you were up to, little brother. I always do."

Ignoring that, Shep took the porch steps two by two. He wasn't really hungry after that breakfast with Rylee, but he'd needed to change the subject.

He opened the front door and stepped inside, letting the screen door slam behind him. Taking his Stetson off, he took a deep breath. He definitely smelled bacon.

"Shep?" his mother called from the kitchen. "Is that you?"

"Yup, just heading upstairs to change."

He was the only one of his brothers who lived in the main house. His room was set apart from the others and felt pretty private, so it was alright for now. Besides, he worked so much, he really only slept there anyway.

"Will you come in here, please? Right now?"

Shep stopped in his tracks. *Uh-oh.* He didn't like that

tone. He wondered if she'd heard the gossip already. If Rylee's best friend knew, there was a good chance his mother did, too.

Slowly, he headed into the kitchen, his boots thudding on the hardwood floor.

Deborah Dalton was standing at the sink, drying her cast-iron skillet with a blue checked towel. She turned with a smile, looking pretty this morning. Her cheeks were rosy, and her blue eyes were bright. Her dark blond hair was pulled into a ponytail at the nape of her neck, making her look younger than her sixty-two years.

Shep leaned against the wall, waiting, but he already knew what was coming. He could tell. It didn't matter if he wasn't in the mood to tell the entire story, he was going to have to tell it anyway.

Warmth crept up his neck and into his face, making him feel like a kid who'd just been caught with his hand in the cookie jar.

His mom set the skillet down and tossed the towel on the counter. Then planted her hands on her hips.

"Is there something you want to tell me, son?"

"Um…"

"You might as well just come out with it, Shepard."

For some reason, he hadn't expected this part would be so hard. What if she could see right through him? What if she thought he was absolutely nuts for getting engaged this fast? What if he couldn't pull this off? Then what? Talk about digging himself into a hole.

"Well—"

"Rylee *Parker*?" his mother interrupted with a grin. "I didn't even know you two were dating!"

He had to stop himself before an automatic *we're not* escaped his mouth.

"It's kind of a long story," he said, feeling the first pangs of guilt for lying to her. He had to remember this was only temporary, that it would all be over soon enough. In the meantime, he'd get a little breather, and that was the whole point. Well, that and getting to kiss Rylee again.

His mother pulled out a chair at the kitchen table and motioned for him to do the same. "I have time," she said cheerfully. "And the cattle can wait."

"Tell that to Boone."

"He'll live. But I might not if I don't get some information out of you right this minute. Now *sit*."

Shep did as he was told, settling back against the chair. His mom continued watching him closely, as if he were about to pull a rabbit out of his Stetson or something. He wasn't sure how it was possible, but maybe he'd underestimated how badly she wanted him to get married.

"You know Rylee is living in Bronco now," he began evenly.

She nodded.

"Well, we ran into each other, and one thing led to another, and we just kind of…picked up where we left off." At least that part wasn't a lie. He resisted the urge to loosen his collar.

"Oh, how romantic," his mom said, clasping her hands in front of her chest. "And you just popped the question? That's so spontaneous of you! I had no idea you had those kinds of romantic impulses, Shep. None at all."

He swallowed hard. "I'm sorry, Mom. It took me by surprise, too." Something else that was true. Maybe this wasn't going to be so bad after all.

"It's all right. I'm just so happy for you. You know I've been hoping for this all along."

"I know."

"So, when are you going to bring her out to see us? It's been so long. I don't think I've seen her since you two were in high school."

Shep shifted in his chair. His mother would want to make a special dinner. It would be a thing. He'd need to give Rylee plenty of notice, so she'd be prepared for the family onslaught.

"Uh…"

"How about next Saturday?"

"Next Saturday?"

"I'll make spaghetti and meatballs. Does she like spaghetti?"

He had no clue if she liked spaghetti. Or meatballs.

"I'll just plan on spaghetti," she said. "And if she'd like something else, I'll make that instead. I'm just so excited about this, honey."

"Thanks, Mom."

"I suppose I should give her parents a call. Wow, I don't think we've seen Norma and Lionel since we moved to Bronco."

"No," Shep said quickly. "I mean, I don't even know if she's had a chance to talk to them yet. You should probably wait on that."

"Okay. Whatever you say."

She smiled, looking for the most part like he'd just made her entire millennium. He was going straight to hell.

"Do your brothers know?" she asked.

"No…"

"When are you going to tell them?"

"Soon."

"Well, don't wait too long, Shep. You don't want them hearing from someone else like I did."

He frowned. "Who *did* you hear it from?"

"Janet's mother. She's in my old quilting group from Tenacity."

Shep resisted the urge to slap his forehead. *Of course.* He'd forgotten about the infamous quilting group, the fastest way to get word around the great state of Montana and then some.

"Anyway," she continued. "Make sure you tell them. I'll tell your father."

He forced a smile. That was going to be the messy part of this engagement ruse. The best part would be seeing Rylee again.

He just hoped she was having a better time of it across town than he was.

RYLEE SAT ON Gabby's couch, holding her little girl, Bella, on her lap. She leaned forward and breathed in the freshly shampooed scent of Bella's silky brown hair as the toddler thumbed through a picture book in quiet fascination.

In the kitchen, Gabby was making them each a cup of coffee, which Rylee needed desperately. She'd been planning on telling Gabby the whole truth, but now, sitting here, she wondered if it might be better to fib, at least for the time being. Bella might overhear their conversation, and that would complicate things. Even though she was only two, she could repeat something. It had happened before. And then there was the fact that Gabby would want to tell Ryan Taylor, her fiancé. Rylee didn't feel right asking her to keep this from him. If she didn't know, that would alleviate that problem right there. Sure, Gabby would be more than annoyed when Rylee ended up telling her the truth, but at this point, it was a calculated risk. She just wished she'd had more time to think this through. She still couldn't believe how fast Gabby had heard about Shep.

"Shoot," Gabby said, holding the fridge door open and frowning at the contents. "We're out of cream. Will milk do?"

"Of course," Rylee said. "Your coffee is delicious even without the cream."

"I don't know about that, but I'm getting better at it. Ryan is a coffee fanatic, so since Bella and I moved in, I've been getting lots of practice. Elsie, *no!*"

Rylee swallowed a laugh as Gabby shoved her little dog gently aside with her foot. Elsie's favorite activity was sticking her nose into the refrigerator. She was a chunk and seemed to be getting fatter by the day. Gabby had a theory that it was because of all the food Bella dropped on the floor, but Rylee thought Elsie just liked to eat. Who could blame her?

"Here we go," Gabby said, walking over with two steaming cups of coffee. "Bella, honey, why don't I turn on *The Wiggles* for you so Rylee and Mommy can talk, okay?"

She didn't have to ask twice. Bella ran over to the television set and plopped down cross-legged on the carpet. "Ready, Mama," she said, giving an adorable thumbs-up.

Gabby turned on the TV with the volume down low and sat next to Rylee.

Rylee took a sip of her coffee and burned her tongue. Frowning, she set the mug on the coffee table. She was nervous, and she was never nervous around Gabby. She hoped her friend wouldn't notice.

"So," Gabby said with a knowing look. "Tell me everything."

"Well…you remember me talking about Shep Dalton, right?"

"Of course. Your best friend from when you were kids."

Rylee nodded and licked the taste of coffee from her lips. "We ran into each other not long ago, and one thing led to another…" She cringed inwardly. Technically, last night would count as *not long ago*, but really. What a whopper.

"One thing led to another," Gabby repeated evenly. "Meaning your engagement?"

Rylee nodded again, avoiding her friend's gaze.

"And you didn't tell me?" Gabby asked.

"It all happened so fast. And I knew you'd understand…" Rylee swallowed hard. Gabby might understand now, but would she when the truth came out? It was a lot to ask. Even for a friend as true as Gabby.

"Okay, I guess I forgive you. But for now, I just want details. Like where's your ring?"

"Oh…uh…" Rylee glanced down at her hand. "I don't have one yet. It happened—"

"I know. It happened so fast. And you're happy, Ry? *Really* happy?"

Rylee took a deep breath. At least she didn't have to fib about that part.

"I am," she said softly.

Elsie jumped up on the couch, gave Rylee a lick on the hand and curled into a little ball by her side.

"So, you're happy," Gabby said. "And now we need to plan for your *wedding*."

"No way. You're the one talking about getting married this summer."

Gabby waved her away. "Please. We can plan together. There must be something in the water, right?"

"I know. What are the odds that we could be getting married so close together?"

"Not just us. Winona Cobbs and Stanley Sanchez finally set a wedding date."

"They have? Oh, that makes me happy."

"Me, too. They really prove that it's never too late to fall in love."

Rylee smiled. Winona Cobbs, Bronco's most famous psychic (and some would say eccentric), was in her nineties. She and Stanley gave Rylee hope that happily-ever-after really did exist in the real world. Gabby was right. It was never too late.

"So," Gabby said, "when do Ryan and I get to meet Shep?"

There was an excited look in Gabby's eyes that made Rylee feel all kinds of guilty. But as she glanced over at Bella, she knew not telling her had been the right call. The little girl was hanging on their every word.

"Who's Ship, Mommy?" Bella asked, her long bangs hanging over one eye.

"Shep, honey. And he's Rylee's fiancé. That means they're going to get married. Isn't that fun?"

If Bella understood what marriage was, she didn't let on. "Can I have Goldfish?" she asked.

"In a minute, sweetie."

"But I'm *hungry*, Mama."

"Just a minute, Bella." Gabby gave Rylee a look. "She's cranky. It's past her nap time."

"I need to get going, anyway. I have to pick up some groceries and stop by the pharmacy before they close. I can never get that done during the week."

That was true, she did have to do those things, but this conversation with Gabby was only highlighting the fact that she needed to call her parents and let them know about Shep, like *now*. They were going to hear about it any day now. She'd already waited too long to say something. She was just going to have to bite the bullet, and this was as good a time as any. She'd give them a call as soon as she got into her car, while she still had the nerve.

"How's the new position, by the way? I'm *so* proud of you," Gabby said.

"It's great. Just busy, but in marketing, that's always a good thing."

They talked about Rylee's marketing plans for upcoming events at the convention center for a minute, then Gabby asked, "Is Geoff Burris still in Europe?"

Bronco's beloved rodeo star and his fiancée, Stephanie, were out of the country, but that didn't mean Rylee could take a breather. The other Burris brothers and the Hawkins Sisters kept the convention center on its toes and Bronco's rodeo fans on the edge of their seats.

"He is. Enjoying the good life for a while." Rylee looked at her watch. She really should get going, so poor little Bella could get a nap. "Thanks for the coffee. It was delicious, as usual. Call you later?"

"Okay. But don't think you're off the hook with this engagement story. You haven't even scratched the surface yet, Rylee Parker. And tell Shep we want to meet him. Your bestie has final approval."

Rylee laughed and leaned over to give her friend a hug. "I'll let him know. You'll like him, I promise." Even as she said it, though, she worried about keeping up this pretense in front of friends and family. A room full of strangers was one thing. People who knew and loved her and Shep was something else altogether.

Grabbing her keys from the coffee table, she said a little prayer that her acting chops would be good enough. And that pretending to be engaged to Shep Dalton would be worth the heartache in the end.

RYLEE SAT IN her little car as it idled at the curb in front of Ryan and Gabby's house. She'd dialed her mother as soon as she'd climbed in, just like she'd planned. But this conversation was proving even harder than she'd thought, and she'd known it wouldn't be easy.

She stared out the window to the mountains in the distance, and listened to the heavy silence on the other end of the line.

"Mom?" she said. "Say something."

Her mother exhaled slowly. "I'm just digesting this, honey. It's kind of a surprise, that's all."

Rylee's belly sank at that. She felt so *guilty*. But she swallowed hard and told herself to power through. This was only temporary, right?

"I know," she said. "I'm sorry it's such a shock. But it's Shep. You know Shep."

"Yes," her mother said, as if she were choosing her words carefully. "We do. But you two haven't seen each other in ages, Rylee."

"We haven't. But we've always had such a strong connection. It was easy taking this step."

"Right. But it's fast."

"It is." There was no use arguing with that, since it was absolutely true.

"And it's what you want?" her mom asked. "Really?"

Rylee had the distinct feeling that her mother was having a hard time believing this. But what part? She thought she'd been convincing enough. But it was probably just her conscience that was making her paranoid. She hated lying, and it felt like she'd done enough of it to last a lifetime in just the last day alone.

"It's what I want," she said evenly. Ignoring the little angel on her shoulder that was shaking a tiny finger at her.

"Marriage isn't easy, Rylee. Your dad and I have gone through some rough patches that we almost didn't make it through. And then when you have kids, well… You know how hard it's been with your brothers leaving the way they have. How hard on the family that's been. All of those challenges are in front of you, and more. You want to be confident in your partner. Sure that you can weather the storms together. You're *sure* about this?"

Rylee could hear the deeper meaning in her mother's

tone. Was she sure that Shep was the one she wanted to weather those storms with? Shep, with his own messed-up family history, and his devil-may-care attitude about life. Rylee felt defensive of him right then, but she could understand her mom's concern. It was natural, even if it wasn't quite fair. Shep had never done anything to hurt her. Still, she guessed it was possible that he could.

"I'm sure, Mom," she said.

"Then if it's what you want, it's what we want for you."

She bit the inside of her cheek. "You mean it?"

"Of course. That doesn't mean we aren't going to worry. We'll worry no matter what. But if you're happy, we're happy."

Rylee smiled, her eyes stinging with surprise tears. She knew this was a leap for her mother, and it meant a lot having her blessing.

And then she remembered this was all just pretend. A very real blessing, for a pretend engagement.

She closed her eyes for a minute and breathed deeply. Saying yet another prayer that everyone would forgive her when the time came.

CHAPTER FOUR

SHEP GLANCED OVER at Rylee in the passenger seat of his truck. It was Friday night, and they hadn't seen each other all week, but had texted for most of it. He'd called her last night and asked if she wanted to go on a date. A pretend date, but still. He'd been looking forward to seeing her for days.

She looked beautiful tonight. They'd settled on a laid-back drink at Doug's in Bronco Valley, but she'd dressed up, and that got him right in the heart. She wore a pretty red dress with a slightly plunging neckline that warmed his blood. Rylee had never been much for makeup, but she had a cherry-red gloss on her lips that made him want to pull the truck over and kiss her long and hard.

He looked back at the road. "Are you ready for this?"

"For what?"

"Our first public outing as an engaged couple."

He glanced over again to see her smile.

"Ready as I'll ever be," she said. "I just hope I'll be convincing enough. It was weird not telling Gabby the truth."

"I know. But I think your reasoning was pretty sound. You'll tell her soon enough."

She nodded, looking out the window into the night. The lights of the farms and ranches were few and far between, and shone like lighthouse beacons through the dark sea of pastures and crops.

"How was it telling your family?" she asked. "You never really said."

At the mention of his family, his shoulders tensed. He'd actually been feeling bad ever since his mom had called him into the kitchen a few days ago, smiling from ear to ear. But he had to admit, it was nice not having to endure the never-ending comments and questions about when he was going to get serious about his personal life, and how much it would mean to his parents to see him happily settled down.

"It was okay," he said. "My brothers were kind of shocked, but happy for me. It felt strange lying to them and my parents. I have to keep reminding myself this is only temporary."

"Right."

"Honestly, though, I never realized just how much my mom has been at me about getting married until now. I knew it was a lot, but it's actually been nearly every day. Every damn day. That's a lot of marriage pressure."

She laughed. "Aww, poor guy. Well, I'm happy to help."

"I'm happy, too. Happy to be taking you out tonight. Have you ever been to Doug's?"

"Nope. I've heard all about it, though. I'm curious about that haunted bar stool."

"Ahh, the bar stool. Just don't sit on it." He winked at her. "Bad luck and tragedy always follows."

"What kind of tragedy?"

"I can think of two marriages breaking up and at least one accident. Best just to steer clear."

Turning his blinker on, he slowed as Doug's finally came into view. He hadn't been here in a while, but it was always a good time. Lots of tasty nachos, good music, decent drinks. It was where Bronco's locals came to unwind on the weekends, and sometimes it got pretty wild, but tonight, all Shep could think about was the woman beside him. How she smelled, like summer itself, and how she looked—gorgeous in the moonlight streaming in through the truck's windows.

He turned into a parking spot close to the front door, where the music thumped from inside.

Turning the engine off, he looked over at Rylee. "I forgot to ask if you two-step."

She raised her brows. "Two-step?"

"Yeah."

"Oh. No, I don't dance. Janet's birthday party was a rarity, believe me. And that was mostly because of the champagne."

"That's probably because you've had lousy partners. Lucky for you, I'm not lousy."

"Shep…"

He grabbed her hand, just like he used to, and rubbed his thumb over her knuckles. "I'll lead. All you have to do is follow me. If you want to, that is…"

Her eyes were dark in the cab of the truck and reminded him of those pools in the river where the current was slow and gentle, and the water was deep and clear. Rylee had beautiful eyes. A man could get lost in those eyes if he wasn't careful.

"I want to," she said.

And smiled.

RYLEE SAT IN the small booth by the window, waiting while Shep got their drinks. The place was packed. The music was loud, and the clientele was rowdy, to say the least. Not exactly the type of Friday night she was used to, which made it that much better.

Looking around, she leaned her elbows on the table. She could feel the country music reverberating inside her chest, thumping out a rhythm with her heart. She couldn't believe she was here with Shep Dalton. And more than that, they were pretending to be *engaged*.

When he'd helped her out of the truck earlier, a few people were walking by, and he'd pulled her close. He'd leaned down and whispered in her ear, his breath warm against her skin, "Have to make it look believable…"

She shivered now, thinking about it. If making it look believable meant more moments like that, she was fully on board. But she had to be honest, she'd been on board with this crazy idea from the beginning. She didn't think she would've been able to say no if she'd tried. But she hadn't tried. She'd just signed happily on, and despite her worry about lying to her friends and family for a few weeks, she was having so much fun. Then, all of a sudden, the thought of having to say goodbye to this pretend relationship, to Shep in general, made her breathless.

She forced herself to sit up straighter. She'd just have to cross that bridge when she came to it. And if she ended up regretting this ruse, this sexy little adventure, she'd have to chalk it up to life experience in the end. Live and learn, and heal from the broken heart.

Frowning, she gazed out the window to the darkened parking lot beyond. She'd had her heart broken before, of course. She'd been devastated when Tyler had called off their wedding. But that had felt more like a rejection of her than like losing something truly special. She'd loved Tyler, but she'd never been madly *in* love with him. What she had with Shep? It was different. Drastically different, even though it was all smoke and mirrors, and that said a lot.

"Can I buy you a drink?"

She startled and looked up to see a stocky cowboy standing over her. He was handsome, with dark hair curling around the nape of his neck and a slightly cocky tilt to his mouth. She thought he looked familiar. Thanks to the convention center, she worked around cowboys like this all the time—bull riders, calf ropers, team ropers. There were so many. For a single woman with a healthy libido, it wasn't the worst job in the world.

Still, she wasn't used to being asked if she wanted a drink, by a cowboy or anyone else. She just didn't put herself out there enough. Since Tyler, she'd only been on a handful of dates, and they'd all ended with her saying she'd call the next day, but never had. She'd learned it was just easier not to let it get that far. That way she couldn't get hurt. Maybe that was part of the reason why this fake engagement was so tempting. It was like she was getting to live out her fantasies vicariously, without any risk to her heart. At least, that's what it would look like on paper. She knew that her heart was very much at risk, whether this was a fake engagement or not.

She smiled, scanning the room for Shep. "No, thank you. I'm actually—"

And then, suddenly, he appeared. Tall, lean, impossibly good-looking. He patted the other cowboy's back good-naturedly. "Sorry, man. She's with me."

"We're engaged," she said. "To be married." She hadn't needed to add that last part, but she couldn't help it. It was too tempting not to.

"Oh, my apologies," the other man said. He tipped his hat and walked away, disappearing into the rambunctious crowd.

"Geez." Shep set their drinks down and slid into the booth across from her. "I leave you alone for two minutes…"

"That kind of thing doesn't usually happen to me."

"Are you serious?"

"Very."

"I have a hard time believing that."

She smiled. "Why?"

"You have to know why."

Rylee had always thought of herself as a wallflower. She felt like she had a tendency to blend in. The red dress tonight was helping, but she wasn't kidding herself that she was suddenly some kind of man magnet.

Shep leaned forward, his gaze suddenly intense. "Rylee..."

"Hmm?"

"You *do* know why, don't you?"

Her cheeks burned. She was glad it was so dim in the bar, or he might've been able to see her blush.

"I don't actually think you do," he muttered.

The music changed to something slow and sweet. She took another sip of wine, liking how it felt going down. It warmed her throat and belly, and reminded her that she was very much an adult now. Not a girl, no matter how shy she felt sometimes. Those days were long gone.

"Will you dance with me?" Shep asked.

"Now?"

"Well, it's not the two-step, but it'll do." He held out his hand from across the table.

She eyed it. Then, after a second, she put her hand in his and let him help her out of the booth.

It felt like every eye in the bar was on them as Shep led her to the dance floor. Without another word, he pulled her close and wrapped an arm around her waist. His belt buckle bit into her hip, leaving her a little dizzy. It was a strangely sensual feeling.

"I've got you," he whispered, leaning close to her ear. "Just follow my lead."

Whether he was talking about the dancing at this point

or their engagement, it didn't really matter. Rylee was completely lost to him right then.

The music thrummed in her ears as she closed her eyes and laid her cheek against his chest. He held her hand tightly in his and splayed the other out on her lower back. His calluses were rough against her palm, his fingers long and blocky and distinctly male. She breathed him in as they moved across the dance floor.

Shep was so confident that she didn't even have to think about where her feet were going next. She found that she loved how that felt. When it came to her career, Rylee had to be dialed in at all times. Since she was in control of so many things at work, she had to be. But when it came to her personal life, she'd forgotten how comforting it was to let someone else show her the way. Even if it was something as small as dancing on a Friday night.

After another minute, the song came to an end, and Shep leaned down and kissed her softly on the cheek. "See?" he said. "You're a natural."

Her face filled with the now familiar heat she felt whenever he did things like this. In front of everyone and with no hesitation at all. Just another thing that she was getting used to. Another thing that she was beginning to love about being in Shep's orbit again after all this time.

"I don't know about that," she said. "You make it easy."

He smiled as they walked off the dance floor and back to their booth.

"It's pretty busy," he said. "I should order our food at the bar, or we might end up waiting forever for a server. Do you know what you want?"

"Oooh, I'd love a cheeseburger," she said. "Everything on it. And fries."

"That's my kind of woman. I'll be right back."

Sliding into the booth again, she watched him cross the

crowded room. He was taller than most of the men there and so handsome that she had to catch her breath. How was it that Shep wasn't taken yet? He'd always been wild and a little reckless, someone she had a hard time imagining any woman being able to tame for any length of time. Was that why his mother was so anxious for him to be married? Was she worried about where that wild streak would leave him in the end?

Rylee was still contemplating this when a young woman stepped up to her booth, smiling wide.

"Rylee Parker? I thought that was you!"

Rylee blinked up at her. She looked vaguely familiar, but she couldn't seem to place her. Maybe someone from the convention center? Or from her apartment complex? BH247 was full of twentysomethings, busy with their careers and lives. Sometimes it was hard keeping track of them all.

"I'm sorry, I…"

"Lisa Frye? We went to high school together. I know it seems like a hundred years ago now."

Rylee smiled. Of course. Lisa Frye. She'd been one of Janet's friends. Popular, bubbly, on the cheerleading team. Not exactly someone Rylee hung out with, but like Janet, she'd always been nice to her.

Lisa looked different now. Gone were the long, blond locks she'd had at seventeen, replaced by a trendy pixie cut and pink-framed glasses. Rylee thought she looked like Tinkerbell, only cuter.

"Can I sit for a minute?" she asked. "My husband is getting us drinks. Might as well catch up."

"Of course! It's so good to see you."

"It's good to see you, too."

"Do you live in Bronco?" Rylee asked, glancing quickly

at the bar. Shep was nowhere to be seen. Swallowed up by dozens of people clamoring for drinks.

"No, we're just here visiting my folks," Lisa said, settling into the booth. "They moved a few years ago. William and I are still in Tenacity. I teach third grade there."

"That's great. I bet you're a wonderful teacher."

"You're sweet. I love it, but some days are easier than others." She smiled and dimples appeared in each cheek. "What do you do, Rylee?"

"I work in marketing at the Bronco Convention Center."

"Oh, wow. So, you know Hattie Hawkins, then?"

"Absolutely. I'm a huge fan of Hattie's."

"Me, too. So is my class. We did a lesson last fall about trailblazing women, and Hattie came to talk to them about rodeo. She had them mesmerized. She's quite a lady."

Rylee grinned. Not only was the septuagenarian Hattie a rodeo legend, but she was also a genuinely great person. Her four daughters, known on the circuit as the original Hawkins Sisters, and her granddaughters, members of the newest generation of Hawkins Sisters, were the same. Hattie had raised a family of strong, spirited women, all while working and excelling in a male-dominated field. Rylee couldn't think of anyone more equipped to speak to a class full of starry-eyed kids than Hattie Hawkins.

"She really is," Rylee said.

"So," Lisa said, leaning forward. "Are you married? Kids?"

Rylee cleared her throat, glancing over at the bar again. For some reason, fibbing about being engaged to Shep was much easier when he was sitting right next to her. Fibbing about being engaged when she was sitting by herself felt less like a playful lie and more like a whopping one.

"Well," she began, "I'm actually engaged…"

She hoped that sounded believable. She'd had a hard time getting the words over her vocal cords.

"That's wonderful!" Lisa said. "Who's the lucky man?"

Licking her lips, Rylee tucked her hands in her lap. She didn't have a ring on. What if Lisa asked to see it?

"Shep," she said. "Shep Dalton."

Lisa's hazel eyes widened. "Shep *Dalton*?"

Rylee nodded.

"Shep Dalton from high school? And *you*?"

She nodded again, beginning to feel a prickle of unease. The way Lisa said that made it sound like she couldn't believe Rylee had landed someone like Shep. And that hurt her feelings in a quick rush that took her by surprise.

"I mean," Lisa said quickly, "it's just that I'm shocked he's settling down, that's all. Not that he's settling down with you. You know what I mean."

"He doesn't seem like the settling down type, I know."

"Well, he didn't used to. But I'm sure he's changed. You're going to love being married. Sometimes I wonder how I ever managed before. Not that I *couldn't* manage before, but I'm just so much happier now, you know? It just feels right. Not for everyone, of course, but I bet you'll wonder why you two waited this long."

Rylee took a sip of her wine. Shep was right. The pressure to get married was everywhere. If this was even a hint of what he'd been getting from his mother, she could understand him welcoming this fake engagement with open arms. It made complete sense.

Lisa looked across the room and waved. "Oh, it looks like William has our drinks. It was so great to see you. Tell Shep I said hello, okay?"

"It was good to see you, too," Rylee said. "And I'll tell him. He'll be sorry he missed you."

With a wiggle of her fingers, Lisa slid out of the booth

and sauntered away, leaving Rylee with an empty feeling in her stomach. She knew the other woman meant well, but the whole interaction had been unsettling. First, with the way she'd reacted to hearing that Shep was engaged to Rylee (of all people!), and then with the whole marriage thing in general.

Sure, she and Shep would have some fun with this for a while, and it would give him a much-needed breather with his parents, but then what? Rylee had always felt fulfilled without being married, but she'd be lying if she said she hadn't longed for that kind of life deep down. She wanted to be a wife, she wanted to be a mother. Tyler hadn't necessarily wanted a traditional kind of family, dismissing her whenever she brought it up. It had made her sad, and left her feeling like she'd have to fight for it when the time came. It wasn't that she didn't think she could be happy without those things, but she wanted them anyway. The fact that this engagement wasn't real only made her want them even more.

Suddenly, she felt melancholy. Looking out the darkened window, she wondered what was messing with her head so much. Was this about turning thirty? If that was it, at least she was in good company. Her entire graduating class was in the same boat.

Or was it something else? Something deeper and more profound?

She watched a car pulling out of the parking lot, its bright red taillights blazing through the night, and before she could help it, she wondered if this sudden feeling could be because of some*one* and not some*thing*. Someone who'd reappeared in her life after being gone for so long. Someone whom she'd had such feelings for…

Maybe it was Shep himself who had her turned upside down.

SHEP MADE HIS way back to the booth, weaving in between people who were getting louder and drunker by the minute. He let his gaze settle on Rylee across the room. She had her chin in her hand and was staring out the window. She didn't look like she was having a very good time.

Frowning, he muttered an apology to a woman for jostling her as he passed, but kept his eyes on Rylee. Maybe he shouldn't have brought her here. They'd decided on something low-key for tonight, but she'd gotten all dressed up and everything. She looked so beautiful in that dress. Maybe he should've taken her somewhere nice in Bronco Heights instead. Of course, that would've been like an actual date, instead of just a pretend date, but still. A real date didn't seem like that much of a stretch. They'd kissed, after all. They were engaged, as far as everyone around here knew. Sure, it might be working backward, but what the hell. He was so attracted to her that backward or forward, it didn't really matter to him. Just so long as he got to spend time with her in some form or fashion, he was happy.

But the question was, was she? Shep felt his jaw muscles clench. Would she even have considered going out with him if it weren't for this game they were playing? Asking himself that question wasn't exactly pleasant, since he'd never relished rejection, and Rylee couldn't truly be interested in someone like him long-term. So, *would* she have gone out with him? He didn't really know. All he knew was that he liked what they had going on right now. He liked it a lot. So much so that he didn't want it to end anytime soon. But the problem was, they'd only agreed to a few weeks. Any more than that, and they'd be digging a hole that wouldn't be so easy to dig their way out of. He was trying to keep himself from thinking about his mother, who would be more than disappointed when they fake broke up.

He stepped up to the booth, and Rylee looked up at

him with a smile. But he'd been right—she looked different. Not unhappy, necessarily, but definitely bothered by something.

He slid in across from her. "The kitchen is pretty slammed, so our burgers should be ready in about twenty minutes. I hope you're not too starved."

"I think I'll survive that long. Thanks for ordering."

He waited, watching her. Her silky auburn hair fell next to her face in a way that made him want to reach out and touch it. In fact, his fingers itched with it. Dancing with her a few minutes ago had lit something inside him that was now burning ferociously. A need that had doubled since they'd met up at Janet's party. Since spending the night together in that little motel bed.

He shifted uncomfortably and took a deep breath, hoping he didn't look as distracted by her as he felt.

"Do you remember Lisa Frye?" she asked, taking a sip of her wine.

"Lisa Frye...from high school?"

She nodded. "She's here with her husband. You just missed her."

"Ahh. How's she doing?"

"She's a teacher in Tenacity. She asked if I was married, and I told her that you and I were engaged."

He smiled, liking how that sounded. "Oh yeah?"

She didn't smile back. Just kept running her index finger around the rim of her wineglass with her gaze averted.

"Rylee?"

"Hmm?"

"What's wrong?"

She looked up at him, her eyes dark. "Nothing's wrong."

"Now, see. I don't believe that. We used to know each other pretty well, and I recognize that look on your face."

"What look?"

"The one that says something's wrong, but you're trying to hide it."

"You could always read my mind," she said.

"What's going on? Did she say something to upset you?"

She shook her head. "No. I mean…kind of, but I know she didn't mean anything by it."

"What'd she say?"

"She just seemed surprised that we were engaged. Specifically, that you would be engaged to me." She tucked her hair behind her ear. "It's silly. But I guess it brought up some of those old insecurities from when we were kids."

He watched her, leaning back in the booth. It was hard to believe Rylee would feel anything but complete and total confidence, as gorgeous as she was. But she obviously didn't have a clue how he saw her. Or how anyone else saw her, for that matter. Maybe Lisa had been surprised, but it made more sense that she'd be surprised that Rylee would have anything to do with him, not the other way around.

But it was easy to forget how Rylee had been as a girl. The glasses and the shy, quiet way about her. The studiousness and seriousness that had drawn him to her in a way that had been hard to deny, even back then. It was true that he'd wanted to see her let her hair down and have some fun, but he'd loved her personality just as she was. She was different. And different in a town like Tenacity was always a good thing. At least, he'd always thought so.

As she gazed back at him now, though, he could see that she still struggled with those differences. He'd known how hard it had been for her; she'd opened up to him about it more than once. Those insecurities were part of what had driven her to go to college out of state. To push herself out of her comfort zone and to get her MBA and come back to Montana a changed woman. A woman who'd left all that

kid stuff behind. But sometimes leaving the kid stuff behind was easier said than done.

He slid out of his seat and came around to her side of
the booth.

"Scoot over," he said evenly. "We're engaged. We
should be sitting on the same side anyway. It's the law."

She laughed and moved over to give him room.

Sliding in, he put his arm around her. Her body was
soft and giving, and he could smell her shampoo. It stirred
something inside of him.

"You," he said, "are stunning. I know you don't believe
that, you've never believed that, but you are. Don't make
me list all the ways."

"Shep…"

"I will, you know."

She shook her head. "Oh God. Don't."

"Why not?"

"It's embarrassing."

"It's embarrassing to hear that you're beautiful?"

She didn't answer that. She just lowered her lashes and
licked her lips, reminding him how much he'd been wanting to kiss her again.

"Let's start with those eyes," he said, pretending to stick
a dagger in his chest. "I mean, come on. Heartbreaker ter-
ritory, here."

She laughed.

"No, I'm serious. You're absolutely gorgeous. But that's
nothing compared to your smarts, Rylee. Your compassion and warmth. Which, by the way, you have in spades."

"Stop."

"Am I getting through? Making a dent in that armor?"

"You've always been able to get through. You're my
Achilles' heel."

"Oooh. I like the sound of that."

She smiled, and he touched her chin with the tips of his fingers, coaxing her to turn her head and look into his eyes.

"Seriously, though," he said, his voice lower this time. "You're the whole package, Rylee."

Her expression softened. Her body relaxed into his, making him wonder how he was ever going to let her go in a few weeks. This wasn't something he wanted to let go of. *She* wasn't something he wanted to let go of. Shep wasn't usually the kind to look too far into the future, but where Rylee was concerned, he couldn't help it. He wanted more.

He swallowed hard, his throat feeling uncomfortably dry. What if he didn't have to let her go? What if this didn't have to end? The thought appeared in his head like a light bulb flashing on, its light warm and bright behind his eyes. *What if...*

Slowly, he took his arm away from her shoulders and reached for his beer. He needed something to wet his tongue. Because the thought that had just occurred to him was beginning to take hold, like a seedling in cool, damp soil. *What if...*

Rylee watched him, her brows furrowed. "What is it?"

Taking a swallow of his beer, he wondered if he should even voice this out loud. It was wild, after all. Wilder than pretending to get engaged, and that was saying something. But if Shep was anything, it was unconventional. He knew that was part of what Rylee liked about him. Or, at least, what she used to like about him. They balanced each other out. She planned things, and he turned them upside down.

"I just had a thought," he said.

"Oh yeah?"

Shifting in the booth, he turned to face her.

"What if we went through with it?" he said.

"Went through with what?"

He waited a beat. Then two. She'd think he'd lost his marbles, but what the hell.

"What if we actually got married?" he asked slowly.

She stared at him. "I'm sorry…what?"

"We made that promise to each other for a reason, right?"

"Shep…we made that promise when we were kids. We had no idea what we were doing."

"We were kids," he said, "but we knew damn well what we were doing. For one thing, we knew each other better than anyone else did. We were best friends."

"Just because we were close—"

"We were best friends."

"Just because we were best friends didn't mean we were serious."

"We were young, but we weren't stupid, Rylee. We knew that marriage could be a practical thing. We also knew that if we got to be a certain age without taking that step with someone else, it just made sense to take it with each other. We already know we're great together. A lot of marriages start out with less than that."

She laughed. "Did you have a couple of shots at the bar or something?"

"I'm stone-cold sober."

"I can't believe you're actually suggesting this."

"Why not? We're not getting any younger. Our families are pumped that we're engaged. Just think how happy they'd be if we actually tied the knot."

"You'd do this just to get them to stop nagging you?"

"No, but that'd be a nice bonus."

She shook her head, but there was a sparkle in her eyes. Maybe she didn't think it was such a nutty idea after all. There was always that possibility.

He nudged her elbow. "No more dead-end dating. We'd always have a built-in plus-one. We'd get to see what's so damn great about being married and still have the safety net of being friends. You're tempted, aren't you?"

"I'm not admitting I'm tempted, but…"

"But?"

"But, there *are* some practical reasons for it."

"See? That's what I'm saying."

"What about all that stuff about you not being the marrying kind?"

He smiled. "That was before."

She touched her temple. "I think I've had too much wine on an empty stomach. I'm actually considering this."

"Look, we don't have to decide anything tonight. But I'm glad you're considering it."

"Wait," she said. "Just wait a minute, Shep…"

He watched her, his gaze dropping to her mouth. If they actually got married, he'd get to look at that mouth every single day. He didn't really care to weigh anything beyond that. At the moment, it was all that mattered.

"Are you *actually* serious about this?" she asked. "I mean, truly?"

He took her hand in his. Before tonight, before he'd seen her in this dress, he would've had to think about that. But that was the thing. He didn't want to think at all. Which a lot of people would say was exactly his problem. Always had been.

Was this just another one of his harebrained ideas that he was going to talk her into? He already knew the answer to that. It was probably selfish, definitely reckless. But he wanted more of her, and she was turning out to be something he was having trouble resisting. And truth be told, he was getting caught up in this engagement thing.

It was fun, wild. And those were two things that Shep had *always* had trouble resisting.

"I'm damn serious," he said.

CHAPTER FIVE

RYLEE STEPPED OUT of her car and into the soft spring afternoon. It was unseasonably warm for April in Montana, and she was only wearing jeans and a sweater, but she shivered anyway, looking over at the sprawling ranch house and the big, fancy barn and riding facility beyond that.

It was her first time at Dalton's Grange, and it was just as beautiful as she'd imagined. Neal and Deborah had bought a gorgeous property with wide-open pastures for their cattle and views of the jagged, snowcapped mountains in the distance.

She took a deep breath, the air smelling sweet, like horses and grass, and tried to ignore the nerves in her belly. Shep had assured her this was just a casual visit. Maybe they'd go on a horseback ride or a picnic or something, but most of his family was in Helena for the weekend for a stock show, so the pressure was off. He'd wanted it to be a laid-back introduction to his ranch, but she was anxious anyway because she knew Deborah had stayed behind, and she was the one person Rylee was most nervous about seeing again.

Her phone dinged from her pocket, and she pulled it out to see a text from Shep.

When you get here, just go on up to the house. I have to check on one of our pregnant cows really quick. Won't be long. Just make yourself at home!

She bit the inside of her cheek, tucking the phone back in her pocket. He'd told her earlier that his mom was in town for the morning, so the house was empty. Still, she'd be back at some point, and then what? All of a sudden, the nerves in her belly multiplied at the thought of making small talk with the woman who thought Rylee was going to be her new daughter-in-law. Poor Deborah. She had no idea she was being deceived. Unless, of course, Shep and Rylee got married after all.

At the thought of Shep's suggestion the other night, Rylee grazed her teeth over her bottom lip. She still couldn't believe that he'd been serious, but he was. Dead serious. She still couldn't get her mind around the idea of marrying Shep. She'd left Doug's the other night without giving him an answer, but ever since he'd dropped her off afterward, she'd been thinking about it. She couldn't *stop* thinking about it. There were two ways to look at this outrageous proposal. One, they'd be digging themselves in even deeper by actually getting married. Something that would require more than a fake breakup to fix. They'd actually have to get an annulment or, worse, a divorce if it didn't work out. And what were the odds that it would work out? Shep hadn't said one word about being in love with her. He'd only mentioned the convenience of it. Because that was what a union between them would be, after all. A marriage of convenience.

Rylee hitched her purse up over her shoulder and began walking slowly toward the house. The *other* way of thinking about it was the most tempting option. They wouldn't have to have a fake breakup. They wouldn't have to disappoint anyone or admit that they'd rushed into an engagement without thinking it all the way through, which was, of course, what everyone would assume. But the absolute best part would be that she'd be getting married to

Shep. No matter what he thought about it, it would be a secret dream come true for her. Getting to marry her high-school crush. She could hardly imagine it without wanting to squeal like a girl. Which was ridiculous, but that was how she felt.

However, she also felt a fair amount of hesitation, which was her brain taking over from her heart. Shep didn't love her. That much was obvious. And did she want to get married to someone who didn't love her, even if it *was* a marriage of convenience? She didn't think of herself as being overly traditional, but she was traditional enough to believe that love and marriage still went hand in hand. Tyler had never loved her, not really. A realization that still hurt to this day. It was something that always made her feel small whenever she revisited the memories of that relationship.

She took the stairs up to the lovely wraparound front porch, where two rocking chairs sat facing the north pasture, just waiting for someone to come sit and rest and contemplate. Hanging baskets full of colorful spring pansies lined the overhang, smelling heavy and sweet. Horses nickered in the distance, and Rylee could imagine living here, sitting on the porch and drinking lemonade on hot summer afternoons or cooking dinner in the kitchen and hearing the thudding of cowboy boots coming down the hallway. It was a big, fancy ranch, but it was also a home where family gathered and lived and loved. Her own modest home in Tenacity felt empty these days, with her brothers gone and her parents rattling around in it alone.

She came to a stop at the front door, where a bronze flower wreath hung, and felt an ache inside her heart that took her by surprise. As much as she loved her apartment in BH247, she missed being around family like this. She missed a wood fire in the hearth on winter nights and home-cooked meals and having someone to share them with. Even a marriage of convenience would still be a marriage. She'd be welcomed into this life; she'd settle into this family. And before she could help herself, she imagined what it would be like to walk through this front door on Shep's arm, as his wife, as his partner.

It was a thought that warmed her through, even as she raised her hand to knock on the door like a stranger would. Shep had said to go on inside, but that felt assuming to her, so she waited a few seconds and knocked again, just to make sure nobody was inside.

When she was positive she wasn't going to be surprising anyone, especially Deborah, she turned the handle and pushed the door open.

Standing in the doorway for a minute, she looked around with her heart in her throat. The house was absolutely stunning. With its rustic leather couches and chairs, and darkly stained wood, it looked like something out of a home decor show. There was a giant antler chandelier hanging from the ceiling, something that would have been too much in any other space but fit perfectly here. She wondered if Deborah had decorated the house herself or had brought in someone to do it for her. Regardless, it was beautiful, and Rylee had to catch her breath at the sight.

From across the house, a door slammed.

"Hello?" she called hesitantly, painfully aware that she was standing in his parents' living room after having just let herself in.

"Shep, honey? Is that you?"

Her stomach twisted. *Deborah.* She must've been out back when Rylee pulled up. Not only was she going to have to explain why she'd walked right in, but she was also going to have to talk about the engagement, which she'd been wanting to avoid for as long as possible. Lying to Gabby was bad enough, but lying to Shep's mother was going to be especially hard to do. Second only to lying to her own mother.

"Um…" She steeled herself. "Actually, it's me, Mrs. Dalton. Rylee Parker. Remember?"

Deborah appeared in the kitchen doorway, looking fit and polished. She wore a pair of dark-wash jeans with a turquoise belt and a pink plaid Western shirt that complimented her dewy skin tone. She looked exactly the same as Rylee remembered.

"Rylee!" she said, slapping her thigh. "What are you doing here?"

Rylee felt herself blush all the way to her ears. "Shep invited me. He's out with the cows. I'm so sorry to surprise you. I knocked, but there was no answer."

"Are you kidding?" She stepped forward and pulled Rylee into a perfumed hug. "You're family!"

Stepping back again, Deborah grinned. "I've been wanting him to ask you over for a proper supper, but he didn't want us bombarding you. I'm just so happy to see you. It's been years! And now this." She shook her head. "Well, I just can't believe it."

Rylee felt her stomach drop like a stone. All of a sudden, the guilt was overwhelming. "I know it must've been a shock, Mrs. Dalton…"

"Deborah, please! It was, but in the best way possible. Come sit down. I'll make a pot of tea. Do you like tea? I can't remember."

Rylee let herself be ushered over to the couch, where she sat, feeling about an inch tall. Deborah was so sweet, so warm and welcoming, and she had no clue that this engagement wasn't real. The whole thing had seemed pretty harmless in the beginning. Fun and carefree, like Shep himself. But now it was obvious that people could be hurt by this. Definitely disappointed.

Deborah sat across from her on the love seat.

"I can't get anything out of Shepard," she said. "Tell me everything. And show me that ring!"

"Oh…uh…" Rylee clasped her hands in her lap. She really needed to fish something out of her jewelry box at home. What kind of newly engaged woman went around without her ring?

"Mom?"

They both turned to see Shep standing there, hat in hand, a ring around his dark blond hair. His face looked flushed. Like he might've run to get here.

"What are you doing here?" he asked. Probably knowing very well that he'd just interrupted an engagement interrogation.

Deborah laughed. "Well, I live here, honey."

"I mean, what are you doing back from town so early?"

"I didn't get groceries… What does it matter? And why didn't you tell me you were inviting my soon-to-be daughter-in-law over?"

Rylee watched him as he walked over then leaned down to give her a kiss on the lips. It was so natural, so believable, she almost forgot it was all for show.

"Hey, baby," he said, then sat down next to her and took her hand. "Sorry, Mom. I just didn't want Rylee feeling overwhelmed or anything."

"Am I that bad?"

"Of course not… It's just that—"

"I'm a little shy," Rylee interjected, trying to help. "But you're absolutely right, I should've come before this."

"Well, you're here now!" Deborah leaned forward, trying to get a look at Rylee's hand.

Shep cleared his throat. "If you're looking for the ring, I haven't gotten one yet."

Deborah stared at him, incredulous. "What do you mean you haven't gotten one yet?"

"I proposed on the spur of the moment. It wasn't planned."

"Still, son. It's been over a week. You need to get this girl a ring."

Rylee resisted the urge to squirm. She felt like she was sitting outside her own body, watching all of this happen to someone else.

"You know," Deborah said, looking thoughtful, "I've got Grandma's engagement ring. It's just gathering dust. It's old-fashioned, so you'd probably want to reset the diamond, but you kids are welcome to it. I know she'd be so pleased about that."

Rylee felt her eyes widen. "Oh… I don't…"

"Mom," Shep said, "that's really sweet. But we'll need to talk about it. You know."

"Of course, of course. But it's here if you want it."

Shep turned to Rylee, looking like he'd bitten off more than he could chew. They'd *both* bitten off more than they could chew. "Want to saddle up the horses?" he asked. "Go for a ride?"

He probably knew how anxious she was to make her escape. The nicer Deborah was, the more she wanted to run away.

"That sounds great."

Deborah smiled. "Okay. Well, you kids have fun. But we're going to have dinner soon, okay? No excuses. With the whole family."

Shep nodded. "The whole family. Got it."

Still holding on to Rylee's hand, he stood up. She stood, too, and leaned into his side. She hoped she looked appropriate. Like a young woman engaged and in love. Instead of how she felt, which was like a huge liar.

After giving Deborah a hug goodbye, she followed Shep out the door and onto the porch. The April sunshine was warm on her cheeks, and the breeze felt good after the sudden claustrophobic feeling of the house.

"Oh my God," Shep breathed. "I'm sorry about that. She wasn't even supposed to be here."

"I feel terrible," Rylee said, following him down the steps.

"It'll be okay. She's excited, but she'd be all right if we broke up. She'd make it."

"If we fake broke up. Since we're not really engaged to begin with."

"Well. Yeah. But you're forgetting, we could go through with it, you know."

"You're nuts."

"Maybe. But you love it."

She smiled, unable to help it.

"Should I list all those practical reasons again?" he continued, walking close to her. She was acutely aware of how his arm felt brushing up against hers. How she'd prefer it around her waist, his thumb moving back and forth on her hip, leaving her skin tingling in its wake.

"I'm aware of all the practical reasons."

"Good. Saves me the trouble."

"I still can't believe you're serious about this," she said.

"You saw my mom in there. You can clearly see what I'm up against. What I've been dealing with this whole time."

"Still, that's not a reason to get *married*, Shep."

"No, that alone isn't a reason. But there are other reasons. Good reasons. You know it as well as I do."

"It's not exactly how I've pictured this marriage thing my whole life."

"Traditional?" He shook his head, putting his Stetson

back on. He pulled it low over his eyes, so he looked sexy and brooding. "No. But what's so great about traditional, anyway? Traditional is boring. And we, Rylee Parker, are not boring."

"Maybe you aren't. But I'm fairly predictable."

"Now, that's where you're wrong. A predictable woman would not have entered into a fake engagement. Nor would she be considering getting married to her fake fiancé. Just saying."

"No, I guess not."

"See?"

"I feel awful about your mother."

"I know. I do, too. But it'll work out. She might not ever have to know we've been fibbing."

"Fibbing is a nice way to put it. We've been lying." She rubbed her temple. "Gabby is going to kill me."

"She won't kill you."

"She will. She'll murder me in my sleep. And I can't blame her. I'd be so mad if I found out she kept something like this from me."

He came to a stop and touched her arm, until she stopped, too. Then took her shoulders in his hands and gently turned her so she was facing him.

"Then let's make sure they don't find out."

She looked up at him. Wanting more than anything to follow his lead, but afraid to at the same time.

"I don't know about you," he said softly, "but I could do without all the damn stuff leading up to marriage. I've been there. I've dated, and *that* bores me. This is anything but boring."

Chewing the inside of her cheek, she let that settle. She thought about Lisa the other night and how clearly surprised she'd been when she heard about this engagement. That had hurt. But could Rylee blame her? She'd always felt the same way. Like Shep would never really be interested in someone like her. And even if their marriage was for convenience only, how long would it be until he got tired of it? Until he got tired of her? The need to protect herself from that eventual pain was overwhelming as he stood there looking down at her. So handsome that her heart literally ached from it.

"I think we might be in over our heads here," she said, forcing herself to look away. "I am, anyway."

Reaching up, he ran the back of his knuckles along her cheekbone. His skin was rough, but his touch was unbelievably gentle. It sent chills all the way to her scalp.

"Do you trust me, Rylee?" he asked.

"It's not about trusting you. We're not kids anymore, Shep."

"No, we're not. And that's exactly why I want to do this."

"Getting married just because it's convenient isn't the right reason to get married."

"Then what *is* the right reason?"

"Oh, I don't know. That you're in love, maybe? That you want to spend the rest of your life with someone?"

"I do love you," he said. "I've always loved you. Best friends, remember?"

It was hard to argue with that. Still, he had to know what she really meant. He was just skirting the issue because this was something he wanted, and that was what Shep did.

"And you're wrong when you say that getting married because it's convenient isn't a good reason to get married," he continued. "But I wouldn't use the word *convenient*, I'd use the word *easy*. Things between us have always been easy, and that's a fantastic reason to get married. I've seen people get married because they fall in love or lust or whatever. And then they've got nothing left when

that feeling fades. We already have a rock-solid foundation. We could build on that. If it doesn't work, it doesn't
work, but at least we could say we tried. And that we kept
our promise to each other. Which I was serious about, by
the way. Doesn't matter that I was a kid. I knew what I
wanted then, and I know what I want now."

She ran her tongue over her lips, and his gaze dropped
to her mouth. Her belly immediately tightened at the expression on his face.

"And I'm what you want now?" she asked.

He didn't answer. Instead, he leaned toward her. So
close that she could feel his breath against her face. She
could see the flecks of hazel in his eyes. It reminded her
of the river rock near their swimming hole all those years
ago. Honey brown and catching the sun like molten gold.

And then, he kissed her. Her heart was beating so hard,
so fast, that she could feel its cadence in her ears. Her pulse
skipped in her wrists as he wrapped an arm around her
and pulled her close. His tongue flicked against her lips,
lightly but insistently, until she opened her mouth and invited him in.

Rylee didn't think she'd ever been kissed like this before. So deeply that she saw stars exploding in colorful
bursts behind her eyes, like firecrackers on the Fourth of
July. She'd asked him if he wanted her, and it turned out
that he didn't have to answer at all. Not with words, at least.

She could feel it in his kiss.

"I CANNOT BELIEVE I had to hear this from Brady Sellers
down at the damn feed store," Morgan said, his baseball
cap pulled low over his eyes.

Shep tucked his gloved hands underneath the twine of
another hay bale and hauled it off the truck. Sweat dripped
into his eyes, making them sting with a viciousness that

made him blink over at his brother now. Morgan looked pissed. And Morgan pissed was not a fun guy to be around. At least, not for any length of time.

"I know," he said, heaving the hay bale toward the barn. It tumbled a few times before coming to a rest near his brother's boots. "Honestly, we weren't expecting it to get around so fast. It just…did."

"Could you please not chuck these things at me?" Morgan said, leaning over to straighten the bale out so it aligned with the rest of them. "There's a way to do this, you know."

"Yeah, I know. The fast way."

Shep grabbed another bale and hauled it over the side of the truck. But this time, he walked over a few steps to set it down neatly next to the others.

"See?" Morgan said. "That wasn't so hard."

Shep rolled his eyes and rubbed the back of his glove underneath his sweaty chin.

"Now, tell me why I had to hear about my little brother being engaged from Brady," Morgan said. "And don't give me the crap you gave Mom about not wanting to overwhelm Rylee."

"I'm sorry." Shep leaned against the side of the Ford for a breath and took his Stetson off. The breeze felt good in his hair. He'd hung his jacket on the fence post a while ago, and he could feel the warmth of the late afternoon sun start to burn the back of his neck. "But you remember how shy Rylee is. And our family? Come on."

"She comes from a big family, too. Lots of brothers, as I recall. She knows how it works."

"All the more reason to keep it on the down-low for a while. But I'm sorry I didn't tell you guys. I was going to."

"Uh-huh."

"I was."

"Right."

"Are you gonna pout now?"

"Shut up."

Shep smiled at his big brother. Giving him a hard time was one of his favorite pastimes. But Morgan was absolutely right. He should've said something. Now all his brothers were pissed at him to varying degrees because they all thought it was their duty to give him marriage advice before he actually got married. The fact that he was already engaged without their nuggets of wisdom strategically planted in Shep's brain irked them to no end.

"This is not something to enter into lightly," Morgan said, crossing his arms over his broad chest.

Shep had to work not to groan. Now that Morgan was married, he thought of himself as an expert on the subject. It was true that he and Erica had a great relationship, and he was helping to raise Josie, her daughter. But Shep could remember a time when Morgan had been just as much of a train wreck when it came to commitment as Shep was. It was hard to listen to his lectures and not want to throw that back in his face a little.

"I know, Morgan," he said.

"You obviously don't know if you just popped the question on the spur of the moment, for God's sake."

Shep bit his tongue. He had a point there.

"Now, Rylee's great—we all love her—but are you absolutely sure this is what you want?" Morgan looked at him hard. Unrelenting. It was the kind of look a father would give his son. Shep's brothers had always been better role models than his own dad.

"I know it's fast," Shep said. "I'm not arguing that. But this is Rylee we're talking about here."

"Yeah, I know. But is it what you want, Shep? Really?"

Shep scraped a hand through his hair. If he was being

honest with himself, he'd say that he hadn't stopped to ask that question since he'd kissed Rylee at Janet's party. Sure, he wanted to sleep with her. And he didn't want any of this to end yet, and getting married seemed like the natural thing to do. Everything he'd told Rylee the other day had been true—they were good together. All the other stuff would work itself out.

But now, with Morgan staring a hole right through him, he had to take a breath and slow down, at least a little, and think about what this really meant.

Marriage... It was a serious commitment, regardless of how he'd been treating it. If it didn't work out, it would mean embarrassment for Rylee. He didn't really give a crap what people around Bronco thought of him, but he cared what they said about Rylee. And he cared that she'd be hurt by it.

He looked out over the north pasture where all the cattle were grazing in the sun. The truth was, knowing all that, he probably shouldn't have pushed this whole marriage thing. But he had. Because at the moment, he *did* think it would work out. There was nothing to complicate it, like most relationships had from the get-go. Rylee wasn't in love with him, something that most likely bothered her, but the way he figured, it only made things easier.

He looked back at Morgan, who was watching him with those eagle eyes. Ready with another epic lecture, no doubt. But Shep wasn't interested. He knew what he wanted, and he wanted Rylee. If that made him a selfish bastard, so be it.

"It's what I want," he said evenly.

Morgan seemed to contemplate this. Then he nodded slowly. "Okay, then. But you need to bring her out for supper, Shep. Let Mom fawn over her a little. Do it right. Rylee deserves that. And honestly, Mom does, too."

Shep tried to ignore a sharp pang of guilt as those words settled. She did deserve that. The only thing was, Morgan had no idea that she and Shep had been leading everyone astray from the beginning. At the thought of his family finding out now, there was an uncomfortable tightening in his gut.

"Soon," Morgan said. "Okay? No excuses."

Shep nodded and put his Stetson back on, hoping his brother couldn't read the look on his face. The one that might betray every damn thought he was having.

CHAPTER SIX

RYLEE WALKED ALONGSIDE Gabby in downtown Bronco Heights, the afternoon sun warm on her shoulders. She winced stepping off the curb when the light changed. She couldn't believe how sore she was from riding the other day. There was a time when she'd been more comfortable on horseback than on her own two feet, but those days were long gone. As evidenced by her screaming hamstrings.

Gabby looked over and smiled. They'd just had lunch and were now window-shopping, one of their favorite things to do on Saturday afternoons. But today felt different. Maybe because there was a fairly significant secret between them, something that Rylee hated.

"I told Ryan we'd be a little longer today," Gabby said. "So he's taking Bella to the park."

"Why are we going to be longer?" But Rylee already knew the answer to that. Gabby had been trying to get her to come downtown for days so they could stop in at Beaumont and Rossi's Fine Jewels to look at engagement rings. And down the street from that was Ever After, *the* bridal boutique in town. Rylee had only ever heard about it before. Shopping there was supposed to be quite the experience. Complete with champagne and pastel macarons up the wazoo.

She shoved her hands in her pockets, more aware than ever that she was ringless. Something everyone probably thought was beyond strange, considering she and Shep were supposed to have been engaged for a few weeks now. Rylee never realized how much people wanted to see your ring when you got engaged. It was the first thing they did when they found out—they grabbed your hand to take a look. Then asked when the big day was.

"Come on," Gabby said. "I know you're not big on jewelry, but this is your engagement ring! We can just take a quick peek inside and see if anything catches your eye. *Please*, Ry?"

"Well…"

Gabby hooked her arm in Rylee's as they passed people on the sidewalk clutching their shopping bags and iced coffees. It was such a nice afternoon, and Gabby was so excited for her. Rylee was caught somewhere between feeling excited herself and feeling like crap for lying to her best friend.

She thought about kissing Shep the other day at Dalton's Grange. And how right that had felt, how perfect. Was it crazy to think something might actually work between them? That they could let this fake engagement carry them away to someplace very real and just as magical?

"Well, what?" Gabby said, looking over at her with an exaggerated pout on her pretty face.

Rylee smiled, unable to help it. "Okay," she said. "Let's do it."

"*Yes!* I didn't want to push, but of course I'm going to push. I mean, I have to be involved in helping you pick it out, right? That seems reasonable to me."

"Very reasonable."

"Can I ask you a question, though? Bestie to bestie?"

"Sure."

The smile faded on Gabby's lips as they continued down the sidewalk, their boots tapping out a steady cadence on the cement.

"Why have you been dragging your feet on the ring, Rylee? Tell me honestly. Is it because you're having doubts about this engagement?"

Rylee's stomach dropped. Gabby knew her so well, of course this question was inevitable. In fact, she was surprised her friend hadn't asked before today. Wasn't going to look at rings probably the very first thing she and Shep should've done together?

"It's so fast," she said. "I'm just nervous."

"I get it. I'd feel the same way. But you love him, right? You love Shep?"

"I've always loved him." That was true. But was she *in* love with him? It was a good question because they were two very different things.

"So, you're just nervous," Gabby said. "Nothing else is going on?"

Rylee shook her head. She couldn't bring herself to deny it out loud.

"Good. Then we can look at rings, and maybe a dress or two before we go home."

"You didn't say anything about dresses."

"No, because I knew you'd probably try to run away, if your body language is any indication."

"I'm not *that* bad."

"Girl, you're stiff as a board."

"I've been the one helping you out of your shell since we met," Rylee said. "When did the tables turn, anyway?"

"Getting engaged to Ryan has taught me a lot. I'm much better at getting what I want now. And what I want is for you to try on these rings."

They slowed as the sign for Beaumont and Rossi's came into view. Rylee's heart skipped in her chest.

"Here we are," Gabby said. "Ready?"

"Ready."

Gabby reached out and pulled the door open. A little bell tinkled their arrival as Rylee stepped inside and looked around. Sparkling glass cases lined the walls, and a crystal chandelier hung low, bathing the entire place in soft light. Expensive-looking paintings hung throughout, and small sculptures accentuated the jewelry cases. They were for sale. Rylee leaned forward and looked at the small price tag on one of them. She almost coughed in astonishment.

"May I help you ladies?"

A tall, graceful woman in an impeccable cream pant-suit appeared from behind the front counter. She wore her hair in a low French twist and looked like someone out of Rylee's mom's favorite rom-com, *Pretty Woman*. Hopefully she wouldn't be as rude as the sales ladies were in that infamous shopping scene.

"Yes," Gabby said. "My best friend is getting married, but she hasn't picked out a ring yet."

The woman smiled wide. "Well, you're in the right place, I assure you. What kind of ring are you looking for?"

Rylee's cheeks warmed. She thought of how sweet Deborah had been the other day, offering her mother's ring. Honestly, that was more in line with what she'd pick for herself. She'd always been a sucker for sentimental things, and she couldn't think of anything more meaningful than a family heirloom like that.

But she leaned forward anyway and peered inside the cases. She didn't think she'd ever seen such beautiful rings in her life. Every size and shape and color imaginable. They twinkled underneath the chandelier lighting, the diamonds and other precious stones drawing her in as if they were magnetized.

"Oh my gosh," Gabby breathed. "Look at that one."

Her friend pointed to a simple oval-cut solitaire that was big enough to choke a horse.

"That's a lovely choice," the saleslady said, leaning down to unlock the case. "And it would look so nice on you with your delicate hands."

Rylee smiled, resisting the urge to look down at her hands. Did she have delicate hands? She'd never thought about it before.

The saleslady brought out the ring, which was even more stunning up close. It was also bigger up close.

"Here," she said. "Why don't you try it on for size?"

Rylee held out her hand, and the saleslady slipped it on. The cold weight of the stone gave her butterflies. Was she *really* thinking about marrying Shep Dalton?

She stood there staring down at the ring, moving her hand back and forth to make it sparkle.

"That. Is. *Gorgeous*," Gabby said. "It looks so pretty on you, Ry."

"It really does," the saleslady agreed. "A truly classic cut, something that's simple, yet refined."

Rylee took a deep, steadying breath. And then, all of a sudden, she was imagining Shep slipping a wedding band atop this ring at the altar. She pictured her dress, which would also be simple, yet refined. Lace, maybe. Or silk. She imagined her friends and family smiling up at her from the church pews, everyone basking in the bride and groom's obvious happiness on their wedding day.

It was such a sweet thought that she startled when Gabby nudged her shoulder.

"Are you okay?" her friend asked. "You drifted off for a second there."

"Oh…" Rylee smiled, embarrassed. "Fine. I was just thinking."

"About?"

"You asked before if I'd been having doubts. Honestly, sometimes I do wonder if I'm ready for this."

She'd recently gotten her promotion at the convention center. She had her own apartment, her own life, and she called the shots. She liked it that way. But now, standing here with this beautiful ring on her finger—which symbolized so much more than just marriage; it symbolized a whole different *life*—she knew she'd been fooling herself for a while now. Maybe she wanted to be a wife and mother more than she even realized.

"I'm just surprised at how much I want it," she continued softly. "That's all. It scares me, whether I'm ready for it or not."

Gabby put an arm around her shoulder. "Of course you want it, Rylee. When are you going to start trusting the good things that happen to you? Not every guy is going to turn out like Tyler. Not everyone is going to break your heart."

She managed a smile. But *scared* really wasn't a strong enough word.

She was terrified.

RYLEE STOOD AT the window in the convention center's nicest conference room, the one that was reserved for the most important meetings with the most important people, and looked down into the spacious indoor arena. Tori Hawkins was running barrels with a gorgeous sorrel gelding that Rylee knew was as green as the day was long. But you'd never know it. Tori, one of rodeo pioneer Hattie Hawkins's granddaughters, had the horse dialed in, tearing around the barrels like a bat out of hell, but never clipping a single one. If Rylee had to guess, she'd say this was another championship duo in the making.

Looking at her watch, she frowned. She had a meeting with Celeste Montgomery this morning, who'd be here any minute. Celeste was a sports reporter for an ABC Chicago affiliate, and she had just arrived in Bronco last month to cover the rodeo beat. Rylee had met her a few times and liked her a lot. But it was clear that she didn't know anything about rodeo. She was a tough cookie though, and Rylee had no doubt that she'd make this assignment work. Besides, in Rylee's experience, most people fell in love with this sport after they'd been properly introduced to it. That wasn't to say that Celeste would, but the odds were definitely in her favor.

"Oh my God, I stopped for a coffee and got caught in Bronco's morning rush hour. Who knew?"

Rylee turned to see Celeste walk through the door wearing a chic blue pantsuit, with a matching jacket and leather tote hooked over her arm. She was still wearing her sunglasses, and her straight black hair was obviously just blown out. She clutched a coffee in one hand and her phone in the other and looked every bit the big-city reporter.

"You're right on time," Rylee said with a smile. "It's so nice to see you again."

"You too, Rylee."

Celeste took off her sunglasses, putting them on top of her head. She had big, dark eyes and a flawless, khaki-brown complexion. She was absolutely beautiful. Rylee glanced down at her own pantsuit, gray and a little drab in comparison. She just wasn't used to calling attention to herself in any form or fashion. But she remembered how it felt when Shep had first seen her in her red dress the night they'd gone to Doug's. His mouth had literally hung open, and he'd stared at her for a good five seconds, making Rylee's face heat in the best way possible. Maybe she should start dressing like that more often. Maybe it was time to start letting her hair down a little. Even if it was just in the wardrobe department. For some reason, knowing that she was involved with a man like Shep gave her courage where she'd lacked it before. That felt good. Actually, it felt great.

"I should've picked up a coffee for you," Celeste said, stepping up to the window and looking down into the arena. "I don't know what I was thinking."

"That's okay. I've had my fair share of caffeine this morning. Any more and I'd probably be able to fly out of here."

Celeste laughed, but kept her gaze on the horse and rider below. "Who's that?"

"Tori Hawkins."

"Ahh. Of the famous Hawkins Sisters?"

"Indeed."

"I can't believe how fast they take those barrels and manage to stay on. I mean, if that was me…"

"Oh, I know, right? I'd fall off right out of the gate."

Celeste turned to Rylee and took a sip of her coffee. Then set it down on the glossy conference-room table with a sigh. "Between you and me, I'm clueless about barrel racing. And bull riding. And calf roping, and…all of it, really. Chicago isn't exactly the rodeo capital of the world. But they wanted someone who wasn't afraid of a challenge, and I guess that was me."

"Well, you'll learn fast. There's still a lot that I'm figuring out, too, but the people around here are friendly and helpful. If you have a question, they'll do their best to give you an answer. And if they don't know, they'll find you someone who does."

"That's good to know."

"How are you settling into Bronco? Are you liking it so far?"

Celeste ran a hand through her hair. "It's different. A lot of cowboys, that's for sure."

"Not a fan of cowboys?"

"Now, I didn't say that." Celeste gave her a knowing smile. "I can appreciate a handsome man when I see one. But the culture is different. It takes some getting used to."

Rylee knew that was true. She'd gone from Montana to California, and that had been a huge shock to her system. She couldn't imagine what it would be like coming from a city like Chicago to a town like Bronco.

"How about you?" Celeste asked. "I know you're not from here originally, isn't that right?"

Rylee shook her head. "No, I'm from Tenacity. A little town not far from here."

"And you're liking Bronco?"

"I like it. It's faster moving than Tenacity, that's for sure."

"I heard someone say you're recently engaged," Celeste said. "Congratulations."

"Oh...thank you."

Rylee sat down next to Celeste in one of the cushy chairs. The leather was cold, and she shivered. She still couldn't get used to how fast this engagement news had traveled. And was still traveling.

"Are you getting married in Bronco?" Celeste asked. "Or are you going back to Tenacity for that?"

Rylee chewed her bottom lip. It was obvious the other woman was a natural reporter. Her questions were direct, her mannerisms a mixture of relaxed and confident.

"I haven't really thought about it yet," she said.

"I'm sure there's a lot to consider, with family and everything."

Rylee guessed there would be. She wondered how her mother would feel about her getting married in Bronco. Or how Deborah would feel about Shep getting married in Tenacity. The latter made more sense because the Daltons were from there originally.

She cleared her throat. The other day, she'd let herself start imagining her wedding dress. Now she was mentally deciding on the location. If only Celeste knew this was a fake engagement. What in the world would she think?

The other woman leaned back in her chair and took another sip of coffee. "So…" she said, putting her cup down again. "Speaking of cowboys, my boss wants an exclusive from Geoff Burris. That's why I'm here. But he's apparently such a superstar that his people keep putting me off."

"Oh. Well, I'm sure it's nothing personal. He's actually in Europe with his fiancée right now."

"I heard that. But I've asked to Skype, or whatever is easiest for him, and still nothing. It's super frustrating."

Rylee frowned. As the Bronco Convention Center's new marketing director, this was exactly the type of thing she needed to make happen for Celeste. Difficult, though, since she knew Geoff was probably tired of giving interviews. It was why he was in Europe in the first place. Celeste was right when she said he was a superstar. Around here, he was *the* superstar.

"I'm so sorry," Rylee said, leaning forward and spreading her hands out on the cold marble tabletop. "Don't worry, though. This is going to work out. If we can't get Geoff to sit down with you, how about one of his brothers? I can assure you they're very knowledgeable, very successful in rodeo, too."

Celeste tapped her index finger against her coffee cup. "Hmm. Normally, I'd be a stickler for Geoff, but I really need this interview sooner rather than later."

"Let me make a call. Set something up for you."

Celeste gazed past Rylee's shoulder and out the window,

obviously weighing this. Then nodded slowly. "Okay," she said. "Thanks, Rylee. I appreciate that."

"Of course. I know you won't be disappointed. The Burris family is wonderful."

"All I know is how they've paved the way for Black rodeo riders in this country, and that's a good story. And I'm all about a good story."

Rylee had no doubt Celeste was about the *best* stories, if the determined look on her face was any indication. She wondered which brother might be the best choice for the interview—Mike, who was engaged to Corinne Hawkins, Jack, or Ross. Ross (a popular bachelor) was also a well-known charmer, which might be perfect for this kind of thing. Of course, Celeste would probably be able to see through all that, but still, a little charm might go a long way. She picked up her phone and added a reminder to call him as soon as this meeting was over. The sooner, the better.

Before she could set her phone back down, it dinged with a text from Shep.

Dinner with the family this weekend? Have you decided whether you're going to marry me or not? Don't break my heart ;)

She must've made a sound, because Celeste looked over curiously.

"It's just my fiancé," she said, managing a smile. "Asking about dinner plans for the weekend…"

Well. Kind of. Not a romantic dinner. Dinner with his entire family. All his brothers and their significant others. But most importantly, Neal and Deborah. If she thought the other day at Dalton's Grange was nerve-racking, just wait until she sat down to an actual meal with all of them.

"That sounds nice," Celeste said. "What's your fiancé's name?"

"Shep. Dalton. Shep Dalton."

Celeste smiled. "You seem nervous."

"I do?"

"You do. Are you okay?"

"Fine. Super."

"Is it pre-wedding jitters? I've heard that's a thing."

If she had pre-wedding jitters, that would mean she was actually getting *married*. Was she getting married? All of a sudden, her head was spinning.

Celeste leaned forward and put a hand on her arm. "Seriously, Rylee. Are you sure you're all right? You're white as a sheet."

"I am?"

"Here. Let me get you some water."

The other woman stood, walked over to the water cooler in the corner of the room and filled a paper cup.

"If you've been busy planning the wedding," Celeste said, bringing it back to Rylee, "you could be overly stressed. Even dehydrated. If it weren't for my coffee, I think I'd forget to drink anything at all. You know how it is when you get busy with work."

Rylee took a sip of the water, which felt heavenly going down. "Thank you. Maybe I am a little stressed."

Celeste sat down again, watching her closely. "That's better. I think the color is coming back."

"Sorry. That's never happened to me before."

"Don't be sorry. Just drink all that water and take a few deeps breaths. That always helps me when I'm feeling panicky."

Rylee breathed in through her nose and out through her mouth. Once, twice, until she felt her pulse begin to slow. Where was this coming from? Was she just nervous about sitting down with Shep's family? That was understandable, but she thought it was more than that. She was pretty sure it had more to do with how she felt about Shep, without him feeling the same way about her. It had been bothering her for a few days now, but she'd pushed it aside in favor of letting herself get swept up in all of this. It was easy to do.

She took another sip of water and smiled at Celeste over the rim of the cup. If she had any hope of salvaging this meeting without this woman thinking she'd come completely unglued, she needed to stop thinking about Shep and weddings and falling in love, and start thinking about how she was going to get Ross Burris to agree to a one-on-one interview with Celeste Montgomery within the next few days. She could worry about dinner at Dalton's Grange later. Right now, she needed to get down to work.

She leaned back and tossed the cup in the garbage, then pushed her chair away from the table. "How would you like a tour of the arena, Celeste? Then after that, I'll give Ross a call, and we can get the ball rolling on your interview."

"That'd be great. Count me in."

Rylee followed Celeste out the door and into the long, air-conditioned corridor that led to the glass elevator. She began telling the other woman all about the convention center's state-of-the-art construction and how they expected it to bring in even more rodeo talent in the years to come. At least it was something to talk about. Something to keep her mind occupied.

But her heart was a lost cause.

CHAPTER SEVEN

"Mom, what's this all about?" Shep asked, looking at his watch. "I still need to shower before Rylee gets here."

"Just come with me for a minute. It won't take long."

Resisting the urge to sigh, Shep followed his mother up the staircase to the second floor, running his hand along the glossy wood railing as he went. He was tired and sweaty after bucking hay with Holt and Dale most of the afternoon, and his shoulders were aching. A long, hot shower sounded good. Followed by a cold beer and his mother's cooking. She'd been in the kitchen all day, making her spaghetti sauce from scratch. The rich, heavy scent filled the entire house, along with the smell of the homemade bread that was currently baking in the oven.

His stomach rumbled. He could almost taste the pasta, the warm, buttery bread and the salad with the tangy vinaigrette dressing that had been his grandmother's specialty. It was almost enough to make him forget that his entire family would be here tonight, grilling him and Rylee until long after the apple pie was served. Maybe he'd get lucky and they'd all be too busy eating to ask a ton of questions. But he wouldn't hold his breath.

His mom turned and gave him a smile over her shoulder. She was practically glowing, and Shep knew why. All her boys were just about married and settled down now. Her mind and heart were finally at ease.

Shep smiled back, feeling a now familiar stab of guilt.

The thought of coming clean now, after all this, was almost too much to contemplate. His mom would be crushed. His dad and brothers would be pissed. And what about Rylee? What kind of fallout would be waiting for her? He knew she'd been worried about lying to Gabby, but what about her parents and her own brothers? It wouldn't be pretty. None of it would be.

Still, deep down, he knew that wasn't a good reason to get married. He was reckless, but he wasn't stupid. The thing driving him now was Rylee herself, and the temptation to have her for his own. He still believed they could make this work if she agreed to it. If they were lucky, everything else would fall into place eventually. And if they weren't? Well, he'd just have to deal with that when it happened.

He followed his mother into her bedroom, the late-afternoon sun slanting in warm rays of gold through the windows. Their cat, Steve, was stretched out in one of the sunbeams on the floor, all four paws in the air. He looked like roadkill. Shep nudged him with his boot as he passed, making sure he was still breathing. The cat chirped a meow and then closed his eyes again, too lazy to move.

"Now, don't feel any pressure to take this," Shep's mom said, walking over to her antique vanity and opening her jewelry box. "But I've been thinking about it since the other day, and in my heart, it just feels right to offer it. You and Grandma always had a special relationship…"

She pulled out a small velvet box and cracked it open.

Inside was his grandmother's engagement ring. He remembered seeing it on her hand when he was little, sparkling against her papery skin. She'd told him the story of when she and his grandpa had met dozens of times. She'd been working at the movie theater in Tenacity when she was only fifteen years old. His grandpa had driven by in a convertible with his friends and had waved at her when she was walking out the front doors. She'd smiled and waved back, and he'd turned the car around so he could ask her out. The rest was history. A love story for the ages.

He stared down at the ring now, suddenly overcome with memories of her, with missing her and her wry sense of humor. Her smiles, which were contagious. And her hugs, which Shep had reveled in as the youngest of five brothers, who got picked on more often than not. He could remember running into her skirts and burying his face in her apron when he was probably as young as three or four. She'd been a huge part of his childhood, an important and loving adult in his life. And he missed her terribly.

His mother watched him closely, probably trying to gauge his interest in the ring. The fact that she would offer this meant so much. But he had no idea if Rylee was even going to marry him, let alone if she'd be interested in his grandmother's ring.

"What are you thinking?" his mom asked softly.

Shep felt the muscles in his jaw bunch. His family wasn't perfect, never had been. He'd been angry at his dad for a long time, finding it hard to forgive him for the way he'd treated his mother in the past. There'd been cheating, lying, drunken foolishness back then. His dad had changed and his parents still loved each other, despite everything. And they loved their sons with a deep and fierce devotion that Shep had always felt to his bones. He was lucky to be a Dalton. And if Rylee gave him the honor of becoming her husband, he knew she'd be welcomed into the family with the same love that he'd always known himself.

"I don't know what to say, Mom," he said, his voice low. "Thank you."

"Now, like I said, don't feel like you need to take it.

But it's here if you want it. Grandpa had it custom-made in 1955, the year they were married. Just so you know."

Shep's grandfather had been a tough old cowboy with a gruff way about him. Except when it came to his wife, whom he'd doted on. Spoiled every day of her life. He wasn't surprised that a stock ring wouldn't have done for his pretty young bride with the raven curls.

Taking the box from his mother's hand, he took the ring out and held it up to the sunlight coming in through the window. There was one large square-cut diamond in the middle, surrounded by smaller diamonds all the way around. His mom had said it was old-fashioned the other day, but he thought it looked surprisingly contemporary. He guessed everything came back in style if you waited long enough. He wondered what kind of ring Rylee liked, what kind of style she preferred. She didn't wear much jewelry on a daily basis, only small earrings and a watch, but he thought the ring would look beautiful on her. But that wasn't a stretch. Everything looked good on Rylee.

He moved the ring back and forth, watching the diamonds create a prism of rainbow color in the vanity's mirror. "I still haven't talked to Rylee about her ring yet," he said. "Can I have a little time? I just want her to be happy with it. And I know she'd love this, but—"

"You don't have to explain. Take all the time you need. It'll be here."

Shep leaned down and kissed his mother on the cheek. She smiled, looking genuinely happy, genuinely pleased with this whole turn of events.

He thought about how his grandparents had met—the story of them waving to each other in the little town of Tenacity in the 1950s, when the world was simpler and their whole lives were ahead of them.

He swallowed hard. He thought about Rylee as a teenager and wondered if she ever thought they'd truly make good on that promise back then. And he wondered if someday, just maybe, they might tell the story of how they met, too.

RYLEE LOOKED DOWN at her dress, something she'd found in the back of her closet and that she'd only worn once before. To a wedding, ironically. She remembered sitting in the back row feeling awkward and out of place. She'd barely known the bride, who'd been a work acquaintance, and she hadn't stayed for the reception. But she'd always loved the dress, a floral print that was flirty and sweet. Paired with her favorite cowboy boots, she thought it was the perfect thing to wear to the ranch for dinner.

She took a deep breath. This was it. The moment she'd been dreading for the last few weeks. Being in the same room with Shep's entire family and actually having to lie to their faces. Rylee hadn't been altogether sure she'd be able to do it when she woke up that morning. The thought of calling Shep and telling him that she didn't feel well had crossed her mind. It was true, she hadn't felt well. She'd been so nervous, her stomach had done somersaults when she'd stepped out of bed. But then he'd texted and said that his mother was making her famous all-day spaghetti sauce and was so happy about this dinner, and Rylee knew she'd just have to power through it.

She reminded herself again that Shep really did want to get married. And not only that—she was tempted to say yes. Which meant this was less like lying and more like… she wasn't sure really. But she knew that in order to get through tonight, she was going to have to put everything else on the back burner and simply wear a confident smile. What else could she do?

She lifted her hand now and rang the Dalton's doorbell with her heart in her throat. After a few seconds, it opened. She looked up to see Neal Dalton standing there, looking larger than life.

He smiled wide, and before she knew what was happening, he'd pulled her into a bear hug.

"Rylee!" he boomed. "It's so good to see you."

Rylee smiled against his denim shirt. He smelled like soap. Neal had always intimidated her a little. He used to be gruff, definitely quiet and on the broody side when she and Shep were kids. But he'd clearly grown a little softer around the edges since she'd seen him last. He was a grandfather now, with salt-and-pepper hair and a matching handlebar mustache, and she wondered if that had something to do with it.

"Hi, Mr. Dalton," she said, pulling away with a smile. "It's good to see you, too."

"Who's this Mr. Dalton fellow?" he asked with a wink. "It's going to be Dad soon enough. At least call me Neal."

"All right. Will do."

"Come in, come in."

He ushered her inside, where the house was bustling. There were a few little ones running around, and about a dozen adults visiting in the living room. The smell of warm bread wafted in from the kitchen and made Rylee's stomach growl, despite her nerves.

Everyone turned when she walked in the door and then made their way over one by one. Morgan, whom she hadn't seen in nearly as long as Neal, gave her a kiss on the cheek and introduced her to his wife, Erica, and their adorable, chubby-cheeked little girl, Josie. And then she was hugging Holt and meeting his wife, Amanda, and his son, Robby, Boone and his wife, Sofia, and Dale and his fiancée, Kendra, who owned one of the cutest bakeries in

Bronco Heights, as well as her daughter, Mila, who was clutching a fat tabby cat in her arms.

By the time Shep came walking down the stairs, Rylee's head was spinning. There were so many of them. Such a big family. Honestly, not too much bigger than her own, but for some reason, things at Dalton's Grange felt larger than life, like Neal himself. Or maybe that was just the weight of the reality on her shoulders. When she and Shep told a few strangers they were engaged at Janet's party, she never would've imagined that lie would grow to be this large or intricate. She ran her palms down her dress as Shep came walking over.

"Hey, beautiful," he said, leaning down to give her a kiss.

At this point, it was hard to tell if that was for everyone else's benefit or her own. Regardless, she felt her knees grow weak, like they did every time he kissed her now. She wondered if her kisses had the same effect on him. She had to ask herself if he would ever love her, or if she was just a means to an end. It was unsettling. Especially now, as he pulled away and smiled down at her, his blue eyes twinkling.

"You made it. And in that dress, too. You look amazing."

He put his arm around her, and she leaned into his side, loving how solid he felt.

"I see you met all the significant others," he said. "And the offspring. Pretty cute, huh? Josie has everyone wrapped around her little finger, let me tell you. And Mila is our animal lover. She's more obsessed with the ranch than Dad is."

Rylee let her gaze fall on the little girl who was now sitting on the couch with the cat, stroking his head and talking to him in soft, gentle tones.

"She's a sweetheart," Rylee said. "It looks like she has a way with cats, too."

"Well, Steve is a bit of a narcissist, so he's all about the attention."

Rylee laughed. "I can't say I blame him."

Deborah came out of the kitchen wearing a lavender apron with ruffles around the bust and made a beeline for Rylee.

"Rylee! I hope you're hungry, honey," she said, taking her hand.

Rylee's stomach rumbled again. "I'm starving. Do you need some help in the kitchen?"

"Absolutely not. That's what Shep's dad is for. And dinner's almost ready anyway. Can we get you something to drink? A glass of wine, maybe?"

"Wine sounds wonderful."

"White or red? I think we have chardonnay and a pinot noir that we bought at a local vineyard last summer. It's delicious."

At the mention of wine, Rylee remembered the chilled bottle in her fridge that she'd meant to bring as a gift. It probably wasn't as expensive as Deborah's, but it was a nice bottle. She'd completely forgotten, though, because she'd been so anxious leaving her apartment that evening.

"The pinot noir would be great," she said. "Thank you."

As if sensing her nerves, Shep tightened his arm around her waist. She could get used to this. They really did make a good team. He seemed to know when she needed him, and she liked to think the same was true about her. It didn't matter that they hadn't seen each other in years. They'd been able to pick right back up where they'd left off.

Deborah disappeared back into the kitchen, and Erica walked up and touched her arm.

"I just *love* your dress," the other woman said. "Where'd you get it?"

"Oh, thanks. I actually ordered it online for a wedding a few years ago. From an outlet that was going out of business, so it was on sale." Her cheeks warmed. Rylee had grown up thrifty. When you came from a family like hers, that had struggled making ends meet, you had to learn to be. She wasn't ashamed of it, but at the same time, she knew there was a good possibility Erica and her sisters-in-law shopped at more upscale places. Places that Rylee hadn't been able to afford before getting her promotion at the convention center.

"Oh, shoot," Erica said. "I wish they hadn't gone out of business. I'd be ordering one just like it."

"Do you even have room for another dress in your closet?" This from Morgan, who was giving his wife a teasing look.

"You hush. There's tons of room in my closet."

"I love you, babe. But stretching the truth is your specialty. You're amazing at it."

Erica rolled her eyes, but there was obvious affection there. A playfulness that Rylee recognized in her relationship with Shep, too. Charm was something the Dalton men had in spades.

Deborah came in holding a glass of wine and handed it to Rylee with a smile. "Dinner will be ready in about ten minutes. You just make yourself at home, okay?"

"Thanks, Mrs. Dalton."

Rylee watched the other woman head back into the kitchen. For some reason, she couldn't stop calling them Mr. and Mrs. As if she was still in the eighth grade or something.

"Nervous?" Shep leaned down close to her ear so nobody else would hear. "You don't have to be, you know. They've always loved you."

"A little," she whispered back. "Aren't you?"

"I can handle them. I'm mostly worried about you. They can be a lot."

He'd always been protective of her, always wanting to shield her from anything that could hurt her. But this was different. This was his family. There was only so much shielding he could do. If they went ahead with this, if they went ahead and got married, she would have to hold her own, no matter what came at her. She'd be a Dalton.

At the thought of that, her stomach dipped.

Shep took her elbow and led her over to one of the big front windows. The view was gorgeous. You could see half the ranch from here, drenched in gold by the setting sun. In the distance, Black Angus cattle grazed, peppery specks against the emerald green pastures. Rylee took a sip of her wine, hardly able to believe she was standing here. That she was contemplating marriage to Shep. That Neal and Deborah might be her in-laws, and Dalton's Grange her eventual home. It was almost too much to absorb, even though she'd had several days to try and do just that.

"Hey," Shep said, gazing down at her. "Is everything okay?"

She nodded. She seemed to be getting asked that a lot lately. "Just thinking."

"About what?"

"You and me. All of this. I can't believe we're doing this."

"Pretending to be engaged? Or thinking about actually getting married?"

"Both."

Shep looked out the window, the muscles in his jaw working.

"What are you thinking about?" she asked, suddenly wanting to know more than anything.

He let his gaze settle on her again. "About whether or not you're going to go through with it."

Her heartbeat slowed. She wanted to go through with it. Who wouldn't want to marry Shep? But on the other hand, it'd be foolish not to consider the consequences. Which was a possibly ruined friendship. Or having to go through an annulment or a divorce and enduring all the talk that would follow. And there would be a lot of talk. Rylee was used to a certain amount of that—she'd grown up in claustrophobic Tenacity after all, and Tenacity was smaller than Bronco. But even so, people would have things to say, and she'd always hated being the subject of gossip. For someone who was shy and quiet by nature, it made her feel exposed and vulnerable. Like she needed to put up walls to defend herself. It felt like she'd done enough of that to last a lifetime.

"What do you say, Ry?" Shep asked, his voice low. "Are you going to marry me?"

It wasn't the proposal she'd always dreamed of. He wasn't on bended knee, holding out a ring. He hadn't professed his love, and neither had she.

"Shep," she began. "Do you love me?"

It was bold. Much bolder than she was used to being, but the stakes were too high now not to know.

He gazed down at her. She knew Shep better than most people did. But right then, she couldn't tell what he was thinking. His eyes were shuttered, revealing nothing. His mouth, normally tilting at one side with a ready smile, settled into a firm line, and her heart sank a little. Just a little. Because, really, she hadn't let herself hope for much more than the fleeting happiness of this fake engagement. If she did, if she let that hope in, she'd be risking pain in the end, and she cared too much about herself to let that happen.

So she continued looking up at him, her chin raised, her shoulders back.

"Rylee," he began. "I…"

She stood there, holding her breath. Whatever he was about to say, she'd be okay. They'd be okay. They were friends, and that was what mattered most in the end. And if she told herself that enough, maybe she'd even start to believe it.

"Dinner!" Deborah called from the kitchen. "Come and get it!"

Rylee exhaled shakily. But her stomach remained tight. Unable to relax because the answer she'd been waiting for hadn't materialized.

Boone walked up and smacked Shep on the shoulder. "Let's get after it, little brother."

Shep took her hand. A silent show of…what exactly? His skin was warm, rough against hers. She wanted to believe that he'd been about to tell her exactly what she wanted to hear. But she wasn't letting herself go there. She couldn't let herself go there.

So she walked into the kitchen beside him and put on her bravest face. Determined not to let anyone see how scared she was. Because, no matter what, no matter how she'd been spinning it to herself, she didn't just love Shep. She was in love with him. And that was the cold, hard truth.

"RYLEE, HAVE YOU thought about where you want to get married?" Sofia asked, handing the basket of garlic bread to Boone, who unloaded three pieces onto his overflowing plate.

Rylee had just taken a bite of her spaghetti and smiled awkwardly, her mouth full.

"Oh," Kendra said. "You guys should definitely get married out here. Can you picture it? A sunset wedding? The ranch always has the prettiest sunsets."

"No, you should one hundred percent get married at that new aquarium!" Mila said, a dot of spaghetti sauce on her chin. Rylee noticed that she liked to say "one hundred percent" a lot. A few minutes ago she'd told her mother that she one hundred percent wanted ice cream with her pie. "My friend Nellie's mom works out there, and she says people can rent it out, and then their family and kids get to visit for free and stuff."

"Honey, your chin," Kendra said. "No, I heard that, too." She turned back to Rylee. "It's not open to the public yet, but when it is, you can rent it out. And since that's where you guys reconnected, wouldn't it be romantic?"

"*Sooo* romantic," Erica said. "And what about your dress? Have you picked one out?"

"We don't even have a date yet," Shep said. "And can you guys let her finish chewing first before you continue with the grand spaghetti inquisition?"

Erica didn't seem to take offense at this. In fact, as far as Rylee could tell, they all treated each other like siblings. Teasing, joking, ribbing each other constantly. Something Rylee could appreciate, since she had brothers herself. She understood the dynamic. She liked the underlying playfulness in the room, the barely controlled chaos. It made her feel at home.

"You mean you don't know when you're gonna get married, Uncle Shep?" Mila said with a frown.

"Well, uh…" Shep looked over at Rylee.

"No, honey," Rylee said. "We're not quite sure yet."

"Oh, then you should one hundred percent get married at Christmas," Mila said with calm, eight-year-old conviction. "Then you'll get presents for getting married *and* presents for Christmas."

"That's an excellent idea, Mila," Shep said. "We'll one hundred percent consider that."

Erica pointed her fork at Rylee. "But the *dress*. Are you going to Ever After? I mean, you should. At least to window-shop. They have the most beautiful things, and Patrice is really wonderful about helping her brides pick out the dress of their dreams. It's a whole experience, believe me."

"Well, if you go," Deborah said, "and if you and your mother want company, I'd love to tag along. By the way, I've been wanting to call Norma, Rylee. Is it okay if I give her a ring? Shep wasn't sure if you'd had a chance to sit down and tell your parents about the engagement properly yet."

At the mention of her parents, Rylee had to force down a stubborn piece of garlic bread and almost choked on it. She'd been eating nonstop since they'd sat down at the table. She was too nervous to sit still.

She took a sip of her iced tea and then set it down again, almost knocking over Shep's in the process.

"I've talked to them," she said, clearing her throat. "I haven't been back to Tenacity since we got engaged, but we've talked over the phone…"

"I'm sure they're just thrilled their baby is getting married," Deborah said.

Rylee forced a smile. They were happy. But she also clearly remembered her mother's worry. If she and Shep were to call off their fake engagement tomorrow, her mom would probably be a little relieved, to tell the truth.

Her brothers, of course, had reacted in the typical big-brother way. *If he hurts you, we're going to kill him* type thing. Deep down, they were teddy bears, and they'd always loved Shep, so she wasn't that worried about them, but even so, they were probably going to pull him aside at some point and threaten him with his life, which wasn't going to be pleasant.

Josie began wiggling in her high chair, and Erica got

up to clean her face and lift her out. The little girl was so cute, looking up at her mother with such adoration, her chubby little cheeks stained with spaghetti sauce.

"Have you thought about a wedding planner?" Erica asked, bringing Josie back to the table and plopping her down on her lap. "I guess you might not need one if it's small and intimate…"

Boone laughed. "Small and intimate? This family?"

Shep gave Rylee an apologetic look. It was a lot. But at the same time, she couldn't help but enjoy it a little, too. Deep down, she felt like a princess. Which was why so many little girls dreamed of this moment practically from birth. The ring, the dress, the venue, the groom… It was all very sweet and magical.

And nerve-racking.

"What do you think?" she asked Shep. "Small and intimate?"

"I don't care. Just as long as you show up."

He winked at her. That familiar, mischievous wink that was so very Shep, and all of a sudden everything else fell away. His family, the dinner, all the worries about how they'd let it get this far, and she gazed over at him. *As long as you show up…*

Was that what she was going to do? Marry him?

She still wasn't sure.

CHAPTER EIGHT

SHEP PULLED UP to BH247, his truck's motor rumbling through the cool night air. He had his window cracked, and he breathed in the scent of the asphalt, of the tidy rows of spring flowers planted out front. So different from the smells of the ranch—the warm smell of hay and animals. Of grass and wood and leather.

He looked over at Rylee, her profile bathed in shadow. She had her hands tucked neatly in her lap, and his denim jacket wrapped around her shoulders. She'd had a couple of glasses of wine, so he'd wanted to drive her home, just to be safe. He'd bring her car back into town tomorrow.

She turned to him, her eyes dark and lovely. Her heart-shaped lips glistening in the gritty light.

"Thank you for such a nice dinner," she said. "Your mom went to so much trouble. I can't imagine feeding that many people on the regular."

"She likes it. She says cooking is her love language. I mean, eating is my love language, but whatever."

She laughed. "Well, she's really good at it. That bread alone…"

"I know." He patted his stomach. "If I wasn't trying to save room for pie, I would've eaten like…well, like Boone."

"Where does he *put* it all?"

"He works it off. Ranching burns a ton of calories."

"And your six-pack is proof."

"Are you trying to say I have a nice body, Rylee?" He flexed and kissed one of his biceps.

"You're a tease."

"Oh, I beg to differ. I'd give you anything you wanted. All you have to do is ask."

He said this playfully, but if she only knew how serious he really was…

They sat there for a minute, a charged silence settling between them. Outside the truck's cracked window, Shep could hear crickets chirping their midnight melody. In the distance, a couple of dogs barked, and beyond that, cars passed on the highway.

Rylee pulled at a thread on her dress then looked over at him in the darkness. "Do you want to come in?" she asked. "For a cup of coffee?"

His heart thumped out a steady rhythm inside his chest. It had been a long time since anyone had affected him like this. Made his heart pound and his palms damp. Just sitting beside her in the cab of the truck had him jumping with anticipation. With excited nerves.

"One hundred percent," he said.

She laughed again, and the sound warmed him through. He liked making her laugh. He liked making her smile. But most of all, he liked when she looked at him like she was looking at him now. Like she might feel the same.

His jaw muscles tightened then, as he pictured how she'd looked earlier tonight. When she'd asked if he loved her. He'd literally frozen. He hadn't known how to answer. And then he hadn't had to answer at all because his mother had called everyone to dinner just in time.

She watched him, probably wondering why he'd grown so quiet all of a sudden. But he kept thinking about that question. And the fact that he hadn't known how to answer—because the answer wasn't that simple. At least, it wasn't for Shep.

Love had always been a complicated word for him. Entangled with the likes of *responsibility* and *commitment*. Both of which he knew nothing about, since he'd grown up looking to his father as an example. Neal Dalton had turned out to be a terrible one, cheating on his wife, breaking her trust, hurting his kids by association. He'd worked hard over the years to make it up to his family, and his wife had forgiven him. But for Shep, there'd been lasting damage. He now had a skewed idea of commitment and responsibility. Both those things were fragile; they could be shattered if you had clumsy hands. He was scared of hurting anyone the way his mother had been hurt. The way he'd been hurt, too. He didn't want to mess anything up, and the easiest way to do that was by not letting himself feel the deep stuff. The scary stuff. The stuff that could actually change him as a person, if he let it.

So…did he love her? He wasn't sure he could answer that question, even now. Even though Rylee deserved an answer. He was asking her to marry him, for God's sake. And he couldn't even let himself utter the word *love*, for fear of falling from this emotional tightrope he'd been walking.

He cut the engine, and Rylee opened her door. He opened his, too, and stepped out into the cool night air, the breeze ruffling his hair. He hadn't worn his hat tonight. He'd actually combed his hair neatly and had worn a starched white shirt. He'd spent the last three hours feeling like an accountant, with the collar itchy against his neck. But Rylee seemed to like it. She'd told him twice that he looked handsome, and he'd caught her a few times watching him from across the room. So it didn't matter if the collar was itchy, or if he looked like he was getting ready to do someone's taxes. She thought he looked good, and that was all that mattered. Maybe he'd have to get out of his ranch clothes more often.

He followed her up the steps to her apartment, trying to be a gentleman and not let his gaze roam all over her back-side, but he was failing miserably. She was so beautiful, he not only wanted to let his gaze roam, he wanted to let his hands roam, too. She only seemed to have grown more attractive as the days passed, as he got to know her better as an adult. She was a stunning woman, inside and out.

Stopping in front of her door, she dug her keys out of her purse.

"It's a good thing everyone thinks we're engaged," she said. "Or this would be a scandal in the morning."

"Why's that?"

"Because everyone knows everyone else's business at BH247. We're probably being watched as we speak."

Honestly, he didn't mind all of Bronco knowing he was being invited into Rylee Parker's apartment, engaged or not. If the rumor mill had him hooking up with a woman like her, he could definitely live with that.

She unlocked the door and stepped inside to turn on the light. He followed her in and looked around. He'd never been to her place before. It was neat as a pin and decorated in soft, feminine colors. The pastel throw pillows on the cream-colored sectional reminded him of Easter eggs. The entire place smelled like cinnamon. There was a big book-case beside the TV full of hardcovers and paperbacks, lit-tle knickknacks and framed photos of family and friends.

He stepped closer to look at them.

"I'll go put the coffee on," she said, shrugging out of her coat. "Be right back."

He smiled over his shoulder, then turned back to the pic-tures. There was one of her in a black cap and gown on her college graduation day. Norma and Lionel were on either side of her, beaming proudly. He remembered them coming to visit his parents at the ranch when he was little, and him getting to play with their sweet daughter, something he'd always looked forward to. There was another picture of her as a toddler, sitting on a countertop in a flower-print swimsuit, holding a phone to her ear. She'd been such a cute little kid, her auburn hair hanging in silky ringlets around her face. But it was the photo next to that one that just about stopped his heart. It was of him and Rylee as preteens on her old gelding, Tuff. Shep was sitting behind her with his arms around her waist, and she had her head thrown back in a laugh. His father had taken this picture, the moment frozen forever in time.

He stood there staring at it, letting himself be transported back to that summer day. He could almost feel Tuff's warmth underneath his legs, the horse's musky scent on his cutoff shorts. He could remember how it felt to be so close to Rylee back then, almost like they were the same person, one an extension of the other. He remembered how it felt to wrap his arms around her, wanting to keep her close and safe. He could hardly believe they'd fallen out of touch like they had. That he'd let himself go a month, let alone twelve years, without tracking her down. What in the world was wrong with him?

But deep down, he knew the answer. He'd known that if he found Rylee again, it wouldn't just be a simple reunion between two old friends. It would go further than that, be much more meaningful. And he'd been right, hadn't he? He'd actually brought up that promise they'd made to each other when they'd been teenagers on the brink of the rest of their lives. He'd brought it up, and he'd gotten her to go along with it.

And now, he was in deep. Very, very deep. What started

out as a light, playful lie had turned into a burning desire that he wasn't quite sure what to do with, even now. Because if it wasn't light and playful anymore, then it would have to mean something. It would have to mean a lot.

Up until now, until he'd seen this faded picture in front of him, he'd been able to fool himself into thinking he could handle the repercussions. He'd been able to talk his way out of anything, even his true feelings for Rylee, whatever those turned out to be. But now... Now he knew there was no talking himself out of anything anymore.

"My favorite picture of us." She came up beside him and hooked her arm in his. "We were so young. Can you believe how innocent we were?"

"Well, you were. Not so sure about me."

She laughed. "You did corrupt me a little."

"A *little*?"

"Believe me, I wanted you to."

He turned to look down at her, and she immediately looked away. The light in her apartment was dim, but he could see that she was blushing furiously.

She chewed her bottom lip, still avoiding his gaze because she'd always been shy like this. He saw her pulse flutter in that delicate hollow at the base of her throat. It tapped like moth wings there, tempting him to bend close and kiss it. To feel her warmth and vitality underneath his mouth.

And then, finally, she looked up at him. Held his gaze with a new confidence he wasn't sure he'd seen before. And maybe that was because she knew she had him in the palm of her hand. He would've done anything for Rylee right then. Anything she asked him to.

"The coffee will be ready soon," she said.

"I don't want coffee."

"What do you want?"

"You have to know." It wasn't exactly a romantic declaration, but Shep wasn't exactly a romantic kind of guy. At least, he'd never been before. He'd been told he was a good time, that he was charming. But he'd never been told that he was particularly romantic. He said what he felt at the moment and wasn't used to sugarcoating anything. Rylee knew that better than most people.

Still, he wished he had the courage to say what was in his heart right then. That he didn't just want her, but he needed her. He was starting to need her in a way that had him spooked, quite frankly.

"You know," she said. "I think back to Janet's party, and how I felt when I saw you again after all this time…"

He swallowed hard. "And how's that?"

"Relieved, almost." She frowned. "Does that sound strange?"

"No. I think I know what you mean. For me, it was like I'd been missing something. And I finally got it back. So *relieved* is a good way to put it."

She nodded, looking far away for a second. He reached up and touched her hair, moved it away from her face until her gaze met his again.

"And then when we decided to get the necklace back—" She stopped short, and her eyes widened.

"What?"

"Oh my God. Shep…"

"What is it?"

"I completely forgot. I still have the necklace. *Here.* I have it here! I forgot to take it back to the mayor."

He laughed. "Uh-oh. Better late than never? That's okay, his wife will just be happy to have it back."

"I know. It's so pretty."

"It is pretty, but a necklace like that is nothing without a beautiful woman wearing it."

She gazed up at him, her lashes long and dark. Her lips parted slightly. That spot at the base of her throat, tempting him more than ever.

"I'd like to see you wearing it," he finished. "And nothing else."

The room suddenly grew so still, so quiet, that he could hear the blood rushing in his ears.

Rylee continued looking up at him, her lovely eyes taking him in. All of him. There was no hiding anything from her anymore, and he wondered if she knew how he actually felt about her now. If she could see through all his crap, down to the bones of everything.

Slowly, she stepped forward. Then reached up and put her arms around his neck. She pressed herself against him, and it was like the other night when they'd danced at Doug's. Except now, they were the only ones in the room. There was no thumping music, no bustling crowd. No sound at all except for the soft inhale and exhale of her breath and that rushing in his ears.

Moving her hair away from her neck, he leaned down and kissed it softly, feeling her shiver underneath his lips. He'd kissed Rylee lots of times since the night of Janet's party. But tonight, it felt different. It felt real, genuine. Like these kisses weren't meant to convince anyone of anything.

Rylee tilted her head all the way back, and he moved his lips up her throat, kissing along her jawline. He breathed in the sweet scent of her perfume. He felt her tremble in his arms, felt her sway when he took her earlobe in his teeth.

"Are we doing what I think we're doing?" she whispered.

"What do you think we're doing?"

"I think you're about to spend the night."

"I think you might be right."

He knew it was a risk they were taking. Their friendship was on the line, and that was no small thing. Sleeping together would change everything. But the question was, would it change it for the better...or the worse?

He slid his hand from the small of her back, down the curve of her bottom, and heard her breath catch in her throat.

He wanted to sweep her into his arms, carry her to the bedroom and close the door behind them. He wanted to lay her on the bed and unzip her dress. He wanted to hear her say his name, over and over again, until she was too lost in pleasure to say anything else.

But he didn't move an inch, even though every nerve ending in his body was humming. He just stood there because he knew how important this moment was. He didn't want her choosing him now and regretting it later. Of course, there was no guarantee she wouldn't regret it later, even if they stood here all night long. But he wanted to hear her say she wanted this, too. He wanted to hear her say that because if she didn't, he'd always wonder, and he didn't think he could live with that.

"Are you sure, Rylee?"

For a few agonizing seconds, he wondered if she might say no. And then what would he do? He knew what he'd do. He'd go home and take a cold shower, and nurse what was left of his heart. It wouldn't be easy, but that was what he'd do because Rylee came first. She'd always come first.

And then, miraculously, she nodded. But her brows were furrowed. There was a tiny wrinkle between them as she gazed up at him.

"What about you, Shep?" she asked. "Are *you* sure?"

It was a simple question, yet had so many implications. He was sure. In some ways, he was more sure of this than of anything else in his life. But he'd be lying if he said those implications didn't worry him plenty.

"I'm sure," he said. It was all he could manage right then.

And it was all she apparently needed. She put her hands on either side of his face, then stood on her tiptoes and pressed her lips to his.

He could feel the eagerness there. The hunger.

Then, in one swift motion, he swept her up in his arms like he'd been dying to do for the last half an hour. He bounced her a couple of times against his chest, making her laugh. His heart hammered at the sound. At the feel of her weight in his arms. Slight, yet so very significant.

"Now," he said with a wink. "Let's go find that necklace."

RYLEE HAD BEEN DREAMING. A wonderful dream that had given her butterflies. They lingered in her belly now, with the early morning light staining the insides of her closed eyelids orange.

She lay there, still and quiet, afraid to move for fear the details of the dream would fade like dreams so often did. She'd been dancing with Shep. But not in a crowded bar with people all around. They'd been dancing at their wedding. She could still hear the music from the live band in her ears. Or maybe it was still in her heart—thumping, thumping, thumping.

She felt her lips tilt into a smile. But this time, it wasn't because of the dream. It was because she'd started remembering something else altogether. Something that was coming back into sharp clarity. Sparkling in her mind and flashing in beautiful bursts of rainbow color.

She and Shep had spent the night together. And it had been wonderful. He'd been gentle and sweet and intuitive about what she'd wanted in a way that had left her breathless and shaking in his arms.

She turned her face into the softness of her pillow now

and let her eyes flutter open to the light coming in through the blinds. In a minute, she'd roll over and curl into his naked side. She'd kiss his shoulder and move her leg over his and feel those rough little hairs tickle her skin.

But for the next few seconds, she wanted to savor the moment. This moment when she felt so excited about the future, whatever that might be. She wanted to soak it all in, until it saturated her completely, and so she'd remember how it felt to be truly happy for the first time in a while.

She took a deep, even breath. And then rolled over to kiss him good morning.

"Shep—"

She barely got his name out before her heart, which had been beating so lightly a minute before, sank like a stone inside her chest.

His side of the bed was empty. The sheets were cold and rumpled. She reached out to touch them and then re-coiled without being able to help it.

Maybe he was in the bathroom? Or the kitchen, making them a cup of coffee? But judging by the thick, ominous silence that had settled over the apartment, it was clear he wasn't in either of those places. He was definitely gone.

Rylee bit the inside of her cheek. She felt cheap, This, despite all the warm feelings that had surrounded her only a minute ago. She'd never had a one-night stand before. She'd never slept with anyone and then woken up to find them gone. Shep had to have known how this would make her feel. He had to have known that…

Trying not to jump to conclusions, she pulled the sheets up to her chest and reached for her phone. Maybe there'd been some kind of emergency and he'd texted after he'd left. Maybe she'd slept right through it. She knew she was grasping at straws, but she couldn't help it.

Her heart sank when she saw there were no text notifications. She sat there for a minute, her eyes stinging.

She and Shep didn't know each other very well as adults yet, and she absolutely didn't know how he usually acted after sex. But this was so strange, so out of character, that she shook her head, for absolutely nobody's benefit but her own. As if to convince herself there was something she was missing.

After a few seconds, she scooted over to his side of the bed and moved the blankets out of the way. And sure enough, there was a note on the nightstand. She'd almost missed it because it was tucked underneath a coaster.

She reached for it and opened it up. It wasn't until right then that she noticed her hands were trembling.

Have to get back for the morning feeding. —Shep

Rylee sat there staring at it as if it were written in a foreign language. She pulled in a breath and let it out slowly. Then took another and another, until she felt herself relax some.

Okay. So, it wasn't exactly an emergency. But it was a completely logical reason to have to leave early. Still, those words were so curt. Like something he'd tell an acquaintance, not a woman he'd just spent the night with.

Frowning, she put the note back on the nightstand. She was so confused. Was he regretting their night together? She didn't want to read into anything, but it was hard not to. Suddenly, what she wanted most was to call Gabby. To tell her best friend what had happened and get her take on this. Gabby had grown so wise about these things, where Rylee felt inexperienced and naive in comparison.

Despite trying to hold them back, tears filled her eyes anyway. But she couldn't tell Gabby anything, could she?

Because Gabby didn't even know the truth about her relationship with Shep. Or why this would be such a big deal in the first place. As far as Gabby was concerned, they were actually engaged—had been this entire time—and him leaving this morning wouldn't mean anything except he had cows to feed.

The guilt from keeping this from her best friend was suddenly so overwhelming that she put her face into her hands and began sobbing like a little kid.

It wasn't just Gabby that she'd deceived. It was her parents. It was Shep's parents. And her brothers and his, too. It was everybody that they knew, and it didn't really matter if they actually ended up getting married or not, their loved ones had still been lied to.

Rylee thought she could handle straightening things out with her family if it came to that. But right then, she didn't think she could keep this secret one minute longer from the woman she'd grown the closest to since moving to Bronco. Rylee shared everything with Gabby. It was time she shared this, too.

She just hoped their friendship would survive it.

CHAPTER NINE

SHEP DROVE INTO the early morning sunlight with his dark aviator sunglasses on and the truck's visor down. He had a splitting headache, despite the two Tylenol he'd taken after leaving Rylee's apartment.

He guessed it was the beer with dinner. Or all the salt in the spaghetti? Or maybe he'd finally woken up to the fact that this whole engagement caper was a hell of a lot more serious than he'd given it credit for. Because the way he felt about Rylee was no longer something he could push to the back burner. It could no longer be treated like some game, engineered for the sole purpose of entertaining him and giving him what he wanted. There were real feelings here. And very real consequences.

He gritted his teeth and felt his jaw muscles tighten almost painfully. Before last night, he could've seen himself falling in love with Rylee. Of course he could. In the future. If everything worked out the way he hoped. After all, falling in love with her would be easy. He was already halfway there. But last night, the second he'd laid her down on the bed and looked into her eyes, he knew that moment was already here, whether he was ready for it or not.

Now, driving back to Dalton's Grange this morning, his hands in a death grip on the steering wheel, all he could think about was the fact that he *wasn't* ready. Because the reality of it, of her, felt like a lightning bolt to his heart. He'd been so stupid. So damn stupid for thinking that he could orchestrate this like some kind of movie. That no matter how it would end, it would be on a positive note. That they'd always be friends, no matter what.

The fact was he was in love with her. And honestly, from the depths of his soul, he didn't know how to be in love like this. He didn't know how to let her in, where she absolutely needed to be. He'd always assumed that when this kind of love happened, if it happened, he'd know how to navigate it.

And now, here he was. So freaked out that he'd thrown off the covers this morning, quietly and like a total coward, and had tiptoed out the door holding his boots so he wouldn't wake her.

Frowning, he stared at the road ahead. He'd left a note. But just barely. The list of things he *should've* said was practically endless. *I love you. I've always loved you. There's never been another woman who's made me feel like this, and I don't know that I can live without you now.*

Of course, he couldn't say any of those things because admitting them to himself was hard enough. Admitting them to her? Impossible. Or at least, that was how it felt now as he continued grinding his teeth and gripping the steering wheel.

So he'd left that stupid note and had hoped she'd accept it for what it looked like. That he'd been in a hurry. And maybe that he was a little bit of an insensitive brute, but a mostly well-meaning one. He just needed to buy himself some time. But what exactly for? What was he going to do when he got back to the ranch?

He already knew what he was going to do. He was going to throw himself into physical labor and try to forget about this feeling unfurling inside his chest. He needed to put some distance between himself and Rylee Parker. He wouldn't let himself think of how rotten that would look to her. Hell, how rotten it would actually *be*. This was self-preservation, plain and simple.

He reached over to where his phone lay in the passenger seat and clicked off the ringer. He just needed some time. That was all. He just needed some time to figure this out.

RYLEE SAT ACROSS from Gabby at a small table at Wild Willa's Saloon. Usually they sat at the famous Get Lucky Bar, which was shaped like a four-leaf clover. But tonight, they'd chosen a quieter spot in the corner where they'd be able to talk.

The drinks at Wild Willa's were good, but the ambience was better. It was a fun place to come after work or on the weekends. When Rylee and Gabby met here, they'd talk about their jobs, their mutual acquaintances, Ryan... Poor Ryan was a frequent and favorite topic of conversation.

Gabby took a sip of her lemon drop martini and licked the sugar from her lips.

"Mmm," she said. "That's *so* good. Best lemon drop around."

Rylee had one in front of her, too, but she hadn't touched it yet. She'd been too busy rehearsing what she was going to say. How she'd try to explain it in a way that made sense. But honestly, she expected Gabby to be angry. Really angry. And hurt, too. Rylee would be, if it were her.

Gabby set her martini down and leaned her elbows on the table. "Okay. Out with it. You've been acting weird all day. Did something happen between you and Shep?"

At the mention of Shep's name, Rylee's heart twisted. He'd sent a brief text yesterday, but hadn't called since they'd slept together. Which was hurtful and more than a little dismissive. She hadn't tried calling him because her defenses were up now. If he wanted to talk, he knew where to find her. Until then, she wasn't going to go chasing him like a lovesick teenager.

Swallowing hard, she tapped the base of her glass. This wasn't going to be easy. But she knew she'd feel better after confessing to Gabby. She needed her friend right now, and if she had to take a few lumps, that was okay. She deserved them.

"Something did happen between me and Shep, but that's not what I wanted to talk to you about…"

Gabby sat up straighter. "Is everything okay?"

"I'm just worried you're going to hate me."

"I could never hate you. Whatever it is."

"You say that now…"

Gabby watched her, a little wrinkle forming between her brows. Somebody had put some money in the jukebox across the room, and it began playing a Garth Brooks song that had been one of Rylee's favorites in high school. It reminded her of Shep and the river and being sunburned and happy. Those had been good times. The best times. Things got so complicated when you got older. She wondered if anyone had ever explained that to her when she was a kid. If they had, she hadn't paid enough attention to remember. When you were seventeen, the thought of turning thirty might as well be like turning eighty. It was too far beyond comprehension, too far beyond the young, tender frontal lobe that only cared about boys and pizza and romance novels. At least, that was how it had been for Rylee.

She looked over at Gabby now and licked her lips. Hoping her friend would understand this. And would forgive her.

"Remember Janet Halstead's birthday party?"

"The one in Wonderstone Ridge?"

Rylee nodded.

"The one where you got engaged," Gabby said. "How could I forget that?"

Rylee's stomach dipped. It was now or never. If she didn't come clean soon, she was going to lose her nerve altogether.

"Well, kind of," she said. "We *kind of* got engaged."

Gabby frowned. "What do you mean?"

"You know that Shep and I grew up together. We were best friends until I left for college in California…"

"Yeah, I knew that. And he was your first crush."

"He was."

Gabby waited, putting her chin in her hand. She probably thought this was the most boring story ever.

Rylee cleared her throat. "Well, when I drove over to his place to say goodbye that day, the day I left for college, we made each other a promise."

"Oh?"

"A promise that if we weren't married by the time we turned thirty, we'd marry each other."

"Wait a minute," Gabby said. "You got engaged because of a promise you made when you were teenagers?"

"Yes. No. Kind of."

"Rylee, you're not making any sense."

"I know. And when I tell you the whole story, you're probably going to be even more confused."

"Try me."

Taking a deep breath, Rylee plowed on. "We made each other that promise. But when we met up at Janet's party, we hadn't seen each other since that day."

"And you decided to make good on it?" Gabby snapped her fingers. "Just like that?"

"Not exactly. We were standing in this crowd, and one thing led to another, and Shep kissed me." Rylee's heartbeat kicked up a notch, and all of a sudden, her sweater felt too warm. "Everyone saw and started clapping, and Shep, well... You'd have to know how much he likes to joke around. He jokes all the time. I think it's how he deals with things. He jokes about them, and they don't seem as real. Or as serious."

Gabby nodded.

"Well, he told everyone he was just giving his new fiancée a kiss. Because of that promise, he said we were engaged. But of course, they all thought we really *were* engaged, because why wouldn't they? We'd had a few drinks, and we got caught up in it. Everyone was so sweet and excited for us, and we didn't think it would go beyond that party. Beyond that room."

"Rylee," Gabby said slowly. "Are you trying to tell me that you were pretending that night?"

Rylee grazed her bottom lip with her teeth. "Yes."

"And are you telling me that you've been pretending this whole time?"

"I'm so sorry, Gabby. But yes."

Leaning back, Gabby shook her head. "But why? Why would you do that?"

"I don't have a great explanation, except that we didn't think it would ever get this far. At first, it was just a fun thing to do. Kind of like when we were kids, something we'd laugh about later. And the next morning, I got your text, and we realized word had already gotten around. That our families probably knew. Our parents. Shep's mom has been on him to settle down for so long, he thought maybe we could just go along with it for a few weeks and then break up, and then that would be that."

"You mean have a fake breakup." Gabby crossed her arms over her chest, giving Rylee a flat look from across the table.

"Yes. That."

"And then what?"

"And then…and then we started spending time together, and Shep started talking about actually getting married. For real."

Gabby rubbed her temple. Not unlike a mother who was exasperated with her teenage daughter. "*Why* in the hell didn't you tell me any of this? I feel like a complete jerk now. I was trying to get you to try on wedding dresses!"

"I know. I'm sorry, Gabby. I didn't say anything at first because it was such a secret, and I didn't want to put you in the position of having to keep it from Ryan. Or risk Bella overhearing us. Or… I don't know. So many things. And then one day turned into two days. And then two weeks, and it got harder and harder to tell you the truth. I was so worried you'd be mad. And you have every right to be."

Gabby sighed and took a sip of her martini. And then another, before putting it down again. "Well, I'm not thrilled. But I'm not *mad*. I just wish you'd trusted me with it. But you're right. I would've wanted to tell Ryan, so there's that…"

Rylee gave her friend a small smile. Maybe it would be okay after all. Having things unsettled with Shep was bad enough. She didn't think she could handle it if she and Gabby weren't speaking.

"So," Gabby continued, "Shep actually wants to get married for real?"

Rylee nodded.

"That's so romantic. He must've fallen head over heels for you, Rylee."

"I don't know. He hasn't said so. He just keeps saying how practical it is, how much it makes sense. I'm so confused."

"But you love him." It wasn't a question. Gabby knew how Rylee felt about Shep.

"I do."

"Then what are you going to do?"

"Getting married would be ridiculous...wouldn't it?"

Gabby shrugged. "I don't know. It's not like you haven't known each other your entire lives. You're friends, and that's half the battle right there. It could be a huge adventure."

"Or a huge mistake."

"But you won't know until you make it."

"True..." Rylee paused, running her hands over the tabletop. "There's something else I need to tell you."

"Oh Lord. I don't know if I can take any more surprises."

"Well, this just happened. So I haven't kept it from you. You're actually the first to know."

Gabby smiled and sat up a little straighter, clearly happy with this turn of events. "Spill."

"We slept together the other night. For the first time."

Gabby's smile stretched wider. She was always beautiful, but when she smiled, she was truly stunning. "Oh, Ry. I'm so happy for you."

Suddenly, and without warning, Rylee's eyes filled with tears.

"Oh no," Gabby said, reaching for her hand from across the table. "What happened? What did he do? Am I going to have to kill him? Because I will, you know."

"No, it's nothing like that." But even as she said it, Rylee knew it *was* something like that. Shep was ghosting her; it was becoming more and more obvious. She didn't know why, but she had to assume the reason was significant. She had to wonder if this had been a mistake for him. Not just sleeping together, but maybe this entire engagement thing. Maybe he was finally realizing that getting married was bananas. Not an adventure like Gabby just said. But just plain bananas.

"Well," Gabby said. "What is it then?"

"He hasn't called. We haven't talked since."

Gabby's expression grew chilly. "I see. I *am* going to have to kill him."

"Don't kill him," Rylee said, trying for a note of levity. "That would get messy, and I can't have my bestie going to jail. Who'd give me outfit advice?"

"Nice try, but I know you're heartbroken about this."

Rylee wiped her eyes. "Maybe a little. But Shep has always been awful at communication. He probably just needs time. And I can give that to him."

"Don't give him too much time. There are a lot of guys who would love to be with you, Rylee. Don't forget that."

Rylee squeezed her friend's hand. Even if that were true, she didn't want anyone else. She wanted Shep. She wanted what she'd dreamed about the other night—the wedding, the life, the happiness. She wanted the fairy tale. But there was one glaring problem with fairy tales.

They weren't reality.

SHEP STEPPED UP to Rylee's door and took a deep breath. There was a good chance she wouldn't be thrilled to see him. After all, he hadn't warned her he was coming. He'd been in town at the feed store and had decided to stop by on his way back to the ranch. They hadn't talked in a few days. Actually, since the night they'd spent together, and he knew it was way past time. If she didn't tell him to go straight to hell, that is. That was always a possibility.

He stood there on her doorstep with a ton of excuses running through his head. *I've been swamped*, or *I've been sick*. Things that would hold water, or were at least halfway true, and would let him avoid the *whole* truth. Which was, *I'm scared...*

Taking his Stetson off, he ran a hand through his hair. He probably smelled like horses. He should've planned this better. But he knew if he'd given himself time to think about it, he would've kept on driving.

Rylee deserved better than what he'd been giving her. But he was so terrified of screwing it all up that he'd just been stuck these last few days. Anxious about moving forward, but not wanting to move back, either. Even his mother had noticed something was wrong, but she hadn't come right out and asked, and he hadn't offered. This was how Shep dealt with issues in his life. Always had. He kept them to himself, and he figured them out on his own. Period.

But the thing was, standing here now, he knew it was time to talk. It was true, he didn't know what he was going to say, and maybe when he opened his mouth, it would be a shock to them both. But if he didn't at least try, he was going to lose her for good. He knew that without a doubt, and he couldn't let that happen.

Steeling himself, he raised his hand and knocked. And then waited with his heart tapping in his throat.

After a few seconds, he heard footsteps. Then a pause, as she presumably looked through the peephole.

When the door finally opened, he realized he was holding his breath.

"Shep," she said coolly.

She had her hair pulled into a high ponytail and was wearing a white T-shirt and jeans with holes in the knees. She looked so effortlessly beautiful that for a second all he could do was stare.

"What are you doing here?" she continued, not slamming the door in his face, but not inviting him in, either.

He looked down at his boots, knowing that all the excuses he'd been contemplating a minute ago weren't going to cut it. But the truth wasn't a possibility, either. At least, not right this minute. He needed... Hell, he didn't know what he needed. He was a mess was what he was.

"It's Saturday, so I came into town to get some grain," he said, "and thought I'd stop by to say hi."

She watched him, obviously wary. "Hi."

"I know we haven't talked. Since..."

"Since sleeping together?" she finished flatly.

Ouch. She wasn't going to make this easy. Then again, he deserved everything she'd throw at him and more.

"I'm sorry about that," he said, pinching the brim of his Stetson between his thumb and forefingers. Trying not to come undone by the scent of her perfume in the air. "I guess I wasn't ready for how all this would make me feel."

That part wasn't a lie, at least. He hadn't been ready. In fact, he'd been so unprepared, this whole thing had damn well knocked him flat on his ass.

"And how's that?" Rylee asked, narrowing her eyes at him.

"Confused."

"That makes two of us."

All he wanted was to step forward and pull her into his arms, where she fit so perfectly. He wanted to kiss that hollow in her throat and breathe her in and feel her body warm next to his. But by the way she was eyeing him, he wasn't sure that would be welcome. Maybe it wouldn't be welcome ever again, and he realized that by being so afraid of screwing everything up, he might've gone ahead and screwed it up anyway.

"Can I come in?" he asked.

She waited, looking like she was thinking it over. Probably weighing her options. Shove him down the steps or offer him a cup of coffee. The jury was still out on that one.

After a few seconds, she stepped quietly aside and motioned him inside.

He stepped past, feeling the tension crackle between them. It was almost palpable.

She closed the door behind him, and when he turned around, she had her arms crossed over her chest. *Nope.* She definitely wasn't going to make this easy.

"How have you been?" he asked. Then immediately wanted to suck the words back in.

"Fine. How have you been?"

He ran a frustrated hand through his hair. This wasn't going how he'd planned. But then again, he hadn't actually planned it, had he? Maybe if he'd start thinking about things before jumping right into them, he wouldn't find himself in situations like this.

The problem was this wasn't just an awkward encounter with someone he probably wouldn't see again any time soon. This was Rylee. His Rylee. He had to make this right, but he wasn't sure how. For maybe the first time in his life, his charm, which he'd always relied so heavily on, was failing him miserably.

"I know you're upset," he said. "And I don't blame you."

"Why would I be upset?"

Heat crept up his neck, and he shifted uncomfortably on his feet. "I'm sorry I haven't called."

At that, she just stood there. It was hard to tell what she was thinking. Her expression was shuttered. *She* was shuttered. She obviously didn't want to give him the opportunity to hurt her any more than he already had, and all of a sudden he felt like an absolute idiot. Sure, this whole thing had taken him by surprise, and he was scared to death, to be honest. But he did know he never should've left that morning. He never should've left her, period.

"Rylee—"

But before he could say anything more, his phone rang from his pocket.

"Sorry," he mumbled, pulling it out to see Boone's name flash across the screen.

Rylee continued gazing up at him, and he thought about not answering, but there was always the possibility it was an emergency. Ever since his mother's heart attack a few years ago, he had a hard time ignoring calls from his family.

Holding up a finger, he gave her an apologetic look. "One second, promise."

"It's okay."

He pressed the accept button. "Hello?" he bit out.

"Jeez," Boone said. The reception was crackly, and wind buffeted the speaker. He was obviously standing outside. "I'm happy to talk to you, too."

"Kind of busy here, man. What is it, Boone?"

"You need to get your ass back here. And bring Rylee with you."

Shep frowned. "Why? What's going on?"

"I can't say. But make it quick."

Shep's stomach tightened. "What's wrong?"

"Nothing's wrong. But can you pick Rylee up? She mentioned to Sofia that she was going to be home today. Something about cleaning her apartment…"

"I'm actually with her now."

Rylee watched him curiously.

"Perfect," Boone said. "Then head back."

"I don't—"

The line went dead.

Shep took the phone from his ear and stared at it for a second. "What the hell?"

"What's wrong?" Rylee asked.

"He wouldn't say. But he wants us both to come back to the ranch. Like, now."

"Both of us?"

He nodded. She didn't look thrilled. After all, they hadn't ironed out a single thing. Hadn't even had a chance to broach the subject of the other night, let alone fix it.

"I can't imagine what this is all about," he said, "but don't feel like you need to come. This is your Saturday. You probably don't want to spend a chunk of it at the ranch." What he was thinking, but didn't say, was that she probably didn't want to spend a chunk of it with him.

"No," she said. "I'll come. Whatever it is, they want both of us there, so it must be important."

He nodded again. She was being so gracious about the whole thing. But he wasn't surprised. Rylee had always been full of grace.

"We can talk after," he said. "Just you and me, okay?"

"Okay."

They stood there for a minute, silence settling between them. He hated how stilted this was, when for the last few weeks the energy that had flowed between them had been so easy and warm. And now they had to go out to Dalton's Grange and keep pretending...

He felt the muscles in his jaw bunch. It had only been a few days ago that he'd been trying to talk Rylee into marrying him for real. And he felt like she might've been tempted to marry him, too. To actually be his wife, for better or worse. In sickness and health. For *real*. Again, he was struck by how flippant he'd been. How arrogant at thinking a marriage of convenience could happen without strings attached. Major strings.

"Let me get my jacket," Rylee said evenly. "I'll be right back."

He watched her disappear down the hallway.

And wondered again how he could've been so stupid.

CHAPTER TEN

RYLEE SAT BESIDE Shep in the cab of his truck, trying to hold back tears. If she weren't so stubborn, she would've let them fill her eyes by now. Maybe they'd even be spilling down her cheeks. But she refused to let him see how hurt she was by all of this. How much this new tension between them broke her heart.

She sneaked a look over at him and wondered again how they'd gotten here. Their night together had been so wonderful, so magical, that she thought he'd have to feel it, too. But there was no rule book that said if one person was in love, the other person had to feel the same. A cruel reminder as she gazed back out the window to watch the businesses and houses in Bronco begin to give way to pastures and lush, green farmland as they made their way toward Dalton's Grange.

Horses and cattle grazed near long stretches of fence line, and the midafternoon sun glinted off the gabled metal roofs of countless barns in the distance. It was beautiful. A gorgeous spring day where the mountains looked more purple than blue, and the snow that graced their peaks reminded Rylee of powdered sugar. A hawk made a lazy circle in the sky above, and she leaned her head back against the rest, taking comfort in the warmth of the sunshine through the window.

Shep reached out and turned on the radio. Probably to fill the empty silence, another arrow to her heart. But there was no use denying it. Things between them were different now. So different that she wondered how they'd ever be able to continue this charade when they got out to the ranch. Everyone would probably know there was something wrong. And then what?

She sighed. She guessed that could be their way out of this lie. They could break up for real (or for fake, she couldn't keep track anymore), and it would all be said and done.

Shep slowed at the long, paved road that led out to the ranch and turned on his blinker. Rylee's stomach dipped at the thought of seeing his parents again. At what their reasoning was for wanting her to come out on a Saturday afternoon. It probably had something to do with the wedding, but what? Maybe they wanted more details or something. Especially if Deborah and Neal thought there was any possibility it would be held at Dalton's Grange. They'd need to start planning. Like, *now*.

Shep cleared his throat. "I'm really sorry about this..."

"Don't be sorry."

Although, the odds were pretty good he wasn't talking about this afternoon. He could be talking about the whole thing, and the thought of that just made her sad. She'd let herself be carried away by this. She'd let herself believe that someone like Shep would truly want to marry someone like her, when they'd always been so different. It wasn't that she didn't think she was good enough for him; it wasn't that. She was confident in the person she was, in the woman she'd become, even though she had to remind herself sometimes. (As a kid, even reminders hadn't done the trick.) But at the same time, she'd always known she wasn't his type. That she lacked the wildness that was so ingrained in his personality. In his very *being*. Even though she was happy with her own personality, she couldn't help but feel like she watered his down some, and that wasn't a good feeling.

The truck made its way down the drive, and the house finally came into view. When it did, Rylee's heartbeat slowed in her chest, and she sat forward to gape at the driveway.

"Uh, Shep?"

He was staring, too. "Oh crap."

The entire drive was full of cars. There must've been twenty of them, and the ones that didn't fit in the big, circular driveway were parked in rows next to the fence line of the south pasture. It looked like a party. A major party.

Rylee's mouth hung open. "What in the world?"

"I should've known this was what they were up to." He rubbed his jaw. "I should've known."

She looked over at him, dread settling like a lead weight in her stomach. "You should've known they were up to *what*?"

But she already knew. It looked like a party because it *was* a party. Probably an engagement party for the two of them. *Oh Lord.* Everyone would be here. All their friends and family. Deborah would've insisted on that part. It would be a big deal, and they would be expected to look happy and in love and very pleasantly surprised.

Rylee had the surprised part down, and even the in-love part. But the happy part? That would be harder to pull off. She felt so unsettled that, again, she had to hold back tears.

Shep pulled the truck over to the side of the drive, behind an expensive-looking Audi, and turned the engine off. The cab was quiet, the sun shining through the windows not nearly as comforting as before. She could feel him watching her. She knew he felt awful about this, and it wasn't his fault. Well, the party wasn't his fault. The other stuff kind of was.

"You don't have to do this, Rylee," he said, his voice gravelly. "I can take you home and make up some kind of excuse. This was a surprise. For all they know, you had something else going on."

"No, Sofia asked a bunch of questions the other night at dinner. She asked if I was going to be home this weekend, things like that. I told her I was doing some spring-cleaning on my apartment today, so they knew I was basically free."

"Yeah, Boone mentioned that. But it still doesn't matter. You can pretend to be sick or something. Anything."

She looked down at her clothes. A T-shirt and jeans. She hoped people wouldn't be dressed up. She didn't look *terrible*, but still. She was completely unprepared. Which, she guessed, was the whole point of a surprise party.

"No," she said. "They went to all this trouble. The least we can do is show up."

He nodded. But it looked like he wanted to say something more. They sat there in silence, sitting so close to each other, but to Rylee, it felt like they were a million miles apart.

"We still need to talk," Shep said.

"Yes."

"When this thing is over…"

"Yes."

He watched her, and she felt the weight of his gaze on her shoulders. When they talked, what would he say? That this had been a mistake from the beginning? That it wasn't her, it was him? Or would it be something else altogether?

She swallowed down the achiness in her throat and unbuckled her seat belt.

"We'd better get in there," she said. "Before they send a search party out."

They got out of his truck. And then they were walking side by side up to the ranch house.

Shep reached over and took her hand. He squeezed it, reassuring her, and she took comfort in his warmth.

The only problem was she had no idea if this was real or all for show.

SHEP GLANCED OVER at Rylee, his hand on the doorknob. She didn't look back. Just stood there, looking calm and very beautiful and resigned to the fact that they were going to have to face whatever was on the other side of this door as a couple. As an engaged couple.

He didn't think he'd ever loved her more, and that was making him nervous. In fact, it was almost making him break a sweat, and he gritted his teeth, trying for a semblance of the vibe she was putting out. *Relaxed. In control. Able to handle anything.*

"Ready?" he asked.

She nodded. "Ready as I'll ever be."

"Is it bad form to get smashed at your engagement party? Asking for…me."

At that, she did look over. Her lips tilted slightly, her eyes twinkling. So, maybe she didn't hate him as much as he thought she probably did. He hoped not. He knew he was doing a pretty terrible job of redeeming himself for going radio silent over these last few days, but once they got this party out of the way, they could sit down and talk. Properly talk. And maybe he'd be able to articulate what he was feeling. Maybe he'd even have the courage to tell her he loved her. But it needed to happen without all this wedding stuff between them. It needed to be just him and her, and he needed to be able to think about what he was actually going to say. Because it had to be real. All this other stuff was like a circus act—a high wire that they'd been trying to walk for the last few weeks. And he hadn't known until right this minute how precarious that had made them. They could lose everything, their friendship, their entire relationship, with one wrong step.

"I can't wait for a glass of wine," she said. "Or two."

"Same. I was just thinking about a beer. Or a shot of whiskey. Or both."

She smiled, and for the first time since seeing her that day, it didn't look forced. "I'm not quite sure how we let things get to this point," she said. "It all seemed so abstract at the time. A little like a fantasy, I guess. But this is about as real as it gets."

"Amen to that, sister."

She licked her lips. "Shep… I don't know if you're still wanting to get married after what happened the other night. But I wanted to tell you… I wanted to tell you that—"

But before she could finish her sentence, the front door swung open. He and Rylee looked up to see his dad standing there, smiling wide. And behind him, Rylee's parents, Lionel looking a little stiff in a pair of Wranglers and a collared shirt.

God, he thought. *Here we go.*

"Surprise!" everyone yelled in unison. And then from somewhere inside the house, music started playing. Country music with an upbeat tempo. Shep could smell barbecue wafting through the house, probably from the grill out back.

"We thought you two were going to stand out here all day," his dad said, taking his arm and pulling him inside. "Come in here and join your party!"

Shep was vaguely aware of someone shoving a cold beer in his hand, and Rylee being ushered in behind him. All of a sudden, she was swarmed by women. His sisters-in-law, his mother, her mother, Gabby… He caught Rylee's best friend's gaze, and he thought it looked a little chilly.

She probably knew about the last few days and was judging him. Rightfully so.

Shep rubbed his throbbing temple.

Someone slapped his back, and he turned to see his cousin Anderson standing there.

"Congratulations, man," Anderson said. "You're finally tying the knot. I didn't think we'd live to see the day, but here it is."

Shep gave him a hug. He and Anderson had always been close. "Thanks for coming, buddy."

"Are you kidding? Marina and I are stoked for you, Shep. Honestly. It seems like so many of our friends are getting divorced lately. We were just talking about it on the way over. It's just nice to see some happiness for a change."

Shep had been so flippant about this in the beginning. He remembered thinking that if it didn't work out with Rylee, they'd just get a divorce. Simple as that. Divorce was obviously necessary for a lot of couples; sometimes marriages just didn't work, and there was no shame in that. But he also knew you shouldn't go into one thinking about divorce first thing. Speaking of flippant...

His neck heated, and his shirt felt itchy, like there might be some bits of hay down his back.

"Yeah," he said, looking over at where Rylee was standing with his mother and Gabby. "I hear you."

"Now, just don't screw it up," Anderson said with a wink. It was meant to be light and teasing. But it hit home like a baseball bat to Shep's chest.

He nodded, managing a smile back. But he felt his teeth grind together, his shoulders tighten. Screwing things up had always been his worst fear. Letting down the people closest to him. Messing things up by getting too invested in them. Was that what he was going to do with Rylee? Was he going to ruin this before it even had a chance to go somewhere? How could he be honest with her, and tell her that he was in love with her, when doing that would mean actually having something to lose? Something significant? The answer was he wasn't sure he could.

He looked over at her again, and this time, she glanced back. She was so gorgeous, so poised. He remembered the little girl who rode her bike with him in the summertime, her copper pigtails flying. And the teenager who swam with him in the river, her skin pale and her body so willowy it seemed like she might blow away in a stiff wind. She'd grown so much since then, but she was also the same in the best ways. She was still the same Rylee… Smart, compassionate, well-read, loving, funny… The list went on and on. Completely different from the women he'd dated in the past.

He watched her, swallowing hard. Rylee was the real deal. The one you brought home to your parents. The one you married, had kids with, had a life with. And then got old with. The one whose hand you held at the very end, when it was all said and done, and you were ready to say goodbye. She was the one.

So why was admitting that so hard? He knew why. It was hard because this wasn't a foregone conclusion for her. And if that was the case, where did that leave him? In love and as unsure of himself as that boy on the bike, that was where.

He rubbed the back of his neck as Anderson told him something about his son Jake's soccer season. He was only half listening. What he really wanted to do was get in his truck, roll down the windows and go for a drive. He needed to think. And being around all these people, as much as he loved them, wasn't helping his mood any.

From somewhere across the living room, someone

tapped a fork on a champagne glass. He looked over to see his dad holding said glass in the air.

"Folks!" he said, his voice booming. "I'd like to make a toast."

A hush fell over the room. Shep glanced over at Rylee again. She didn't look thrilled. In fact, she looked like she might want to run away just as much as he did.

"This engagement came as a bit of a surprise," his dad continued, "but we honestly couldn't be happier. We've known the Parkers for a long time. Some of you know that we were neighbors in Tenacity. And, well, Rylee grew up with Shep. Deborah thinks it was meant to be."

A collective *aww* moved through the crowd, and Shep's mother smiled wide. He didn't think she'd ever looked happier. She wanted this so much. He knew her heart attack had something to do with that, and the fact that she'd faced her own mortality on the highest level. She wanted her family happy, all her boys settled. It was important to her.

Shep's stomach dropped into his boots. How would she feel if this marriage immediately ended in an annulment? Or worse, a divorce? What would that do to her?

"Son, I know this party was a surprise," his dad said. "But we knew you and Rylee wouldn't have wanted a big fuss, so this was the only way your mother could work it out. We actually scaled it way down, if you can believe that."

Collective laughter.

"So, a toast…"

Everyone who had a champagne glass or a mug of beer or a glass of soda raised them in the air. Shep had to admit, the whole thing was pretty festive. If it weren't his own engagement party, and if he weren't so upside-down about the whole thing, he'd probably be having a great time.

"To Shep and Rylee," his father said. "We love you both."

The entire room erupted in cheers, and Shep took a long drink of his beer. It warmed his throat on the way down. Rylee was immediately enveloped in hugs, and he could barely catch a glimpse of her from across the room anymore.

"Wait, wait, wait…" This from Holt, who was standing next to the rest of his brothers. His voice was also deep and booming—apparently a Dalton trait. "We want to know when the big day is. Especially if it's gonna be at the ranch. We'll have to clean the place up, put a dance floor in the barn, tell the horses to hit the road…"

More laughter. But the question made Shep's ears burn. *The big day…* Such a simple question for anyone actually getting married. Of course people were expecting to know. He and Rylee were newly engaged, but they'd had plenty of time to narrow it down. Come up with a wedding month at least.

A few weeks ago, Shep wouldn't have had any problem lying about this. He would've simply put it in the "harmless" category, along with everything else. But today, he couldn't seem to open his mouth to utter a single word.

He looked over at Rylee as the room settled down again. As people waited for a response to a seemingly simple question. She was watching him back.

He shifted on his feet, his face growing uncomfortably hot. They were all waiting for him to say something. Anything. Rylee was waiting, too, and he knew what she was waiting for was much more meaningful. She was waiting to see how he'd react to this. To all of it. And all of a sudden, the entire world seemed to be holding its breath as Shep struggled to get a damn clue.

"Cat got your tongue, little brother?"

More laughter. But this time, it was clearly awkward. The moment felt strained. And still, he couldn't seem to get his mouth to cooperate. It was embarrassing. Where were the fun little fibs he and Rylee had been telling for the last few weeks? Where was his characteristic cockiness? It wasn't just that he hadn't answered Holt yet, it was also how he probably looked standing there that was making all his friends and family stare at him now. He felt like a deer in the headlights. And he was sure he looked worse. Much worse.

"Rylee?" Holt said. "Help us out here, since your fiancé seems to have lost all ability to speak. Have you two set a date or what?"

All the curious gazes in the room shifted to Rylee then. Shep's gaze shifted to her, too. As if she might hold the answer to all the questions in his heart. As if what she might say (or not say) would determine the course of the rest of his life.

He watched her, his heart thumping inside his chest. The blood rushing hotly in his ears. The fear that had washed over him the morning after sleeping with her was almost tenfold now. It was carrying him away with all the power of a swollen, rushing river. Intuitively, he felt like he was about to lose her after all.

Her eyes grew glassy. Her chin started trembling. She was obviously trying not to cry.

Enough. He needed to say something to avert whatever was happening here. It didn't matter if it was the truth or another lie, he just needed to protect her the best way he could. Better late than never…

He took a breath, but before he could say anything, she held up her hand. It was for his benefit, he could tell. She probably knew exactly what he'd been thinking just now.

"I'm sorry, everyone," she said. "I know you took time out of your day to come here. And Neal and Deborah, I'm especially sorry to let you both down…"

Shep's mother's expression fell. The tension in the room was now palpable, and Shep felt mildly sick to his stomach.

"But we're not getting married," Rylee said, her voice trembling.

There was an audible gasp. And then Rylee pushed her way through the crowd and was out the front door before Shep could even comprehend what just happened.

Her mother followed her out in a rush, and then the door closed again, leaving everyone standing there quiet and stunned.

Shep could feel their gazes on him. He was numb all over, his stomach turning.

"I'm sorry," he said. Then found there was simply nothing else to say.

He pushed his way through his friends and family, and opened the front door to a blast of cool, spring air. Rylee was standing with her mother on the porch, crying. Her eyes were red and puffy, her face wet with tears.

She looked up at him, but shook her head. "No, Shep."

"Rylee…"

"Mom, can you please take me home?"

Norma frowned, wrapping an arm around her daughter's shoulders. They both walked past him without another word. Heading down the front porch steps to the sea of cars in the driveway.

Shep watched them go, feeling so confused that his throat ached. He hadn't cried since middle school. Not even when his mother had been in the hospital after her heart attack. He was used to keeping his feelings inside, underneath the surface, where nobody could see them and where even he couldn't be bothered by them very often.

But right then, he felt about as raw and vulnerable as he ever had, and he knew as he watched Rylee climb into her parents' Suburban that this was a turning point in his adult life. He had two choices...

Go after her.

Or let her go and let this crazy idea of a marriage, which had little to no chance of actually working—no matter how much he might want it to—go with her.

CHAPTER ELEVEN

RYLEE SAT BESIDE her mom, watching the farmland pass by in a blur. Her eyes had been full of tears ever since they'd driven away from Dalton's Grange, and she kept having to brush them away to be able to see at all.

Her mother looked over at her now. Rylee knew she was worried. But to her credit, she hadn't said anything—she'd just held Rylee's hand, probably sensing that she needed a good cry before she could say anything at all.

Finally, Rylee took a deep breath and wiped the last of her tears away. She didn't think she'd ever experienced this kind of feeling before. Her heart wasn't just broken. It was shattered. And the shards were like thousands of needles inside of her, piercing her consciousness, reminding her with every second that she'd let herself fall in love and hope for something that just wasn't meant to be.

"Are you ready to tell me what's going on?" her mother asked softly. "What happened back there?"

Rylee clasped her hands in her lap, wondering how much she should say. She didn't really think there was any point in telling her the engagement had been fake. It would be hard for her mom to understand, and even harder for Rylee to explain. Her heartbreak was real, and that was all that mattered right now. All her mom needed to know. The rest was history, anyway.

"He wasn't ready," she said. It was the truth. He wasn't

ready. Apparently, he just didn't know it until they'd slept together. That was the most painful part.

"Oh, honey…"

"It's okay, Mom. I'll be okay."

"I know you will. You're strong—you've always been strong. But this is a lot."

There was silence for a minute, her mother staring at the road ahead. Rylee picked at a hangnail on her thumb until it started to sting. The windows were cracked, and the fresh air felt good against her feverish cheeks.

"Can I just ask…" her mother finally said. "Why? What happened? I mean, you said he seemed so excited to get married. What changed his mind?"

Rylee didn't know the exact answer to that, but she could guess well enough. Maybe he didn't feel the same about her as she felt about him. That seemed like a logical explanation. Or maybe the thought of marriage in general, to her or anyone else, was starting to be a little too real for comfort. That was also a logical explanation. Or maybe it was a combination of the two. Who knew?

It didn't matter though. She'd been able to see everything she needed to see in the living room of his parents' house a half hour ago. The look on his face, his body language when Holt had asked when the wedding would be. And then he simply hadn't been able to open his mouth to answer at all. He'd looked shell-shocked and frozen in place, obviously struggling with the question, when he'd been able to lie about all of this so easily before. It had been one of the most humiliating and hurtful moments of Rylee's life. She hadn't been able to get out the door fast enough.

"I'm not sure," she finally managed. "Things have been different between us this last week, and I knew something was wrong. He's been distant…"

Her mother frowned. Her hair blew in front of her face, and she pushed it away again. "Your father and I were worried this was all happening too fast," she said. "I didn't want to say anything because you don't need our permission, or even our blessing, to live your life the way you want."

"But I did want your blessing."

"I know, and you know we love Shep. But he's always been like this. A risk-taker, when you've always been so careful."

Rylee looked over and gave her a small smile. "Except when I was hanging out with him."

"Yes, exactly that. He used to be able to get you to do things I don't think you normally would have. He had a way of leading you into trouble, and your dad and I were worried this engagement might be history repeating itself. I mean, you barely know each other now. You only reconnected recently."

"I know." It was true. All of it. But still, Rylee felt herself growing defensive of Shep, despite everything. His wildness was what she loved about him. And he hadn't led her into this engagement. She'd gone willingly enough. She'd known the risks, the risks that went along with being with a man like Shep, and she'd accepted them happily. Because it meant being with Shep, and that was all that mattered.

Except now her heart was broken, and those risks seemed a lot more glaringly obvious in hindsight. How could she have ignored her instincts so easily? How could she have been so naive?

"I'm sorry about this, Mom," she said. "I shouldn't have rushed into it."

"You don't have to be sorry. But, honey...do you love him?" Her mother looked over at her then, her eyes unmistakably sad. "Because if you still love him, and you two talk it out…"

Rylee shook her head. She couldn't, she *wouldn't* let herself hope for more from Shep. He'd made it very clear over the last few days how he felt. And if she had trouble getting the message before, she'd gotten it today. No, talking wouldn't make a difference. Sometimes actions spoke louder than words. She'd seen a glimpse of his fear and doubt today, and she wouldn't let herself be on the receiving end of that any longer than she already had.

"There's really nothing else to say," she said. "He's not ready, but it goes deeper than that. Sometimes love isn't enough. We're just too different, and it kills me to say that, but we are."

Her mother nodded slowly. It made sense.

The only problem was, Rylee didn't quite believe it.

SHEP RODE ALONGSIDE his dad, their horses plodding along in unison. The sun was unusually warm this afternoon, and he took his Stetson off to feel the breeze in his damp hair and wipe the sweat from his brow.

His dad had asked him to come along to check the fences, which usually took a few hours. But they'd only been out for about twenty minutes before Shep realized the fences weren't the real reason they were out here. This was his dad's way of initiating a conversation with him about Rylee. He'd bet money on it. And now, all he wanted to do was turn his little chestnut mare around and urge her into a gallop back to the barn. Conversation be damned.

Instead, he put his Stetson back on again, pulling it low over his eyes, and leaned forward in the saddle. Alice's ears flicked back and forth as she waited for him to tell her what to do. She could probably feel the tension in his body, his legs stiffer in the saddle than usual. In fact, his shoulders and back felt stiff, too, and he'd had a continuous headache for about three days now. But he wasn't surprised. He hadn't slept well, had barely eaten since the engagement party from hell. All he could think about was Rylee. Her name throbbed in his mind, like a fever dream that he couldn't shake.

His father leaned on the horn of his saddle. His white gelding, Blanco, lifted his head and tugged on the bit in his mouth, wanting to pick up the pace.

"Whoa, whoa," Neal said in a soothing voice. When he talked to his horses, it was like he was a different man altogether. He was intuitive with animals, exceptionally gentle. When Shep was growing up, he sometimes found himself jealous of them, realizing even at a young age how silly that was, but not being able to help it, either. His father was a tough man in most ways, like most ranchers were, and hadn't left a lot of room for affection for his boys.

Shep understood that better now that he was a man himself. He understood how messy that kind of emotion could be, how much it could complicate everything. At the same time, he couldn't help but feel a little resentful about how that lack of affection was embedded in his very essence. Maybe if he'd learned as a kid to be more in touch with his emotions, and less afraid of them, he wouldn't be in this mess now.

"Son," his dad said, "I haven't wanted to push, but I'm worried about you."

Shep nodded, keeping his eyes on the fence line ahead. "I know you are. But I'm okay."

They were quiet for a minute. Shep knew this kind of talk didn't come naturally to his father. He had to work at it, and Shep wasn't making it any easier by not opening up. But honestly, thinking about Rylee constantly was hard enough. Talking about her was damn near impossible.

"Do you want to tell me what happened?" his dad asked, his saddle creaking underneath him as Blanco stepped over a small log in their path.

"Dad…"

"I know you probably don't want to go over the details, and that's okay. I'm not asking you to. I just want to know what's going on. You seemed so happy before. And now…"

What was he supposed to say to that? It was true. He was miserable. The second Rylee had left Dalton's Grange that day, he'd become a shell of his former self. Trying, without much luck, to get back to how he'd been before he'd run into her at Janet's party. Because it was looking like they'd parted ways now for good. She wasn't answering his calls, and he'd finally just decided to give her space. If that's what she needed, that's what he'd give her.

He took a deep breath, taking in the smell of the grass and of the horse underneath him. Even though the temperature was well over average for spring in Montana, there were angry-looking clouds in the distance. The smell of rain on the breeze promised a storm soon.

"You're right," he said, trying his best to keep his voice even. "I was happy."

"Then what happened?"

Shep shrugged, guiding Alice around another fallen log. He wasn't sure how much he should say. Or how much his dad expected him to say. Heart-to-hearts weren't exactly their style. Still, it felt good knowing this engagement to Rylee wasn't just a footnote in his dad's life. He obviously cared, even though it was hard for him to come right out and say it. He and his youngest son were so much alike, it was scary. And that wasn't a comforting thought. Neal Dalton had changed for the better over the years. But there was no denying the man he used to be.

Shep had the same blood flowing through his veins. Did

that mean he was going to make the same idiotic mistakes as his dad? It was the question he'd been asking himself since spending the night with Rylee. The question that had been haunting him since he'd seen her last, driving away in the passenger seat of her parents' SUV. He'd been so tempted to go after her that day. But he'd talked himself out of it because he'd convinced himself that staying away was for her own good. He'd wanted to protect her, to keep her from any pain that he might inflict without even trying.

Shep glanced over at his dad and frowned. He looked tired. Weary. Which wasn't like him. It was enough to make Shep pull lightly on Alice's reins and bring her to a stop.

"What is it, Dad?" he asked.

His father pulled Blanco to a stop, too, and the horses stood side by side, sniffing each other's noses.

The older man sat there and looked out over the pasture to the mountains in the distance. The muscles in his gray, stubbly jaw bunched and then relaxed again. His shoulders were slumped a little, making him look older than he actually was. For a rare moment, Shep was overcome with emotion for his dad. They'd always had a complicated relationship and had sometimes gone for weeks without speaking. But they loved each other. That had never been a problem.

"I know I've made some mistakes with you, son," his father said, his voice gravelly.

"Dad…"

"I have. We both know it. The way I raised you…well, it's probably why you're having such a hard time talking to me now. You're not exactly an open book, Shep."

No, he never had been. So he just sat there, shifting his gaze to the mountains, too. Wishing that relationships, that love of all kinds, didn't have to be so hard.

"Your mother was always the better parent," his dad continued. "She was the nurturer. The one you boys came to when you'd get hurt or into a fight. She picked up the slack when I wasn't around. Physically and emotionally. I know I failed you in a lot of ways."

Shep lowered his head, watching the breeze move through Alice's rust-colored mane. Watching her fuzzy ears flick back and forth. He felt her breathing underneath him, felt her skin twitching at the flies. Everything seemed magnified right then—the sound of the birds in the trees and the insects in the grass. It felt dreamlike, sitting here talking to his father about the past. Something that Neal Dalton didn't love bringing up. He was ashamed of the things he'd done, and preferred keeping them firmly behind him.

But now, sitting here on the back of his favorite horse, it seemed like he was having a moment. For whatever reason, he could see himself in Shep's circumstance. Or, at least, he could see his shortcomings in Shep's shortcomings, which might've been deeper than he'd ever looked before. Shep didn't know if that made him feel better or worse.

"What I'm trying to say," his dad went on, "is that I'm sorry for a lot of things that happened in your childhood. And I'm not sure what I would've done without your mother. She was the glue that held our family together for a lot of years."

Shep nodded. He could remember days when it felt like they were a single-parent family. It hadn't been easy. Even after they'd won the money. And then his mother had her heart attack, and everything had changed. They'd moved from Tenacity, bought Dalton's Grange, and it was like the sun had come out after a long, dark storm. His dad woke up from whatever stupor he'd been in and had started paying attention to his wife and family. In a lot of ways, it was like he was a different person, whom Shep was still getting to know to this day.

He sensed how close his dad's feelings were to the surface now. This kind of display was so unusual that he was afraid to say anything back, for fear of breaking the spell. It was nice hearing him say things like this. It was nice hearing him acknowledge how wonderful his wife was and how grateful he was to her for the years she stuck with him, when quite frankly, not many women would have.

They sat there for a minute, quiet. The horses shaking their heads every now and then and jingling their bridles. Then, Shep's dad turned in his saddle and pushed his cowboy hat up on his forehead.

"If you love Rylee," he said. "If you truly love her, you should try and make it work."

Shep considered this. He did love her. He knew that now. There was something that happened to you when you were faced with losing someone that made everything else come into sharp focus. It was probably the exact same thing that had happened to his dad.

The problem was Shep didn't know how to navigate it. How was he supposed to love her the way he wanted to love her and not be terrified of losing that feeling someday? Or worse, losing her? It went against every single instinct he had to protect himself. It was an awful feeling to be so sure about something, yet so unsure of it at the same time.

"I love her," he said. "But I'm not sure she wants it to work."

"Are you positive about that?"

"I'm not positive about anything. Except how amazing she is. I'm not quite sure what she sees in me."

"Shep," his father said, his voice suddenly sharp. "Don't be stupid."

Shep raised his eyebrows.

"You heard me. You're a good man, and I think it's pretty obvious that she loves you. But I can understand the doubt. Hell, I doubt myself all the time. I'm a flawed person. But I decided I'm not going to live my life in fear of what might or might not happen. Especially with things that are out of my control. The only thing you can do, Shep, is try to be a good human. A loving person. To appreciate your friends and family, and the rest is going to be out of your hands. The sooner you accept that, the sooner you can stop running away from your life and get down to living it."

Shep sat there in stunned silence. It was maybe the most advice he'd ever gotten from his father. Ever. It was absolutely the most heartfelt thing he'd said in a long time. And it made absolute sense. Was that what was happening here? Was Shep running away from life?

He looked out over the pasture as Alice shifted restlessly underneath him. He'd never thought of himself as fearful. In fact, he'd always thought of himself as exactly the opposite. Strong, independent, a bold streak a mile long. But the truth was, when it came to women, he'd never let himself get close enough to risk a damn thing. And wasn't that the definition of fear itself?

"I don't want to lose her," he said quietly.

His dad nodded, then pulled his hat low over his eyes. "I know you don't." And then, without another word, he nudged Blanco forward. The horse obliged with a soft nicker.

Shep sat there watching them go, thinking of what had just happened between him and his father. Thinking about what had happened between him and Rylee over these last few weeks, and how much it had changed him. He hadn't realized it until right that minute, but it had. *She'd* changed him. The question now was, was it too late to convince her of that?

With a squeeze of his legs, he nudged Alice forward, too.

RYLEE REACHED OUT and rubbed a clear spot in the foggy windshield. The wipers were going as fast as they could, but her car was having trouble keeping up with the sudden nasty weather.

Leaning back again, she looked over at the small box in her passenger seat. The pearl necklace that she was just now getting around to returning to Mayor Smith and his poor wife. She was embarrassed it had taken this long to bring it back. But to be fair, her mind had been kind of occupied with other things lately.

At the thought of the necklace, her stomach dropped. It was impossible not to linger on the memory of Shep teasing her about wanting to see her wearing it and nothing else the night they'd slept together. She'd been so happy in his arms that night. Almost euphoric. And then it had all come crashing down.

She looked back at the road, feeling an ache rise in her throat. She swallowed it back down with a new, welcome stubbornness. Any time she felt like dissolving into tears over Shep, she simply refused to give in. She couldn't thank any particular strength for that; she was just tired of crying. It was getting her nothing but swollen eyes and a chapped nose, and she was desperate to move on from him and this whole ridiculous engagement.

The problem was, though, she couldn't.

Trying to ignore the painful squeeze of her heart, she peered through the frantic windshield wipers to the street beyond, looking for the mayor's address. It'd be dark pretty soon, and then she'd have an even harder time seeing where she was going through this downpour. Not the best time to be driving to Tenacity after this, but she was long overdue for a vacation, and her parents had been wanting her to come home for a while now. Truthfully though, the timing was perfect, since the thought of staying in Bronco a second longer was too much to bear. She needed to get her head on straight again, and she was hopeful that might happen a little faster in a familiar setting, with the comfort of her mom nearby.

She squinted through the dusky evening light, seeing the mayor's house finally come into view. It was big and fancy, and wasn't very distinguishable from the other big, fancy houses on the street. But the address was right there, in bold black numbers on the garage.

She eased up to the curb and cut the engine. Then sat there for a minute with the rain drumming on the roof. She felt blue from the miserable weather and lonesome beyond belief. She missed Shep so much that sometimes she didn't think she'd be able to stand it one second longer.

Lifting her chin, she forced a deep, even breath. It was true that she hadn't answered the handful of times he'd called. But he hadn't shown up in person, either, and that was what really needed to happen for any of this to get sorted through. But, she reminded herself again, there wasn't really anything to sort through, was there? After she'd left Dalton's Grange the day of the party, it had taken a while for everything to sink in. But when it had, she realized how truly crazy this whole thing had been from the beginning. She'd let herself fall in love with an idea. A romantic notion that their promise had actually meant something. When in reality, the promise they'd made the day she'd left for college had simply been a way for her and Shep to make their goodbye easier. Lighter. More bearable.

And she'd wanted so badly to believe it had been real that she'd let herself fall back in love with him.

She stared through the rain streaming down the windshield. She simply hadn't realized how easy it would be to love Shep again. She'd let her guard down. But then again, she hadn't thought she would need to protect herself from him. She hadn't thought he'd hurt her like this. Which was stupid. Looking back, she should've known he wouldn't be able to commit. Even to a pretend engagement or marriage. Shep wasn't the settling-down type, never had been, and she'd *known* that. So she guessed a good portion of this was on her. Plain and simple.

She reached over and tucked the small box into the inside pocket of her jacket, then opened the door into the rain. It immediately hit her in the face—big, cold drops that chilled her to the bone. She needed to remember to keep an umbrella in her car. She never thought of it until it was actually raining, which made her want to groan.

Holding her jacket collar snug around her neck, she ran up the walkway to the front door. When she got there, she shook out her hair and rang the doorbell. She probably looked like something out of *Night of the Living Dead*, but she knew the mayor would be so happy to have the necklace back, he wouldn't care.

After a few seconds, the door opened and Mayor Rafferty Smith stood there looking at her curiously, a glass of what appeared to be bourbon in his hand.

"Hi, Mayor," Rylee said. "I'm Rylee Parker. I met you a few months ago at the convention center. I'm the director of marketing—I'm not sure if you remember. Chuck Carter gave me your address…"

His bushy eyebrows shot up. "Rylee! Of course. What are you doing out in this weather? Come in, come in."

Rylee stepped inside and was immediately met with

the smell of woodsmoke. A cozy fire was crackling in the fireplace, and soft lighting glowed throughout the living room. The rain tapped on the windows outside, and all of a sudden, she felt so tired she thought she could curl up on the overstuffed sofa and fall asleep right then and there.

"Please, sit," the mayor said. "My wife is playing Bunco with friends tonight, or she'd make you some of her famous peppermint hot chocolate. It's a perfect night for it."

Rylee sat on the sofa, grateful for the pulsing warmth of the fire. She hadn't realized she was shaking until right that minute.

"Thank you so much," she said. "But I can't stay long. I'm heading to Tenacity after this, and I think it's only going to start raining harder. I want to get a jump on it."

"Oh?" The mayor sat opposite her, the ice tinkling in his glass. "What's in Tenacity, if you don't mind me asking?"

"My family. I try and get back when I can, but work keeps me pretty busy."

"I can imagine." He smiled, obviously curious as to why she was there, but doing his best not to show it. Rylee had always liked him. He seemed like a nice man.

"I'm sorry to just appear on your doorstep like this, Mayor, but—"

"Rafferty, please."

"Rafferty. But I have something for you. I think you'll be happy to have it back." She pulled the box out of the pocket of her jacket and handed it over. "It's a long story, but I think this belongs to you. Or to your wife."

"Is this what I think it is?"

Rylee watched him open the box and pull out the pearl necklace with a gasp.

Looking up at her, he shook his head. "Where did you find it? I didn't think we'd ever get it back. We'd just about given up hope."

"I went to a birthday party a few weeks ago and saw a friend there." She swallowed hard. The fact that she was now calling Shep just a friend sent brand-new shock waves through her heart. "He'd seen this necklace at a vintage shop and bought it for our other friend's birthday present. When he described it, I told him it sounded like the necklace you bought your wife for your anniversary."

"Thirty years…" the mayor said.

"Yes. A really special anniversary, and a special anniversary gift."

"So, it ended up at a vintage shop, huh?"

"It did."

"And then it ended up at this birthday party."

Rylee nodded.

"And now it made it all the way back to us, thanks to you."

"I'm just sorry I didn't bring it back sooner. I've been…" Her voice suddenly hitched in her throat, and she found that she couldn't finish her sentence. She looked down at her hands in her lap, unable to hold the mayor's gaze anymore for fear she might start crying. And that would just be mortifying.

He leaned forward, putting his elbows on his knees. "You've been what?"

The rain continued tapping on the windows outside. Insistent, chilly. But it was so cozy and welcoming in this living room, and she felt such genuine warmth coming from the man across from her that she looked up and answered honestly.

"I've been distracted. I'm going through a breakup."

He frowned. The firelight flickered across his weathered features, and he nodded knowingly. "Oh, I've been there. Well, not for over thirty years, obviously. But I'm sorry. I know how much it hurts."

Rylee wondered if the pain was etched all over her face. Probably. It felt like she was walking around with a neon sign pinned over her heart that said Warning: Handle with Care.

The mayor looked down at the pearl necklace that was still laced through his fingers and squeezed it in his fist. "You'll probably think I'm crazy," he said. "But I'm starting to think this necklace might be a good luck charm."

"Oh?"

"Do you believe in things like that?"

Rylee had carried around a tiny piece of her baby blanket in her wallet for years because her nana had quilted it, and she thought it was good luck. So, yeah. She did believe in things like that.

"I do," she said. "But what makes you think it's good luck?"

He shrugged and took a sip of his bourbon. "I don't know. Just a feeling I have. I mean, for one thing, it managed to find its way back to us, and what are the odds of that? Like finding a needle in a haystack."

She nodded. *And then some...*

"I'm just saying," he continued, "don't be surprised if your own luck changes pretty soon, young lady."

"What do you mean?"

"I mean this breakup might mend itself. You never know." He winked. "Necklace magic."

For the first time since sitting down, Rylee wondered how much he'd had to drink. The necklace having some kind of special power was a fun thought, but not quite something a totally sober adult would adhere to.

She smiled and looked over at the fire. "I'm not sure he's interested at this point."

"Oh, I doubt that. Sometimes it just takes a man a while

to realize what he's got. And then a light bulb goes off. At least, that's what happened with me and my wife."

Rylee glanced back at him.

"And remember," he continued, "thirty years. We've been married a long time, so I know what I'm talking about. She's the love of my life, but I almost walked away in the beginning because I was petrified. And I'm telling you, that's pretty common."

She knew that was true. More than true. In fact, it was like Rafferty Smith had morphed into some kind of bourbon-drinking, super-power-believing relationship guru in the last five minutes, and it was hard not to laugh at the ridiculousness of it all. Her heart felt lighter for the first time in days, and she got up to give him a quick hug.

"Thank you, Mayor," she said.

"Rafferty."

She smiled, pulling away again. "Rafferty. Thank you."

"Thank *you*. For bringing the necklace back. And for reminding me how lucky I am. You just keep your chin up. It'll work out for you, too. I promise."

Rylee looked down at the necklace in his hand. She'd love to believe it had some kind of magic that would rub off on her and Shep. It had brought them back together, after all. But there was so much doubt and fear to get through. She was scared of this. It wasn't just Shep who was struggling. She was struggling, too.

Forcing her gaze away from the lovely string of pearls, she zipped her jacket up to her chin. She had a long drive in this rain and a lot of thinking to do.

"Have a good evening, Rafferty," she said. "And happy belated anniversary to you and your wife."

He stood and smiled down at her. "You drive safe, now."

CHAPTER TWELVE

RYLEE TURNED THE radio down. The rain was coming harder now, and it was so dark that she was having trouble seeing the fog line on the road ahead. She was almost home. Only fifteen minutes away, but it felt like a lifetime with the highway so eerily deserted like this. The clouds and rain were choking out the light of the moon overhead, making her heart beat nervously inside her chest.

Ever since she'd left Bronco, she hadn't been able to stop thinking about Shep. About what it was that had happened between them. Even now, she wasn't exactly sure. Had it been a fling? An actual relationship created from a fake one? Or had it simply been a way for Shep to sow some wild oats, like he was so prone to do?

It hurt to think that maybe it hadn't meant as much to him as it had to her, but at this point, she had to consider the possibility. She had to face the fact once and for all that Shep didn't seem to feel the same about her. He didn't love her. It was a bleak realization and a sad acceptance. Especially after sleeping with him and falling even harder than she ever would've thought possible.

Frowning, Rylee squinted through the darkness and rain. The wind buffeted her little car, and she squeezed the steering wheel with both hands, trying to stay within the lines. If she'd known it would get this bad, she would've waited until morning to leave. But she'd been so ready to get out of Bronco that she hadn't been thinking clearly.

She'd only been thinking of Shep and the unrelenting pain in her heart.

The wind gusted again, this time pushing the car toward the middle of the road, where the water was collecting in dark, ominous pools. Rylee felt the tires leave the asphalt in a brief hydroplane before she got control of the wheel again. She glanced over at her phone in the passenger seat, wondering if there was service all the way out here.

And then the car hydroplaned again.

SHEP ROLLED OVER in bed and opened his eyes to the gritty light of dawn filtering in through the window. The storm last night had pounded the ranch, sending torrents of rain against his bedroom window and keeping him awake until almost three. He'd finally fallen into a restless sleep and had dreamed of Rylee. She'd been trying to call him, and every time he picked up the phone, it went dead, and he couldn't call her back, no matter how many times he tried. It was the kind of dream that left a bad feeling, even long after waking up.

He was so tired now it felt like he was blinking through sandpaper. His muscles were weary and achy. Even his bones didn't seem to want to cooperate inside his limbs, and for the first time in a long time, he felt old.

He was going to be thirty in a few weeks. And thirty was hardly old. But for some reason, Shep felt every single year like a weight strapped to his shoulders. Symbolic and unwavering. Not letting him forget the fact that he was facing this milestone alone. Sure, he had friends and family. But he didn't have the one person who understood him better than anyone else in the world. And that was Rylee. It was all his damn fault that she wasn't waking up beside him now. Curled into his side, her hair fanned out over her pillow in waves of auburn silk. How could he have let her go? The best thing that had ever happened to him, and he'd let her slip right out of his hands.

He pushed himself up on his elbow and stared out the window. The sky had cleared, and he could see the mountains in the distance, cutting a crisp blue line against the grainy dawn sky. He couldn't stop thinking of what his dad had said yesterday. *The sooner you accept that, the sooner you can stop running away from your life and get down to living it.* Those words had echoed in his mind over and over again last night. Until his body had practically hummed with them, until they'd seeped into his subconscious, and he'd fallen asleep with them tapping against his heart, like the chilly spring rain tapping against the window.

Get down to living it...

He lay there now, feeling a strange kind of peace wash over him.

Because he knew what he had to do to get right again.

SHEP STOOD OUTSIDE Rylee's door and knocked again. This time harder. When he'd gotten in his truck to come into town, he hadn't really considered the possibility that he wouldn't be able to find her. It was anticlimactic. And frustrating as hell.

He raised his hand to knock again, when someone cleared their throat behind him.

He turned to see Gabby standing there, holding the hand of a little girl who couldn't be more than two or three. She smiled up at him. She had chocolate smeared around her mouth.

"She's not home," Gabby said, her voice unmistakably cool.

Shep took his Stetson off and clutched it to his chest. It wasn't like him to feel this uncertain about things. But right now, standing in front of this woman who had nothing but daggers in her eyes for him, he knew he needed to tread lightly. She probably knew where Rylee was, and if he wasn't careful, she'd tell him to go straight to hell.

"Hi, Gabby," he said. He looked down at the adorable little girl who looked so much like her mom. "Who's this?"

"This is Bella. Bella, say hello, honey."

"We came to get Rylee's UFP box," the toddler said, waving with a sticky-looking hand. Shep felt his insides melt. What a cutie. She was almost cute enough to make him forget why he'd come in the first place. Almost.

"The UPS box," her mother corrected gently.

He fixed his gaze on Gabby again and hoped that he looked appropriately pathetic. "I was hoping you could tell me where she is."

Gabby watched him, narrowing her eyes a little. She was obviously weighing whether or not to say anything. But after a moment, some of the stiffness left her shoulders and she sighed.

"You really hurt her, you know."

"I know."

"And I shouldn't tell you sh—" She stopped herself and glanced down at her daughter. "I shouldn't tell you diddly-squat."

Shep smiled. He was making progress. "I know that, too."

"But you look like a man who might be trying to redeem himself, so…"

"I am. I really, really am, Gabby."

She frowned then and grazed her bottom lip with her teeth. "Then I'll tell you…she's fine. She's okay. But she had an accident on the way to her parents' place in Tenacity last night."

Shep's heartbeat slowed, and he felt himself go cold all over. *Accident… Tenacity…* He'd had no idea she was even going back to Tenacity. But then again, why would he? He hadn't come to see her until just now.

"An accident?" he managed. "Is she all right? What happened?"

"Her car went off the road in the rain. She's got some bruises, but other than that, she's fine. She's really lucky."

Shep barely heard that last part. He was already heading down the apartment steps toward his truck.

"Thank you!" He waved over his shoulder.

"Shep," Gabby called after him. "She might not want to see you."

"I know, and that's okay. But I need to tell her something."

Shep climbed in his truck and turned on the engine, revving it without meaning to. He could barely keep his foot off the gas pedal.

Rylee sat on her parents' couch, a fire crackling in the fireplace beside her. Her mother had brought her a quilt and a cup of tea a few minutes ago, and she was having trouble keeping her eyes open.

She took a sip of the tea and winced. Every muscle in her body was sore. But nothing was broken. Her neck moved back and forth just fine; she could wiggle her fingers and toes, and aside from a small cut on her temple where she'd hit her head against the window, most of her bruises were hidden by clothing. So, all in all, she was doing okay. It could have been so much worse. Her Toyota was probably totaled though, since it was older, so she'd have to figure that out. But her raise at the convention center would cover it. She just hated to say goodbye to that car. She'd had it since her high-school graduation, and she'd taken a lot of road trips in it. She felt like she'd grown up in that car.

She thought about pulling up to Shep's house in it on the day she'd left for California. He'd leaned against the hood, his skin a deep golden brown. His hair had been longer back then, curling around his ears in sandy blond tufts. He'd been so sexy that she remembered having to literally look away for fear he'd be able to tell what she was thinking.

It had been years, but she was finally able to admit how in love she'd been as a teenager. It'd been way more than a schoolgirl crush. For a long time, Shep had been her very best friend. He'd been her family and her confidant. She'd loved him for everything he was, and that included all his faults, which she'd been able to see clearly, even at seventeen. She'd simply cared for him in a way that she'd never cared for anyone before or since, and that made her heart ache even more this morning. Knowing that she'd been so close to being with him, *really* being with him, and it had all crumbled at her feet. The only thing left was dust.

She stared into the fire, its sparking orange flames licking the air. She hoped eventually they'd be able to get past this and be friends again. In some capacity, at least. But some time had to pass first, and she needed perspective to be able to heal. The heartache wasn't going to kill her. At moments, it felt like it might, but it wouldn't. She'd move on, and she'd learn from this. She'd protect herself at all costs, wouldn't love so easily next time and wouldn't give so much of herself so fast. All rules to live by. Rules that she'd discovered a little too late this time around.

From outside, she could hear the faint sound of a vehicle coming up the dirt drive. The neighbor's shepherd mix, Henry, barked in the distance.

Rylee sat up straighter, pain screaming through her core, and listened to the slight rumbling get louder and louder. It wasn't a car coming down their driveway—it was a truck.

She froze, her heartbeat thumping in her ears. It wasn't beyond the realm of possibility that Shep would show up here. Then again, he hadn't shown any interest in seeing her since their engagement party. Even though they'd agreed on talking things out before they'd gotten there. The events of the afternoon had blown that plan right out of the water.

She sat completely still, hating herself for how much she wanted it to be him. Despite everything. And that broke her all over again.

Her mother came into the living room, apparently hearing Henry, too. He was a good watchdog. Almost never wrong. Any time he got to barking, there was a reason to look out the window.

Her mom stood there, the expression on her face drawn. "He's here," she said. "I don't suppose you'll want to talk to him. I can say you're not up to it…"

Rylee let out a breath. So, he'd come to Tenacity. She prayed she had the strength to resist his charms this time. But maybe he just wanted to talk like he had before. And that made perfect sense. They *should* talk. Everything just felt so turned around and upside down, she didn't know if she was even up to that. The only thing she knew for sure was that she didn't want to hurt again like she'd hurt after that party.

"I'll see him, Mom," she said. "It's okay."

Her mother watched her closely for a few seconds. And then, there was the sound of a truck door slamming. Of boots thudding up the porch steps. And then, there was a knock on the screen door.

"Are you sure about this, Rylee?"

She swallowed with some difficulty. Her tongue felt

thick and dry in her mouth. "I'm sure." That was a lie. But it was what it was.

Nodding, her mom opened the door. From where she sat on the couch, Rylee could see Shep standing on the porch with his hat in his hand. He wore a blue plaid shirt and worn-out jeans. His dark blond hair bore its characteristic hat ring that always made her heart skip a beat.

"Hi, Mrs. Parker," he said.

"Shep."

"I came to see Rylee. I know she might want to tell me to jump off a cliff, but I was hoping that could be in person."

Her mother gave Rylee a sidelong glance. She wanted to protect her daughter. But at the same time, she knew how she felt about this man. He had the power to make her miserable. Or ridiculously happy. It was a crapshoot.

She turned back to Shep, her stance rigid. "You know she had an accident last night…"

"I do."

"So you can probably guess she's exhausted."

"I won't stay long. I just want to see her. I should've come before this. I wish I had a good reason for staying away, but I don't. At least, not one that you'd probably want to hear right now. But I'd really like to talk to her. And then I'll go back to Bronco, and you won't see me again unless she wants you to. I promise."

Rylee's mother stood there, holding the screen door open a crack and contemplating that. Rylee watched them both, her heart beating in her throat.

"Okay," her mom said after a long minute. "Come on in."

The look of relief on his handsome face was so obvious that Rylee wondered again why he was here. Was this a visit to ease his conscience? Or was he after something else altogether?

She sat up straighter, the pain in her muscles making her want to whimper. But she clamped her lips together as he stepped through the door. His deep blue gaze swept the room and then came to rest on her. She felt it settle there like something warm and comforting and longed for. She'd missed those eyes. That supremely confident look on his face. But he also looked different somehow. There was an expressive, vulnerable tilt to his lips that she'd never seen before. He smiled, but the cockiness was gone. So was the playfulness. In their place was something more serious.

He walked over and leaned down to give her a kiss on the cheek. His stubble scraped her skin in that delicious way that she'd come to love so much.

Setting his hat on the end of the couch, he pulled in an audible breath. "Can I sit?"

"Of course."

She was vaguely aware of her mother leaving the room. Giving them privacy to talk. She heard her bedroom door close from down the hall.

Shep sat beside her, and she could immediately feel the heat radiating from his body. It was almost like the warmth from the fire, only better. She hadn't realized how sad she'd been, how empty she'd felt, until just now. Which made her wary. Without meaning to, she leaned away a little, wanting to stay as aloof as possible, but knowing how futile that probably was.

After a few seconds, she glanced over at him. His eyes were full of concern. He kept looking at the cut on her temple, and she reached up and moved her hair over it.

"I came to your apartment this morning and saw Gabby," he said. "She told me what happened."

Rylee nodded. "I had to talk her out of coming. I'm fine, though. Really."

"You don't look fine."

"It scared me, but I'm okay."

"Well, I'm not okay. I'm not okay by a long damn shot."

She pinched the edge of the blanket between her thumb and forefinger, wishing she at least had some mascara on. Or some lip gloss. Or something.

Shep leaned forward and put his elbows on his knees. Then scrubbed both hands through his hair. She could smell the soap on his skin, the faint scent of hay and leather and man. It made her stomach drop like she was on some kind of roller coaster. And she guessed that was exactly what this was. A Shep Dalton roller coaster, full of twists and turns, ups and downs.

"I don't know what I'd do if something ever happened to you," he said, his voice low. He looked toward the fire, and she could see that he really meant it.

"Shep—"

"No. I need to say some things. And then you can tell me to get out, or whatever you want to tell me. And believe me, I'll understand if that's what it comes to. But I need you to know why I acted the way I did at the party."

All of a sudden, Rylee wasn't sure she wanted to know. Maybe some things were better left unsaid. She and Shep could forget about being lovers and go back to being friends, which was what they'd always been good at. They could chalk these last few weeks up to some kind of adventure gone awry and get back to the comfortable place they'd been their entire young lives. It was possible. Anything was possible.

"Sometimes I wonder if you know how special you are," he said.

She had a strange feeling he must be talking about

someone else. Because she'd never thought of herself as anything much to write home about. She knew she was smart, but a lot of people were smart. She was reasonably attractive, but not nearly as pretty as most of Shep's girl-friends were growing up. She was funny enough to be entertaining in a pinch and sensitive enough to cry at sappy commercials, but special? Not really.

But here was this man, this man whom she thought of as nothing *but* special, uttering these words and wanting her to believe them. It was a tall order when you'd spent your whole life thinking of yourself in a certain way.

"You are, you know," he continued. "You always have been. Even when we were little kids, there was something about you that stuck. When you left for school, I missed you so much it was like a part of myself left, too. And when I saw you again at Janet's party…" He shook his head. "It was like that part of me, that puzzle piece, slid right back into place again."

Rylee's heart was beating so fast, it felt like it might pound right through her chest. Shep was describing the exact feeling that she'd had for him back then. And the exact feeling she'd had when she'd seen him at the party. She'd felt like a piece of her had been returned. Like she was complete again after all this time.

And now, here he was. Putting words to those feelings that had been huddling at the deepest, farthest corners of her heart. It took her breath away. But at the same time, she didn't want it to be taking her breath away. She wanted to be stoic. In charge of her emotions. Unable to be swayed by that look in his eyes that was melting away all of her defenses. She thought she'd been prepared for this. But she hadn't been prepared at all.

"I didn't know you felt that way," she said.

"You wouldn't. Because I don't have a great track record of being honest about how I'm feeling."

She gave him a small smile. Truer words had never been spoken.

"It scared me, Rylee," he said. "All of it seemed to happen at once. In the beginning, the engagement seemed harmless and fun. But then it started to mean something. It started to mean everything... And we spent the night together, and before I knew it, I was falling for you."

Rylee's pulse slowed. *Falling for you*... She could hardly believe what she was hearing. It was too good to be true. And in her experience, any time something seemed too good to be true, it usually was.

He ran his hands down his thighs, like he might be nervous. Shep wasn't the type to get nervous. At least, she'd never known him to be, and she knew him pretty well. But this conversation was blowing everything she thought she knew about him right out of the water.

"But there's one problem with falling for you," he said.

"What's that?"

"You're too good for me."

She stared at him. She'd always thought it was the other way around. He was too good for her. Too handsome, too sexy, too charming. The list went on and on. She'd never really let herself imagine a relationship with Shep because she thought he was out of her league, always had been. Yet here he was, telling her these things. Making her question everything. Definitely making her forget to be wary, and that was a very dangerous thing.

She looked down at her hands in her lap, the quilt a colorful backdrop against her pale skin. She wanted to believe this. She *so* wanted to believe it. But love was a tricky thing. No matter how strong it was, no matter how sweet, it usually came with a healthy dose of fear. At least, that was how it was for her. She thought about what the mayor said last night, about how his own fear had almost derailed his relationship so long ago. And now look at him and his wife—married thirty years. It was a comforting thought.

"Say something," Shep said.

She could feel his gaze on her. Questioning. Heavy. She wasn't sure what he wanted her to say, but so many things were swirling around in her mind right then that she didn't think she could articulate any of them if she tried.

"It's just hard for me," she finally managed. "To believe you'd ever think I was too good for you."

"Why? Why is that so hard to believe?"

She laughed. "Shep. We're *so* different. You were always the popular one. The fun one. The one everyone wanted to be around. I was never like that. I blended. Everywhere I went, I blended in. The only reason I wasn't completely invisible was because I was so close to you. You made people notice me by association."

He watched her, looking incredulous. "Rylee…"

"You have to remember that about me. And I'm okay with it. I'm comfortable in my skin now. I'm happy with who I am. But too good for you? Is that just a line?"

Slapping his thighs, he stood up with a groan. Then walked over to the window and looked out toward the pastures in the distance. Rylee's family's ranch was small. Much smaller than Shep's had been, and nothing in comparison to Dalton's Grange. But it was beautiful land. Some of the prettiest in Tenacity, and she loved it completely. Having Shep standing there, with the ranch stretching in front of him through the single-pane windows, was doing something to her heart.

"You know," he said, turning to her again, "one of the things I love about you is that you don't know how amazing you are. How beautiful you are…"

Her stomach dipped at that. Another drop on the Shep Dalton roller coaster.

"It's the strangest thing. It's like you don't know when other guys look at you. Or when other women are jealous of you. And to me, it's the most obvious thing in the entire damn world." He fixed her with a hard look. "You're the entire package, Rylee, and you don't even know it."

"Shep..."

"And I came here to tell you that I'm falling in love with you."

She blinked up at him. It felt like all the oxygen had been sucked out of the room, and she was breathing through a straw. Her lungs weren't working right. Her throat wasn't working right. He was falling in love with her? Why now?

He frowned and rubbed the back of his neck. "And I'm pretty freaked out right now, Rylee. Because before, when I was pushing to get married, I was only thinking about today. Not about tomorrow, and who doesn't think about tomorrow when they're talking about marriage? It was stupid. I wasn't treating it with the respect it deserves. Or treating you with the respect you deserve."

Swallowing hard, she sat up straighter. Her nose stung, her eyes stung, like she might start crying, and she didn't want to do that. She wanted to be clearheaded for this. This was a conversation that had been a long time coming. Maybe her entire life. She thought of the string of pearls that she'd brought back to the mayor last night and how he'd told her they might be good luck. Was it possible that he'd been right? That a stroke of luck or fate or magic, even, had brought her and Shep back together again? Her heart warmed at the thought.

"I wasn't treating it that way, either, Shep," she said. "There were two people pretending to be engaged, not just one. But I don't regret it because it was maybe the most fun I've ever had. And I've had a lot of fun with you."

He smiled, those two long, irresistible dimples cutting into his cheeks. He looked so young, standing there in the afternoon light, that her throat ached. She wished it could be like this forever. With the two of them on the cusp of something special. With time stretched ahead of them like a long country road. It was scary to think of what could happen if she let herself trust this, if she let herself trust him.

"Why did you do it?" he asked. "Why did you go along with it?"

It was a fair question. And one he probably thought he already knew the answer to. Rylee had gone along with a lot of things he suggested over the years, after all. But this time was different. And she could admit that to herself now. A few weeks ago, it had been hard to admit anything. But now, she could.

She grazed her bottom lip with her teeth, focusing on the feeling. On the taste of her ChapStick on her tongue. She took a deep breath and prayed that when she said what she was about to say, she would be strong enough to walk away from this if it wasn't right for her. Just because you cared about someone deeply didn't always mean you belonged with them. Even if it was Shep she was talking about. They simply might not be right for each other, and at the end of the day, that was okay. It didn't mean she cared for him any less.

"Rylee?" he asked. Waiting. Expectant.

If she'd been standing up right then, her knees might've buckled. She was glad she was sitting down.

"I went along with it," she said quietly, "because I love you. I've always loved you."

He stared down at her. The logs shifted in the fireplace, sending sparks floating into the chimney.

This was the most honest she'd ever been with Shep. It felt strange telling him how she really felt, when she'd spent so long keeping it inside. She never thought she'd tell him this secret. She never thought she'd even admit it out loud, but here she was.

"You've always loved me…" he repeated slowly.

She nodded.

"Since we were kids?"

She nodded again. Thinking of all the time they'd spent together back then, all the adventures they'd gone on. How she felt like she'd follow him anywhere, on any path, no matter how dark and winding. And then, they'd been on the brink of marriage. *Marriage.* She'd been about to follow him into that, too. It was a testament to how much power he had over her. She reminded herself how important it was now not to follow, but to walk side by side.

"You were my best friend, Shep," she said. "You were there for me when I felt the loneliest of my whole life. When I felt awkward and weird and didn't have any other friends. You were always there for me. How could I not love you?"

He listened, letting the words settle. Now he knew. Now there really was nothing left unsaid, and that was a good feeling for her. No matter what ended up happening between them, they were finally being honest with each other.

He walked over and sat down again. This time closer. His thigh brushed against hers, and even through the quilt, there was a familiar electricity there. Her chest tightened with longing. She thought she'd always long for Shep in some form or another. Maybe that part was just meant to be.

"So, you've always loved me," he said quietly. "And I'm falling in love with you. Tumbling head over heels, more like it."

The corners of her lips tilted at that.

"So, now what?" he continued. "What do we do about this, Rylee Parker?"

She took a deep breath. That was a good question. The best question she'd heard in a long time because the possible answers could take them in so many different directions.

"I just know that I want you in my life," she said. "It's more colorful with you in it."

He smiled. He was gorgeous, all tanned and scruffy, his hair messy from his Stetson. He smelled so good that Rylee was having trouble not throwing her arms around him, but she was trying to show some restraint. At least a little bit. She needed some control right now to get through whatever was going to happen next. Because, despite all of this, nothing said they would end up together. That wasn't promised. Nothing was promised.

"I want to show you something," Shep said. "You're probably sore as hell, but I'll carry you there if I have to. Are you up to it?"

She watched him, her heart swelling. When it came to Shep, her heart had trouble not swelling. It was as simple as that.

"I'm up to it," she said.

CHAPTER THIRTEEN

SHEP WALKED BEHIND Rylee up the forested path, watching her wince when she stopped to take a breath. He hadn't been kidding when he'd offered to carry her back at the house. And then again when they'd gotten out of the truck. But she'd just laughed and insisted on walking on her own. Probably a good idea. If she'd been in his arms, he would've had trouble not kissing her neck, her cheeks, her lips. It was driving him crazy being this close and not touching her at all. But he wanted to show her the tree first. In order to tell her what he hoped for their future, she needed to understand how he felt about their past.

"Are you sure you're okay?" he asked.

"I'm all right. Just a little sore."

"It's just a few more yards."

She looked up through the canopy of pine trees and smiled. "When you said you wanted to take me to our old stomping grounds, I was thinking more along the lines of the strip mall or the movie theater. Or maybe the river. I haven't been up here in ages."

"I know. Me neither. It's kind of out of the way, and parts of it are being developed. But the trail is the same. And so is the meadow. For now, at least."

"It would break my heart if anyone built on that meadow."

"They might someday. Tenacity isn't as small as it used to be. But at least we'll have the memories."

"And we have a lot of those."

They did. They had so many. Their lives had been so intertwined that sometimes Shep forgot which memories were Rylee's and which were his.

She put her head down and stepped forward on the trail. He followed her, breathing in the scent of the pine and moss. It was so beautiful up here, so peaceful. He and Rylee had spent a lot of time wandering these woods in the summers. Maybe not as much time as they'd spent at the movies and at the river, but a fair amount. They'd come up here when it was hot in town, and when they'd had too much sun and water, and they'd sit in the meadow grass and talk. They'd had some of their best talks up here, with the stars just beginning to pierce the evening sky and the moon lifting its pale face in the east. Shep coveted those long-lost moments. And he coveted this place.

Slowing, he touched her elbow then came to a stop on the trail. The mountain air was cool against his skin. Birds and squirrels rustled in the bushes to their left, and the sun was trying its best to peek through the steely blanket of clouds overhead. Overall, this spot hadn't changed at all since he and Rylee had hung out here as kids. It was untouched by time, and Shep knew what a rarity that was in this day and age.

He turned to his right, to the meadow that was visible now through the trees. The grass, deep green from the recent spring rains, was punctuated by fragrant wildflowers that moved in the breeze. Even though the air still held a chill, the warmth in the sunshine carried a hint of the seasonal change on the way. It was a perfect afternoon as far as he was concerned. A perfect place, with perfect company.

He let his gaze settle on the aspen tree closest to them. The one with the large knot in its trunk about halfway up.

It was the first one you came to when walking along this trail. The first one in the grove surrounding the meadow. And he'd carved something into it a long, long time ago. When he'd been a kid, and when his best friend had meant more to him than just about anyone else in the world.

"Rylee," he said.

She turned, her cheeks flushed and her eyes bright. He could smell the faint scent of her perfume mixed in with the sweet smell of the wildflowers and grass. Her lips were full and pink and glistening, and she looked so pretty right then that she just about killed him dead.

He reached for her, and she put her hand in his. He just hoped he wouldn't screw this up, like he'd screwed up so many other things lately.

"I wanted to bring you here," he said, "because it's always been a special place for me."

She smiled. "Me, too."

"I know we've talked about our childhoods and the things that were hard for us. But I'm not sure you ever knew how worried I was that I'd end up like my dad."

She watched him, her eyes full of understanding. He was lucky to have a friend like Rylee. Sometimes he wondered if she knew him better than he knew himself. Having a person like that in your life was special. It made him feel like he had everything to lose. And maybe everything to gain.

"He's changed," he continued. "He's gotten better with age, and he finally grew up. But for a long time, he made my mom miserable. He made our entire family miserable, and I never wanted to be like that. But when I was a kid, I thought it was a foregone conclusion. I refused to imagine myself married in the future, or even in a relationship that mattered, because it always made me so unsettled to picture that kind of life. Where I could have such a negative effect on other people. People who loved me, and who I loved back. After a while, I stopped thinking about it consciously. It just...*was*."

Rylee nodded, listening in that way that made him feel like he mattered. That he was important. That he was loved. It gave him the courage to pull her closer, until he could feel the softness of her body next to his. She fit perfectly there, making him think about those negative expectations that had always been a part of his narrative. Making him think about what it would be like to finally say goodbye to them, once and for all. He thought it would probably be a wonderful feeling, changing and growing like that. And he knew Rylee was the only woman he'd be able to make that change for.

"That's why I left the morning after we slept together," he said quietly. "It was just easier than facing this dumb fear that I've always had. Can you forgive me? For leaving you like I did?"

She reached up and touched his face. The tips of her fingers left his skin tingling. They left his heart tingling.

"I can't believe you've ever been scared of anything," she said. "To me, you've always been fearless. But you telling me this... I have to be honest. It makes me love you even more, Shep. And that scares *me*. Because I didn't think I could love you any more than I already did."

He laughed. "Well, then. I think this might be the perfect time to show you what I brought you up here for."

"It's not the meadow?"

"No. Look."

He pointed to the aspen tree next to them. The one with the knot in its trunk. Below the knot was a heart carved into the snow-white bark. And inside the heart was another carving. *S+R*.

Rylee gasped. "Did you..."

"I carved that when I was ten. Back when I thought just about anything was possible. Before I got jaded by things."

She stared at it. "Shep…"

"So, you see," he said, leaning down to kiss her temple, careful to be gentle with the cut there, "I think I've always loved you, too."

She smiled, looking happier than he'd ever seen her. But the wariness was there, too. And she had every right to be wary of him. He was wary of himself. But something was different now. He could feel it.

"I don't know," she said, her voice low. "Do you think something could work between us? Do you think we should start dating?"

Shep wrapped his arms around her waist. They were good together. They'd always been good together. Maybe this was what people meant when they talked about fate. Suddenly, that old fear he'd battled for so long began receding as he stood there with her in his arms. As he clearly pictured them in the future. Together. Happy. It was something he never thought would be in the cards for him, but that was the thing with change. True change. It could take you by surprise in the best possible ways.

"You want me to be honest with you?" he asked. "Really honest?"

"You know I do."

"Then I have to say I don't want to date you, Rylee."

Her expression fell. Her body stiffened. But before she could pull away, he held her fast.

"I want to marry you," he finished softly. "I don't want to be your boyfriend. I want to be your husband."

She stared up at him. "You want to get married," she repeated. "For real…"

He nodded. Then leaned down and kissed her on the

lips. Tasting her. Loving her. When he pulled away, her eyes were red-rimmed and glassy.

"I'm just sorry it took me this long," he said, "to see what I had in front of me this whole time."

Swallowing visibly, she reached up and wrapped her arms around his neck. She was shaking. He could feel it.

"Maybe we just needed a little push," she said. "I'm not sure I would've had the courage without one. And then there was the necklace…"

"The necklace?"

She smiled. "Maybe that was the little push. Fate or magic. Or whatever you want to call it." She told him then, about what the mayor had said about the necklace's power.

"I like that. Magic." He spread his hand over her lower back, rubbing his thumb against the sliver of skin above her jeans. "And all before we turn thirty."

"Just in the nick of time."

"So…" He looked down into her clear blue eyes. "Does this mean you're saying yes?"

"Are you asking me to marry you, Shep Dalton?"

"I am. I'm asking you to marry me. Except I don't have a ring. Again." He laughed. "I guess you'll have to trust me on that part."

"It's a leap of faith."

"Will you take it with me?"

The sound of the forest enveloped them like a hug. Their aspen tree shivered in the breeze. Pretty soon, it would be alive with leaves that would turn red and gold in the fall. But for the summer months ahead, they would be as green as the swimming hole he and Rylee had shared as kids. As the river that had always led them home again. They'd grown up in two very different families, but they were the same in so many ways. Those similarities had brought them back together again. And yeah, Shep thought, maybe that was magic. Maybe it was fate. Whatever it was, he was grateful it had touched his life like it had. And had brought Rylee with it.

Her smile widened, and it was like the sun coming out from behind the clouds. Until right then, he hadn't realized how worried he was that she'd say no. They'd had a rocky start with this whole marriage thing, after all. And it was fast. Some might say lightning fast. But if you considered the fact that they'd known each other, and loved each other, since elementary school, then it really wasn't fast at all.

She stood on her tiptoes and kissed him softly. Sweetly. "I will," she said. "I absolutely will."

RYLEE STOOD IN front of the giant living-room window and looked out over the lush green expanse of Dalton's Grange. Today was one of those late spring Montana days that was so rare she wanted to stop time altogether, just so she could sit in the sun and soak as much of it up as possible. Days like this got her through the long winters, when it seemed like the snow would never stop falling and the wind would never stop howling. But they always did. Spring always came. And with it, days like this. Full of warmth and hope and promises of the future.

Footsteps approached behind her—boots thudding on the hardwood floor. She knew it was Shep long before he wrapped his arms around her waist and moved her hair aside to kiss her neck. Lately, it seemed like she could sense his presence before he'd even entered the room. It was like he was a part of her. And she was a part of him.

"What are you doing?" he asked, his mouth close to her ear.

Everyone was talking and laughing across the room. Enjoying the party and the food and the company. They'd come to celebrate Shep's thirtieth birthday, but he seemed to be more focused on Rylee than anything else. Not that she was complaining. She could get used to this kind of attention.

"Just thinking," she said, turning her face into his.

"About?"

"About how we got here."

"To the party?"

She laughed. "To this point in our lives. How funny it is that it all ended up like this."

"Engaged."

She nodded.

"I think it makes perfect sense," he said evenly. "It was meant to be."

It was one of his favorite things to say now. That they were meant to be. And she couldn't argue. She agreed with all her heart. But sometimes, she couldn't understand how she'd gotten so lucky. She felt like the luckiest woman in the world, and that still felt delicate. Like it all might come tumbling down again if she wasn't careful.

But whenever she thought about it that way, whenever she felt the fear taking over, she remembered what Shep had said in their meadow a few weeks ago. He'd asked her to trust him. And that was exactly what she intended to do. She loved him. And that meant putting her faith into this relationship. As new and tender as it was. If they could both do that, put their faith into it, it would grow into something special. Even more special than it already was. Like that pearl necklace that she thought about all the time now, it would grow into something magical.

He kissed her cheek, and she closed her eyes, reveling in the feel of his lips on her skin. How his stubble scraped against it, and how his breath was warm in her ear. She loved Shep with her whole heart. And every time she thought about becoming his wife, she wanted to pinch herself all over again. It was her childhood fantasy coming true. The sweetest promise being kept.

"I think I'm supposed to say something before my mom cuts the cake," he said.

"That cake looks amazing."

"It does, doesn't it? When you turn thirty, everyone gets excited about things like cake. Including the birthday boy." He winked at her. "You'll see when it's your turn."

"I know. I'm right behind you."

"Only a few more weeks and you'll be entering another decade, baby."

"At least you're blazing the trail for me."

"That I am."

"Shep! It's time, honey!" Deborah called from across the room. Her voice carried over the country music playing on the stereo. She was so happy to be giving Shep this party. Even happier that Rylee was here to help him celebrate. She'd told her over and over again. It was nice for Rylee to feel like she belonged here. Like she was already family.

Before leaving Tenacity, she'd told her parents that her and Shep's engagement was officially back on. She could tell they were still worried it might be too fast. Her dad was especially hesitant about it, and she could understand that. It took a lot for him to come around to most things. She just hoped they'd feel more comfortable with it soon, since Gabby, as the maid of honor, was on fire to make an appointment at Ever After to try on dresses. Her mother had promised to drive up to Bronco for that. Rylee wouldn't have it any other way.

Shifting, she laid her head on Shep's chest and gazed out at all the people in the room. All of Shep's family and friends were there, along with townspeople from Bronco. Gabby was there, with Ryan and Bella, and so were Rylee's parents. Even Winona Cobbs and her fiancé, Stanley San-chez, were there. Winona and Stanley were finally get-ting married in July. Some people didn't think they'd ever get around to making it official, but July was just around the corner, and they looked pretty happy as far as Rylee could tell.

It was a good turnout. A lot of people loved Shep. But she didn't think anyone could love him more than she did. For the first time in a very long time, she was looking for-ward to her future, and all the unknowns that might come with it. Because if she was facing it with Shep, she knew they could make an adventure out of just about anything. Even the hardest days.

He gave her a squeeze and kissed the top of her head. "I'll be right back."

She watched him make his way across the room—hand-some, broad-shouldered, confident, sexy. *Her Shep.*

Gabby walked over and elbowed her gently in the ribs. "You're glowing, girlfriend."

"I am?"

"You absolutely are. I don't think I've ever seen you this happy, Rylee."

So, it showed. But she guessed that made sense. Every-thing felt so close to the surface lately. Like it had just been waiting to rise to the top. The happiness, the joy. The love.

Gabby put an arm around her as they watched Shep step onto a stool and lift a champagne glass in the air. He tapped it with a fork, and a hush fell over the room.

"I think he's your destiny," Gabby whispered. "And that's pretty romantic."

Rylee smiled, her gaze resting on the handsome cow-boy who had stolen her heart all those years ago. And had kept it tucked in his pocket ever since. It belonged to him, she thought. And it always would.

"Thank you all for coming," he said. "Thirty years old today. *Ouch.*"

Everyone laughed.

"When I was younger," he continued, "and when I thought about this day, the only thing I knew for sure was that I didn't want to celebrate it without my best friend by my side. And now, I can happily say that she is. Because she's not only my best friend, but also my fiancée. It's been a little bit of a learning curve for us, but I can't imagine spending the rest of my life with anyone else. Rylee, would you come up here for a minute? I have something for you."

Rylee stared at him. Gabby gave her a little push, until she finally stepped forward through the throng of people and up to where Shep was standing.

He stepped off the stool and grinned down at her. Playful, mischievous Shep. Always keeping her on her toes. Always keeping her young at heart. When he looked at her like this, anything was possible.

"I should've given this to you weeks ago," he said.

He took her hand and placed something in her palm. Something cool and tiny. She looked down at it and felt her heart skip a beat. It was a ring. A beautiful antique ring that immediately took her breath away.

"It was my grandmother's," he said. "She would've loved you, honey."

There was a collective *aww* that moved through the room as Rylee felt people craning their necks, trying to get a glimpse.

With her heart thumping in her ears, she slipped the ring onto her finger and held it up to the light. The diamonds glittered like stars, the white-gold band glinting in the sunlight coming through the window. She didn't think she'd ever seen anything so lovely in her life. It was exactly what she would've chosen for herself. Exactly.

She turned to Shep with a terrible ache in her throat. For a second, she worried she wouldn't be able to speak. To tell him how much she loved the ring and how much she loved him. How excited she was to become his wife. But then, she didn't have to.

Slowly, he took her in his arms and leaned down to kiss her.

The room erupted in applause, and she felt herself being lifted off the ground. Her feet dangled in the air as he held her against his chest. She felt laughter bubble up from the deepest parts of her. It was the same feeling she'd had when they'd held hands and jumped off the rock into their swimming hole. The same feeling she'd had when they'd stood in his driveway the day she'd left for college, when they'd made their promise to each other. It was a feeling of weightlessness. Of pure, unrelenting joy.

When he set her down again, people made their way forward to congratulate them. Her parents, smiling and happy. His parents, looking proud of them both. Their friends and family. And then Winona Cobbs, in a flowy white dress and chunky costume jewelry that sparkled in the afternoon light. Even in her nineties, she was still a very beautiful woman, and Rylee found herself looking down at her in wonder. She knew some people in town thought she was eccentric, maybe even a little nutty, but Rylee had always thought she was wise. She'd seen so much in her lifetime. She had so much to share.

"Congratulations, sweetheart," Winona said with a smile. Her soft, powdery wrinkles deepened then. Her cheeks were flushed pink, and she wore an understated lipstick that reminded Rylee of roses.

"Thanks so much, Winona."

Shep took her thin, delicate hand and kissed her knuckles, just like Prince Charming. "I'm so glad you could make it," he said.

She smiled wider, obviously taken with his charm, just like everyone else. "I wouldn't miss it, Shep. We get to celebrate your birthday *and* your new life with this lovely girl."

Rylee leaned into Shep's side, and he put his arm around her waist. They stood there with Winona, who suddenly looked wistful.

"Being young and in love is a wonderful thing," the older woman said. "Josiah and I...well, it's a long story, meant for some other day..."

Rylee watched her. A curious expression crossed the older woman's face, just as the music changed to something slower and softer. When Winona had been a young woman, she'd had quite the secret romance with a rancher named Josiah Abernathy. Most everyone in Bronco knew about it now, but there was still an air of mystery surrounding their love affair, even all these years later. Rylee would love to hear the story if Winona ever decided to tell it.

She reached out and touched Winona's arm. The other woman jumped a little, as if startled from her thoughts.

"Are you okay?" Rylee asked.

"Oh, I'm fine, sweetie. Just taking a trip down memory lane." She glanced behind her at Stanley, who was helping himself to a piece of cake. She frowned, and Rylee thought some of the cheerful color had drained from her face. But maybe that was just her imagination.

"Well," Winona said, turning back to them again. "You two enjoy the party. Happiest of birthdays to you, Shep."

Rylee watched her go, her billowy white dress making her stand out like an exclamation point in the room full of Wranglers and plaid shirts.

"Now, there goes a very interesting woman," Shep said, pulling Rylee close.

"You can say that again. She has a lot of secrets."

"Yes, she does."

Rylee turned to Shep and tilted her head back to look up into his handsome face.

"You're thirty today," she said.

"That, I am."

"I'll be thirty in just a few weeks."

"Indeed."

"And we're getting married." Her voice caught in her throat. She felt such naked emotion right then that it probably should have embarrassed her. But she didn't care. She wanted him to know. She wanted him to know everything that lay in her heart.

He cupped her face in both hands. Then he moved his thumbs across her cheekbones and leaned down to kiss her lightly on the lips.

"We're getting married," he murmured against her mouth.

"Is it too soon to make another promise?"

He smiled. "Never. What is it?"

"Promise we'll always be together."

Rylee was a realist. She knew life would throw things at them that they weren't prepared for. Or that might change their existence forever. Things that weren't anyone's fault, they just *were*. So maybe it wasn't fair to ask for that. But deep down, she knew that Shep would know what she meant.

She wanted to know that they'd always love each other. No matter what. No matter what might happen in the future. Whether they could control those things or not. She wanted to know that their love would transcend time and space. That it would transcend circumstance and just *be*.

Like the color of the river in the summer or the scent of their meadow in the spring. It would always be.

"That," Shep said softly against her ear, so only she could hear, "is a promise I can keep."

* * * * *

Don't miss the stories in this mini series!

MONTANA MAVERICKS: THE ANNIVERSARY GIFT

Welcome to Big Sky Country, home of the Montana Mavericks! Where free-spirited men and women discover love on the range.

The Maverick's Marriage Deal
KAYLIE NEWELL
March 2024

The Maverick's Thirty-Day Marriage
ROCHELLE ALERS
April 2024

Starting Over With The Maverick
KATHY DOUGLASS
May 2024

MILLS & BOON

The Rancher's Secret Crush

Cari Lynn Webb

MILLS & BOON

Cari Lynn Webb lives in South Carolina with her husband, daughters and assorted four-legged family members. She's been blessed to see the power of true love in her grandparents' seventy-year marriage and her parents' marriage of over fifty years. She knows love isn't always sweet and perfect—it can be challenging, complicated and risky. But she believes happily-ever-afters are worth fighting for. She loves to connect with readers.

Dear Reader,

I confess that I've been known to fall down more than one research rabbit hole during the course of writing a book. It has in fact happened with each book I've written, despite my best intentions and repeated warnings to myself not to get too sidelined by horse videos or the latest wedding dress styles.

In *The Rancher's Secret Crush*, reserved city girl Elsie Parks takes after my own heart with her penchant for reading and learning before she jumps into anything. When Elsie ends up on a working farm, it's not the steep learning curve that unsettles Elsie. It's professional bronc rider Ryan Sloan, with his passion for adventure and his soft spot for Elsie, who has her researching ways to guard her heart. Now if these two opposites can realise that their hearts are meant for each other, they just might discover a love they never expected.

It's springtime in Three Springs, Texas, where the bees are buzzing, the tractors are tuned up and there's always room on the porch swing. So, grab a tall glass of iced tea and come on over. We'll leave the porch lights on.

Cari Lynn

DEDICATION

To the readers who believe opposites attract
isn't only for science.

Special thanks to my fellow writers for their
friendship and encouragement. To my husband for
explaining those tractor videos to me and
my daughters for offering plot solutions on
demand. I'm grateful for your enthusiasm
and continued support.

CHAPTER ONE

LEAVE IT INSIDE the gate.

Those had been Elsie Parks's exact but haphazard words not twenty minutes ago to Trey Ramsey of Ramsey and Sons Auto & Heavy Machinery Repair. Elsie had been moderating a dispute between her two young nieces over crayon ownership and checking the visitor policy at Belleridge Regional Hospital. That was where Elsie's brother—and her nieces' dad—was currently a patient.

Not that any of those details mattered if Elsie couldn't even get out of the driveway. She put the car in Park, told the girls to stay buckled and stepped out to confront the massive green tractor standing in their way.

The very one that Trey Ramsey had repaired. And the same one the very nice mechanic had left just inside the gate like Elsie had instructed. Completely blocking the driveway. Elsie squeezed her forehead. Behind her, car doors opened, and footsteps scrambled across the gravel drive. Soon enough, her two nieces bracketed her on either side.

Gemma smashed her polka-dot bucket hat lower on her blond head and bumped her skinny elbow into Elsie's side. "You gotta drive it, Auntie."

Elsie gaped at the giant tractor. One tire was wider than her six-year-old niece was tall.

"She can't," Autumn countered. At eight years old, Autumn was already proving to be analytical and serious-minded, same as her father had always been. Autumn pointed toward the tractor. "It's headed for the ditch. If auntie doesn't turn it just right, she'll end up in the ditch too."

The ditch was the least of Elsie's issues. The main one being Elsie had never operated a tractor, let alone sat in one. She wasn't even sure how to climb aboard to get inside the enclosed cab. Elsie turned and surveyed her surroundings.

Her nieces moved with her. Gemma rolled up onto her tiptoes and whispered loudly, "What are we looking for?"

"Another way out of here." Elsie tracked the thick three-rail wood fence that framed the acres upon acres of Doyle Farm. Her aunt and uncle had started with twenty acres and expanded during their thirty-year marriage. The property was now well over a hundred acres.

"There isn't another exit," Autumn declared, her words tinged with pride. "Dad says it's like a castle here. One way in. One way out."

"Can we have a tea party when we get home? It's what all princesses who live in castles do." Gemma jumped and clasped her hands together. "Pretty please. We can invite Cowboy Prince since Dad can't come."

The sun beat down on Elsie's head, making her wish she'd grabbed a hat like Gemma. She could already feel her skin tightening and her face heating. Even though it was spring in the Panhandle and that Texas heat hadn't even been dialed up quite yet. Still, spring or summer, she'd never tanned gracefully. Simply turned a fascinating shade of beet red before peeling and returning to pale. *Remember to take care of your porcelain skin, Elsie. You must always protect your assets.*

Elsie touched her cheek. Sunscreen certainly wasn't going to help her now. Besides, she'd grown up and learned to rely on things like hard work, wise decisions and determination. She said, "Gemma, let's table the tea party until after we visit your dad, okay?"

Gemma opened her mouth to argue.

Autumn leaned around Elsie and added, "We have to see Dad, Gem. 'Cause he's lonely and bored in the hospital without us."

"Don't forget you promised your dad you'd bring him pictures for his wall." Elsie touched Gemma's thin shoulder and added more cheer to her words. "Maybe you could go draw another one inside the car while I move the tractor."

"Can't we watch?" Autumn yanked on the waist of her shorts, tugging the baggy denim higher on her hips. "I could help guide you."

"I want you both to wait inside the car. Where it's safe." Elsie cringed. But it was too late to take back her words.

"You can't move the tractor, Auntie. You can't." Gemma knocked her hat off, latched her arms around Elsie's waist and clung tight. "It's not safe."

Unfortunately, two days ago, Gemma's dad had told both his daughters that it was perfectly safe for him to be up on one of the greenhouse roofs on the farm. It had been mere minutes after his bold declaration that one of the older rafters gave way and Elsie's brother fell through the roof to the cement floor below. Miraculously, Bryce had only suffered several badly bruised ribs and multiple fractures in his ankle. Now Bryce was in room 414 at Belleridge Regional Hospital, preparing for an early morning surgery on his ankle. As for Bryce's six-year-old daughter, well, Gemma now fully distrusted all claims about safety.

Elsie lifted Gemma up into her arms and hugged her. Her nieces had been through so much. First their parents' divorce that was finalized just before last Christmas. Then their sudden move at the start of the new year from the only home they'd known in the suburbs of Philadelphia to a farm in the Texas Panhandle. Now their dad's accident. More than anything the girls needed stability and reassurance. Elsie walked closer to the silent tractor. Autumn trailed beside Elsie, her shoulder brushed against Elsie's arm every other step.

"The tractor is safe." Bold statement. Up close the tractor loomed into even more intimidating. What could her brother possibly need with a tractor that massive? He'd never even owned a riding lawn mower before. What was she supposed to do with it? Elsie worked a confidence she wasn't entirely feeling into her words. "See, it's turned off right now. It can't hurt anyone."

"We should leave it off." Gemma rested her head on Elsie's shoulder.

"We could," Elsie started. "But then we wouldn't get to see your dad today."

"Then he'll be really sad." Gemma wiped her hand under her nose. Her voice descended into pitiful. "I miss my dad."

"I know you do." Elsie squeezed the little girl harder and reached for her own resolve. So what if she didn't know anything about tractors. She had to do something. She hugged Gemma once more. "I promise I'm going to get you to the hospital this afternoon so you can give your dad the biggest hug ever."

Gemma nodded and swirled Elsie's ponytail around her fingers. "The tractor won't hurt you, right?"

Elsie shook her head then lowered her niece to the gravel. "Now head on over to the car. I put your backpack of coloring supplies on the front seat."

Gemma picked up her hat and raced to the bright blue Jeep Bryce had purchased for what he'd dubbed his career pivot from financial advisor to full-time farmer.

Autumn lingered beside Elsie. Her hands on her hips, she studied the tractor then tipped her head toward Elsie. "Maybe you should call like Dad did."

"What do you mean?" Elsie studied the tractor and searched for a way inside. Her brother had hit the height gene jackpot in their family. What would've been a simple extended step up was more like a big leap for Elsie. She rolled onto the balls of her feet. The soles of her cute sandals had little flex and even less bounce. Perhaps a running start then.

"Dad made a phone call, and a cowboy came over. Then the cowboy drove the tractor for Dad." Autumn tucked her brunette chin-length hair behind her ear and nodded sagely at Elsie. "You should call a cowboy too."

Elsie rocked back and forth. *Run. Jump. Grab.* Nothing to it. Surely, she could reach the door handle on the tractor cab. It was just one jump. *Ouch.* Elsie winced and brushed away the sharp pebbles that slipped between her sandals and bare toes. "I don't know a cowboy to call."

"All the cowboys live next door," Autumn added. "One of 'em has a beard whiter than Santa." The little girl paused and patted her stomach. "But his belly is too flat so he can't be the *real* Santa. We get to call him Cowboy Santa, even though his real name is Sam."

Sam Sloan and his family had property that bordered her aunt's farm. The two families had been neighbors for decades according to her aunt. Elsie's brother always hung out with the Sloan brothers during their summer trips to their aunt and uncle's farm. As the younger sister and only girl for miles around, Elsie had often stayed with her aunt. She'd always preferred reading on the back porch and helping her aunt in the greenhouses. Until the summer after Elsie's freshman year in high school. When she'd encountered one Sloan brother alone at the Sloan family pond.

Elsie tightened her ponytail and pushed her memories aside. "Well, we don't have Santa or Santa's helpers right now. It's just us and a tractor."

"But Auntie." Autumn tapped Elsie's arm. "What about Cowboy Prince?"

"We don't need a cowboy rescue." Especially not from some cowboy prince Elsie didn't know. All she had to do was jump. Grab the handle. Climb inside. On three. Elsie inhaled a deep breath and fixed her gaze on the tractor. Target set, she shook her arms out at her sides and crouched lower. "Watch. I'll show you. We got this."

One. Two. Three.

Elsie sprinted to the tractor and leaped. Miraculously her fingers wrapped around the door handle. She gripped tight and managed to find a place to prop her feet. Adrenaline propelled her upward. Autumn clapped and cheered her on. Swinging the door wide, Elsie climbed inside, albeit awkwardly. Scraping elbows and knees on her way in. She'd have more than one bruise from this exercise. No matter. She'd made it.

But her victory celebration was immediately cut short. The inside of the tractor looked more technologically advanced than a space shuttle cockpit. And at least as complicated. Elsie dropped onto the captain's chair. Sweat beaded along the back of her neck. The heat wasn't too stifling inside the enclosed cab. Yet the air was stale. Defeated? Not yet. All she needed was an instruction manual. Good thing she excelled at online searching.

Propping the door open with her foot, she called out, "Autumn. Look for a name on the tractor."

"But Auntie," Autumn hollered. "You can…"

Elsie's foot slipped the same time she jostled her phone from her back pocket. The door slammed shut on Autumn's words. And her cell phone landed with a *thunk* up under the console. Elsie scrambled to locate her phone. And the cab door swung open behind her.

"Well, if it isn't Elsie *won't-dance-with-me-ever* Marie Parks."

Elsie stilled. No one had called her that in forever. Not since that one particular summer. When only one person—with a very similar deep Texas drawl—had ever dared.

Slowly twisting around, she took in the full-fledged cowboy propped in the open doorway. His chestnut-colored cowboy hat rode low on his forehead, shadowing his bearded face. Dust and pollen stuck to his plaid shirt, with the sleeves rolled to his elbows, and his jeans as if he'd been walking through a dry field. Oh, but she knew him. Her heart raced. Her mouth felt as dry as the dust caked on his worn boots. "Ryan Sloan."

His grin lifted into both cheeks. His teeth flashed white. "You remember me."

Ryan was hard to forget. Even though he'd only ever been nothing more than her one-time crush. When she'd been young and foolish enough to accept his dares at his family pond one summer evening. She'd been excited and giddy and thrilled to have his undivided attention. Until his girlfriend had arrived. Then Elsie had discovered firsthand why it was called a crush. The pain had been oddly difficult to dismiss. And Elsie had decided cowboys weren't worth the trouble of a real heartache. Her voice cracked. "Ryan. What are you doing here?"

He nudged the brim of his hat higher on his forehead. Revealing a pair of all too dreamy, but deceptively shrewd, hazel eyes. "Sundancer and I were just passing by."

Elsie glanced out the window. Saw a stunning palomino grazing not far from Autumn. Not surprising. Ryan had always been a cowboy first. And his partner his trusted horse.

"I tried to tell you, Auntie." Autumn's enthusiastic shout

reached Elsie clearly and concisely. "Cowboy Prince is here. Now he can rescue you." Autumn skipped over to Sundancer, tore a fistful of grass from the ground and carefully fed it to the horse.

Except Elsie rescued herself these days. No prince, cowboy or otherwise, required. Still, she couldn't quite clear the surprise from her words. "You're the cowboy prince I've been hearing about."

"One and the same." The corner of his mouth hitched into his beard. "We can talk about all that later."

Talking later. With Ryan. That sounded appealing. Or would have if Elsie's crush on Ryan hadn't expired well over a decade ago. If she had returned to Three Springs for more than her family. If she wanted to get entangled in some sort of cowboy situation. *With him.* More sweat dampened the back of her neck. Despite it not being mid-summer and the temperature not even close to sweltering.

Ryan eyed her. "Well, are you going to tell me?"

"What?" *That you've strolled through my thoughts over the years. Slow and unrushed. Like the spark of a good memory. The kind worth revisiting again and again.* Elsie rolled her lips together and willed the flush she felt out of her cheeks.

"Tell me what exactly you are doing in here," Ryan said.

"In case it isn't obvious, I have a bit of a tractor situa-tion." And definitely *not* a cowboy one. Elsie waved her hand around and tried to stir the suddenly stifling air. "Now, all I need is an instruction manual to get out of it."

"That's your plan then. Reading your way out of this." He braced his arm on the door frame and looked her over. "I see some things haven't changed much."

Elsie refused to squirm and instead returned his steady regard. Eye for eye. Beat for beat. Same as she'd met his stare years ago. *You read too much, Elsie Marie. You can't really want to be alone all the time. Come on. You might have fun.* Elsie had only ever grinned and turned the page of her book. *I'm not alone. I have my books. You should try sitting still once in a while, Ryan. You might like it.* Ryan had always laughed. *Only place a cowboy sits is in the saddle.* And then he'd hop onto his horse and leave her alone. Like she preferred. Until she hadn't.

She lifted her chin and nudged aside her memories. "Yes, that's my plan. Read the instruction manual. Drive the tractor."

"Still doing everything on your own too," he mused, seeming intent to point out what hadn't changed about her.

While Elsie couldn't help but notice what had changed about him. Specifically, the boy she'd known had grown into a man. Where he'd once been cute and boyishly charming, he was now so very handsome, in a rugged, outdoor, hands-on kind of way. The exact kind of way Elsie had no business noticing. Elsie crossed her arms over her chest before she reached out, touched his arm. Tested her theory that beneath his sun-soaked skin was all muscle.

He rubbed his hand over his mouth. "What's your plan B then?"

"What?" Elsie met his gaze.

"Elsie Marie, I know you." He leaned farther into the cab, closing the distance between them.

And Elsie almost leaned toward him. As if she meant to meet him halfway.

Those gold flecks in his gaze sparked. His words were wry. "You always have multiple plans, Elsie. So much so, your plans *have* plans."

Only she hadn't planned on running into him so soon. So quickly. With barely enough space between them to draw a decent breath. Let alone think clearly. She swiped at her damp neck. Wanting desperately to blame the unrelenting sun for rattling her. "There's nothing wrong with being prepared."

"Let me see your phone." He extended his arm toward her. Palm up.

Now was her chance. To finally know. To take his hand in hers and know for certain if his grip was as strong and secure as she'd always imagined. To know for certain if their hands fit in that easy, perfect way that just felt right. The way she'd always wanted her hand to fit inside her ex-husband's and never quite did.

Definitely not a chance she would ever take, especially with Ryan Sloan. Who took relationships less seriously than a bear took a bee guarding its hive. *Love. Why would I want that, Elsie Marie? I have bronc riding. That's my life. All I'll ever need.* And given that Ryan was currently ranked number one in bronc riding and very single according to her brother, Ryan had certainly proven his words true.

Besides, everything Elsie needed waited in New York. The city was her calling. The country his. Their time together would only ever be temporary. As always. It was best not to hold his hand. Best not to know. After all, she never liked starting things that could not be finished.

She set her phone carefully on his palm. "If you can tell me what kind of tractor this is exactly, I can read the manual on my own."

"You don't need a manual." He tapped quickly on her phone screen, then handed her phone back. His expression was neutral. His voice causal. "You have me."

Have him. No. He wasn't hers. She didn't want to think of him like that. That implied things like dating and relationships and those extra messy emotions. The ones she'd gotten completely wrong before. No matter. She'd filed away love in the *been there, don't need that again* folder along with her divorce papers more than a year ago.

"I added myself to your contacts. Now one of your plan B's can be calling a cowboy." A close-lipped smile worked across his face. He motioned toward her. "Scoot over."

Elsie never budged. "Why?"

"So I can give you your first tractor driving lesson." He folded his tall frame into the suddenly too-small cab.

Sweat dampened her entire back now. Yet he looked unbothered as if he was somehow immune to the heat. Elsie blurted, "We can't."

He paused and arched an eyebrow at her.

He was close enough to hug now. Without any effort. Just a small stretch. For a welcome back embrace between friends. First, she wanted to hold his hand. Now hug him. What was next? *Exit now.* She had to get out. Get herself back together. She rushed on, "I can't leave Autumn alone with your horse."

"Sundancer is gentler than a kitten and better trained than a show dog." He motioned toward the window. Outside, Autumn picked a dandelion and blew the fluff into the air all while the horse grazed calmly beside her.

"Still, I should wait here. Gemma is coloring in the car. She might need me." Elsie scooted to the edge of the chair and shifted toward the door. Only to pause when her toes touched the tips of his boots. Two problems faced her. Getting around her cowboy. And getting down.

He lifted his arm as if reaching for her.

Elsie held her breath and waited. Braced herself for the connection. She had always wanted to know...

But he simply touched his hat and adjusted it lower on his forehead. "Let me get out of your way first. Unless you need help climbing down."

Elsie exhaled and shook her head. "I can manage."

With a quick nod, Ryan backed out of the cab and was on the ground in seemingly one agile leap. Elsie on the other hand found herself indecisive about how to even climb down. Forward or backward. She finally chose backward. Only to have her sandal slip off the first step. She would've fallen unceremoniously into the dirt if Ryan hadn't reached up, caught her around the waist and set her safely on the ground.

One shift. One lean back against him. Then she would be inside his embrace completely. One more thing she didn't need to test. She took a quick breath and released it. Finally, she glanced over her shoulder and worked to keep her words light and easy. "Thanks for the assist."

His fingers flexed at her waist. His mouth opened.

But Autumn's excited words filled the silence. "Cowboy Prince, did Auntie stall the tractor like she does Dad's car?"

Elsie cringed. Then stepped away from Ryan. She set her hand on her niece's shoulder. "We only stalled twice."

"In the driveway," Autumn supplied.

Elsie glanced at Ryan. He smoothed out his grin. Elsie shoved her shoulders back. "It's been a minute since I've driven a stick shift." More like years since she'd driven her own car. Let alone one with a manual transmission. She'd lived in Seattle until last week. Walked to work. To restaurants. To everything. And if she'd wanted a ride, she opened the app on her phone and scheduled a pickup.

"I offered to give you driving lessons all those summers ago," Ryan teased. "Maybe you should've said yes."

She'd been fifteen and more worried about what Ryan thought of her outfit than perfecting her shifting skills. And he would've been a distraction she hadn't needed. Then or now. "It's coming back to me."

"I'll be happy to give you a refresher," he offered.

More time with Ryan. Not what she came for. She was there to watch her nieces. Until her Aunt Marlena and Elsie's mom returned from their extended overseas vacation. Then the two sisters would care for Bryce and look after the girls. For now, Elsie would do what she always did. Keep her senses about her. "If you could move the tractor so we can get to the hospital to see Bryce, that will be more than enough."

"Well, the offer stands," he said. His gaze gleamed. "You know how to reach me if you change your mind."

Not happening. One cowboy rescue was more than enough.

Ryan shifted his smile toward Autumn. "Want to take a ride in the tractor? Think of it like a carriage for a cowgirl princess such as yourself."

"Can I, Auntie?" Hope widened Autumn's eyes. "Please?"

Elsie looked at Ryan.

"She'll be fine," he assured her. "I know what I'm doing."

That made one of them. Elsie finally nodded.

Ryan guided Autumn up into the tractor. Elsie walked over to Sundancer on the other side of the driveway.

Within seconds, the tractor engine started. Autumn waved excitedly from her perch next to Ryan. He maneuvered expertly around the Jeep, missing the ditch entirely, and stopped beside the car. Autumn shouted out the window at her sister. Gemma cheered from the front passenger seat. The tractor rumbled up the driveway and out of sight. The large wheels kicked up a dust cloud in their wake.

Minutes later, the pair finally appeared on the crest. Ryan held Autumn's hand while she skipped beside him.

"I finished two drawings, Auntie," Gemma shouted and waved the papers at Elsie. She was out of the Jeep and racing up the drive toward Ryan and Autumn in a blink.

The girls' bright laughter floated like the plump white clouds across the spring blue sky, drawing out Elsie's own reluctant smile. It was the first time she'd heard her nieces truly laugh since she'd arrived late yesterday afternoon. It rankled slightly that it was their cowboy prince, not Elsie, who was responsible for her nieces' sudden good moods.

Watching the animated trio, Elsie's smile expanded. Before she checked herself.

Sundancer nickered and pawed the ground beside her as if wanting Ryan's attention too.

Elsie patted the horse. "Don't worry, Sundancer. He's all yours."

After all, the very last thing Elsie wanted was her own cowboy situation.

CHAPTER TWO

"COWBOY PRINCE. COWBOY PRINCE." Gemma hopped toward Ryan like a chirpy house finch flitting through his late Gran Claire's gardens. Gemma's spindly arms flapped at her sides. Her drawings snapped in the warm breeze. "Look. I put you in my pictures too, Cowboy Prince."

Cowboy Prince. Ryan still hadn't quite adjusted to his newly anointed nickname. Cowboy he was, from his old, broken-in boots to his bloodlines. But a prince? Never that. Cowboy daredevil would've been more appropriate. At least until recently. He sidestepped his current identity crisis, knelt and caught Gemma as she careened into him. Taking the crinkled paper from her, he said, "I haven't been in a drawing for a really long time."

Gemma braced her small hands on his shoulders and tipped her head to study him. "Why not?"

Ryan worked his expression into serious then shrugged. "I suppose because no one in my family draws pictures anymore."

Although with his sister-in-law Tess expecting twins soon, he supposed that would change in the coming years. As for Ryan, coloring for fun had ended in grade school around the time he had discovered the thrill of the rodeo. And rodeo became the only thing he ever wanted to do.

Gemma's nose crinkled. "Then how do you make your walls happy if you don't have any pictures on them?"

He was happiest outside. Covered in dirt, horsehair and

nature. Not a wall in sight. He glanced at the thick layer of dust stuck on his boots. Not exactly the polished look of a prince. Still, the concern in Gemma's fawn-wide brown eyes caught his attention. Unsure of the right answer to soothe the sweet little girl, he asked, "Do you think my walls are unhappy?"

She chewed on her bottom lip and nodded solemnly.

"What should I do?" he asked.

"Put pictures on them, silly." Gemma tapped her drawing and grinned. "You can have this one."

"But this is for your dad," Ryan countered.

"I'll make Dad another picture on the way to the hospital. I don't get sick reading and stuff in the car like Gem and Auntie." With that declaration, Autumn leaned against Ryan's shoulder and pointed at her younger sister's artwork. "Besides, you gotta have that one. You're in it."

"I'll put it on my wall tonight." Ryan grinned and looked at the picture. Two stick figures, one with a cowboy hat and the other with a crown on her yellow hair, stood in a field of bright sunflowers. Each flower had a smiley face drawn in the center. Even the sun in the corner beamed. It was a burst of happiness on paper. He added, "I like the crown you're wearing in this picture, Gemma. You look just like a princess."

"That's not me." Gemma giggled. "That's Auntie Elsie and you."

Ryan shifted and glanced down the drive where Elsie stood beside his horse. Elsie stroked her fingers down Sundancer's muzzle. The horse leaned into her touch as if already drawn to her. Ryan knew the feeling. He'd always been aware of Elsie. Too aware. And at all the wrong times. Like now for instance. When he was lingering for no apparent reason. When what he needed was to get back to his career. Back to the circuit. Where he belonged.

"You can look at my picture when you fall asleep. And dream about holding hands with Auntie Elsie." Gemma twirled around in several circles, wobbled to a stop and speared her arms over her head. "Then you'll wake up happy."

A belt buckle. A jackpot. A perfect eight-second ride on a bucking bronc. That had been Ryan's dream for as long as he could remember. Now certainly wasn't the time to go looking for some new dream. Or worse someone. He was good as he was—riding through life solo. On his own terms.

Besides, the truth was Elsie and Ryan only worked in a dream. Elsie was high-rises and corner offices. Sophisticated. Polished and poised. He was backroads and pastures. Straightforward. Rough and unrefined at times. Those roads weren't meant to intersect. Let alone connect. Ever. He pulled his gaze back to Gemma's picture. "So, this is me and your Aunt Elsie then."

"Holding hands." Gemma beamed then grew serious again and lowered her voice. "Auntie used to hold Uncle Andrew's hand, but no more. I think she cried a lot too. Now she won't be sad if she holds Cowboy Prince's hand."

Maybe not in a colorful picture. But Ryan was far from a prince. Never claimed to be one. He rubbed his palm on his jeans. As for Elsie, she should be holding a real prince's hand. One who would care for her heart properly. She certainly deserved that. Deserved more than a reckless cowboy like Ryan with calloused fingers and a heart too cordoned off to ever find. The last thing he ever wanted was to make Elsie sad. Nothing for it but to keep his distance.

"Well, thank you for my picture. I'm sure my wall will be very happy to have it." He folded the picture, tucked it into his shirt pocket and stood. Then walked between the girls back down the drive. "Now it's time to get you two to the hospital to see your dad."

And past time for Ryan and Sundancer to get on their way. There was no need to stick around as if he was suddenly interested in reconnecting more with Elsie. As it was, he already knew the highlights reel of her life.

He'd kept low-key tabs on Elsie over the years. Never asking her aunt or uncle or even Bryce about her directly. Yet whenever Elsie's name came up in conversation, he always paid attention.

He knew Elsie had earned both her college degree and master's degree in hospitality and event management in an impressive five years.

Knew she worked in Seattle as an event manager for an upscale worldwide hotel chain. She'd always been driven and hardworking.

Knew also about her private wedding in Paris. Even in a simple black-and-white bridal photograph her aunt had shown him, Elsie had taken his breath away.

Lastly, he knew about her divorce.

He frowned. That was the only piece that didn't quite fit. Surely her ex-husband regretted his decision every single day. Because that was the thing about Elsie. Beyond her pretty looks and natural poise, Elsie Marie Parks was what his grandpa would call a keeper.

Which made her entirely wrong for Ryan of course.

The only thing Ryan was interested in keeping was his top ranking in bronc riding. Yet to do that, Ryan had to rediscover his edge and get back in the saddle. The one he hadn't been in for more than a month. After he'd messed up during a stunt on a Western movie set and ended up injuring Sundancer. His stomach pitched sideways. And that edge—the one that had kept him razor-focused and at the top of his bronc-riding game for so many years—remained silent and flatlined. Same as it'd been since the accident.

Gemma rushed over to Elsie and showed off her artwork.

Ryan reached for Sundancer's reins and tipped his hat at Elsie. "Looks like you're clear to get on your way." Same as him.

He needed to get on his way to finding himself again. Time was running out. He had two weeks until he had to be back in the saddle. Back in the chute. Anticipating that first jump of his horse for an eight-second ride at Belleridge Rodeo Rides for A Cause.

If only the rodeo wasn't a charity event. If only Ryan hadn't agreed to compete for Martha Claire Horse Haven. The very same horse sanctuary named after his own late Gran Claire. The one he volunteered at whenever he was home. The one that needed another new stable. Because Ryan had promised homes to five aged-out broncs from the circuit. Then perhaps he could've bowed out. Blamed an old injury. But he refused to let down his family, his hometown or those circuit horses. He had to ride. But first he had to figure out how.

"But you can't leave." Gemma turned toward him. Disappointment widened her already impossibly round eyes. "You'll miss the tea party later."

Ryan rubbed the back of his neck. "I could come back."

Gemma's eyebrows pinched together. "You said that last time and didn't come back."

Bryce had granted Ryan a tea party rain check last week. Because Ryan had told Bryce he was finally getting back in the saddle. Finally practicing for the upcoming Rodeo Rides for A Cause at the newly restored Belleridge arena. Bryce had believed him. Heck, Ryan had believed it too.

Until he'd gotten home. Saddled Mischief, his mustang. Walked to the practice arena. Started overthinking. Second-guessing. And backpedaling. Not a good look for a supposed champion bronc rider. Fortunately, he excelled at keeping things like that to himself. He tapped Gemma on the nose. "But I apologized for missing the tea party and even brought you a box of chocolate peanut butter candy. Your favorite."

Gemma's face softened.

"You could come to the hospital with us now, Cowboy Prince." Autumn snapped off a dandelion and handed it to her sister. "You and Dad can talk about the bees."

"They always talk about the bees," Gemma added. Her words rushed out in a forlorn breath that scattered the dandelion fluff into the air.

The girls weren't wrong. It was entirely intentional on Ryan's part too. If his friend was thinking about the bee business and his own life, then Bryce was less likely to go poking into Ryan's problems. Ryan switched the reins to his other hand and his gaze caught on Elsie.

She studied him closely. Suspicion crossed her face. "I should've known this was all your idea."

What? That he wasn't there by chance. That he'd purposely walked by the farm. Yesterday. And today. That he would've walked by again tomorrow. And the day after. All for a not-so-impromptu run-in with her. Ryan smoothed his expression into impassive.

"The beekeeping," Elsie clarified. "You're the one who gave Bryce the bee business idea."

No. He couldn't claim that one. But he had helped Bryce refine it. Showing her brother several other potential income streams for his beekeeping endeavor. Ryan took in Elsie's flushed cheeks and the flash in her silver gaze like the start of a spring storm brewing. Her mind was already set. No use arguing now. He pressed his lips together and waited. He'd always been partial to a midnight storm.

"You convinced my brother to do all this. To take such a risk," Elsie charged. "You could always convince him to do anything."

But not Elsie. Never her. Despite his best efforts. Which had only intrigued him more. Yet it was for the best he hadn't succeeded. Then saying goodbye to Elsie might've actually hurt once upon a time. But Ryan had vowed long ago that goodbye would never get to him. Never hit him hard enough to ever matter.

Elsie rolled on. "Then you talked Bryce into uprooting his entire life and family to relocate here."

"You say *here* like it's a bad thing." But it was. To her. *I won't be back. There's nothing here I could ever want.* Those had been Elsie's parting words that last summer she'd spent at her aunt and uncle's farm. After Ryan had made the mistake of asking when she'd return. He tapped his hat up, met her gaze. Didn't back down. "I won't apologize if that's what you're looking for. Bryce is better off living here."

She stepped toward him. Her gaze sparked again. "That's debatable, given my brother is currently in the hospital."

"Bryce is happy here, Elsie." *You could be too.* Strike that thought. Her happiness was *so* not his concern. Still, beneath the frustration he saw the worry for her brother on her face. Heard the unease in her words. And just like that he wasn't quite ready to leave her. He said, "Since you clearly don't believe me, there's only one option. I'm going with you to the hospital. Then we can ask Bryce together about his recent life decisions."

Autumn and Gemma cheered. Then Gemma shouted,

"We'll go make room for Cowboy Prince in the car." The two girls raced toward the Jeep.

Elsie lost her bluster. Touched her forehead. Searched his face. Relief and resistance clashed in her gaze. "You can't come with us."

Try and stop me. His grin was gentle. "Sure, I can. You know I care about Bryce too." *And you if only from a distance.*

"What about your horse?" Elsie flicked her wrist toward his horse. Then rubbed the back of her neck. "You can't just leave Sundancer here."

Ryan peered at her closer. She looked flustered now. He turned and guided Sundancer up the drive. Time to get moving before she came up with more excuses to deny him. "I'll put Sundancer in the pasture. There's nothing he can get into there."

"But no one will be here with him." Elsie caught up to him and followed Ryan to the back gate of the pasture. "To look after him."

"He'll be fine." Ryan released the halter from Sundancer and checked his gait. The gelding's limp wasn't visible. It hadn't been for the past few days. Of course, Sundancer hadn't been saddle tested yet. Or ridden. Still, the horse certainly seemed to be on the mend faster than Ryan.

Elsie gripped the top post of the fence. Her attention was on Sundancer. "It doesn't feel right."

There was a distance in her tone. A tension in her fingers. Even more in her words. Nothing he would have noticed if he wasn't so aware of her. And so very intent on not facing his own predicaments for a little while longer. Ryan checked the lock on the gate and turned toward her. "What's really going on, Elsie?"

"We aren't meant for farming, Ryan." Elsie pushed away

from the fence and rounded on him. "We weren't farm raised. You know that better than anyone."

"Neither was your Aunt Marlena." Ryan motioned behind him. Only the roof of the striking stone two-story house was visible in the distance. He knew the land and the house as well as his own. Bryce and Ryan, along with Ryan's four brothers, had spent as much time roaming these acres growing up as they had exploring the Sloan land. He added, "Look at what your aunt built here."

"This was all my Uncle Robert," Elsie countered. "Aunt Marlena and Uncle Robert built all this together. Bryce is alone now that my mom and aunt seem to have acquired an insatiable travel bug."

"Not really." Ryan lifted one shoulder and stepped around her, heading back to the Jeep. "Bryce has good neighbors and friends here. People looking out for him."

"Except no one was here when he fell through the greenhouse roof." Frustration was thick in her words. And in the crunch of her steps on the gravel drive.

"You'll have to take that up with your brother," Ryan said. "In the meantime, give this place a chance. It might change your mind."

Elsie flipped her ponytail back over her shoulder. Certainty coated her words. "My mind is set on New York."

He shouldn't have been surprised. Her gaze had always been fixed well beyond Three Springs County lines. He tried to sound indifferent. "What's in New York?"

"My new job." She slanted her gaze toward him. "I was going there when I got the call that Bryce was in the hospital."

This was a detour. A temporary stopover on her way to where she wanted to be. This was what his Gran Claire would've called good information. *Any information is good, Ryan, even when it's not what you want to hear.*

Can't expect to make good decisions without knowing all the facts. He asked, "When do you start?"

"I'll leave when Aunt Marlena and my mom get back from their vacation late next week," she explained.

She would be back on the road. Alone. But who would be watching over her? Not him. With luck, he would be on the road too. Getting back to his own life on the rodeo circuit. The only one he ever wanted.

"I want you to know." She glanced at him. "If Bryce is truly happy here, I'll do my best to support him."

Ryan nodded. Did his best to do the same for her now and pushed more positivity into his tone. "Congratulations on your new job, Elsie. I'm sure you will be very happy in the city."

"That's my plan." Her smile was small and brief. "To be happy."

Before he could press her about *not* being happy, she tossed the car keys at him then quickly added, "I think it would make everyone in the car happy if you drove us to the hospital."

Ryan caught the keys and opened the front passenger door of the Jeep for Elsie. "Your chariot awaits, my lady." That drew out her laughter. To his delight.

"Thank you, Cowboy Prince." Her gaze gleamed before she climbed into the car.

Ryan grinned, more than glad to spend a little bit longer with Elsie.

As for his own happy, he'd always found it in the saddle. And that was exactly where he would find it again. Because a horse and a rodeo were all a cowboy like him ever needed.

CHAPTER THREE

"Turn it up, Auntie," Gemma chanted from the back seat. "This is my favorite song *e-v-e-r*."

"Dad says he can't think with the radio turned up too loud," Autumn chided her sister.

Elsie was starting to think too much. And worry. About her brother. Her nieces. Herself. Four years separated Elsie and her older brother. When their parents divorced, Bryce had preferred their father's quieter house. Elsie had shuffled between houses yet never quite found her footing in either place. And the siblings grew further apart. Attending different colleges hadn't helped. Neither had job relocations that widened the distance to state lines. Now they weren't exactly tight as far as siblings went. They cared for each other. Albeit from afar. Showed their affection mostly over text and occasional phone calls on holidays and birthdays. But Bryce's accident had scared Elsie. A lot. Elsie wanted to change things between them before it was too late. She only hoped her brother did too.

That worry swirled around her racing thoughts. Elsie reached for the volume button on the radio and slanted her gaze at Ryan. "Do you mind?"

He shook his head and grinned. "It feels like a volume up, windows down kind of day."

That sounded carefree. Worry free. She couldn't remember the last time she'd enjoyed a day like that. Certainly not with her ex-husband. They'd been too focused on their careers and work goals to ease off, even for an afternoon. She eyed Ryan. "Do this often?"

"Not as much as I should," Ryan admitted.

Surprise filtered through her. The boy she'd known had hardly ever been serious about anything, except his horses. The man now looked guarded as if he carried secrets that weren't so light and easy. But Elsie was there to mend things between her and her family, not discover more about her cowboy. She tapped her finger on the volume button and said, "Sing it if you know it."

With that, the windows rolled down. The radio went up. And the girls belted out the words to the pop song and wiggled their shoulders to the upbeat tune in the back seat. Slowly, Elsie's shoulders relaxed. By the next song, she was tapping her foot to the beat.

Two songs later, she was windblown, singing with her nieces and urging her cowboy to join the chorus. He didn't shy away and instead matched the singer's deep timbre with his own equally rich voice. All to the girls' delight and Elsie's disbelief.

Ryan Sloan could sing. And his was not a voice reserved only for showers and solo car karaoke sessions. She wanted to find another song. One of his favorites perhaps, if only she knew it. She wanted to listen to him sing more.

But he pulled into the hospital parking lot. And Elsie remembered there was nothing else she wanted when it came to her cowboy. Certainly, no further singing sessions that might make her wonder what else she didn't know about him. Oh, her curiosity was certainly caught now.

That was bad. Elsie was a learner, and the more puzzling something was, the more she wanted to understand it. But there was no manual on cowboys. Besides, her cowboy looked more like a closed book. Best all-around if she reined in her curiosity. She worried if she started learning about her cowboy, she might not want to stop.

The windows went up. And that worry stepped forward again. Searching for a distraction, Elsie unbuckled then leaned around her seat. She asked, "You need help picking up those crayons?"

The girls had spilled their crayons and markers when they'd started dancing. "No thanks. We got it." Gemma bent down, reached under her seat, and handed a green crayon to her sister.

Autumn arranged the crayon in the large box and frowned at Elsie. "Dad says if we make the mess, we gotta clean it up too."

"That's the rule." Gemma sat up, holding several more crayons. "And we gotta follow the rules or Dad gets mad."

Elsie left her nieces to their cleanup, opened her door and stepped out. Suddenly restless yet rooted in place.

Ryan rounded the front of the Jeep and approached her. "You okay?"

"Hospitals. Nerves." Elsie stuck to the obvious reasons for sudden hesitation. The ones easiest to explain. Admitting she was anxious to see her brother for the first time in person after more than three years, well that would only lead to questions. Especially from Ryan, who always put his family first. Elsie was trying to do that now. She wanted to get it right. She just wasn't certain how. She added, "Not the best combination for me."

Ryan lifted his cowboy hat and ran his fingers through his hair. "I think I should warn you."

"Hospitals make you nervous too." She winced at the hope she heard in her words. As if she wanted that to be what connected them. What made her feel not quite so alone. Not so completely out of sorts.

"They don't bother me anymore." He settled his hat back on his head.

"How did you get over it?" she asked.

"Too many injuries." He touched his thigh as if testing an old injury. "Been here more than I'd like to admit."

"Still, you keep competing." Same as she kept proving she was alright alone. "I admire your resolve." And she liked to think she had some herself. She released the car door.

"Rodeo is what I do," he said simply. Firmly.

The edges of his mouth tightened. A brief tensing. There and gone. She would've missed it if she hadn't been watching him so closely. Locked on to him as if he was somehow her anchor inside all her sudden insecurities and uncertainty.

Ryan scratched his fingers through his beard. "But back to your brother. Bryce is pretty banged up. He's going to tell you he looks worse than he feels."

Elsie was still missing a few details about Bryce's accident. But she knew Ryan had gone to the hospital after her brother's fall. While a volunteer EMT had stayed with Autumn and Gemma at the house until Sam Sloan, Ryan's grandfather, had arrived to watch the girls. It had been Sam who'd called Elsie to tell her what had happened. It was several more hours before she'd been able to speak to Bryce. Elsie frowned. "How bad is it?"

"Lots of bruises all over. Stitches on his face. Cuts and scratches on his arms." Ryan motioned toward his boots. "And some sort of drain in his ankle that Grant can explain a lot better than me."

Grant was Ryan's younger brother and one of the best orthopedic surgeons around. Fortunately, Bryce was under Grant's care and Grant would be handling her brother's ankle surgery the following morning. Elsie's nerves stretched tight. Surely once she saw her brother, the worry would even out.

"I just wanted you and the girls to be prepared," Ryan added.

She hadn't prepared the girls. She wasn't certain they'd ever been in a hospital before. Let alone to see someone they loved. She'd been so focused on getting *to* the hospital, she hadn't given much thought to what happened *when* they arrived. "What's the process here?" Elsie drew a breath and glanced at the girls slipping on their backpacks in the back seat. "Do I go in first? Do we all go in together?"

"How about I take the girls to the gift shop," Ryan offered. "They can pick out balloons for their dad, while you go see your brother."

She was supposed to be looking after her nieces. That was why she came. But she could use the help. And a moment alone with her brother would be welcome. "I owe you."

"It's no big deal." Ryan's eyebrows lifted. "Believe it or not, the gift shop sells the best caramel almond popcorn around. Gran Claire always got us some to share when she had to bring me here as a kid."

Claire Sloan had been full of warmth and welcome. The first time Elsie had met Ryan's grandmother, she'd hugged Elsie tight. Then told her: *We only use the back door around here. The front door is for strangers. If you've come inside my home, you're no longer a stranger.* Elsie had always marveled at how instantly she'd felt at home in the Sloan farmhouse. She'd never felt that anywhere else, not even the house she'd shared with her ex-husband. Yet she searched for that feeling. Even still.

Ryan stepped around her, opened the car door for the

girls then glanced at Elsie. "I think I'm going to reserve the right to call in that favor."

The smile in his words paired perfectly with his half grin. And the combination was much too appealing. Before Elsie reconsidered that expiration on her old crush, she said, "Call it in soon or I'll be gone."

Her words hovered between them. More like a warning than a casual reminder. Still, she needed to hear it out loud. She was leaving. Whatever she felt now was surely just as temporary.

Minutes later, the girls were spreading hand sanitizer all over their palms in the hospital lobby then heading to the gift shop with Ryan. While Elsie pressed a visitor's sticker onto her shirt and tapped the elevator call button. On the fourth floor, she greeted the nurse behind the desk and located her brother's room at the far end of the hall.

One deep inhale. One longer exhale. Then she stepped over her nerves and walked inside. Only to pull up short. Ryan hadn't exaggerated. If anything, Ryan hadn't been detailed enough. Her brother looked as if he'd crashed through multiple roofs headfirst.

"I look so much worse than I feel." Bryce watched her from behind two black eyes. One cheek was swollen. The other stitched from his hairline to his jaw. He started to smile, then lifted his hand toward his cheek and added, "I promise."

"That's exactly what Ryan told me you were going to say." Elsie moved to her brother's bedside and took his hand—the only part of him not bandaged—and squeezed his fingers. "The girls are in the gift store with Ryan. They'll be here soon. But seriously, are you in a lot of pain?"

"Not right now. Thanks to the pain meds." Bryce tipped his head at the IV bag hanging on the pole beside the bed and connected to the line in his arm. "And if I don't move too much. Or breathe too deeply, that helps."

Elsie winced.

"I'll be fine soon enough." Bryce tightened his grip around her hand. "I'm just glad you're here, Els. I can't thank you enough for changing your plans for us."

It was the first time Bryce had ever called Elsie and asked for her help. The first time she'd ever heard her brother say: *We need you, Els.* She couldn't have refused. Wouldn't have even considered it. Now that she was with him, she was even more certain she'd made the right decision. She was exactly where she needed to be.

"Everything okay with work and your new job?" Concern shifted through his words.

"I pushed back my start date." Elsie straightened the covers on Bryce's bed and avoided looking at the contraption holding his swollen ankle off the bed. "My new boss was very understanding."

"Well, I'm grateful to you and your new boss." Bryce dropped his head back on the pillow and tugged at his hair. "I don't have time to be down like this. There's so much to do. It's the start of the bee season."

"I'm here now," Elsie said, adding more reassurance to her words. "That should help, right? You can concentrate on getting better."

"I can't believe you're so open to helping." Bryce's gaze brightened inside his black eyes. He pressed a button and raised the head of his bed until he was sitting up. "But I really need it, so I'm taking you up on it."

Elsie fussed more with his covers and ignored the pinch of guilt in her chest. Had he needed her help before and been afraid to ask her? Afraid she would've turned him down. Or perhaps he simply hadn't wanted to bother her. It was just that Elsie and her brother always fended for themselves. They had, she supposed, ever since their parents' difficult divorce, when, in the chaos and uncertainty, it had become abundantly clear it was everyone for themselves.

Still, she was there now. This was her chance to make things right. To be there for her brother and nieces. Perhaps even make up for the years when she hadn't been.

Bryce rolled the small table closer with his good hand and tapped on his notepad. "I've got spreadsheets all prepared for you."

Detailed and task oriented were two of her mathematically-minded brother's top skills. Spreadsheets one of his superpowers. Finally, something felt familiar. Elsie grinned. "You actually created individual spreadsheets for how to care for the girls."

Bryce lifted his gaze from his notepad briefly. His thoughts preoccupied. "No, the spreadsheets are for the farm."

"The farm," Elsie repeated.

"Didn't you check your email?" Bryce asked. His fingers tapped against the computer screen again. Surprisingly quick given the rest of him was bandaged and hurt. His mind, it seemed, was still in overdrive. "I sent you an overview about an hour ago."

When she was trying to teach herself to drive a tractor. "I haven't had time to look at my email."

"Open it now." Bryce motioned toward the empty chair but kept his attention fixed on his notepad. "We can talk it through together quickly before the girls get here."

Elsie pulled her phone from her pocket and double-clicked on her email app. Sure enough Bryce's email was at the top of her unopened list. The subject: Farm to Do.

Monitors beeped in the quiet room. Elsie scanned the lengthy email. Paused and read it again. Only slower. Still, she couldn't quite wrap her mind around any of it. She looked at her brother, searched his head for a wound that the doctors might have missed. Maybe a concussion that made him forget her skillset was hospitality, not horticulture.

Only Bryce stared back at her, patient, calm and expectant. His pale blue gaze surprisingly clear and lucid, despite the pain medicine. He didn't wince from pain. Or smile and tell her he was only kidding. Her brother had never been much of a joker. And his email was no prank. She was there for more than babysitting. But she wasn't even confident she had the childcare piece in hand. Her time spent around kids was limited. Unease slipped through her.

Where to begin? Elsie glanced at her Farm to Do email and decided the only place to start was at item one. "Let me make sure I've got this straight. That I'm reading this right." Elsie searched for her most composed expression. Her most coolly collected tone. "You want me to make more space for the bees." Whatever that meant.

Her brother's eyebrows lifted. His barely-there nod encouraging.

Elsie cleared her throat and focused on item two. "Then you want me to expand the pollinator gardens." No matter she was an at-home houseplant killer. Not intentionally. She either overwatered or under watered. After her latest plant flop, she'd decided it was best for nature if she admired the flowers in the botanical gardens instead.

"It's more like a pasture than a garden," Bryce explained. "We want to add more mountain mint and white clover along with the flowers I've listed for you. The different blooming times allows extended harvesting and foraging for the honeybee colonies in the bee pasture."

"Right. Bee pasture." Elsie inhaled around the panic stirring inside her. She was there to watch her nieces. Not sow a pasture.

"The local nursery, Cider Mill Orchard, doesn't have the plants I want," Bryce continued. "I'll email you a list of other nurseries that aren't too far of a drive from the farm. We need those plants in the ground this week or we'll really be behind schedule. We can't afford that."

Elsie was already feeling behind. Far behind. She dropped her free arm to her side, forcing herself to look open and receptive. Not stubborn and resistant. She could do this. For her brother. "And item three."

"The seedlings." Bryce ran his hand through his hair and ruffled the light brown strands on the top of his head. "I updated their care spreadsheets this morning too."

"The seedlings have spreadsheets." It seemed the entire farm had its very own spreadsheet. Her brother was nothing if not thorough.

"I've got several seedling test groups in the greenhouses. Different food. Water schedule. Light." Bryce's voice got more animated. "It's all on the spreadsheet."

Color coded, she would bet. When her brother focused on something, he went all in and gave it his full attention. His clients from his financial advising days had certainly benefitted from his dedication. She asked, "What are these seedlings for exactly?"

"Bee garden starter kits," Bryce said. "We'll give out the seedling starter kits with every honey purchase. That was Ryan's idea."

Ryan. The cowboy seemed to be full of ideas.

"No, that's not entirely accurate." Bryce chuckled. "Ryan suggested harvesting the seeds and selling the kits as another way to monetize our beekeeping business."

What did a rodeo cowboy with a fondness for adventure and adrenaline rushes know about monetizing beekeeping? While Elsie felt like she suddenly knew nothing.

She ran her fingers over her forehead. "You keep saying *we* and *our*. Whose business is this exactly?"

"It's mine." Bryce lifted his eyebrows up then stiffened as if the action stretched his bruises too much. "Well, it was Aunt Marlena's, but I took it over. But you already know that. It's a family thing."

She shook her head at her brother's uncharacteristic rambling and bumped the bewilderment from her words. "Selling seeds is a profitable business then."

"You'd be surprised." Bryce tapped on his notepad again. "But we need quality seeds, which means we grow and refine our flowers and seeds to produce the best product. Then we sell those."

"Of course." Elsie studied her brother. He sounded excited about growing seedlings. Looked happy, despite his banged-up face, about it too. Ryan hadn't been wrong.

Now it was up to her to stand behind her word. She'd told Bryce she'd do anything for him when they'd talked after his accident. And she'd given Ryan her promise to support Bryce if he was happy. Time to prove she meant what she said. That her brother could count on her. Surely, he wouldn't have given her anything he didn't think she could handle.

The door to his room opened slowly. A bouquet of balloons filled the doorway before Gemma squeezed inside. Autumn close on her heels. The girls halted and slipped behind Elsie. Their eyes wide, their faces pale. Elsie wasn't quite sure what to do. Or say.

Affection spilled across Bryce's face. "Daddy doesn't look so good, does he?"

Autumn continued to study her dad and shook her head.

Gemma wrapped her arm around Elsie's waist and rested her cheek against Elsie's side. "Your face is puffy and mad, Daddy."

"Yeah. It sure is, Gem-Gem." Bryce shifted in the bed. A small smile worked across his mouth. "But those shiny balloons are making my eyes very happy."

"I picked out the balloon in the shape of the rainbow, Dad." Autumn edged closer to the bed, her hands clutched behind her back. "'Cause it has all your favorite colors in it."

"It sure does." Bryce's voice was soft, gentle.

"I picked out the sun balloon," Gemma announced and joined her sister. Then wrapped her arms around herself. "Now you'll be warm 'cause the sun is so hot in Texas."

"I'm already feeling so much better." Bryce reached his good arm out to his daughters. "And guess what?"

Autumn took her dad's hand. Gemma bounced and said, "Your face isn't mad no more."

"There's that." Bryce chuckled. "And I don't have any bandages on my right hand, which means I can still color with you."

Her brother colored. That was unexpected yet heartening. Elsie hadn't known what kind of a father Bryce would be. Their own father had been a man of few words and even less affectionate. Whereas their mother was charismatic, capricious and often unreliable. Fortunately, their father had provided a stable place growing up, even if his house felt more like a museum than a kid-friendly home.

"We got pictures, Daddy." Gemma turned and took her backpack from Ryan. Then the girls returned to Bryce's bedside to show off their artwork and debate the best wall to display the pictures on.

Elsie moved closer to Ryan and whispered, "I think I might need those tractor lessons from you after all."

Surprise crossed Ryan's face. He lowered his voice. "What did I miss?"

Before Elsie could explain, the door opened again. A

nurse in light blue scrubs backed into the room with a large cart. "Okay, Bryce. I've logged into my investment website. Now, let's create my portfolio. I sure like the sound of that." The nurse turned around, touched her dark hair that was graying at the temples and blanched. "Sorry, didn't realize you've got company. Pay me no mind."

"Everyone, this is Ms. Liza. The best nurse on the floor," Bryce said. "She puts up with me."

Liza greeted the girls first, then shook her head and chuckled. "Your daddy is one of the easiest patients I've got."

"Liza and I struck a bargain," Bryce added. "Extra cookies at lunch in exchange for investment guidance. I'm getting the better end of the bargain."

"It's more like an investment tutorial." Liza laughed and punched a code into the machine on her cart. "But I can come back after lunch."

"Lunch." Gemma pressed a hand on her stomach. "Do we get lunch too? My tummy is hungry."

"Sorry, only Dad gets lunch in here." Liza leaned down between the girls and whispered, "Don't tell him, but the food is better down the street at All-Day Corner Diner. You can get fancy milkshakes there with whipped cream and double cherries."

"Dad always steals my cherry," Autumn replied. "Then pretends he didn't eat it."

"Not this time." Liza's laugh filled the room and she glanced at Elsie. "But you should hurry if you want to beat the lunch rush."

"Can we go please?" Both girls asked in unison.

Elsie glanced at her brother. He nodded then covered his yawn. "I'll check in with you guys later."

Ryan gathered the girls and steered them around the medical cart into the hallway. Elsie followed.

Bryce called out, "Els, I forgot about the wind barrier."

Elsie paused in the doorway and set her palm flat on the door, propping it open. Then she glanced back at her brother.

"It's no big deal. I just want to ensure we've got the best wind barrier around the hive colonies," Bryce rushed on. "I'll email you the details."

Elsie swallowed her urge to holler: *No more emails*. He'd hit her email quota for the day. Then she glanced back at her brother. Watched him wince for the first time. Saw the pain he was working so hard to hide. If building spreadsheets kept his mind busy, she'd let him send another hundred. She smiled and softened her words. "That would be great. I'll email you back if I have questions."

In the meantime, Elsie needed a crash course on all things farming. Fortunately, she knew a cowboy to ask. Now all she had to do was keep her interest in check. Otherwise, she might find herself needing a crash course on how not to fall for a cowboy.

CHAPTER FOUR

RYAN WAS NO sooner in the hallway outside Bryce's hospital room when Gemma slipped her hand into his. Autumn took hold of his other hand and eased further into his side away from a complicated looking medical cart and two interns, their expressions intent and serious, standing outside another hospital room. Ryan tightened his grip as if he was a prince ready to protect his princesses from whatever scared them.

Up ahead at the nurse's station he saw a familiar figure and relaxed. He squeezed the girls' fingers lightly and said, "Want to meet the doctor who is going to fix your dad's ankle so he can go home soon?"

Both girls nodded.

Stepping up to his younger brother, Ryan cleared his throat and said very seriously, "Dr. Sloan, I've got two very important people here to see you."

Grant looked up from his paperwork on the counter, lifted his chin in acknowledgment to Ryan then turned his full attention to the girls for proper introductions. Complete with formal handshakes. Then Grant said, "Now, I believe you were just visiting my patient, Mr. Bryce Parks."

Gemma giggled, kept her hand inside Ryan's and swayed her hips side to side. "That's Daddy, Doc Grant."

"Right." Grant kept his expression neutral and ran his palm over his silk tie. "Anything you think I should know about your dad? I want to make sure our patient gets the best care ever."

Autumn lifted her hand and leaned in to whisper loudly, "He's sneaking cookies with Ms. Liza. But when we sneak extra cookies, we get scolded."

"And we gotta put the cookies back." Gemma joined in, her words solemn and grim. "Even if we accidentally took a bite of the cookie we weren't supposed to have."

Ryan rolled his lips together to squash his smile.

Grant ran his hand over his mouth. "What should I do, do you think?"

Autumn lifted her chin. Certainty filled her words. "Make Daddy give 'em back."

"But he's got to help Ms. Liza with her portfolio." Gemma stumbled slightly over the portfolio part then rushed on. "Because Ms. Liza is really nice."

"That she is. I'll see what I can do about the cookies," Grant said and shook their hands to seal the deal. "And I'll fix your dad's ankle so he can chase you two around the farm again soon."

"Dad doesn't run." Gemma giggled again, hips swaying. "But he does play hide-and-seek if we get our chores done."

"Well, you might need to play board games until your dad is fully healed." Elsie stepped beside Ryan and smiled warmly at his younger brother. "Hello, Dr. Sloan."

"It's Grant." Ryan's brother stood and greeted Elsie with a quick hug. "We're neighbors and practically family. We used to swap science fiction books, remember?"

Elsie laughed. "Of course, I remember."

Ryan hadn't known. He started to frown then caught himself. He wasn't seriously jealous of a memory, was he? *Impossible.* Ryan had never been jealous in his life, especially not of his own brother.

"You were the only person I knew who read faster than

me," Elsie added, affection in her words. "I can't tell you how many sleepless nights I had trying to keep up with you."

Grant had kept her awake. That frown worked across Ryan's face.

"I've got a well-stocked library at our new house if you need any reading material," Grant offered. "Come on over any time."

"I just might take you up on that." Elsie smiled. "I could use a good distraction."

Then why not call me? Ryan had ideas. All sorts, like a late-night stroll through Marlena's gardens. Or stargazing. Back porch swinging. He could keep going. Ryan's frown deepened. If only he'd stopped there. But his words kept falling out. "Elsie is going to be busy with the farm and the girls. Most likely won't be much time left for reading."

Elsie frowned at him.

Grant tipped his head and eyed Ryan, his gaze slightly narrowed as if Ryan was a grumpy patient withholding information.

Ryan pushed back his shoulders. *Stop talking. Don't make it worse.* "I'm just stating the obvious. There's a lot of work to be done. I saw Bryce's spreadsheets."

At the mention of Bryce, worry skimmed across Elsie's face and settled into the crease between her eyebrows. Ryan felt it like a wasp's sting—sharp and consuming. He wanted to comfort her, but his brother stepped in first.

"Bryce is going to be fine. He's going to heal and recover from this." Grant held Elsie's gaze an extra beat as if he understood she needed reassurance.

Ryan wanted to reassure Elsie too. But in a different sort of way. The way that had his arm curved around her waist. And her tucked right into his side. But not for long. She wasn't meant for a cowboy like him. And if he held her, he might not want to let go. Even when he had to. Ryan eased away from Elsie, reestablishing that distance.

Grant leaned toward the girls again. "Now, Gemma and Autumn, does your dad let you have sugar before lunch?"

"We're having milkshakes with extra cherries for lunch." Excitement widened Gemma's eyes. "My tummy can't wait."

"Then how about a lollipop you can keep for later." Grant straightened, reached behind the nurse's station and picked up a jar of colorful lollipops. He held the jar out to the girls then offered it to Elsie. Grant added, "The nurses around here try to hide these from me, but I always find them." Grant tucked one in the pocket of his white lab coat.

The brothers might not share the same clothing style, but they did share similar sweet tooths. Ryan reached for a lollipop, but his brother swung the jar out of his reach.

Grant shook his head and waggled his finger at Ryan. "None for you, big brother, until we discuss my wife."

"It's not my fault." Ryan lifted his hands. "I tried to tell Maggie and Vivian you are scared of cuckoo clocks."

Grant's face darkened.

Maggie and Grant had gotten married in a winter wedding that past February. Vivian was his youngest brother Josh's girlfriend. Ryan knew both women from the rodeo circuit and now he was grateful to have them as part of the family. Still, they were a force when they set their minds to something. And they'd set their minds to the two vintage cuckoo clocks they'd discovered in a family storage barn. Ryan added, "Maggie and Vivian wouldn't believe me. They badgered me until I got the clocks working properly."

"I should have known you turned those clocks on." Grant eyed him and wrapped his arm around the lollipop jar the same way he used to guard the cookie jar from Ryan growing up.

Ryan glanced at Elsie. "Grant here can't balance the weights precisely on the cuckoo clocks. It takes a deft hand, which is ironic given he's a renowned surgeon."

"My hands are deft enough," Grant countered. "I don't want the weights balanced. Because I do not want the clocks chirping."

"They cuckoo," Ryan corrected, more than happy to tease his brother. It was familiar and natural. Unlike his feelings toward Elsie. The ones he was putting at a safe distance.

"Call that sound those clocks make whatever you want." Grant held his hand out for the girls' candy wrappers. The girls seeming to have missed the part about lollipops later. Grant added, "There's still something creepy about those clocks."

"The clocks always scared Grant when we were kids." Ryan chuckled. The two clocks had hung in the living room of their great-grandmother's house. Their own Gran Claire had adored them. Ryan said, "Shouldn't you have gotten past this irrational fear by now?"

"I'm afraid of zombies." Autumn sucked on her lollipop then added, "Dad says I'll outgrow it. Maybe you just need to grow more, Doc Grant."

"That is a very good thought." Grant grinned at Autumn then shot a look at Ryan. "When I grow taller than Ryan, I can hang the clocks in his house where he can't reach them. And they can cuckoo all hours of the day and night. Then we'll see who's laughing."

His own home. Ryan hadn't given that much thought over the years. But he had to now. He couldn't very well live with his older brother Carter, his wife, Tess, and their kids for the rest of his life. He just assumed when the time came, he would know exactly what he wanted to do. But now he faced decisions beyond where to live and he wanted to run in the other direction. Hardly mature, he admitted. Yet he wanted to believe entirely effective. And so, for the moment, he'd keep looking the other way.

"Maggie loves those cuckoo clocks," Ryan argued and pointed at his brother. "You love your wife. You need to learn to love the clocks too so that Maggie is happy."

"Just like that, you brought us full circle, big brother." Grant rubbed his chin then pointed back at Ryan. "Maggie isn't happy right now and it's entirely your fault."

Ryan crossed his arms over his chest.

"Maggie claims you're refusing to practice with her," Grant went on. "And she refuses to lose because you're an arrogant cowboy who thinks because he's a champion bronc rider, he can win at any rodeo event there is. Her words, not mine."

Elsie shifted and stared at him. Her surprise in her partially opened mouth. Her amusement in her arched eyebrow.

"I'm not refusing." It was more like avoiding his sister-in-law. He had agreed to partner with Maggie for the team roping event in the charity rodeo long before his movie stunt mishap and Sundancer's injury. When he'd still been in the saddle and riding without fear. He shifted and told himself not to fidget. His brother would surely notice. He said, "I've been really busy."

"I don't care. All you have to do is practice roping with Maggie for an hour. Show her you've got skills. Prove to Maggie that you guys can win at the rodeo," Grant ordered then he slowed his words as if to ensure Ryan was listening. "Just make my wife happy."

Autumn took Ryan's hand and tugged until she had his attention then she asked, "What's roping?"

"It's where two cowboys or cowgirls ride their horses

and try to catch a steer with their ropes," Ryan explained. "A steer is a boy cow with horns."

"Ryan is on a roping team with my wife, Maggie," Grant added. "Maggie is a champion team roper."

"Cowboy Prince is a champion too." Gemma grinned and turned to Elsie. "Can we watch Cowboy Prince and Ms. Maggie go roping?"

Grant's eyes widened. Oh, his younger brother hadn't missed Ryan's new nickname. And Grant wasn't about to forget it anytime soon either.

"I didn't know you roped too." Elsie searched Ryan's face. "I'd love to see that."

So would Ryan. The key to roping was riding a fast horse. But Ryan still hadn't been on a horse, fast or otherwise. But that was his secret. One he fully intended to keep to himself. "Tickets are on sale for Belleridge Rodeo Rides for A Cause. It's a charity rodeo. All the proceeds will go to the charities the competitors support."

"Who are you competing for?" Elsie asked.

"The Martha Claire Horse Haven," Ryan replied.

"It's named in honor of your grandmother." Approval was there in Elsie's sincere words.

He'd known she'd easily make the connection. Ryan nodded. "We'll compete in our best event and then there's a mixed team roping event. Only one person on the team can have competed on the professional circuit in roping before. Maggie is one of the best women ropers riding today."

"That's amazing," Elsie said. "I'd like to see Maggie compete too."

"You don't have to wait until the rodeo to see Cowboy Prince or Maggie rope," Grant offered, a little bit too gallantly. "You can come watch him and Maggie practice at our private arena on the Sloan farm."

"Can we pet the horses too?" Gemma clasped her hands together.

Grant nodded. "Maggie might even let you ride with her, if your aunt agrees."

Autumn and Gemma cheered then lifted their hope-filled gazes to Ryan. Totally not fair. How was he supposed to disappoint them? But take his first ride in over a month with an audience? Especially one that included Elsie. What would she think of him then?

"Well, Cowboy Prince, stop shirking your duties and give the people what they want." There was a challenge in Grant's growing grin. "Maggie and Vivian are painting the nursery for Tess today and then they're heading over to the arena to practice before dinner."

Vivian was a talented barrel racer. On her way to being one of the best too. Perhaps he could arrange for Elsie and the girls to watch Maggie and Vivian practice. Make it a cowgirls' day of sorts. He rubbed his chin, stalling and searching for an excuse. "Today won't work. I'm giving Elsie tractor lessons this afternoon."

"But it sounds like Maggie needs you." Elsie set her hand on Ryan's arm. "She's counting on you. You can't let her down."

He was already letting everyone down. Himself included. Ryan didn't need witnesses for his current downfall. But he hadn't hit the bottom yet. He could still turn things around. He would. On his own.

Grant handed Elsie a fistful of lollipops. "I always liked you, Elsie."

"You're alone at the farm, Elsie. You need help too," Ryan said then looked at his younger brother. "If Grandpa Sam and Uncle Roy get wind of Elsie's tractor woes, they'll want to teach her themselves."

"Good point." Grant frowned and returned the candy jar behind the nurse's station. "We definitely can't have that."

"Did something happen?" Elsie asked.

"Carter took their tractor privileges away," Ryan explained, not feeling the slightest bit guilty he'd turned the conversation away from him and roping practice. "Indefinitely."

"Because those two and tractors get into too much trouble," Grant volunteered and unwittingly helped Ryan. To Ryan's relief.

"Ryan can fill you in on the specifics of Grandpa Sam and Uncle Roy's tractor adventures." Grant tore off a piece of paper, wrote on it and handed it to Elsie. "In the meantime, that's my number and Maggie's. Call us anytime. For anything. We're happy to help too."

But Ryan wanted to be Elsie's first call. Her anytime. For anything call. Her go-to person.

"You say that now until I call you late at night after you worked all day." Elsie chuckled.

Even then, Ryan wouldn't mind. He ground his teeth together. He had bigger things to worry about than who Elsie chose to phone for assistance. He had a saddle to get into. Horses to ride. An equine sanctuary to help fund. A new stable to establish. And five horses counting on him for a home.

"I'll send Maggie if it's after hours and go back to sleep," Grant teased.

"Thanks." Elsie tucked the paper into her purse. "I really appreciate it."

"It's what we do around here," Grant said, serious and sincere. "We look out for each other." With a promise to take good care of Bryce, Grant picked up a clipboard and headed down the hallway to see his patient.

Ryan took each of the girls' hands in his and walked to the elevators.

As for looking after Elsie and the girls, he would do that through lunch. Then he'd return them to their farm, give Elsie a quick tutorial on tractor driving and finally get back to his day.

Regarding the whole keeping his distance from Elsie thing, surely, that wouldn't be hard. Nothing he couldn't manage. After all, Elsie was headed to her life in the city. Soon enough.

And for as far back as Ryan could remember, his direction had been the rodeo, not ever the city. And not even a pretty woman from the city like Elsie Parks would get him to turn around now.

CHAPTER FIVE

THE WALK TO All-Day Corner Diner was short. They placed their orders quickly after being seated at a table. And the service proved even faster. Ryan wiped a napkin across his mouth and was about to push his plate away when Autumn dropped the rest of her club sandwich on it.

"I'm full and you look hungry." Autumn grinned at him. "You gotta finish it now that it's on your plate."

"Is that a rule?" Ryan glanced at Gemma.

She nodded in solidarity with her older sister and dipped a french fry in the last of her milkshake.

Ryan picked up the sandwich. "Well, I don't want to be a rule breaker."

"Since when?" Elsie's gaze connected with his. Amusement curved around her words. "I've never known you to follow the rules."

"There's a lot you don't know about me," Ryan said. Her eyes widened. He saw the curiosity. The interest she tried to hide before she studied her phone again. Satisfied he wasn't the only one feeling something and working to hide it, he polished off the sandwich in two bites.

"Did you know the new utility tractor has a swivel captain's chair and panoramic roof? It looks like a sunroof in a car. I never used my sunroof when I had a car." Elsie swiped her finger across her phone screen. "It says the operator can view the full cycle of the loader, which has dynamic weighing technology." Her eyebrows pulled together at that last part. A cue that she was intent on learning more. Sure enough, she rapidly opened a new window on her internet app.

"It means you can get an accurate weight of whatever you've got in the bucket." Ryan set his hand over Elsie's phone screen, stopping her from reciting more tractor highlights. "What are you doing?"

"I was searching for a user's manual on the tractor dealer website." Elsie tried to peel his fingers off her phone. "But now I'm reading a utility tractor sales brochure."

"Elsie, you can't learn to drive a tractor from reading." Ryan tightened his grip. "That's not how you learned to drive a car."

"Sure, it is." She stopped trying to free her phone and sat back. "I read the driver's manual and also the car owner's manual for Dad's sedan before I ever even sat in the driver's seat of his car."

"What driver's manual?" he asked, not even bothering to mask his baffled expression.

"The *Driver's Handbook from the Department of Motor Vehicles*," she recited, her words dry and monotone. She swiped a sweet potato fry off his plate and aimed it at him. "Every state has one. If you had read it, you might not have gotten those tickets that one summer when Bryce had to drive you around."

"I got two speeding tickets that summer." Ryan held up two fingers and eyed her. "Because I was a teenager who treated the speed limit signs on the backroads as suggestions. And for the record, I don't do that anymore."

"Do what?" Elsie bit into the french fry and watched him. A faint gleam in her gaze. "Drive on the backroads or speed?"

"Speed," he replied and held her gaze. "I still like a

drive on the backroads. Only slow and preferably not alone these days."

She swallowed but never looked away. "Where would you go?"

"This time of year, there's nothing like dusk at Silent Rise Canyon. A warm blanket and picnic basket is all we would need. If we're lucky, we'll catch a storm out on the plains at sunset. Incredible view," Ryan said and lifted one shoulder. "Nothing fancy, but it's a drive worth taking and definitely an evening well spent."

Elsie picked up her water, sipped then watched him over the rim of her glass. "Do you go there often?"

"Haven't been in a very long time," he admitted. And he'd always gone alone. Because he'd never been interested in sharing the moment with anyone. Until now. "What's an evening well spent look like to you?"

"My evenings are mostly spent working on the events I'm managing." She fiddled with her straw. "All work, no play tends to be true in my case, but I'm not complaining. I've always found my job really rewarding."

"While you're here, you might want to take an evening off of work just to test my theory," he suggested.

"What theory is that?" she asked.

"That slowing down can be a reward all on its own." He dropped his napkin on his plate.

"I wouldn't think a champion bronc rider has the luxury to take things slow," she countered.

"I don't." He grinned. "But like I said, the appeal is in not being alone."

Her mouth opened in the smallest O. Curiosity worked across her face. But the waitress arrived. They declined refills on their drinks and Ryan accepted the check.

"We should get to it." Ryan smiled. Elsie looked slightly distracted as if maybe she was considering the appeal of backroads and sunsets. *Wishful thinking*. And not something he gave in to. Ryan pulled out his wallet, slipped money into the billfold and pushed his chair back. Then said, "After all, the only way to learn to drive a tractor is to drive one."

Elsie blinked and picked up her purse. "You didn't need to pay for us too."

"I ate almost all the food on this table." Ryan chuckled and watched Gemma hop from her chair. "Elsie, I finished your milkshake, Autumn's club sandwich and Gemma's cheeseburger."

Gemma rushed around the table and grabbed Ryan's hand. "We were full, and you were hungry, and it was on your plate, Cowboy Prince."

Ryan squeezed Gemma's fingers. "I appreciate you looking out for me, Princess Gem."

"Well, thank you for lunch," Elsie said. "Next time is on me."

Next time. That made it sound like this was more than a one-time thing. That she wanted it to be more too. Not likely. Still, one could hope, even if it was a bad idea. And he knew it.

Ryan held the door open for the girls. When Elsie stepped through the archway, he couldn't resist. He leaned in and whispered, "I'm already looking forward to next time."

Her cheeks heated. Like she stood under a heat lamp. How he liked that. He followed Elsie, who hurried to join Autumn ahead of him. The pair led the way back to the parking lot. Elsie kept the pace brisk, and he recalculated that distance. Trying to decide just how much space he needed between him and Elsie to keep his interest in her to himself. Where it belonged.

Because following that road was only going to end in

things he spent his whole life avoiding, like regret and heartache. And something about Elsie told him that she could very well be his heartbreaker. But only if he let her in. Good thing he knew better than to open that door.

Back inside the car, Ryan confirmed all seat belts were buckled then Autumn asked, "Is it still a windows down, volume up kind of day?"

Elsie shifted in her seat and considered Ryan. A challenge was there in her words. "Only if Cowboy Prince sings with us."

"Deal." He liked the surprise on her face a bit too much. If only she knew that singing would keep his interest in her tethered. Keep him from getting to know Elsie any better. He started the car and backed out of the parking space. "If we can slip in a few country songs too."

"Done." Elsie plugged her phone into the car audio system and opened her music app. "Everyone gets to pick a song they want to hear."

"Let the car karaoke begin." Ryan drove out of the parking lot and onto the main road.

Car karaoke continued all the way back to Three Springs. Ryan kept his word and sang every word in every song, even embellished several songs with a few extra lyrics to the girls' delight. They were belting out the verse of an upbeat country song about dancing in the moonlight when Ryan drove under the Doyle Farm arched wrought iron gate.

At the top of the drive, Elsie sucked in her breath. Then she simultaneously gasped and coughed. Pointed out the window then stammered, "There's a goat standing on the top of my U-Haul."

If Ryan hadn't believed Elsie earlier about New York, he had no choice now. Her U-Haul moving truck was all the proof he needed. Elsie was destined to keep on moving. Far from Three Springs. Now all Ryan had to do was be careful and avoid the kind of goodbye that could hurt.

"That's Smarty Marty," Autumn shouted. "He got out again."

Smarty Marty looked as if he'd tripped inside a white paint can. He was all black except for his tail, one back leg and his ears. And he watched them with an alertness and arrogance only a goat could perfect.

"Marty is so smart." Autumn laughed and jumped out of the Jeep. Then added, "He gets out of their pen then lets the others out to play too."

"One day, Smarty Marty walked the others all the way to Cowboy Prince's yard." Gemma's head popped between the front seats. Her gaze bright. "Cowboy Prince had to drive them all back home. Remember that, Cowboy Prince?"

Gemma was out of the car before Ryan could reply. He followed the girls into the yard.

Elsie scrambled out of the car and joined them. "How many others are there?"

"Ten. But two are lazy and don't ever leave the pen." Gemma clapped and pointed at the caramel-colored goat sitting on the front porch. "There's Butter-Belle. She's so sweet."

"We gotta gather goats, Auntie." Autumn set her hands on her hips and stared up at the top of the truck. Excitement wound around her words. "And put 'em back in their pen."

"Gather. Goats." Elsie glanced at Ryan and rubbed her throat as if that was where her words were stuck. "I've never… How exactly do we…"

"It's easy, Auntie," Gemma declared and sprinted toward the porch. "Watch me."

Except it wasn't easy. It was somewhat exasperating. Entertaining, but mostly exasperating. The girls squealed.

The goats bleated. And everyone ran. It was more a game of chase than catch. And difficult to tell if the goats or the girls were having more fun. Finally, the girls wore themselves out, retreated to the porch swing and helpfully called out goat sightings.

A quick search on her phone and Elsie raided the girls' backpacks for snacks. Then she lured one goat at a time with a trail of raisins that led toward Ryan. Leaving Ryan to take care of the capturing and releasing back into the pen. After he praised each goat and treated them to bites of an apple Autumn had given him.

Finally, Elsie counted ten goats in the goat pasture and declared goat gathering concluded for the day. She walked back to the house beside Ryan and bumped her shoulder against his arm and said, "I don't know if I'm more sweaty or dirty. I need a long, hot shower. Then I'm putting my feet up and not moving for the rest of the night."

There was something appealing about the idea. Sitting with her. Their feet up. Leaning into each other. Talking the night away. They rounded the house and Ryan caught sight of her moving truck, sitting there like a giant billboard. *Right*. Best to keep on moving himself.

Elsie walked up the stairs to the porch.

Ryan stepped back. "I'm going to get Sundancer from the pasture and walk on home."

"Walk?" Elsie turned toward him. Confusion curved across her face. "Why aren't you riding?"

Loaded question that was. And not one of those truths he was about to share. He said, "Sundancer is injured. Walking is part of his rehab. As it turns out, I also aggravated an old leg injury so walking suits me too."

"But that's several miles away." Elsie set her hands on her hips and watched him.

"Sunset isn't for a while yet." Ryan continued his retreat

toward the pasture. "Don't forget I know all the shortcuts between our property and yours."

"But aren't you tired?" she asked.

"Not especially." Ryan tapped the brim of his cowboy hat. "Sweet dreams, Elsie Marie."

Then he turned on his boot heels and kept walking until he reached the pasture. One loud whistle brought Sundancer to him. He picked up the halter he'd hung on the fence post earlier, adjusted it on Sundancer's head and led the horse down the drive.

And hoped he would be tired when he got home. Too tired to let his heart do any of that wishful thinking about things like backroads, slow drives and Elsie. All the things he shouldn't want.

The cowboy and the girl from the city. Impossible combination that.

Still, he patted the picture in his pocket. The one Gemma had drawn of him and Elsie. He'd hang it on his wall in his bedroom. And if he dreamed tonight of impossible things, well, what was one more secret to keep.

CHAPTER SIX

SCHOOL LUNCHES PACKED. *CHECK.*

Chickens fed. *Check.*

Goats counted and thankfully still contained. *Double checked.*

Elsie crossed off the morning task list Bryce had left her and walked back to the house. Now it was time for the school drop-off then a grocery store run. They'd decided on breakfast for dinner last night after Elsie had discovered the pantry and refrigerator were more sparse than stocked.

Only two car stall outs later—one in the school car line and the other at the only stoplight in downtown Three Springs—Elsie congratulated herself on her success and parked in front of her aunt's house. Groceries unloaded and put away, Elsie stood at the kitchen island and considered the spreadsheets spread across the granite countertop. The doorbell interrupted her, keeping her from having to decide where to get started on her brother's farm to-dos.

She opened the door to find a pair of older cowboys. Both holding their cowboy hats against their chests and wearing wide smiles.

The one with the pure-as-snow beard touched his bolo tie clasp and cleared his throat. "Elsie Marie, you most likely don't remember me."

"Sam Sloan." Elsie returned his smile. "Or should I call you Cowboy Santa?"

Sam's eyes twinkled much like she imagined Kris Kringle's would. He spread his arms wide. "It's sure nice to see you back home."

She skipped over correcting him. He'd always told Elsie that Three Springs was her home. She stepped onto the porch and into Sam's embrace. He was older, but his hug held the same warmth and kindness she remembered. "I wish it hadn't been an accident that brought me back."

"Your brother is strong. He'll recover. And you're here now. That's what matters. No use dwelling on the reasons." Sam settled his cowboy hat over his white hair and introduced her to his brother, Roy Sloan.

"Pleasure, Elsie." Roy tapped his hat against his chest then placed it on his head, covering his thick, curly, salt-and-pepper hair.

"What brings you by?" Elsie asked then frowned. Her shoulders slumped. "The goats got out, didn't they? You had to bring them back."

"Goats." Roy scratched his weathered cheek. "We don't know anything about goats."

Elsie sighed her relief.

"We're here for the tractor." Sam's eyebrows lifted.

"That one over there." Roy pointed at the green tractor Ryan had parked yesterday in front of the greenhouses. "Trey Ramsey joined us for breakfast at the Lemon Moon Diner this morning. He told us he got your tractor all fixed up and returned to you right quick."

Elsie's relief faded and a hint of unease spread across the back of her neck.

"Have you taken it for a test drive yet?" Sam asked, his words mild and pleasant.

"You need to know if it is working proper," Roy added.

"Ryan drove it yesterday," Elsie explained. "I'm sure it's fine."

"Then it's all ready to go for your lessons today." That

gleam flashed in Sam's gaze again. He held his arm out as if he was asking her to take a spin across the dance floor. "Shall we?"

But Ryan was supposed to teach her to drive the tractor. Yet they'd been sidetracked goat gathering and all of a sudden Ryan had been wishing her sweet dreams and leaving. And Elsie had let her cowboy go before she'd invited Ryan to stay for dinner. To stay longer. With her. As if she wanted to spend more time with him. As for those tractor lessons, those hadn't been rescheduled.

"Ryan mentioned you needed tractor lessons." Roy hooked his thumbs around his large bronze belt buckle and lifted his chin. "So, we've come to offer our assistance."

"But I thought..." Elsie paused.

Ryan had never told her the tractor stories about the two older cowboys. No, Ryan had distracted her with talk about country backroads and sunsets yesterday at lunch. Then he'd sidetracked her with the goats. When he'd befriended each goat, he'd been so gentle and sweet. And Elsie had just stared, caught completely off guard. Her cowboy was a daredevil. A risk-taker. Not a softy.

Elsie pressed her fingers against the bridge of her nose and blocked thoughts of Ryan. His grandfather and uncle were there now. Looking so very earnest and sincere. She didn't want to hurt their feelings. She was definitely going to give Ryan a piece of her mind when she saw him again. She disliked disappointing anyone, especially these two kind cowboys. She continued, "Grant and Ryan mentioned yesterday that..."

"That we can't drive the tractor," Roy finished for her, his tone helpful, not resentful.

Elsie nodded.

"That's just a bit of a misunderstanding." Sam brushed his hand through the air as if he shooed a fly away. "We can't drive a tractor at the distillery. My grandson Carter is worried about his precious whiskey barrels."

"But out here with all this wide-open land…" Roy spread his fingers wide and chuckled. "There's nothing to stop us out here."

"Or for us to run into," Sam added then rubbed his hands together. "How about we get those lessons started?"

"I should probably call Ryan." Elsie reached for her phone in her back pocket.

"He won't answer." Sam glanced at the watch on his wrist. "He's at the sanctuary."

"Tori, the manager at the sanctuary, picked up another rescue early this morning and the poor mare is real spooked in the trailer. Been kicking something fierce the whole ride back," Roy explained. "Ryan is there to calm her and get her settled in her new home."

"Ryan's got a touch with the wild, tricky ones. Understands them better than anyone around these parts." Pride framed Sam's words. "But it sounds like he'll have his hands full with that poor Arabian this morning."

Elsie frowned, tried to block her worry for Ryan. "Will he be safe with that horse?"

"He's got the training and the know-how," Sam said, his expression encouraging. "He just needs to keep his focus. Can't risk any distractions. That's when injuries happen."

Elsie slid her phone back into her pocket. Suddenly calling Ryan didn't seem like a good idea. "What kind of lessons are you thinking?" Something like turning the tractor on and off would be a helpful start.

"Well, what's needing to be done around here?" Sam asked and watched her, a knowing look in his gaze. "I'm certain your brother left you a list. He always was prepared and organized, even as a child. Always hoped he'd rub off on my grandsons."

Elsie pulled a folded piece of paper out of her other pocket. The one Bryce had titled Quick Reference Farm Task List.

Sam took the paper, scanned it and handed it to Roy. Then he announced cheerfully, "We can start with the bee pasture. Clearing it."

"You want to expand the bee pasture. Today." Elsie worked the alarm and surprise from her expression. "Right now."

"Just clearing it." Roy grinned. "Then we'll till it. Then we'll seed it. Can't seed with the weeds. Not a good combination."

Elsie nodded as if she completely understood.

"Gotta start someplace." Sam tucked her list in the top pocket of his chambray shirt. "Work's not gonna get done standing around reading lists."

That was true. Elsie needed to get to work. She needed to start. She'd given her word to her brother. Promised she'd do whatever it took to help him. And no one else was on her porch offering their services. How much trouble could they get into in a wide-open pasture anyway?

"We'll show you everything you need to know. There's nothing to it." Sam offered her his arm again. "We can even take pictures of the cleared field and send them to your brother. Imagine his surprise."

And then her brother could stop worrying so much. He'd already left her several voice mail reminders and sent more emails that morning when he should've been concentrating on his upcoming surgery. Now Elsie could finally prove she had things under control around the farm. That she didn't require any more cowboy rescues. That she could be counted on. Elsie curved her arm around Sam's and said, "Let's go clear a bee pasture."

"Now, that's the spirit." Roy took Elsie's other arm.

The two older cowboys hooted and escorted her to the tractor. They patiently explained the proper way to climb into the tractor. Then pointed out the different panels, switches and buttons. How to start the tractor. How to turn it off. And back on. Then it was out to those wide-open fields. Sam perched right beside her in the tractor cab.

Who got to ride with Elsie had been the only disagreement between the two older cowboys. Finally, they agreed to split up the lessons. Sam took the ride to the pasture with Elsie and Roy would take the ride back to the house. In the meantime, Roy was following behind them in her aunt's UTV.

"I'm doing it," Elsie marveled and bounced lightly in the captain's chair. The tractor rumbled and rolled forward. "I'm actually driving a tractor."

"Nothing to it." Sam beamed beside her. "You're a natural."

"I read up on this particular model last night." Elsie peered out the window and promptly lost that thrill of achievement. She frowned. "But the manual did not go over what to do about that."

Sam leaned forward. "That's just a little mud from the storms we've been getting recently."

It was more than a little. The muddy land stretched longer than a football field, reaching the fence on one side and the wooded area on the other. And it was wider than the tractor was long. Elsie slowed to a stop. "Maybe we should go around this."

"Can't drive the tractor through the trees." Sam scratched his cheek and tipped his head toward the door. "Then there's the fence in our way over there."

"Turn around then," Elsie suggested and peeled her fingers from the steering wheel.

"Best to cut it straight down the middle," Sam said, confidence in his words. He lifted his arm and pointed out the windshield. "The pastures are just on the other side. Not too far now. All you got to do now is go full steam ahead."

Full steam ahead. Elsie had never done anything full steam ahead. She'd always stopped, assessed and reassessed. Then maybe she went ahead. *Maybe.* But never right into the mud. Into the mess. Elsie frowned and chewed on her bottom lip. "Sam, maybe you should drive for this part."

"If you're sure." Sam patted her arm.

Elsie nodded and edged toward the door. "I think I'll just wait with Roy."

"I'll meet you two on the other side." Sam slid into the chair, his words eager and excited. "You and Roy can drive through the woods and skip the mud entirely."

Elsie made her way down the side of the tractor. This time more gracefully than she had with Ryan the day before. Roy met her near the tractor. She said, "I'm letting Sam take it from here and tackle the mud."

"Might as well watch over here and make sure he gets through it." Sam motioned Elsie off to the side.

"You don't think he'll make it?" Alarmed, Elsie followed Roy. "But Sam told me it's not…"

The tractor engine rumbled, cutting off Elsie's words. And it rolled full steam ahead into the mud field. Just as Sam had predicted. Only the tractor lost steam somewhere in the middle of the muck when the tractor wheels started spinning, spraying clumps of mud in every direction. And all forward progress ceased. Worse, the rotary cutter they'd attached to the tractor hitch sank and completely disappeared beneath the thick watery muck.

Elsie slapped her hands over her mouth and caught her gasp.

Roy yanked his cowboy hat off his head, stomped toward the UTV and tossed his hat on the driver's seat. "Looks like I gotta get into the driver's seat now and fix things, as usual."

Alarmed at the barely concealed delight in Roy's words, Elsie rushed after the older cowboy. "Are you sure that's a good idea?" How in the world was he going to get to the tractor? It wasn't a swimming pool. It was a mud pit. He couldn't possibly be happy about this.

"Someone's got to get in there or we'll be out here all day. No one wants that." Roy went to the edge of the mud pit. Elsie trailed after him. Roy added, "And it's just a little mud."

Why did they keep saying that? Elsie had a little mud on her jeans. But there was nothing little about the muck facing her.

Roy waved his arms over his head until he captured Sam's attention. Then he yelled, "Come on out, so I can get in there and drive it right."

"Think you can do better." Sam climbed out onto the tractor steps. "I'd like to see you try." With that Sam jumped down into the mud. And then sank. First his boots disappeared. Then his knees. Finally, the mud stopped rising just below his waist.

Panic squeezed around Elsie. She flailed her arms in front of her as if she intended to grab Sam's hand. But she was much too far away.

"Now look what you did," Roy grumbled.

"Don't just stand there," Sam shouted back. "Get me a rope and pull me out. I'm getting mud in places I don't want."

Roy turned and stomped back to the UTV. Elsie hot on his heels. Roy opened the toolbox in the UTV bed. "Who stocked this? There's nothing useful in here."

Elsie stepped around to the other side of the small bed

and pulled a frayed rope from under the toolbox. "What about this?"

"That'll have to do." Roy managed to get back to the edge of the mud. He swirled the rope over his head as if he was catching a steer then released it. Sam lifted his arm. But the end of the rope landed several feet short of its mark.

Elsie cringed.

"You have to get closer," Sam called out. "I can't move, let alone hardly bend."

"Gimme a minute." Roy tapped the toe of his boot into the mud in front of him as if testing the temperature of bath water.

Elsie stood close enough to Roy to easily grab him around the waist. Ready to pull the older cowboy back if he waded in too far.

"Hurry up, will you," Sam said, his words surly. "It's not deep over there. I drove right through it."

"Fine." Roy tromped farther into the mud.

Elsie reached for him, but her fingers caught a fistful of air. "Roy. Stop."

But the older cowboy had already stepped in too far. And he too sank. All the way past his knees and almost to his waist. Just like that. The rope dangled from the hand Roy lifted over his head. From Elsie's angle, Roy looked to be even deeper in the muck than his brother. Elsie paled.

Sam's eyebrows bunched together. "Didn't see that coming."

Roy twisted to look at her. "Best step back, Elsie. We don't need you sinking too."

Too late. Elsie glanced down at her feet. Her running shoes were no longer visible. The muck was up around her ankles. And her shoes were practically rooted in thick sludge and sinking more. Elsie shoved her hand under the surface, loosened the laces on both shoes and worked one foot free. Then she stepped back and added an awkward, desperate lunge toward solid ground. Her other foot slipped free of her stuck shoe, and she landed with a decided thud on her backside.

"Nice dismount," Sam offered. "You okay, dear?"

Elsie nodded and stopped short of rubbing her sore backside. She'd lost both shoes and a sock, but at least she was on solid ground. Wiping her filthy hands on her jeans, she asked, "What should we do now?"

"Don't suppose there's another rope in there?" Sam said, his words hopeful.

Elsie shook her head and used the back of her hand to push her hair out of her face.

"It's probably a good time to mention that the key to the UTV is in my back pocket," Roy added. "Given how the rope toss turned out, it's probably best if I don't go throwing the key around too."

"Never thought I'd see myself stuck this far in a mud puddle," Sam said and started to laugh.

"Me either." Roy's laughter streamed out.

And Elsie shook her head. How could they laugh at a moment like this? Still, she felt her own laughter swirling inside her. But her amusement quickly soured, and her stomach turned. She had to call Ryan. Get help. And confess what she had done. How could she tell Ryan what had happened with his grandfather and uncle? How could she not? She needed another cowboy rescue, even if she didn't want to admit it.

"No one is staying stuck for long." Elsie tugged her phone from her pocket and worked to sound confident. "Not on my watch."

"Who you callin'?" Sam shouted, a hint of panic in his words.

"Ryan." Elsie wiped more mud from her fingers and tried to keep the phone screen clean.

"Not that one," Sam countered. "Call my other grandson Grant. He's always been the calm, more reasonable one."

"Grant is in surgery," Elsie said. Or would be soon. He'd texted Elsie when she'd been at the grocery store to let her know that Bryce's surgery was moved to the afternoon.

Still, Elsie had known she should've gone to the hospital for Bryce's surgery. But her brother had told her it was a waste of her time to sit in the waiting area. Even though Elsie could've been reading up on tractor ownership, best beekeeping practices and how to train goats. But Bryce had insisted between the girls and the farm there was too much for her to do in Three Springs. And Grant had promised to personally call Elsie when her brother was out of recovery and back in his room.

"Well, that won't do. Can't bother Grant when he's in the OR," Roy mused. "What about Caleb?"

Caleb was one of the youngest Sloan brothers. One of the identical twins. Caleb had always been funny and laid-back growing up. Perhaps he could break the news to Ryan instead of Elsie. *Coward. Absolutely.* She asked, "Do you know Caleb's phone number?"

Sam frowned and shook his head. "Why do I need a phone number when I can just holler for my grandson in the house?"

"Don't look at me." Roy speared his fingers into his hair and fluffed the curls higher. "My mind is good, but not my memory these days."

"Looks like it's Ryan." Sam sounded irritated. "Got no choice now."

"What happens when Ryan gets mad?" Elsie asked, wanting to be prepared.

"Ryan gets real quiet. Same as his Gran Claire used

to," Sam offered. "I prefer the shouting. The heavy silence makes a person twitch something fierce." Sam watched her. "And that's when the guilt sets in something bad."

Elsie pressed her hand to her stomach then hit Ryan's number on her contact list.

Sam lifted his chin. "But we ain't done anything wrong. Just got a little stuck is all."

"Nothing to feel the least bit guilty about either," Roy charged on. "You tell him that too, Elsie. That it's not our fault."

But it was her fault. She should've stopped this. Never accepted their offer to teach her to drive a tractor. *I'm sorry. I'm sorry. I'm sorry.*

The line clicked on. Ryan's voice filled the speaker. "Elsie. Is that you? You okay?"

Elsie lost her apologetic chant and stammered, "Ryan. Hey." Elsie looked at Sam. He nodded at her, his gaze encouraging. Elsie spoke around her sudden unease. *Tell him.* "Ryan, I'm hoping you can meet me out at the farm. There's a bit of a situation here."

A scratch came across the line. "What kind of situation exactly?"

One you are definitely not going to like. Elsie started to sweat.

"Tell Ryan to bring an extra-long, heavy rope." Sam shouted into the sudden silence. "Two ropes. Three if he's got 'em."

"Elsie." Ryan's voice rushed over the speaker. "Elsie. Is that my grandfather?"

"Yeah." Elsie pressed her lips together, swallowed. Worked her words from her tight throat. "I'm with Roy and Sam."

That silence descended across the phone line. And Elsie started to fret and fidget. Just like Sam warned.

Sam shouted again, "Tell him not to bring Carter."

Another beat of silence and Ryan asked, "Did he just say he doesn't want Carter?"

Ryan's words sounded careful and tight as if he spoke through clenched teeth. Elsie nodded and cringed, even though Ryan couldn't see her.

"Anyone but Carter," Roy hollered.

Elsie lifted her hand and made the universal shush sign, trying to quiet the duo. That silence stretched again. But Elsie was fully in it now. "Ryan," she started.

"Do I want to know what's going on?" Ryan finally asked. His words were even softer and even more contained.

Elsie hedged, "Not really."

"Is everyone okay?" The concern in Ryan's words calmed her.

"We're good," Elsie said, glad she could offer that much, then she added, "Just stuck at the moment."

Another scratch came over the line as if Ryan was on the move. Walking most likely. He asked, "Where are you exactly?"

"Hold on," Elsie said and covered the speaker with her palm. She looked at Sam. "Where are we exactly?"

"Tell Ryan to head to the north pasture and cut across toward the old wheelhouse," Sam called out. "He can't miss us."

"Got it," Ryan said, an urgency to his words. "I'm on the way."

The call disconnected before Elsie could thank him. She worked a small grin across her dry mouth. "Help is on the way."

"Now, don't look so worried, Elsie." Sam swirled his hand over the sludge-covered surface. "This is nothing but a mud puddle."

"That's right." Roy nodded. His words were confident and amused. "Sam and I got stuck in a real mudhole once before. Now, that was a real problem. Remember that, Sam?"

The two brothers laughed at the memory. Yet looking at the pair of older cowboys and the immovable tractor all Elsie could see were problems. And the biggest problem hadn't even arrived yet.

CHAPTER SEVEN

IT WASN'T LONG before the deep hum of a truck filled the air. Elsie stood and turned. Make that two trucks. Heavy duty and powerful and carrying three Sloan brothers.

Ryan emerged from a silver truck and set his hands on his hips. Elsie shifted her attention to the steel blue truck. The driver climbed out, his face set in a hard mask beneath his cowboy hat. Elsie recognized Carter Sloan, the oldest Sloan brother, from his dark hair touching his shirt collar and his commanding presence.

The passenger door of Carter's truck opened, and Caleb hopped out. His handsome face broke into an inviting grin before he released a wallop of deep laughter. No sooner did Caleb pull out his cell phone and move carefully to the edge of the muck. His brothers followed behind him.

"Caleb, what are you doing?" Sam asked, exasperation thick in his words and expression.

"First I'm taking pictures." Caleb's words were gleeful. "Then I'm going to video this. For Grant and Josh because they aren't here to witness this fiasco in real time."

"Stop messing around, Caleb," Sam ordered. "We need to get out of here."

"Should've thought of that before you climbed in." Carter's words were gruff, his exasperation an equal match for his grandfather's. And his stance was unyielding.

Carter Sloan had always been intimidating growing up. Always focused and always looking out for his brothers.

Then Elsie had gotten to know Carter better and decided the oldest Sloan was mostly bluster. At least she'd thought so. Except she wasn't so certain right now.

Sam pointed at Ryan. "We told you not to bring Carter."

"Should've known Ryan wouldn't listen," Roy grumbled. "He never listens to us."

Ryan lifted his arms. "Was I supposed to bring Tess?"

"Tess is pregnant with twins, she needs her rest." Sam matched his grandson's frown.

Wrong thing to say.

Carter's face darkened more. His voice lifted. "Tess can't rest now. She's at home worried about you two."

That silenced the older cowboys. But there was no reprieve. Carter swung around and narrowed his gaze on Elsie. "Why did you let them drive a tractor? What were you thinking?"

"Don't raise your voice to Elsie." Ryan stepped to her side and faced off with his older brother. "You know how persuasive those two can be." Ryan glanced at her. His voice gentle. "It's not your fault, Elsie."

And just like that, something inside Elsie burst. Maybe it was the stress. The panic. Whatever it was, she gave into it completely and wholeheartedly. Her voice raised, matching Carter's. "Of course, it's not my fault." She advanced on her cowboy. "Because it's entirely your fault, Ryan Sloan. Yes, it is. This is all on you."

That brought Ryan around to face her fully. And caught the immediate interest of both his brothers who never hesitated to step to either side of Ryan as if to defend him. Ryan stared at Elsie. His voice lowered. "Mine? How can this be my fault?"

"You distracted me," she accused. With talk about back country roads and slow, long drives to the sunset. With him. Then he'd befriended each goat. So sweetly and tenderly. And she'd wanted to impress him. Show her cowboy that she was more than capable. More than worth his notice too. Nope, not going there either. She squeezed her forehead and searched for something not too revealing. "At lunch. You interfered with my tractor research."

A slow smile worked across his face before he smoothed it out and set his expression back to impassive.

"We can assign blame later," Sam interrupted. "Like after lunch."

"I am getting rather hungry," Roy mumbled.

"You two are lucky we're not leaving you right where you are," Carter quipped. "To think about what you've done."

"I'm really sorry about all this. I should've stopped them." Elsie reached out and touched Carter's arm. "How can I make it up to you? I can make dinner for everyone tonight."

Carter tipped his head and eyed her. His voice softened. "My wife's stomach is sensitive these days. It's the twins she's carrying. She's only been eating chicken."

Elsie nodded and grinned. "My Aunt Marlena says I make her chicken and dumplings better than she does."

Carter smiled, genuinely and openly. "What time should we be here?"

Dinner was no sooner set than the Sloan brothers focused their attention on the trio of trouble in the mud field. How best to pull out Roy and Sam, then work the tractor free. Ryan pointed out that the tractor was stuck on some sort of mound in the middle of the field, which had led to the tires losing traction. And the sunken rotary cutter was contributing to the tractor's awkward angle.

Caleb handed his phone to Elsie and instructed her not to miss a single second. Then grinned and lifted his eyebrows up and down. "Record everything, Elsie. I'm counting on you. This is bargaining power later. We'll want this."

In the end it was Ryan who came up with the plan. And then the brothers got to work, using their trucks, tow hitches and communication that told Elsie the brothers always worked as a team. Not that they didn't stop and debate several times. And laugh. That was a surprise to Elsie. They joked and laughed the entire time. As if once they knew their grandfather and uncle were not in serious danger, they relaxed and found the humor in the situation.

Roy and Sam were pulled free and waited with Elsie. Then the brothers concentrated on extracting and unhitching the rotary cutter before working on the tractor. And that laughter continued through it all. No matter how much mud covered them or how many tries failed to budge the tractor. But finally, even the tractor found purchase and rolled free of the sludge. Fishing for Roy's favorite boots brought about the most laughter and arguments on how best to retrieve them. Elsie even offered a few suggestions, happy to join in.

It was decided Roy and Sam would ride in Carter's truck bed back to the Sloan farmhouse where the two cowboys could then be hosed off out in the driveway. Caleb jumped into the UTV after Roy used his muddy hand to fish the key out of his pocket to drive it back.

The only awkward moment came when Ryan noted Elsie's bare feet and swept her easily up into his arms. And her laughter got swept away by those butterflies flapping in her stomach. "Ryan. I can walk."

"Not barefooted," Ryan insisted. "Not around here."

"I've been barefoot for a while now." Elsie wiggled her mud-coated toes. But that only stirred those butterflies more. "And I'm fine."

"You're lucky." Ryan frowned, tightened his hold on

her and headed to his truck. "You have no idea what's out here. Barbed wire. Nails. Thorns. I can keep going."

"I got it." Elsie felt him tense. And then she gave in. Wrapped her arms around his neck and settled in. Just for a moment. Just to calm him. And herself. After all, she'd never been swept off her feet. Not in any sense. Right now, it was heady and thrilling. A little bit irresistible. And this seemed as close as she was ever going to get. Best to take it in.

Ryan deposited her in the passenger seat and buckled her seat belt for her as if he wanted to keep her where he put her. Before she could protest, he brushed his thumb across her cheek, stalling her words. Then her forehead, the caress just as gentle and light, making her breath catch. And he kept right on fussing over her. Tucking her hair behind her ears. Sliding a towel under her bare feet.

Elsie willed her heart to stop racing. She always did the fussing. Prided herself on not needing to be looked after. She should put a stop to things right now. But her cowboy made her *feel*.

Feel cared for. Feel important. Feel worth the inconvenience.

Finally, his gaze tracked over Elsie from her head to her toes, slow and steady, as if assuring himself she really was fine. Then he stepped back, shut her door and came around the hood of the truck to the driver's side.

But feelings were inconvenient. And uncalled for. Ryan was a friend who'd come to her rescue again. Nothing there to let her heart get confused over. *Follow your heart, Elsie, but don't leave your brain behind.* Her mother always followed that advice up with a reminder: *If I'd stopped to think straight, I would've seen clearly that your father and I were too opposite, and that spark between us was just too weak. It blew out easier than a tea light.*

She'd listened to her mother and believed she'd been wise about her first husband. Yet she'd ended up divorced and discovered her heart and her mind were not in sync when it came to relationships and love. And could not be trusted.

Ryan climbed inside and started the truck. "Caleb and I will come back out here and get the tractor."

Elsie nodded and forced herself to think straight. To get back to her task list. Back to the things that mattered. "I need to pick up the girls from school and head to the hospital to see Bryce. Then we'll go to the store and get started on dinner for tonight."

"Can I bring anything?" He slipped on a pair of sunglasses.

"No thanks." Elsie rubbed the dirt on her jeans. "I've got everything handled."

Or she would have everything handled. That included her growing feelings for a certain cowboy. Because falling for her cowboy would be more than unwise.

And she'd vowed not to let love outsmart her ever again.

CHAPTER EIGHT

RYAN PARKED HIS TRUCK, carried Elsie to the front porch despite her protests and because he wanted to. Because he wanted her arms around him again. Because he wanted to hold her close and tell himself one more time that she was fine. Unharmed. Safe. As if she was his to be concerned about.

When she was inside the house, he jumped into the UTV with Caleb and headed back out to the north farm fields. Caleb's fast driving and the wind blowing in his face made any conversation less than ideal. For that he was thankful.

He needed a minute to collect himself. It'd been an emotional storm from the time he'd seen Elsie's number flash on his phone screen earlier to pulling his truck in at the mud pit. He'd gone from delighted to hear her voice to concerned to bone-deep worried to riled to relieved. When he considered all the things that could've happened to Elsie and his family, that anger threatened to creep back in. He reminded himself again that everyone was good. Dirty, but good.

The mud field came into view. Ryan lightly punched his brother's shoulder. "Drop me here."

Caleb pulled to a stop and frowned at him. "The tractor is on the other side."

"I want to look for Elsie's shoes." Ryan jumped out and headed for the spot where Elsie had been sitting. He knew it'd been too much to expect his brother would leave him alone and head back to their family's farmhouse.

Caleb was quickly at his side and jabbing his elbow into Ryan's ribs. Speculation in his words. "So, you and Elsie."

There was no Elsie and him. Ryan shoved at his brother. "Just look for Elsie's running shoes so we can get the tractor, hightail it out of here and shower."

"You may not know this, but I'm an excellent multitasker," Caleb boasted, his words teasing. "For instance, I can look for shoes and talk about things like you and Elsie."

"We are not discussing that." Ryan followed several small tracks deeper into the mud. "We are just retrieving her missing shoes for her."

"Why? They're most likely ruined," Caleb said.

They wouldn't have been if Elsie hadn't been out there in the first place. She didn't belong in tractors and mud fields. She belonged in his arms. *No.* She didn't belong there either. She wasn't meant to be traipsing barefoot through the sludge. She was meant for formal affairs where she could shine, showing off her style and her elegance. Even if she'd looked happy and content with mud streaked across her face and her arms wrapped around his neck. Time to stop. Reset. Focus. She was headed back to the city soon. Ryan back to the circuit. And all this would simply become a moment. A memory. Nothing more. Ryan grumbled. "Just keep looking."

His little brother searched the muddy water and kept right on talking too. "Still, I'd like to mention that you carried Elsie twice. I really think that's something to discuss."

"That was the polite thing to do." Ryan sighed. "She was barefoot." And Ryan had seen an opportunity and he'd taken it. Selfish, sure. He'd do it again too. Without hesitation. And now he was getting in deeper and deeper.

Not good. Yet he wasn't sure how to stop himself. There'd always been something about Elsie.

"You never even gave Carter or me a chance to do the polite thing," Caleb chided.

Wasn't that a fact. If anyone was carrying Elsie, it would be him. Now he sounded possessive, not polite. Ryan ground his teeth together. How could one woman turn him inside out in no time at all? "Leave it alone, Caleb." And he would leave Elsie alone too. Surely, he could manage that much.

"Fine," Caleb agreed too easily. Then grinned at Ryan. "I've other things to discuss with you anyway. Like how worried you were when Elsie called."

"We were all worried," Ryan reminded him.

"True." Caleb nodded and stuck his hand into the sludge. "But you were riled, big brother. You never get riled up about women. Horses yes. Women never. There isn't one I can recall."

"Think harder." Ryan tossed a rock across the mucky water and tried not to get irked by his brother's refusal to let things go.

"I got nothing." Caleb pulled his arm from the mud and revealed his empty hand. "Nor can I think of anyone who you've been worked up about ever."

"What about Mom?" Ryan offered.

"Mom doesn't count." Caleb chuckled. "Mom is the reason you don't get riled up about women in the first place."

Ryan didn't deny his brother's claim. Their mother, Lilian Sloan, had left her five young sons with her parents one summer and never returned. She'd gotten divorced from their father, lost focus of her family and concentrated on her medical career instead. Ryan had lost count of the nights that he'd had to soothe his upset little brothers, Caleb being one of them, when they'd cried for their mom. All while tucking away his own emotions to keep his brothers from feeling worse. That kind of thing tended to leave a mark, he supposed. Still, their grandparents had stepped in to raise Ryan and his brothers. What Ryan felt for his late Gran Claire and Grandpa Sam was more than he could ever put into words.

"It's only Elsie. She is the only woman I've seen you actually riled up about." Caleb paused, wiped the back of his hand across his forehead then added, "But then Elsie was sure riled up with you too earlier."

Elsie had been riled. Sparking like one of those midnight thunderstorms he liked so much. And she hadn't backed down. Came right at him. Right into his space. Ryan couldn't remember ever wanting to kiss a woman more. It'd taken all he had not to haul her into his arms and do just that. But he had more restraint than that. And a certain degree of self-preservation. Kissing Elsie would no doubt sink him.

Right now, he could only imagine what he couldn't have with Elsie. If they kissed, then he would know. And some things just weren't good to know. No matter what his Gran Claire had claimed. That was information he did not need.

"Hard not to like Elsie even more after she faced off with you, big brother," Caleb added, all too cheerfully. "Definitely admire her spirit."

So did Ryan. And that was a bit of a problem. There was too much he already admired about Elsie. Too much he still wanted to learn about her. His hand collided with something familiar. "Got it." He pulled one of her shoes from the mud, tossed it to Caleb, then eagerly reached for the other. "Take these back for Elsie. I'll get the tractor." And finally end their conversation.

"Don't take too long clearing that bee pasture for Elsie," Caleb ordered and turned to walk backward in the direction of the UTV. His words wry. "After all, you wouldn't want to be late for dinner. Nothing at all polite about that."

"I'm not..." Ryan stopped talking and let Caleb's laughter roll around him. Because he was. He was absolutely going to clear the field for Elsie.

MORE THAN AN hour later, Ryan parked the tractor outside Marlena's greenhouses and forced himself to look right at Elsie's packed U-Haul as he walked by it to get into his truck.

Forced himself to remember that Elsie was moving on. Very soon. And that he wanted nothing more than an uncomplicated goodbye. That meant no more carrying Elsie around. No more getting to know her. No more complicating things between them. Time to treat her like nothing more than a neighbor—friendly but respectful of each other's personal space.

Back on Sloan land, Ryan checked on his horses in the stables then headed to the farmhouse to shower and change.

Carter sat on the porch, his hair damp and mud-free. His ankles were stacked on the outdoor coffee table. His laptop was propped on his lap. And an open chip bag and bowl of salsa were within easy reach. At Ryan's approach, he glanced up and said, "Hey, little brother, it's your turn."

His turn. Ryan paused on the other side of the table and eyed the chip bag. But his hands were still filthy. He studied his brother. "Is this about Mom and her house-hunt-help text from earlier?"

As yet there'd been silence in response from all Ryan's brothers and himself. They weren't convinced their mother truly intended to move from New York City back to the Texas Panhandle. The very place she'd turned her back on decades ago.

And Ryan wasn't exactly certain he wanted to encourage his mother. He'd stopped hoping years and years ago that his mother would change. He hardly wanted to start hoping again. Although now, with Tess expecting twins soon, their mother would become a grandmother. And he couldn't stop wishing that Lilian Sloan would prove to be a better grandparent than mom. His future nieces and nephews deserved that much.

"Not what I was talking about." Carter closed his laptop and slid the computer onto the table. "But now that we're on the subject of Mom…"

"I can meet with Mom's real estate agent for her." Ryan wiped his hands on his jeans, but the dirt remained stuck to his palms.

"Why would you do that?" Carter asked, his surprise obvious.

And not all that unexpected. Ryan hadn't gone out of his way for Lilian Sloan since she'd suddenly decided to come back into her sons' lives over a year ago. He was still adjusting to her presence. Still undecided on exactly how he felt about her return. He shrugged and decided on honesty. "Maybe if our mother sees there's nothing here for her, then she'll give up on the idea of moving back permanently."

Carter scratched his cheek. "Or you might find Mom her dream home and give her a reason to stay."

Ryan grabbed Carter's iced tea glass instead of the chips and took a long drink. "You don't actually believe that, do you?"

"I've recently decided that when it comes to our mother, anything is possible." Carter lifted one shoulder. "But if you're set on taking the lead on the house hunt thing, I won't stop you. And I doubt the others will either."

He wasn't exactly set. But Lilian Sloan provided a ready

excuse to avoid roping practice and things he wasn't ready to face yet. Still, he knew the clock was ticking. Time was running out. And ready or not, he was going to have to figure out if the bucking-bronc-riding cowboy who attempted daredevil stunts was who he used to be. And the answer terrified him. Because if he wasn't *that* cowboy, who was he? And would he be enough?

Yeah, he was going to have to face his fears. Real soon. Ryan tapped a piece of ice into his mouth and crunched down hard. Just not tonight. "If you weren't referring to Mom just now, what else is going on?"

"It's your turn to watch Grandpa and Uncle." Carter dropped his feet onto the porch, pulled a chip from the bag and considered Ryan. "They're up to something."

"And you want me to find out what," Ryan guessed.

"I want you to keep an eye on them," Carter said. "Make sure they don't get into any more situations like today."

"Fine." Ryan readily accepted again. For too many reasons beyond ensuring his family's safety. Reasons like needing just one more excuse not to get in the saddle. Reasons like needing distance from a certain neighbor.

Carter chewed on his chip and studied Ryan. His gaze narrowed. "Why aren't you protesting? Telling me to ask Caleb instead?"

Ryan finished the rest of Carter's iced tea and wished for indifference to tinge his words. "Maybe I'm curious to see what Grandpa and Uncle Roy got planned now."

Carter sat back and drummed his fingers on the chair rest. "You could ask them what they are up to now."

"Like they'd tell me outright," Ryan countered. "And we both know they won't tell you."

"I already tried asking them. They told me they were only being good neighbors and I could learn a thing or two from them." Carter shook his head and rubbed his chin.

"But you're making this too easy, little brother. First Mom. Now this. You're avoiding something."

If you only knew how many things. Ryan crossed his arms over his chest, met his older brother's stare and kept his expression neutral.

"Or someone." Carter grinned and lifted his eyebrows. "Interesting."

"There's nothing interesting about anything," Ryan said. "You've got the distillery and you need to be available for Tess. The twins are due within the month. Caleb has been working at the fire station a lot. Josh and Vivian left for Arizona. Grant is busy in the operating room. That leaves me."

"Makes sense. You're right." Carter shrugged then stood and clapped his hand on Ryan's shoulder. "Still, I find I'm really looking forward to dinner tonight with Elsie. It'll be fun to catch up with an old friend, don't you think?"

There would be no more catching up. It was simply dinner with the neighbor. "I'm sure it'll be fine." Or it would be if Ryan could remember those neighborly boundaries. Besides, a cowboy with an identity crisis was hardly the kind of partner someone as successful and put together as Elsie would ever want.

"We're going to head out early," Carter said. "Tess and Maggie want to pick up a few things for Elsie. Hostess gifts they told me. Need us to get you something too?"

Ryan shook his head. "Already got one on my way home."

"Now, that is very interesting." Carter wrapped his arm around Ryan's shoulders. "Care to share what you bought for an old friend you aren't interested in catching up with?"

"Nope." Ryan shoved his brother away and walked into the house. His muddy boots dropped in the mudroom, he headed upstairs to his room.

He shouldn't be looking forward to dinner with Elsie. Not even a little bit. But he was.

And that was what his Gran Claire would've called trouble brewing. *That there is nothing but trouble brewing, Ryan. Best not go stirring it up either. Otherwise, it'll boil over and then you've got yourself nothing other than a mess. And you've never been good at cleaning up a mess like that.*

CHAPTER NINE

HER COWBOY WAS LATE.

No apology. No excuse.

He simply slipped inside the house as if he always came and went on his own terms. Even in her house. Then he slid easily into the empty chair at the head of the table on the far end. Shared a fist bump with Autumn. Then Gemma. Accepted the salad bowl from Carter and what Elsie hoped was a lecture on punctuality.

Elsie would've liked to lecture him herself. It would be long and lengthy. And detailed about how he must stop making her feel. Nervous. Excited. Irritated. Frustrated. Relieved when he finally arrived. Disappointed he wasn't closer. Exasperated by her own roller coaster of completely uncalled for emotions.

If they weren't each seated at the head of the table, but on opposite ends. If his entire family wasn't there as witnesses. If she had him alone.

Alone. With her cowboy. That she intended to avoid. Otherwise, she might forget everything she meant to tell him and do something foolish. Like run her hand through his wavy deep brown hair, tangling her fingers in the thick strands that touched the collar of his striped navy button-down shirt. A color he should definitely consider wearing more often. *Enough.* Her cowboy had gotten to her plenty for one evening. Time to put a stop to that. Elsie concentrated on her bowl of savory chicken soup and scooped a plump dumpling onto her spoon.

Sam dipped a butter knife in the whipped butter Elsie had made for the homemade biscuits and slanted his gaze along the length of the table. Then he looked at Elsie. His voice lowered conspiratorially. "Roy and I hooked up the tiller after we arrived this evening, in case you're of a mind to drive that tractor again tomorrow."

"Have to get back in the saddle, or rather the seat," Roy said, his voice just above murmur level. He lifted his eyebrows at her. "That's the way of things. Today was nothing but a little setback. We'd never get anywhere if we let those thwart us."

"But we never cleared the field." Elsie set her spoon down and kept her voice tuned to quiet. "You told me that's the first step."

Sam grinned wide. His eyes brightened. "Ryan took care of that earlier today."

"Why would Ryan do that?" Elsie whispered and worked to keep her focus on the older cowboy, not the one who already stole too much of her attention.

Sam reached over and patted Elsie's arm. "That's what a cowboy does for his cowgirl."

"I'm not his…" He certainly wasn't hers either. Elsie shook her head. Still, her gaze landed on Ryan at the end of the table and stuck.

Gemma had shifted her chair closer to Ryan. The pair was busy coloring, their heads pressed together, their focus on the paper in front of them. Gemma traded Ryan's yellow crayon for a green one. Her cowboy never missed a beat, simply kept drawing and listening to Gemma chatter away. As if he always colored with six-year-olds at dinner gatherings. And those feelings stirred again. Elsie reached for her wine glass and barely swallowed her sigh inside the chilled white wine.

"You and Ryan will have to sort out your relationship particulars." Roy squeezed her arm and drew her attention to him. "But if you'd like our assistance, we're available."

"We're quite familiar with the nuts and bolts required for a solid, strong relationship," Sam added quickly, as if not wanting to be left out. "And we know more than a thing or two about the finer points of love."

Elsie shifted her gaze from one to the other, took in their sincere expressions and wisdom-tinted gazes. Then realized they were more than serious. The pair was ready and willing to offer love advice. To Elsie. About Ryan. She sipped her wine again. A deeper, longer drink. And considered how not to disappoint the two well-meaning cowboys she really liked.

But relationship advice wasn't necessary. Elsie was putting all her stock in her career these days. Her mother had given up everything for love, including her theater career, only to have Elsie's father give her up. Fortunately, Elsie had her event manager job at the hotel when her ex-husband walked away from their marriage. A career could be counted on. Elsie couldn't claim the same about love. She said, "You'll be my first call if I ever require relationship advice."

"Just keep in mind, if you're calling about Ryan, then we might need more than one call," Roy offered and scraped his spoon across the bottom of his bowl.

"Roy isn't wrong. My grandson is like a wild mustang." Sam nodded, his expression and words resigned. "He just needs the right cowgirl with enough patience and time to understand him."

Time was not what Elsie had. As for patience, that was not always her best trait. And cowgirl she was not. She was batting zero on the list of things Ryan's cowgirl should be, according to his grandfather. The man who most likely knew Ryan best. She wasn't who Ryan needed. She knew it. Understood it. Yet her gaze drifted back to him. Fortunately, Gemma and he seemed intent on creating their personal collection of artwork.

"Now we can help with your relationship business, but I'm afraid we can't continue with the tractor lessons." Sam rattled the ice in his bourbon glass. His words disgruntled. "Even though we'd sure like to."

"But if you have a mind for improving what we already taught you on the tractor," Roy started then paused. His bushy eyebrows lifted, widening his eyes. "There's another bit of land that sure could use your attention."

Elsie finished her wine and worked to keep her curiosity in check. "Where would that be?"

"Not two turns to the west of your bee pasture." Roy waggled his eyebrows. "Close and easy to find."

"Where exactly is that?" Elsie asked. Unsure how she was going to get the tractor out of the driveway, let alone drive it to another field. Still, she'd driven today. And Roy hadn't been wrong when he told her that she had to get back in the tractor seat. There was work she'd promised to complete.

"You head to the north end of your bee pasture and keep straight for another hundred or so yards." Sam drew an imaginary line on the tabletop then picked up the crystal saltshaker and set it down in his finger's path. "At the copse of trees, which you cannot miss, head west."

"That's left," Roy chimed in.

Elsie nodded. Sam grinned and continued, "Then follow those trees until you see the old wheelhouse near the stream. Can't miss the field."

Elsie pushed her bowl away and took in the two older

cowboys. Before she could ask more about the land, Carter interrupted.

"This is the best chicken and dumplings I've had, Elsie." Carter dragged a piece of a homemade biscuit through his empty bowl. There were murmurs of approval and praise around the table.

"When did you become such an accomplished cook?" Grant helped himself to a second serving of chicken and dumplings.

"Aunt Marlena taught me to cook when I came here for the summers." Elsie wiped a napkin on her mouth. Then after her parents divorced, she always cooked at home. For herself and her mom. But not for fun, rather for necessity. Otherwise, every meal would've been breakfast cereal—her theatrical mother's preferred go-to fast food. Still, Elsie had always found a certain comfort and satisfaction in the preparation and sharing of a good meal with friends and family.

"Wait." Carter picked up the rest of his biscuit and eyed her. "You were making these biscuits back then and never thought to share with me. Not once. Even though I taught you to drive."

Elsie chuckled and sat back. "Would those biscuits have made you a nicer driving instructor?"

"I was plenty nice." Carter popped the biscuit into his mouth and grinned around the bite.

"Why do I not believe that, husband?" Tess shoved playfully against Carter's shoulder.

"It wasn't my fault." Carter rested his arm on the back of Tess's chair and picked up his bourbon glass. "If Elsie hadn't been on a mission to strip the gears in my truck with every shift she made, I wouldn't have yelled so much."

"That was not her fault," Maggie said, coming to Elsie's defense. "She was just learning. You should've been more patient with her, Carter."

Tess nodded her agreement and frowned at her husband. Elsie had only just met Tess and Maggie, yet she couldn't deny she'd felt an instant connection with the two women. They'd brought her a brand-new pair of proper work boots for the farm to replace her ruined running shoes. And white chocolate truffles handmade by Tess that, according to Maggie, solved any problem. Even more, they treated Elsie like she was already family, offering to help, take her to lunch, listen. Whatever she needed, she was not to hesitate and simply let them know.

"It wasn't all bad." Carter tipped his glass in a toast to Elsie. Laughter swirled in his gaze. "Tell them what you did, Elsie."

"I might have threatened him." Elsie felt her cheeks warm. Carter had always treated her like his little sister. In return, she thought of him as another big brother and often talked to him like she would her own brother. Elsie lifted her chin. "I told Carter that if he didn't stop barking at me, I was going to drive straight to Claire and cry all over his grandma's shoulder. Then I was going to tell Claire that her grandson was nothing but a big meanie."

Laughter spilled around the dining room.

"I'm sure that threat got him to act right." Sam tapped his glass against Elsie's.

"Gran Claire taught us all to mind our manners and be kind." Grant took Maggie's hand in his. His words wistful and affectionate. "Gran Claire definitely wouldn't have tolerated her grandson being a big meanie. I wish Elsie had told her. I would've loved to have been there for that lecture."

"You got enough Gran Claire lectures all on your own,

Grant," Carter said, his words dry. "Besides, I was perfectly polite after Elsie threatened me."

"Instead of snapping, he groaned every time I stalled," Elsie added. "Which was a lot."

"But you learned to drive a manual transmission that summer." Carter pressed his hand to his chest and toasted himself. "So it seems I wasn't all bad."

"A skill that is coming in rather handy right now." Elsie lifted her wine glass toward Carter. "If I didn't thank you before, I am now."

"Wait." That one drawn-out word rolled across the table like the thud of a wild mustang galloping across a field.

Everyone shifted to look at Ryan. Gemma had moved back to her original spot and continued to color. Ryan leaned back in his chair, his arms folded across his chest. His fingers stroked through his beard. He looked casual, almost disinterested. All except for the glint in his gaze. The one fixed fully on Elsie.

You've certainly got his attention now. And those feelings—the ones Elsie refused to acknowledge—swirled faster. Those butterflies fluttered.

His fingers stilled inside his beard. His gaze narrowed ever so slightly. His words sounded careful. "You let Carter teach you to drive. But when I offered, you flat-out refused me."

Elsie swallowed and tried not to fidget under the weight of Ryan's stare. Of course, she had refused him. She always thought of Carter like a big brother. As for Ryan, she always thought *about* him. Too much. And her teenage heart was too tender back then. Elsie opened her mouth to explain.

But Caleb saved her. "Did Elsie refuse to dance with you too, Ryan?" His words were casual and almost too cheerful. "Because I taught her how to dance. Same as Carter taught her to drive." Caleb turned an all-too-innocent look at Elsie. "Remember when we danced together, Els?"

Elsie nodded. Her gaze collided with Ryan's and stuck. She felt her cheeks warming all over again and said, "Your Gran Claire taught us to dance, Caleb."

"Still, you were my partner, Elsie, for every dance lesson we shared," Caleb continued, seemingly content to keep on elaborating.

The heat in Elsie's cheeks spread to her chest. And Elsie second-guessed the sleeveless, V-neck wrap dress she'd chosen to wear for dinner.

"You must remember that." Caleb's words were persistent and ongoing. "Gran Claire always complimented me on my proper hold when we practiced together."

The extra emphasis Caleb put on together was hardly necessary. Elsie would've frowned at the youngest Sloan brother, but she couldn't quite pull her focus away from her cowboy.

Ryan's eyes widened. The briefest flare before his expression shifted into impassive once more.

She might have believed her cowboy didn't much like what he was hearing. Might have not minded his misplaced jealousy if she considered him more than a friend. If she wanted to feel something more for him. And if she wanted to know her cowboy felt something for her in return.

Instead, Elsie decided to put an end to things and said gently, "Caleb, I think my toes are still bruised from when we danced together back in high school."

There. The smallest of grins on her cowboy's face. The tiniest of twitches across his mouth that faded before it caught fully. Elsie had no time to celebrate her small success.

"I've come a very long way since high school, Els." Caleb pushed his chair back, stood and thrust his arm out toward Elsie. Then grinned and said, "Dance with me and I'll prove it to you."

"We can't dance here," Elsie protested.

"Why not?" Sam asked, his words mild. "Seems as good a place as any."

"Used to dance with my sweet Millie in our kitchen. Bumped against a cabinet or two, but we always just kept dancing." Roy smiled into his bourbon glass as if watching the replay of an old memory.

"But…" *I want to dance with…* Her gaze found Ryan again.

His arms were still crossed loosely over his chest. He looked distant and disengaged. Much like he'd been since he'd arrived. All except for his intense gaze. The one that captured hers and refused to let go.

"Don't you remember how to dance, Elsie?" Caleb asked, his words taunting and teasing. "Or are you afraid you'll step on my toes?"

Elsie held Ryan's stare. His eyebrow arched as if challenging her hesitation. As if daring her. Elsie pushed her shoulders back. She would dance with Caleb and anyone else who asked her. She would dance all night if she must. If only to prove she didn't want Ryan to be her first or last dance.

"I didn't step on your toes back then, Caleb. Nor will I now." Elsie rose and moved around the large table into the open space between the family room and dining area. "Autumn, play a country song. A fast one." Autumn ran over to the smart speaker on the bookshelves, Gemma on her heels. Then Elsie stepped into Caleb's hold and smiled. "Try to keep up, Caleb."

And he did. Led her in a two-step and country swing blend perfectly. No bruised toes. Only laughter and twirling and cheering from their audience. Caleb finished the dance with a brilliantly executed dip. She was out of breath when Caleb righted her. And told herself she was relieved when she saw Ryan had cleared part of the dining table and was already disappearing into the kitchen.

Not my concern. Still, she gathered more dishes and stalked right after her cowboy. She dropped her stack of plates in the kitchen sink and cornered Ryan between the island and the refrigerator. "What is your problem tonight?"

"I don't have one." He braced his hands on the granite countertop behind him and leaned back. "Do you?"

Oh, she had a problem. A cowboy-sized one. For certain. But that was for her to sort out herself. Later. When she was alone and not so intent on reading between the lines. Surely, she hadn't truly felt butterflies because of him earlier. Now only frustration flickered through her. "No. I'm having a delightful evening."

"That's good." His words sounded bored. He tipped his head toward the dining room. "Sounds like they are playing another song. I'm sure Caleb would dance with you again. You should head back out there. Enjoy the rest of your evening."

"What about you?" *Would you dance with me? Just once. So, then I would know...* Elsie cut off that thought. She had to stop feeling so much around him. Stop imagining what wasn't there. And start thinking straight.

"I see Marty is out of the goat pen again." His focus shifted to the wide window over the kitchen sink. "I think I'll go and gather the goats."

"Right now?" She worked to hide her exasperation.

He nodded.

"Is that really what you want?" *What if I wanted it to be me?* She searched his face.

His chin dipped, quick and certain. Then he released the

counter and eased around her without making the slightest contact.

She could've reached for him. Stopped him. To what end? To ask him to dance with her only to realize she wanted another and another. But she had her own life—and career—to build in New York.

The one she'd diligently researched and mapped out. The one that would prove she could live outside the pages of her books. Outside her comfort zone. *You're too content watching life being lived around you, Elsie. But I'm ready to go live it.* Without her, it turned out. Her ex-husband had never asked Elsie to join him. Never asked what she'd been ready for.

But Elsie was ready now. To create her own success in a big city where she could thrive. Yet a cowboy like Ryan wasn't meant for city life. He was meant for everything she couldn't offer. Like open country roads, long sunrise horseback rides and her trust.

Her trust that what she felt between them was something more than a flicker. Something worth risking her heart for. Because she was done handing over her heart only to have it returned broken. Something about her cowboy warned her that he could steal her heart and break it before she even knew it.

Elsie kept her arms at her sides. Then twisted and watched him leave. Best get used to it. After all, she would do her own leaving one day soon enough.

At the back door, he turned around and watched her for a beat. Then one more. Finally, he said, "What I really want is to kiss you, Elsie Marie. But sometimes we just don't get what we want."

CHAPTER TEN

THE NEXT MORNING, Ryan walked Sundancer up the Doyles' driveway and veered straight for the tractor. Elsie sat in the captain's chair, the cab door propped open courtesy of her new work boots from Maggie and Tess. She wore a blue plaid flannel shirt, the sleeves rolled to her elbows, and a faded burgundy baseball cap, her ponytail pulled through the back. Casual suited her. Same as the emerald green silky dress she'd worn last night had suited her. She was pretty. He supposed she would always be that to him. He'd come close enough. He stopped yards from the tractor.

"Elsie." Ryan set his hands on his hips and stared up at the tractor cab. "What are you doing?"

"Working up my nerve to drive this thing." Elsie's hands fluttered in the air then settled on her jean-covered legs. She tipped her head and considered him. "What about you?"

The same. Working up my nerve to apologize. But I meant every single word last night. Not the apology he should give her. He went with the first thing that came to mind, stalling until he found the right words for that apology he owed her. He said, "I'm worried about a mare at the sanctuary. Midnight Rose is not settling in well with the other horses. Even the stables stress her out." Details were vague on the mare up until her arrival at Martha Claire Horse Haven, but Ryan didn't need specifics to know the mare's life had been far from ideal. "I'm trying to figure out how best to help her."

Elsie adjusted the brim of her baseball cap. "Get her a goat."

Ryan gave up. Gave in. And climbed up into the tractor cab. To be closer to Elsie. Like he wanted. He asked, "Did you say goat?"

"Yes." Elsie shifted in the chair and picked up her cell phone from the cup holder. "Goats make excellent companions for horses. I was reading all about goats last night."

About last night. Up close, he noticed how ridiculously big her plaid shirt was. She'd clearly borrowed it from Bryce's closet. It was knotted at the waist and unbuttoned to her stomach, revealing a pale pink tank top underneath. The ill-fitted shirt, designer jeans and scuff-free boots reminded him she'd stepped into this life temporarily. And soon she'd be leaving Three Springs and him behind.

Yet when he looked at her, he still wanted to kiss her. Same as he had last night. That hardly meant it was the right thing to do. For either of them. Still, that apology drifted away on the crisp morning breeze.

"Listen to this." Elsie crossed her legs. The toe of her boot tapped the air in time to the tap of her finger on her phone screen. "I found this blog last night. The top five reasons to get your horse a goat as a companion."

Ryan had a top five list too. Five reasons Elsie and he wouldn't work. Five reasons he should walk away and keep his distance from her. One reason was parked in the driveway with a goat standing on it. Yet despite the logic and his common sense, Ryan stayed. If he lingered longer, then maybe he would find that one reason they were meant for more than a goodbye.

Elsie paused and glanced at him. Her gaze expectant. "What do you think?"

I think that I still want to kiss you. Very much. Would you mind so much? He leaned against the door frame and said, "The rescue doesn't have goats."

"I do." Elsie pointed out the windshield toward the U-Haul truck where Smarty Marty was currently standing as if playing king of the mountain. Elsie added, "We have an empty stable and a pasture that's suitable. Sundancer seemed to enjoy it."

"I can't bring her here." He rubbed his fingers across his bearded cheek. *I shouldn't be here.*

"Why not? There are no other horses to scare her. And she'll have goats for company." Elsie tapped on her phone screen again. "Sometimes a change of scenery is all that's needed."

Perhaps that was what Ryan needed. A change of scenery. Or perhaps it wasn't a change. It was just getting back to the circuit and back to what he did best. Back to the place where he never questioned whether he belonged or not. Where he knew the rules and the expectations. Where it wasn't about his heart, but rather his dedication. His perseverance. Being fearless. For eight seconds, not a lifetime. Because love couldn't guarantee his heart would ever be enough for someone else. After all, he'd loved his mother and that hadn't been enough for her. He sidestepped his thoughts and concentrated on Elsie. "But a horse means more work for you."

Her eyebrows lowered beneath the brim of her baseball cap. She frowned at him. "You already did my work. So, it seems I need something else to do."

There was too much irritation around her words not to be genuine. Ryan stared at her. "You can't be angry with me for clearing the bee pasture. I was helping you. You should be thanking me."

"I didn't want you to do it for me." Her frown deepened. "And I'm certainly not thanking you."

"I can see that." Amusement softened his words, but his own exasperation quickly followed and took hold. "You can't actually want to drive a tractor. Plow fields. Farm. You admitted you were not born into this life." One more reason they wouldn't work. This was never the kind of life she wanted. And it was the only life he knew.

"Of course, I don't," she charged then brushed her hand over her face and seemed to lose a bit of her steam. "But it's not about that."

"This conversation isn't making any sense." Nor was he. They made no sense together. And yet when he looked at her...

"How about this then?" She stiffened in the chair and eyed him. "It's about proving that I can do something more than read a how-to book. That I can be counted on too. That I can handle things on my own and be trusted to get it right." She paused, tightened her ponytail and adjusted her hat as if putting herself back to rights then added, "Surely that makes sense. Or maybe it does not. Because you always get things right, especially out here. Where you belong."

He'd gotten a lot wrong lately. Ryan held her stare for an extra minute then said, "Don't move." He was out of the cab and on the ground before she could respond. Within minutes, Sundancer was secured in the same pasture as days earlier, and he was back inside the tractor cab with a silent Elsie. He propped himself next to the captain's chair, motioned to the control panel then said, "Well, turn it on."

She slanted her gaze toward him. Her voice breathless and low. "What?"

"The bee pasture has only been started," he explained then added a small smile. "Now you're going to finish it."

"Right now?" Excitement and reluctance wobbled through her expression and words.

"Can't think of a better time, can you?" He sounded concise and challenging. Then he crossed his arms over his chest as if intent on waiting her out. "Time to prove yourself to yourself, Elsie Marie."

Elsie stuck her phone into the holder and scooted back in the chair. "What are you going to do?"

"Consider me your onboard help desk. Here for advice." Nothing more than a good neighbor being helpful. Ryan pushed his hat lower on his forehead and stared out the windshield, rather than at the stray piece of Elsie's hair that touched her cheek. "But you are in the driver's seat. What happens next is entirely up to you."

And that's where Ryan was going to leave things. With Elsie. Entirely. Because Elsie had always been the one to do the right thing. To follow the rules. To be sensible. And Ryan had always been the risk-taker. The jump-and-consider-the-consequences-later one.

But the consequences of jumping with Elsie, well, those were ones even he might not recover from. Good thing he knew Elsie was smart. She would know someone like him was all wrong for her. He should be more relieved. He shouldn't want to prove that he could be who she needed. Because that would be all kinds of wrong. For both of them. And that meant Ryan would do what he did best in relationships—keep things between them light, easy and casual.

Several hours later and the bee pasture prep completed, Ryan lifted his hat off his head and brushed his hand through his hair. Beside him, Elsie concentrated on driving the tractor with the same intensity she had since they'd started. She was completely by the book. Although, she'd stopped reciting proper tractor operating tips she'd collected from the owner's manual. When he'd run out of farm facts to fill the silence, he'd turned on music inside the cab. Still, her shoulders were too tight and her grip tense as if she feared relaxing.

Ryan paused the music on the console and asked, "So are you going to tell me why we are now working on Sloan land? Or do you want me to guess?"

"How do you know this is Sloan land?" Elsie kept her attention trained on what was ahead and steered in a perfectly straight line that would have impressed the most seasoned farmhand.

"Bryce and I used to have epic battles on the property line out here." Ryan chuckled. Their battles had lasted hours in the summers and often stretched over days. Truces were called for afternoon cannonballs in the Sloan family pond, lunch, or worse, chores. But the friends had always stepped in to help each other finish their chores in order to get back to the fun faster. Ryan grinned at the memory. "True turf wars were waged in these parts on more than one occasion."

"Who won?" A smile played across Elsie's face.

He liked that. Making her smile. Would've wanted to do that more if he wasn't determined to be more detached neighbor than interested friend. He said, "I won, of course."

"Of course." She chuckled, the sound natural and relaxed.

He liked that too. His own smile came easily.

"And if I asked my brother?" There was a tease in her words.

"Bryce will lie and claim a false victory," Ryan said, dryly and decidedly.

Her full laughter spilled free, falling around him like an unexpected spring shower. That sound he really liked.

Far too much. And he was drawn in again, despite his determination to remain detached.

She slanted her gaze at him, her amusement faded. "Sam and Roy told me I could practice my tractor skills out here. I never got a chance last night to ask them more about this land."

Ryan ran his palms over his jeans and considered the property. Not far ahead, nestled among the treetops, the pitched roof of an old, all-too-familiar barn came into view. Ryan pointed out the windshield. "Head that way."

"Is that a barn?" Elsie leaned forward in her chair as if wanting a better view. "Why would someone put a barn all the way out here? All by itself. That's odd."

"I don't know." Ryan smiled and shrugged. "But growing up we never cared about the reasons the barn was built, only that it was here."

Elsie frowned at him.

"I'll have you know that barn served several important purposes over the years for Bryce and me," Ryan stated, unable to keep the humor from his words. "Among other things, that old barn was our hideout, neutral ground during those epic turf battles, and a dungeon when we were rogue pirates."

"There was certainly a lot going on out here." Elsie shook her head. Her grin stretched wider. "Clearly, I had no idea."

"Hey, I tried to invite you to come along." Ryan lifted one shoulder, nudging aside his old disappointment at her refusals then added, "But you were always more interested in your books than joining our adventures."

"Well, you never mentioned anything about rogue pirates." Elsie slowed the tractor to a stop.

"Well, I can't promise we'll find any pirates, but it's worth exploring." Ryan reached for the door rather than hold his hand out to her. "You can wait here or join me. Your choice."

"Lead the way." Elsie motioned to the door. "But if I find pirate treasure in there, I'm not sharing."

"Fine." Ryan leaped to the ground. He was glad to share this moment alone with her. And wasn't that far from the neutral neighbor he intended to be. Still, he waited within easy reach of Elsie and watched her climb down.

Her boots barely touched the grass when Ryan turned, heading toward the old barn. A path had been cleared toward the side door of the stone and slate rectangle building. The glass in the windows had been gone long before Ryan and Bryce had claimed the space as their own fortress. The second-story loft only covered half the space and few floorboards had remained when they'd been kids. But the waterwheel on the other side of the barn had transformed the barn into something more. And ignited their imaginations same as the water from the stream had turned the wheel in a slow, constant roll.

"That's a waterwheel." Wonder splashed through Elsie's words and expression. "You never told me about that."

There was a lot he hadn't told her. Even more he couldn't tell her. Still, he grinned. "Would that have enticed you to come out here with me?"

She ducked her head and hurried over to the waterwheel, but not before he caught the blush tinting her cheeks pink. And didn't that jump-start his own foolish thoughts. Still, he followed Elsie over to the stream's edge. The wooden wheel creaked. The water spilled gently from the wheel slates. The stream gurgled. It was peaceful and calming. And very inviting.

The perfect place to gather your thoughts as his Gran Claire would've told him. *Always good to sit for a spell,*

Ryan. Every now and then. Make sure your heart and your mind are in tune.

Before he invited Elsie to sit beside him for a spell to see if they were in tune, Ryan turned and pointed at the warped wooden door. "Want to hunt for that treasure now?"

Elsie laughed and motioned in front of her. "After you."

"I haven't been inside here in years." Ryan nudged the door open then peered inside to check for fallen beams or other potential mishaps. The space was surprisingly debris-free.

"Is it the same as you remember?" Elsie joined him. Her face lifted to the pitched roof and thick rafters still bisecting the ceiling.

Ryan turned a slow circle then brushed his fingers across the stone wall. "Feels smaller than it did when we were kids."

"You've grown a bit taller since then." Elsie chuckled and moved farther into the rectangle barn.

"I suppose that's true." Ryan wandered over to the ladder still leaning against the stone wall. The one they used to scale to reach the rickety loft. Looking up at it now, he was amazed they hadn't collapsed through the worn floorboards to the cement floor below. The entire space seemed to be one safety violation after another. When had he started seeking those out first? "And it doesn't help that I seem to have lost my imagination."

She paused and considered him. Her face shadowed by her baseball cap and the dimly lit interior. "You sound disappointed."

"More nostalgic…" He looked up at a cobweb in the window. Water droplets glistened on the intricate webbing. "For those times when you believed you could be anyone or anything. All you had to do was imagine it. There was nothing to stop you."

"What's stopping you now?" Her voice was all too perceptive.

"Nothing." He shrugged one shoulder, nudging against his uncertainty. Then added more conviction to his words. "I am who I always wanted to be."

"Then there's nothing left to imagine," she said quietly.

Except when he looked at her. Then he imagined. Things like a life partner. A real commitment. His own family. All the things he never really considered. All the things he always avoided. After all, the only commitment he'd ever been able to keep was to his rodeo career. Same as his mother had only ever stayed true to her medical career. His apple hadn't fallen far from that tree. And the thought of failing Elsie left him cold. Nothing to do but tuck his foolish imaginings away. Concentrate on what he did best: rodeo.

Elsie stood in front of a wooden worktable that spanned the length of one wall. Amusement and confusion blended in her expression. "I'm trying to imagine what Sam and Roy plan to do out here. This is where they told me to bring the tractor the other night at dinner."

Ryan walked over to the table. He picked up a handful of tiny yellow flower petals from the wooden work top and scattered them across his palm. Thanks to Elsie, he now had a fairly good idea what his grandpa and uncle were up to. "My guess. They want to make dandelion wine."

"Seriously?" Elsie peered at the flower petals he held.

"They found an old family recipe a few years back." Ryan picked up an intact dandelion flower from the work top and held it out to her. "They've been wanting to brew something, but Carter hasn't let them use the distillery or its equipment."

"So, they found a workaround," Elsie said, approval in her words. She touched her fingertip to the dandelion blossom. "They certainly are enterprising."

"Among other things." Ryan brushed the petals off his hand and wiped his palms together. No use lingering and encouraging his own wayward wishes or those of his grandfather and uncle. "We should get going. I need to head over to the sanctuary this afternoon."

He had a meeting with the contractor about the new stable barn build. The one the sanctuary could afford if Ryan took home the grand prize at the rodeo in two weeks. And the same one that would house the five aged-out broncs Ryan had committed to giving a new home to. All part of his family's legacy. But it only happened if Ryan located his nerve and got in the saddle again.

Elsie walked over to him, pulled his attention back to her. She said, "We can't just leave this unfinished for Roy and Sam."

"Why not?" Ryan asked. "We can't encourage them. This barn wasn't safe when we were kids. It's undoubtedly gotten worse over the years."

"But you can make sure it is safe," Elsie countered. "Make sure they are safe out here."

For now. But who would watch his grandpa and uncle when he was on the road? Back on the circuit full-time where he needed to be. He knew how to be successful there. But Elsie tempted him to think beyond the arena. Beyond that eight-second ride. He stopped himself. He always faltered in relationships. And letting down Elsie wasn't something he ever wanted to do. Promises were something he couldn't give her.

He nudged the toe of his boot into a pile of dirt. "I don't know, Elsie. This place needs more than a deep clean."

"Come on, Ryan," Elsie urged. "You know how happy it would make them."

And her too. He could see it all over her face. Hear it in her voice. But her happiness wasn't his to ensure. He crossed his arms over his chest. "I'll talk to Josh and see what I can do." When her smile spread wide and her mouth opened, he held out his hand, palm up. "But I'm not making any promises. If it is not safe out here, then there will be no dandelion wine making happening."

"I believe in you," Elsie said, quickly and decidedly as if doubting him was an impossibility. Then she pulled out her cell phone and tapped on the screen.

But all Ryan seemed to have were doubts. Especially where Elsie was concerned. Looking at her now, he doubted they were so very different after all. Simply two people content to make others happy until they discovered a bit of their own. *I could be happy with you.* He shut down that thought and ordered his heart to get back in line. Then he cleared his throat. "What are you doing?"

"Researching dandelion seeds." Elsie swiped her finger across her phone screen. Her eyebrows knitted together. "We will want a high-quality seed for the wine."

"It's a weed," Ryan said, his voice dust coated like the stone walls surrounding him and his heart.

"It's a weed that turns into something delicious." Elsie followed him outside.

"Have you ever tried dandelion wine?" Ryan asked.

"No, but it sounds good." Elsie grinned at him over her phone. "Listen to this."

Ryan paused and considered her. He was beginning to like those three words—*listen to this*—more than he should. Every time she repeated that phrase her gaze lit up and her voice sparked. And she captured his full attention. Completely and undeniably.

"'Dandelion wine is a citrusy, floral spring tonic. Not too sweet. Its golden color is both warm and rich,'" Elsie read from her phone. "Doesn't that sound delightful."

He was beginning to think she was delightful. And wasn't that just about as unacceptable as weeds in his Gran Claire's gardens? He turned and headed for the tractor. "It's still a weed."

"It's a weed with a worthy second act." Elsie bumped her shoulder into his arm. "We should all appreciate that."

And before he got to appreciating her enthusiasm for dandelion wine and how much he liked being with her, he said, "You do realize that your family can shut down the whole operation if they choose to, don't you?"

"How is that?" Elsie tucked her phone back in her pocket.

"Water rights." Ryan hitched his thumb toward the waterwheel. "The stream is on Doyle land. And I imagine there were disputes centuries ago right here in this very spot over the land and the water."

"Or maybe the previous owners worked together," Elsie mused.

"That sounds very optimistic and idealistic." And she looked very adorable and all too approachable. Ryan retreated.

"Perhaps I should advise my brother and aunt to demand a percentage of the profits from the sale of the dandelion wine." Elsie climbed up into the tractor cab.

"You should probably demand a bottle of dandelion wine first," he suggested. "You might not even like it."

He definitely couldn't say the same about Elsie. He liked her. Too much already.

And now he'd gone and complicated that goodbye. Only one thing to do. Demand his heart stand down.

Otherwise, he just might find himself in trouble—the heartbreaking kind of trouble.

CHAPTER ELEVEN

RYAN HAD NEVER been one to second-guess his decisions. Until recently. And the frequency seemed to be multiplying by the day. Take right now, for instance. Ryan glanced at the time on his watch. His frown deepened.

He certainly had not planned on touring houses for sale all morning with his mother's real estate agent, Fletcher Belfer. As for his mother, she was back in New York overseeing her medical practice.

Now it was well past the lunch hour and he was still looking at houses. Worse, he and his mother were also currently live on video chat. Ryan already had to postpone his visit to the sanctuary to check on Midnight Rose. And had to ask Maggie to meet Paige Bishop, the local veterinarian, at the Sloan stables for Sundancer's weekly checkup.

Adjusting his grip on his phone, Ryan moved from the office and continued to film his walk-through of the first floor of the renovated townhouse in downtown Belleridge. As for Fletcher, he'd stepped outside to take an important phone call. *Lucky him.*

"Ryan." His mother's crisp voice streamed across the speaker. "Step back and pan across the entire kitchen again. Only slower this time."

Ryan did as his mother requested. He moved farther back into the living room and lifted his phone to capture the kitchen. And kept silent.

He had not planned on this. He'd counted on his meticulous mother instantly disliking every single place. Instantly discounting each one as unsuitable for her. And that in turn would have immediately proven Ryan correct. That his mother really had no intention of *actually* relocating to the Texas Panhandle to be closer to her family.

But his mother was acting interested. And very involved. Now Ryan was second-guessing his decision to take the lead on this particular task. And seriously reconsidering calling Caleb for backup. Especially now that Fletcher appeared not to be returning anytime soon from his urgent phone call, leaving Ryan to deal with his mother alone.

"How many people can fit around that island, Ryan?" His mother's voice disrupted the silence. She added, "I can't tell from this view."

"I'm not sure. Maybe six could stand around the island." Ryan tipped his head and studied the granite-topped island.

There was room enough for two stools. Three would definitely be a crowd. But he could see the appeal. It would be an ideal spot for a relaxed evening. With room enough for a couple to cook comfortably together. Then enjoy a good bottle of wine and good food together. It would be quiet. Intimate. Romantic. With the right person. Someone like Elsie, he supposed, if he wanted a night like that. In a place like this.

Ryan shook his head. He had all the room he could want in his trailer on the circuit. "Is it really important how many people fit in the kitchen?"

"Well, I'd certainly like to know what size dinner party I can host in the space," Lilian countered, her words mystified as if she couldn't understand his question.

Or perhaps it was that they didn't understand each other. That wasn't much of a surprise. They were no more than strangers who happened to share a bloodline. He was at home in an arena on horseback. She thrived in an operating room in the city. If he hadn't been desperate for one more reason not to get back in the saddle, he wouldn't have agreed to this. But now, he was in over his head and sinking fast.

"Mother, this townhouse has the essentials," Ryan said then recited the same things he'd told her earlier. "A completely upgraded kitchen. Full-sized bathrooms and a two-car garage." *Can we please stop pretending now? Stop pretending you intend to move here.*

"What about the outdoor living space?" his mother asked, as if she was genuinely engaged and considering this property as her potential new home. "Does it flow from the living area outdoors? Or is it disrupted? It looks to be disconnected."

Ryan squeezed his forehead with his free hand, twisted to film the family room and strove to be patient. "There are sliding glass doors leading right out to the screened-in patio."

"But would there be ease of movement for my guests with furniture in place?" his mother asked, seeming far too intent on continuing to discuss the property. She added, "I need to know about the flow in the main rooms. The energy. The feel of the house."

Ryan flipped the phone around and looked directly into the camera. "It is an end unit and a solidly built townhouse." That should end the conversation. Stop the farce.

"That sounds just adequate." His mother's lips pulled together, and she shook her head. "That won't do. We'll need to keep on looking."

Why wasn't she giving in already? Ryan decided on a gentle nudge and suggested, "Or we could put this whole house hunt thing on hold."

His mother's shoulders stiffened. Then she peered closer

into the screen as if he'd suggested she add ice cubes to her champagne. Her words were measured. "Why would I do that?"

Because you have no intention of following through. Of committing to mending the family fences, as it were. Those words stuck to the back of his dry throat. As if that little kid he used to be still held a shred of hope that Lilian Sloan could change. That Lilian Sloan meant to keep her word this time.

Some of his family members were more optimistic about Lilian's intentions, Ryan however was not one of them. "I just think it might be better if you were here to look at the homes personally."

"I plan to do that." Lilian's smile returned then she straightened away from the camera. She lifted her arm and flicked her ring-free hand toward the screen. "I've several things to do on my end over here. I want to ensure a smooth transition with my practice. I'll still be consulting and advising of course, but there are details I must oversee to ensure my patients are getting the best possible care when I'm not here. And I really need you to help me narrow down the search to our top five."

Five. She wanted a top five list. Ryan wasn't certain he had time to find one, let alone five possible homes for his mother. He studied her, took in her composed expression and steady stare. Surprise filtered through him. "You're serious about this."

"Quite serious," Lilian said firmly and without hesitation. "Now, call me tomorrow after you've walked through the next group of listings. We can decide if there are any places I need to see on video chat afterward."

And so it seemed the house hunt would go on with Ryan leading the charge. He nodded. Because she seemed to be expecting his acknowledgment. And he wasn't about to back out and hand the task over to one of his brothers. If she reconsidered—which Ryan believed was still very much a possibility—his brothers would only end up disappointed in her again. And his brothers being hurt was—as it always had been—unacceptable.

"Also, you might consider bringing someone along with you to walk the properties," Lilian suggested, her thin eyebrows lifted. "Vivian or Maggie perhaps."

Both Vivian and Maggie liked Lilian Sloan. However, when it came to taking sides, Vivian and Maggie often agreed with and protected Ryan and his brothers. And in turn, Ryan looked out for the two women whom he thought of as his sisters. "Vivian and Josh are in Arizona with Vivian's family. They won't be back until late next week for the rodeo. And Maggie has been busy helping to organize the rodeo and practice."

"We don't want to take Maggie away from that." Lilian smiled fondly. "She's so very dedicated to her roping career and now rodeo management it seems." Lilian paused then tilted her head. "Surely you know someone who can join you and provide answers to my questions."

"I'll see if I can find someone," Ryan said then added a warning. "But you might just have me. And that might have to be enough." *For once.*

"Well, I'm sure you and I can learn to speak each other's house language," Lilian said, her words encouraging and pleasant. "Even if it takes dozens more house showings, I'm certain we will find a rhythm. Until tomorrow then." With that his mother wished him a good afternoon and disconnected.

Ryan would have better luck finding a rhythm on a wild mustang than with his mother. But there was nothing for it now. He had to see this through. Wait his mother out. Wait for her to change her mind and back out. Then he'd deliver the bad news to his family somehow. Because family first wasn't just something he said, it was something he lived. Just as his grandparents had taught him.

Outside, Ryan replaced the key in the lockbox on the front door then waved to his mother's real estate agent still sitting in his sedan. Arrangements made to talk about the next listings in the morning, Ryan climbed into his truck and checked his messages. And his heart sank. Midnight Rose hadn't eaten her evening feed or her morning feed. It wasn't a trend that could continue.

He opened a new text message and typed: Taking you up on your offer to use your stables. Will be by this afternoon. Then he pressed Send and told himself he was acting only on the mare's behalf. It was in the mare's best interest to be moved to Elsie's quiet, empty stables.

It certainly wasn't good for him.

To be around Elsie and pretend that he wanted nothing more than to keep his distance. That he thought of her as only his best friend's little sister. Nothing more. Still, he would do just that because it was what was in the best interest for them both. Their roads were crossing now, but not for the long haul.

Back on Sloan property, Ryan parked outside the stables. His door was only barely open when Maggie left the stable and let out an excited whoop. Ryan climbed out of his truck and greeted his sister-in-law.

"Sundancer has been cleared completely," Maggie announced. Then she raised her arms over her head, shimmied in circles and added, "Dr. Paige declared him in full health not an hour ago." Another circle shimmy then Maggie stopped and pointed at Ryan. "Now you can saddle up too. You haven't limped since you brought Sundancer home."

Ryan stilled. That was excellent news about Sundancer.

Everything he'd been waiting and wanting to hear about the intelligent and hardworking gelding. Yet it was nothing he'd been prepared to hear. Because he wasn't quite ready himself.

He yanked his hat off and ran his hand through his hair then did what he was becoming rather skilled at recently. He stalled. "I can't saddle up. Not today anyway."

"But you said you would ride when Sundancer could ride." Maggie's head tilted to the side. Her lips pursed as if she was trying out her next statement. "Those were your exact words. That day is here."

The day for second-guessing was certainly here. Once more Ryan was questioning why he'd asked Maggie to meet with Dr. Paige Bishop instead of rescheduling for the afternoon. And why he ever thought it would be a good idea to tell Maggie he'd ride when Sundancer could. "Can't ride today."

Maggie narrowed her gaze. Her words sounded careful and reserved. "Why not?"

"I want Elsie to ride Sundancer first," Ryan said and quickly warmed to his off-the-cuff explanation. "Elsie is lighter, and I can check Sundancer while she's in the saddle. I don't want to push him too hard too fast." As for himself, well, he'd always been driven to push himself harder and faster than everyone else. Once he located that overdrive button, he'd press it again. And all would be as it should.

"When have you ever done that to a horse?" Maggie crossed her arms over her chest. Her brow furrowed. "You put your horse's comfort and health before your own. Always."

Except when he'd been careless and too full of himself. When he'd pushed too hard and believed he was too good for anything to go wrong. Then Sundancer had gotten hurt. And it was Ryan's fault. That guilt surfaced again. He knew the risks to himself and accepted those willingly. But injuring a horse was hard to accept. He glanced at Maggie. "Then you know it makes sense to put Elsie on Sundancer first."

"What else is going on?" Maggie asked, her words soft. Her gaze piercing and all too perceptive.

Maggie and Ryan had been friends for years on the circuit. They'd seen each other at their best and their worst and everything in between. And understood each other. Yet, Ryan hadn't told Maggie the truth about Sundancer's injury. Nor had he confessed his role in the accident. That was one burden he had to bear on his own. Ryan held her stare and tried to deflect. "Why does there have to be something else going on?"

"You're not acting like yourself." Maggie walked closer to him, her focus steady. "And I'm not the only one noticing and commenting."

"Look, I've had a frustrating day already, walking through houses and condominiums for my mom." Ryan shut his truck door, but nothing blocked the discontent he'd felt since the accident. "Can we not do this right now, Mags? Please."

"Sorry." Maggie winced. "Why did you agree to take that on for your mother anyway?"

"The truth?" Ryan said grimly.

Maggie nodded.

"I didn't think she was serious." Ryan shook his head. Disbelief growing. "And now I'm not so sure." Despite all the reasons not to believe in his mother, there was that worrisome pinch of hope. One he couldn't quite seem to toss aside and ignore.

Maggie opened and closed her mouth. "What now?"

"We have lunch. I'll make the sandwiches." *And prove*

I'm not rushing off to see Elsie. That I can in fact ignore my feelings for my city girl. He turned toward the farmhouse and said, "Then you help me load Sundancer in the trailer on your truck and come to the sanctuary with me."

Maggie took the conversation detour in stride. "What's happening at the sanctuary?"

"Midnight Rose is worse." Ryan frowned. He'd brought the mare to the sanctuary after another rescue had requested help with the overly nervous, easily spooked mare. He'd been certain she would settle right in. No problems. No more stress. It hadn't gone as planned. Something of a theme of his lately. "She isn't eating. And she's more anxious than when we picked her up. We're out of options on-site, but we need to do something for her. And Elsie offered her stables."

"So, you're bringing Sundancer along in the hopes that he'll help calm Midnight Rose," Maggie said, her words pensive.

Ryan nodded. And he was bringing Maggie along as a buffer between him and Elsie. As a reminder to him not to sweep Elsie up into his arms for a been-thinking-about-you embrace. Or worse, a been-dreaming-about-this kiss. Ryan lengthened his strides. "It's probably a long shot."

"I think it's a good idea." Maggie matched Ryan's quick pace easily and effortlessly. "Perhaps Sundancer here will be all Midnight Rose needs."

"I doubt it will be that simple." Ryan frowned then searched for more confidence. He was responsible for the mare. Surely, he could help her. Surely, his gut instinct for horses hadn't disappeared too. "If she tolerates Sundancer being in the stall beside hers then that will be a promising start."

"Sometimes the ones you think would never go together get along the best." Maggie hurried ahead of him and reached the back door first. "And seemingly mismatched pairings not only have things in common, they also find the perfect fit together." With her hand on the door handle, Maggie kept the door closed and met Ryan's gaze. "I'm not just talking about horses either, Ryan."

"If you're trying to be subtle, Mags, it's totally not working." Ryan chuckled and crossed his arms over his chest. He was more than willing to let his stomach growl if only to set his misguided, happy-to-be-in-love sister-in-law straight. He said, "Just to be sure we are clear, I will tell you this. Elsie and I aren't a pairing—mismatched or otherwise. And we definitely are not together."

"But you could be." Maggie widened her stance in front of the door as if more than ready to press her own point upon him. "You could be together. With Elsie."

"No. We can't be," Ryan stressed, pushing more conviction into his words. "What we can be—what Elsie and I are—is friends. We are two friends helping each other out. Nothing more."

Maggie considered him. Her mouth pulled in as if she was working through possible arguments.

"There's nothing more to talk about, Mags," Ryan said. "Elsie is just a friend." The same as any other.

As for wanting to kiss his friend, well, that was only a temporary hiccup. When he got back to the circuit and what he'd always done, then he'd remember where he belonged. And what he always wanted. The rush of one more ride. The thrill of one more win. A rodeo lifestyle all his own. And no regrets.

Maggie studied him then finally shrugged one shoulder and opened the back door. "If you say so."

He certainly did say so.

Not that his heart seemed to be paying him any mind. Still, there was no thrill in risking his heart.

As for those regrets, well, that was simple. He wouldn't allow there to be any.

CHAPTER TWELVE

ELSIE STEPPED OUT of the stairwell at Belleridge Regional Hospital and exhaled long and deep. Then told herself she was winded from climbing four flights of stairs, not from Ryan's text. And her heart was beating faster thanks to those same stairs, not from the thought of seeing her cowboy again. If ever there was a sign she needed to get back on a consistent exercise program, she had one now.

Elsie made her way down the hall and greeted the nurses behind the desk. Her phone she kept in her purse. Not for safety reasons, but to keep herself from texting Ryan back with something foolish like *Looking forward to seeing you.* Or *Can't wait to see you.* Or worse, *You're welcome to stay for dinner. Then we can talk about that kiss.*

Nope. That conversation wasn't happening. Elsie moved out of the path of an empty gurney and turned down the hall toward her brother's room.

For a cowboy who'd claimed he'd wanted to kiss her, Ryan had acted completely disinterested afterward. Sure, he'd been patient and attentive in the tractor the other morning. Yet despite the closed-in cab, there had been no contact, accidental or otherwise. No leaning into each other's space. No closing the distance. He'd been polite and informative. Reciting tractor statistics and farming essentials as if he understood that information grounded Elsie. That the more she knew, the less uncertain she felt.

Only her cowboy left her uncertain. And too aware

that when it came to matters of the heart, Elsie often read things all wrong. For now, she'd stick to the facts. Ryan had taught her to drive a tractor then he'd left. And they hadn't spoken for several days since. Except for his recent text about bringing Midnight Rose to stay at her family's stables that afternoon. There was nothing that suggested he even still thought about wanting to kiss her. Therefore, she would stop thinking about him doing just that.

Mind made up, Elsie knocked on her brother's door then walked inside his hospital room. The laughter and animated voices caught her off guard immediately. Yet the two familiar, lively women, each one propped in a chair on either side of Bryce's bed, were immediately recognizable. The Baker sisters were long-time friends of her Aunt Marlena's and two of Elsie's favorite Three Springs residents. Elsie's smile stretched wide. "Breezy. Gayle. I didn't know you would be here today."

"We just got back from our great-niece's wedding in Austin." Breezy adjusted the fire-engine red framed glasses propped in her short, spiky white hair and laughed. "We told our niece to get married in Marlena's greenhouses. The gala Vivian staged in those greenhouses was quite stunning."

Elsie had seen the photographs from the holiday event in her aunt's greenhouses that past Christmas. It'd been quite the transformation and nothing short of inspiring for Elsie.

"Instead, our niece staged quite a spectacle, taking over every public space at the hotel." Gayle's lips pursed and she tapped her finger, the nail painted a bold purple color, against the edge of her moon-round eyeglasses. "Could've used your eye for editing, Elsie. You always know how to finesse things into just the right blend of lovely and refined."

There was nothing garish or pretentious about the Baker

sisters. They claimed to be as homegrown as Texas tumbleweed and iced tea. Always looked after everyone as if they were their own. And Elsie adored them.

"But never mind all that." Breezy edged around the bed and squeezed Elsie tight. "It's been too long of a spell since we've seen you, dear. Much too long."

"But she's lovelier than ever, don't you think, Breezy?" Gayle elbowed her sister aside and hugged Elsie with a strength that belied her petite frame. Then she reached up and patted Elsie's cheek. Her gaze tender. "It's good to have you home again, dear."

"I'm glad to be here," Elsie said, surprised by how much she meant it. She greeted her brother then said, "It sounded like I interrupted quite the lively conversation. Anything I should know?"

Breezy shooed Elsie into her chair then joined her sister. The pair each perched on a side of the chair and appeared completely comfortable. Breezy said, "We have a nephew that spends his pennies before he's earned them. He could surely stand a sit-down with Bryce for a bit of financial advising."

"Don't let them fool you, Els." Bryce lifted his eyebrows slightly. The swelling around his eyes had gone down yet the bruising was an assortment of blue and purple shades. "Breezy and Gayle were taking copious notes and I have no doubt they'll do quite well with the financial advising all on their own."

Gayle preened and chuckled. "Even so, Bryce has kindly agreed to be on speakerphone during our sit-down with our nephew."

"We find it wise to always have backup. Sometimes our nudges aren't enough to set 'em straight." Breezy laughed, the sound unrestrained, and waved her hand as if orchestrating the melody. "But now that you're here, dear, we can discuss the booth."

"Booth," Elsie repeated and looked at her brother.

Bryce shrugged at her and didn't bother to hide his confusion. Instead, he fluffed the pillow behind his head and leaned back as if settling in for an entertaining afternoon.

"The booth at It's Blooming Spring Garden and Food Festival that's happening this coming weekend." Gayle smiled and traced her finger around the embroidered cherry blossom on the bib of her white denim overalls. "I found these at the cowgirl boutique booth last year. Then Maggie's older sister Kelsey upscaled them for me with her fancy hand stitching. You won't find a more skilled embroiderer than our Kelsey."

Elsie couldn't disagree. The overalls looked like something sold in a chic boutique in the city. She nodded and held her silence, familiar with the two sisters' meandering style of conversation. Talking to the lively duo was always a bit of an adventure, filled with detours and alternate routes that eventually circled back around to where the conversation started. All Elsie had to do was sit back and enjoy the ride.

"It's Blooming Spring is the largest spring festival in the surrounding counties." Breezy spread her fingers wide. "It draws thousands and thousands of visitors every year. There's even a live concert Saturday night. And this year is their twenty-fifth anniversary."

"Always puts me in the mood for spring," Gayle mused and tapped the toe of her slip-on foam clog as if already listening to that live band. "I look forward to this weekend every year. And there's even more to look forward to now." Gayle's foot paused. Her pencil-thin eyebrows lifted, and her voice dipped into a confidential whisper. "What with Bryce's honey being a finalist in the competition and all."

The retiree's toe went back to tapping. And Elsie hit that first speed bump. She glanced at her brother. "You entered a competition?"

Bryce shook his head and tugged on his hair, messing up the strands even more. "When would I have done that? I've been in here for days."

"He didn't enter his honey," Breezy announced then wrapped her frail arm around her sister's thin shoulders and beamed. "We did."

"And now you need a booth at It's Blooming Spring for the whole weekend of the festival and samples," Gayle added. Excitement pushed her words into each other. "Lots and lots of honey samples will be needed for the attendees."

A booth. Honey samples. The whole weekend. *Bump. Bump. Bump.* The conversation was suddenly full of speed bumps and potholes. Elsie rolled her lips together, but that unease zigzagged through her.

"You will also need product to sell." Breezy tipped her chin down and eyed Elsie. "No good giving out honey samples if no one can take any honey home, right?"

At Elsie's small nod, Breezy's grin burst free. Approval worked across her papery face.

"Monty Westwood did that one year." Gayle blinked behind her round lenses and shook her head. When she spoke she sounded woeful and aghast. "Monty refused to hand out samples. Claimed the attendees could buy his barbeque sauce if they wanted to taste it. Well, you can imagine, he wasn't invited back to the festival after that."

Elsie wasn't sure what to imagine. She rubbed her forehead and tried to extinguish her dismay. "Can we start with the competition? Maybe you can share how that all came about." Elsie slanted her gaze at her brother. He looked as mystified as Elsie, yet slightly less dismayed, and slightly more than a little amused. She continued, "I'm sure Bryce is as curious as I am."

"Oh, that. The contest is for the best new local specialty food product in the surrounding three counties." Breezy touched the rings on her fingers and lifted one shoulder. "Gayle and some of the others in town were convinced the contest was fixed."

"On account of no Three Springs businesses ever finaling in the competition for more years than we could remember," Gayle added, displeasure framing her frown.

"It certainly was quite the dry spell for our town and county included." Breezy shook her head then grinned. "Until Tess Sloan entered her divine chocolate truffles last year and finally managed to break into the finals."

"She should've won too," Gayle harrumphed. "Verna Sanford stole first place, with her lavender rhubarb tea. But then Verna is from the same county that hosts the festival. As you can imagine, those rumors about the contest being fixed started up again."

Elsie was starting to imagine more potholes in her path.

"So, we decided we should try again," Breezy explained. "For the sake of proving our theory. And we entered Bryce's honey into the contest this year."

"Now you've finaled, Bryce." Gayle clapped then pressed her clasped hands against her chest. "And this certainly feels like it's Three Springs's year to win at long last."

"Thank you for believing in my product enough to enter it." Bryce smiled then gingerly touched the stitches on his cheek. "I'm honored to make it this far in the competition."

"You'll feel more honored when you win." Breezy leaned forward and patted his arm. "The winner receives a cash prize and a feature in *Lasso Your Lifestyle* magazine. That's good exposure for your business."

"As is the festival booth," Gayle chimed in. "Can't forget about that. I'm sure Elsie can design something for you."

"Me?" Elsie stammered.

"Who else, dear?" Gayle blinked at Elsie calmly. "Your brother certainly isn't up for the task. Besides, it needs to have flair and pizzazz. You must entice people to walk up to the booth. It must truly stand out. That's more your expertise."

Elsie coordinated conferences, corporate retreats, galas and weddings. Festival booths were nowhere on her résumé.

"And you'll need a partner," Breezy declared. "But not a silent one like your brother has."

Her brother had a business partner. Why hadn't he told her?

Bryce shifted in the bed, suddenly looking slightly uncomfortable.

"Breezy is right. You need a partner to help you work the booth," Gayle continued, drawing Elsie's attention back to her. Her grin expanded into mischievous. "Nothing for it now, dear. You need to call your cowboy."

Her cowboy. Elsie felt as if she'd tripped face-first into another pothole.

Before she could respond, Breezy jumped in. "The workload is always better when shared. And when you do it with a handsome cowboy at your side, it's always more fun."

"No need to get tongue-tied, dear," Gayle said in an understanding tone. "If it was Bryce running the booth, we'd tell him to go get himself a cowgirl to share the work with."

Bryce cleared his throat. "I've got two little cowgirls at home already. That's more than enough for me."

"You've got two sweet daughters, Bryce. There's no

denying that." Breezy chuckled and patted her palm over her chest. "But there's room in your heart for that someone special. You just haven't met her yet. But when you do, I promise you'll make room."

Bryce's gaze widened on Elsie as if seeking a silent rescue from the pair's matchmaking endeavors. But Elsie feared turning the sisters' romantically-inclined attention back on her. Elsie ran her palms over her jeans. "Anything else I should know about the festival?"

"We've already forwarded the email from the festival coordinator to Ryan." Breezy smiled.

"Already?" Elsie asked. What about calling her cowboy?

Gayle nodded. "We figured Bryce's partner would want to know too, even if he's a silent one."

"Ryan is your silent partner." Elsie stared at her brother. Waited for his nod.

Bryce looked guilty as charged. "Ryan is an investment partner."

Elsie welcomed the news. Or told herself she did. After all, she'd been right not to read between the lines where her cowboy was concerned. He'd helped her only to watch out for his business investment. He really hadn't been there *for* her. She swatted away that dash of disappointment. "Well, then I guess I'll talk to Ryan about the particulars for the booth."

And completely disregard those particulars about kissing her cowboy.

CHAPTER THIRTEEN

CALL A COWBOY. It'll be fun. That was what the Baker sisters claimed. Yet Elsie wanted to call *out* a cowboy. That, she thought, might be satisfying.

Elsie pulled into the circular driveway in front of her aunt's house. A silver truck and long horse trailer were already backed in beside the stable barn. Looked like Maggie and Ryan had arrived while Elsie had been in the elementary school car pick-up line, waiting for her nieces. And if she was of a mind to call out her cowboy, now was her chance.

"Cowboy Prince is here already!" Gemma exclaimed from the back seat, her excitement obvious. "With the horses too."

"I can't wait to meet Midnight Rose." Autumn's delight infused her words.

Seat belts unclipped and suddenly there was an unmistakable scrambling sound in the back seat.

"Everybody pause," Elsie ordered. The engine cut, she twisted around in her seat and pointed at the boots she'd tossed into the car earlier. "First things first. Take your sandals off and put your boots on. No bare toes in the barn."

The girls made quick work of swapping their shoes. Elsie nodded and used her most serious tone to keep her nieces pinned in place. "Remember what we talked about. Midnight Rose frightens easily. You need to keep your voices

down and listen to everything Cowboy Prince tells you."
Elsie looked from Autumn to Gemma. "Understood?"

"We won't do anything unless Cowboy Prince tells us
it's okay," Autumn promised.

Gemma nodded and reached for the door handle. "He's
coming this way, Auntie. I'm just gonna say hi."

"Me too." Autumn pushed open her car door.

The pair was out of the car, hollering their hellos and
racing toward Ryan before Elsie could stop them. Elsie
sighed into the empty car. "So much for using their indoor voices." She climbed out and closed the car doors
her nieces had left open. Then paused, her gaze fixed on
the trio.

Ryan swept both little girls into his arms for a group
hug, drawing out their collective delight and laughter.
Gemma's boots barely touched the ground when she
tugged Ryan's arm, pulling him down so she could climb
onto his back for a piggyback ride. He only laughed and
obliged, securing Gemma on his back before standing up.
Autumn latched on to his hand with both of hers. Her feet
swirled in some sort of quick step in the dirt while she
chatted away to her rapt audience of one.

And suddenly Elsie wanted to join her cowboy for an
embrace of her own. So much for calling out her cowboy.
Elsie shook her head and stayed where she was.

A familiar blonde walked out of the stable and waved
to Elsie.

Elsie hurried over to greet Maggie and put even more
distance between herself and her cowboy.

Maggie adjusted her cowboy hat and grinned. "You
better be careful, Elsie, or you're going to have a houseful here soon."

A houseful. There was something pleasant about the
idea. But nothing Elsie could afford to linger on very long.

This wasn't her place to fill with all those things that would make it a home. Like family and friends. Pets and companions. Laughter and love. Her gaze skipped over to her cowboy and held. "Ryan told me the horses won't be here permanently." Neither would Elsie.

"Well, don't be surprised if you get used to having horses around," Maggie said. "And want to keep them."

She was already getting used to having her cowboy around. But there would be no keeping him. Or this life. It wasn't what she wanted, was it? "I'm worried the girls might have that problem." *Not me.* She paused, stretched the wobble from her smile then continued, "Bryce may need to give in and get them a pair of barn cats or puppies sooner than he planned."

"It would be hard to refuse those two adorable kids much." Maggie chuckled then glanced at Elsie. "Grant tells me that Bryce has been a model patient."

"Because Grant has given my brother full access to his computer," Elsie said. "Now he can build his spreadsheets, run honey sales models and forecast future earnings."

"Bryce is very talented at that. He already built a budget for Grant and me, as well as designed our investment portfolio." Maggie laughed and touched her cheek. Her wedding ring sparkled in the sunlight. "Never thought I'd have that. I feel very grown up and very prepared for those next stages in married life thanks to your brother's guidance."

"Bryce has always been good at helping people plan wisely for their futures." Elsie had planned wisely too for her own future. And her plans hadn't included a cowboy or an extended stay in Texas. She would be wise to remember that.

Maggie's eyebrows lifted above her sunglass frames, and she tipped her head toward Ryan. "Speaking of being good at things, that cowboy over there has always been good with horses and kids."

"What's he not good with?" The words slipped out before Elsie could stop them.

Maggie slid her sunglasses lower on her nose and eyed Elsie over the tinted lenses. Her words sincere. "A cowgirl's heart."

Good thing Elsie wasn't a cowgirl. Nothing for her to fear. She offered Maggie a small smile. "Well, that was honest." But hardly unexpected.

"I really like you, Elsie." Maggie nudged her sunglasses back into place. "While I think you and that charming, but extremely guarded, cowboy over there could be really good for each other, I also believe it's good to be prepared. To know exactly what you are getting into."

Ryan strolled closer and lowered Gemma to the ground. His gaze shifted from Elsie to Maggie and back to her. "What are we getting into now?"

They definitely were *not* getting into matters of the heart. Especially not ones involving a cowboy complication. And there would be complications with her cowboy. The kind caused by difficult goodbyes and inevitable heartbreaks. Best not to go there. Not now. Not ever. Elsie said, "We were about to get into proper horse care."

"And on that note, I'll take these two lovely ladies to visit Sundancer." Maggie grabbed Autumn's hand then Gemma's and added, "We're going to talk about what Sundancer can eat. What he can't eat. What his favorite snacks are. Then I'll show you how he likes to be groomed."

"What about Midnight Rose?" Autumn frowned. "Doesn't she get favorite treats too?"

"We'll let Ryan handle Midnight Rose for now," Maggie said.

"Because Midnight Rose likes Cowboy Prince the best.

Do you know why?" Gemma lifted her arm, raising Maggie's arm too. She spun in a quick circle beneath their joined hands then answered her own question. "It's because Cowboy Prince makes her feel safe."

He certainly had a knack for that. Elsie tethered her thoughts before they spiraled away from her. Still, her gaze was hooked on Ryan. He was strong. Yet it was his confidence and certainty in how he carried himself that drew her to him. He knew who he was. Where he belonged. She envied that. But she was determined she would have it for herself too. In New York.

Her gaze connected with his. That awareness spiked. And that was bad. She looked away before she got tangled up in that cowboy complication after all.

Maggie spun Gemma one last time then wrapped her arm around the little girl's waist. "Once Midnight Rose gets used to you and your sister and your goats, she's going to like you best too."

That brought out Gemma's ear-to-ear grin.

Autumn scratched her nose. "Which goat do you think she'll like the best?"

"Smarty Marty will greet her first," Gemma decided. "But Auntie calls him a rascal and she uses her mad voice when she says it too. Then she says he's lucky he's so cute."

"I'll leave you two to it then." Maggie waggled her eyebrows at Elsie and laughed. Then the trio walked toward the pasture, debating who was the friendliest goat in the flock. And who would make the *best* best friend for Midnight Rose.

"Have something against rascals?" Ryan tapped the rim of his hat higher and studied her.

"Yes, especially the cute ones that make me chase them around the backyard all night," Elsie said.

"You could just let him roam around," Ryan suggested. "Save yourself the frustration."

"I tried that." Elsie wiped her hand over her mouth, but her smile still broke free. "And found him standing beside my bed the next morning, chewing on my favorite pair of leggings."

Ryan's shoulders shook. Then his laughter spilled free.

"It's not funny." Elsie failed to sound admonishing. "I liked those leggings, but now there's a hole in the backside. I'm still mad at him too."

"I'm sure he feels bad." Ryan on the other hand hardly looked contrite.

Elsie rolled her eyes. "I know he doesn't. I caught him two days later trying to eat my scrunchie."

"Could be he just wants your attention." His eyebrows twitched. His gaze warmed.

Elsie's cheeks heated. "Well, that's not the way to go about it."

"Care to tell me what is?" His words came out in a slow drawl.

This. Right here. Treating me as if I'm the only one who matters. Elsie blinked, batted away those butterflies and fluttery feelings tangling inside her. She fumbled for her phone rather than reach for his hand to anchor her. "Right. We should get to Midnight Rose." She swiped across her phone screen, but her knees still felt slightly wobbly. "I was researching anxious horses in the car line earlier. Listen to this."

Silence swirled between them.

Her breath caught. His smile was tender. Affectionate. Unguarded. And aimed directly at her. Her voice was no stronger than a puff. "What?"

The corners of his mouth curved into his beard as if he had more than one really good secret and no intention of sharing. Then one of his eyebrows arched. "You were going to tell me something you read."

Elsie blinked.

"During your horse care research," he added.

Horse care. Right. Elsie came to her senses. What could she possibly tell him about horses that he didn't already know? Silly Elsie. He wasn't the one complicating things. She was. Turning this into something it wasn't. Time to stop. "Never mind. It's nothing."

"But you thought it was important." He crossed his arms over his chest and widened his stance as if preparing to wait her out. "So, I'd like to hear it."

He didn't mean that. Couldn't mean that. She waved her hand. "I'm sure you've already covered it on your spreadsheet."

"Spreadsheet," he repeated, not bothering to mask his confusion.

"You must have made a spreadsheet for the horses and their care for me," Elsie explained, letting her own frustration roll through her words. "As my brother's business partner, you would know he puts everything on spreadsheets, especially for me."

"I'm only supposed to be a silent partner." He scratched his cheek and frowned. "But there doesn't seem to be anything silent about it."

"Why didn't you tell me?" she asked, finally calling him out. Just as she should have earlier. Then she wouldn't have gotten lost in his warm gaze. Or his charming ways. Or let herself get carried away.

He shrugged. "I didn't think it was important."

Or rather he didn't think she was important. At least not enough to be let in on the secret. One more reason not to read between those lines. It was past time to get back to matters other than her heart. There was a festival booth to build. Honey to sell. A competition to win. And an anxious horse that she felt compelled to help. "I already turned music on in the stables for Midnight Rose. It's supposed to help soothe horses. But I should warn you. The stables aren't as nice as the ones your family has."

"The stalls here open to individual paddocks," Ryan said, his words reassuring. "That will allow Midnight Rose to come and go for her food and water when she wants. On her own terms. I'm hoping she won't feel so trapped."

"That's good." Elsie started walking toward the stables. "It's important to know where you stand, isn't it? Even for a horse."

"Elsie." Ryan touched her arm and stopped her. "You're upset I didn't tell you about the partnership with your brother."

I'm upset I thought, even for a second, I could matter to you. Elsie shook her head. "It's fine." *I'm fine too.*

After all, sharing things wasn't what they did. And nothing she wanted to do. Not with him. That implied things like a relationship. That she was part of a *we*. But she was comfortable on her own. Preferred it like that, in fact. "Let's get Midnight Rose settled in. I'm sure you have more important things to be doing."

He opened his mouth then closed it. His gaze searched hers, sharp and alert, then finally he said, "I'm right where I want to be."

And for a second time those lines blurred. Until Elsie checked herself. Tethered herself back to the facts. He was there because he'd delivered Sundancer and Midnight Rose. Reminded herself his priority was the horses. As it should be. As was hers too. The horses and the bee farm linked them. Nothing else. She said, "I'm going to have her eyes checked. I was reading about equine eye issues causing some horses to spook."

"You don't have to do that," Ryan said. "I can handle her care."

"She's living on my family's property," Elsie argued. "I will look after her." *You too if you let me.*

"Why would you do that?" Ryan asked. He set his hands on his hips. "You have more than enough going on already."

Because she was inexplicably drawn to the mare. The same as she was to him. She nudged that realization aside. "It's important to know you are wanted, Ryan. Everyone, including horses, needs to feel that."

"I agree," he said softly.

Maybe it was the sincerity in his expression or that tenderness in his eyes, but Elsie let her words slip free. "I want Midnight Rose to know that she can belong here if she chooses." She inhaled, tried not to fidget under his unrelenting stare then exhaled, revealing another truth. "If I can help Midnight Rose find her place, then maybe I can find…"

"Your place," he finished for her.

He understood her.

She nodded. "I know what it's like for her. It's unsettling and scary shuffling from one home to another. Not knowing where you fit. Then realizing you don't and probably never will."

"Was that what it was like after your parents' divorce?" he asked, his voice gentle.

"My dad didn't know what to do with me. Dresses, braids and tears mystified him," Elsie admitted. "He was brilliant at solving a math equation. But faltered when it came to soothing a scared little girl."

His only daughter who'd only ever really wanted a warm hug from her father. To have someone hold her and tell her it would be alright. Even if it'd been a lie. That was all Elsie had ever wanted growing up. Instead, her father kept her at an arm's length, providing the material things she needed growing up but without the affection.

Ryan stepped closer to her, but he didn't reach for her. "What about your mom?"

"Mom let me go to the theater with her as long as I stayed quiet backstage." Elsie lifted her shoulder as if her past wasn't of any real consequence. Yet still she shared it with him. "So, I stayed out of her way too. I would read in the prop room until the final curtain dropped." And lose herself in the pages of her books. Chapter after chapter. Book after book.

"Did you ever feel like you belonged someplace?" he asked.

"Here." Elsie lifted her arm and motioned around her. "With my aunt and uncle during our summer visits. They made me feel like I belonged." *Like I was truly wanted.* She'd forgotten just how much her time spent on the farm had meant. Until now.

His smile was soft and sincere. Surprise skimmed over his words. "There's something about this place, isn't there?"

"You feel it too?" Elsie closed the distance.

"Always." He lifted his hand.

Elsie held her breath.

"Auntie. Cowboy Prince." That shout came from Gemma.

Followed by Autumn's excited command, "Hurry up. You gotta see this."

Ryan's hand landed on his hat, smashing it lower on his forehead.

Elsie jumped away, spun around and hurried toward the pasture. Ryan kept pace beside her. Autumn hopped up and down and waved them on.

Gemma decided they weren't moving fast enough and sprinted toward them. She grabbed Elsie's hand then Ryan's and tugged them both forward. "Butter-Belle and Midnight Rose are friends now. You gotta see." Gemma steered them toward the pasture gate and pointed through the fence posts. "See."

Sure enough, Midnight Rose stood at the far end of her paddock. Her graceful black head stretched over the fence posts, grazing on grass. Butter-Belle grazed not inches from her.

Ryan set his arms on the top rung of the fence and leaned toward Elsie. "And look who's not all that far away either."

Sundancer was grazing in the main pasture. Only ten feet from the gate that opened from Midnight Rose's paddock into the pasture. Elsie smiled at Ryan. "This just might work."

"Yeah." His warm gaze skimmed over her like a caress. "It just might."

CHAPTER FOURTEEN

EVEN THE DEVIL knows when to walk away, Ryan.

And that was the problem with Ryan, according to his Gran Claire. Despite knowing he should walk away, he never did.

Like right now.

"I'm going to head out and get in some practice before dinner." Maggie pushed away from the pasture fence and pulled her keys from her pocket. "Ryan, are you joining me for some roping practice?"

Here was when he walked away. He shook his head. "Can't. I need to build a festival booth with Elsie."

Elsie aimed a surprised look his way. "How did you hear about that?"

"I got a text message from Bryce earlier to check my email." He tugged his phone from his pocket and waved it at her. "Then Breezy and Gayle called to give me a direct order. I was told to help Elsie with whatever she needs for as long as it takes."

Elsie pressed her lips together as if fighting back her smile.

"I'm definitely not messing with an order from the Baker sisters." Maggie chuckled and lifted both her hands, palms out. "We can practice tomorrow. Should I tell Tess to expect you for dinner this evening?"

Ryan watched Elsie and waited. Here was her out. Her

chance to decline his help. And send him on his way. That would've been the sensible thing.

Elsie chewed on her bottom lip, looking indecisive and adorable.

"I'm really doing you a favor and saving you a call." Ryan leaned toward Elsie and kept his voice low. Only for her. At her raised eyebrows, he added, "Now you won't need to call a cowboy like the Baker sisters instructed you to do."

Her smile finally broke free. Followed by her soft laugh as if the joke was theirs to share alone. And that indecision disappeared. He really should leave now. Before he decided he wanted to share even more with Elsie.

"Unfortunately, I don't think we will be done before dinner, Maggie." Elsie counted off the list of items on her fingers. "We still have to go through the feeding schedule for the horses. There's the seedlings to water. The goats to gather. The honey inventory to locate. Homework to complete. And that festival booth to design."

"Sounds like a busy evening for you two," Maggie mused then jingled her keys. "Don't forget to stop and eat at some point. If the Baker sisters find out that tonight was all work and no play, they just might send you two on a real date."

Elsie blushed and knocked the brim of her baseball cap lower on her forehead.

Maggie didn't bother to hide her amusement. She hugged the girls, wished everyone a good night and strolled away. Her laughter trailing behind her all the way to her truck.

Autumn tucked her hair behind her ear and studied Ryan then Elsie. Finally, she asked, "Auntie Elsie, are you and Cowboy Prince dating?"

"No. We're working together." Elsie looked everywhere

but at Ryan. "And we're going to need your help and your sister's tonight."

"But, Auntie, don't you want to date Cowboy Prince?" Gemma's nose scrunched up. Confusion coated her words. "Everybody wants to date a prince."

Ryan stilled. Held his breath. And waited on Elsie.

Elsie fidgeted. Tightened her ponytail. Touched her cheek. Then finally caught herself and jammed her hands into the back pockets of her jeans.

But the girls had already moved on. To Ryan.

Autumn tipped her head and assessed him as if she was a matchmaking understudy of the Baker sisters. Her words clear and clever. "Cowboy Prince, do *you* like Auntie Elsie?"

"I do." Very much. And much more than was wise.

"Then you and Auntie should go on a date," Autumn announced. Pleasure brightened her expression.

"Autumn, thanks for finding me a date." Elsie's hand landed on Autumn's shoulder. A hint of alarm leaked into her words. "But now isn't really the time for this."

Ryan couldn't think of a better time for this. And judging from the resolve on Autumn's face, the little girl was just as undeterred. He kept his focus on Autumn. "I can take your aunt on a date, in fact." At Autumn's cheerful double fist pump, he asked, "When do you think we should go on this date?"

"Tonight," Gemma declared and sashayed between Autumn and him.

"It's a school night, Gem." Autumn frowned at her sister.

"We never get to have fun on school nights." Gemma's shoulders deflated. She nudged the toe of her boot into the dirt.

"Speaking of which, we have that work we should really be getting too." Elsie motioned toward the main house as if urging them away from a hazard zone.

"But you could go on Saturday night," Autumn offered and held her ground. Gemma clapped and jumped back into dizzying twirls. Autumn added, "That's when dates happen on TV. But then Dad always changes the channel, so we don't know what happens."

Elsie's chin dipped toward her chest. She reached up and pressed her fingers against her forehead as if she wasn't sure what was happening. And she required a moment to reset her thoughts. Or perhaps her plans.

But Ryan had plans of his own. He stifled his amusement and said, "Saturday it is."

Elsie gaped at him, then her eyes narrowed as if to warn him the conversation wasn't over.

He grinned at her and said, "Now that date night is settled, we should get on with our evening. We have lots of work to do after all."

Elsie shook her head. Her exasperation more than obvious. She spun on her boot heels and headed toward the main house.

"What about dinner?" Gemma poked her finger into her stomach. "My tummy gets hungry when we gotta do lots of work."

"We will definitely have dinner." Ryan bent down and let Gemma climb onto his back. He stood and caught up to Elsie and added, "Work makes me hungry too."

"But we can't eat and work at the same time." Autumn skipped between Ryan and Elsie. "That is Dad's rule."

"'Cause dinner is for sharing, not working," Gemma chimed in. Her words loud in Ryan's ear. Then she shifted to look at Elsie. "Right, Auntie?"

"That's the rule," Elsie said, still seemingly exasperated and slightly distracted. Perhaps by the idea of Saturday date night.

But did she want to go on a date with Ryan or get out of it? He wasn't sure he wanted the answer. Still, he wanted a date with Elsie. Knew it was selfish. Though he couldn't deny he wanted more time with her. That goodbye was looming, but it wasn't there yet. He asked, "Are we sharing our food?"

"No." Gemma giggled, and her arms tightened around his shoulders. "We're sharing stories about our day."

"Or our dreams," Autumn said then pointed at him. "But only the good ones. Not the scary ones. Nobody likes those."

"We talk basically," Elsie explained. "That's the rule at the dinner table."

He was already looking forward to the experience.

Hours later, that dinner with Elsie and the girls was looking less and less like a sit down affair and more like quick takeout.

The afternoon had slowly started to slip sideways not long after Autumn and Gemma went inside to change out of their school clothes. It began when Gemma couldn't find her favorite pair of overalls she always wore to work on the farm. That launched a full house search, only for Gem to discover them in the hall closet where she'd hastily stashed them with the bath towels.

Crisis averted and their work clothes on, the group ventured to the attic for supplies to use for the festival booth. Autumn opened a box marked Craft Supplies and discovered a large spider nestled among the colorful furry balls and tissue paper. Consequently, the girls had refused to go back into the attic. And demanded a rehoming of the spider outdoors and far enough from the house that he wouldn't be enticed to return anytime soon.

Finally, Elsie set the girls up on the lawn with the paints to fill in the festival sign she'd already traced out in pencil. That left Elsie and Ryan to locate the honey inventory. They'd found the cases neatly stacked in the storage shed near the honey house. They were each carrying the last of the cases from the UTV to the main house when the first clap of thunder cracked across the sky.

The storm rolled in quickly and chased the girls inside. That left Elsie to rescue the festival sign and Ryan to herd a screeching Smarty Marty and his escapee pals, who for reasons unknown feared even the tiniest of raindrops, back into their shelter. Then he coaxed Midnight Rose into her stall next to Sundancer's, closed the stable doors and turned up the volume on Elsie's classical station.

By the time he walked out of the stable, the rain had picked up. His shirt was damp halfway to the main house when he spotted Elsie in one of the greenhouses. Just as he crossed the threshold, the greenhouse door snapped closed behind him. A bolt of lightning streaked through the darkness. Thunder boomed. And the lights overhead flickered and cut off.

"Was that the..." Elsie glanced up, but her words were drowned out by sound of the sudden downpour of water. Inside the greenhouse. Soaking them and everything else.

Ryan tipped his head down and watched the water stream off the brim of his cowboy hat. He felt his laughter swell deep inside him. He'd always enjoyed spring thunderstorms.

Elsie sputtered and wiped the water off her face. "What is going on?"

"Sprinkler system." Ryan pointed at the intricate polished piping crisscrossing the glass ceiling.

"Why is it on now?" Elsie frowned and brushed her wet ponytail over her shoulder.

"Probably an electrical short and wiring mix-up." Ryan set his hands on his hips and shook more water from the brim of his hat. "I told Bryce to have Josh check his work after he installed the new sprinkler system himself."

"Looks like we don't need to water." Elsie pulled her damp shirt away from her stomach. "What now?"

"You head on in to check on the girls. The generator should've kicked on at the main house when the power went out." Ryan held the door open for her. "I'll find the water shutoff out here and meet you back at the house."

It wasn't long before Ryan stepped under the covered porch, even his socks inside his boots were soaked. But there wasn't time to dwell on that. The thunder boomed. The lightning lit the sky. And the rain kept falling in heavy sheets.

Elsie swung the back door open. Autumn and Gemma clung to either side of her, their eyes peeled wide. Elsie held up her cell phone with the flashlight on. From the darkness behind them, Ryan already guessed what she was going to tell him.

"We don't have power." Elsie's fingers tightened around her phone. Yet her words were calm and mild as if she wasn't the least bit concerned. "The generator isn't on. The fuel level is on empty."

One more item most likely on Bryce's to-get-to-later spreadsheet. But now there would be no getting around it. Power outages weren't uncommon where they lived. Surely Bryce hadn't forgotten that.

Ryan swiped his hat off his head, shook off the water and set it on the hook inside the door. Then slipped out of his boots, peeled off his socks and walked barefoot into the house. "Then we'll just have to find as many candles as we can." Ryan tugged his cell phone out, turned on the flashlight and handed it to Gemma. "Let's team up and see who finds the most candles. Winners get double dessert."

That distracted the girls as intended. It wasn't long before they had piled quite a candle collection on the dining room table. Then declared it Princess Pizza Night thanks to Elsie having all the ingredients on hand and her brother having bought a propane pizza oven over Christmas. That announcement set the evening back on track. As did the dry clothes Ryan borrowed from Bryce's closet.

Ryan secured the last blanket over the princess fort he'd constructed in the center of the family room and let it drop over the opening. The blanket muffled the girls whispering inside. He joined Elsie on the oversize L-shaped couch.

An open case of honey sat on the coffee table. It was one of over a dozen cases she'd opened. She stared at the glass honey jar in her hand and shook her head. "I cannot believe my brother didn't notice that the labels were printed wrong."

Ryan dropped onto the sofa and picked up a honey jar. "It's hard to miss. Sweet House of Bees Pure Honey, Prefect Treat for all Ages."

"Children under one year old can't have honey." Elsie peeled the label off the jar and then scraped at the last stuck bit. "Surely he meant to put that warning on the jar."

"It's required." Ryan worked the label off the glass.

"I suppose we can have a labeling party when the new, correct labels arrive." Elsie picked up her wine glass and settled back into the sofa. "Thanks for everything today."

"Glad I was here." He wiped a rag over the jar and dropped it into a box. Then glanced over at Elsie.

Her head was resting against the cushion. Her long wheat-colored hair fell in waves around her shoulders. A soft smile teased the corners of her mouth. She'd changed into a pair of lilac-colored wide-leg pants, a cream-colored cropped tank top and a lilac cropped sweater. Comfy-chic she'd called it. Now she looked relaxed. Content. He drank his wine. "You look happy."

"I am." She leaned in toward him. "I feel like we accomplished a lot this afternoon. It's satisfying."

Ryan nodded. "Is your job in the city satisfying?"

"It's different." She sipped her wine then touched the corner of her lip. "It feels good when one of my events happens without any issues. And it's rewarding knowing that I put together something that mattered to other people. That gave them a moment to remember."

"But," he said.

She swirled the wine in her glass and stared into it as if gathering her thoughts. "But I don't get to experience those events. I don't get to take part. Those events happen at the luxury hotel I work for, but they aren't for me. Today I was part of things that mattered *to me*." Her glass stilled and she shrugged. "Probably doesn't make sense."

"No, it does." He leaned over and tapped his glass lightly against hers. "Here's to doing more things that matter."

"With the people who matter," she added then sipped her wine and watched him over the rim. "Can I ask you something?"

Yes, you matter to me too. He straightened away from her and nodded.

"Why the rodeo?" she asked. "Why bucking broncs?"

"I'm too tall for the bulls."

She arched an eyebrow at him. "That's not what I'm asking."

They'd reached the sharing part of the evening it seemed, after all. And perhaps it was the candlelight. Or the rain pattering against the windows. Or the remarkable woman beside him. But for the first time in longer than he could remember, Ryan shared parts he rarely revealed to anyone. "I was hooked from my first ride on a pony that bucked harder than some grown bulls I've ridden. I was five. It was the summer before we moved here permanently. We were only visiting our grandparents for two weeks. I begged Grandpa Sam to let me ride every single day until we left."

And then he'd begged his parents to let him stay longer. Then back in the suburbs of upstate New York, he'd wished every night to go back to his grandparents to ride horses and bulls forever. He hadn't known then that his wish was about to come true faster than he'd ever imagined. And just what he would lose when his wish for forever was actually granted.

He sipped more wine and continued, "When we came back the following summer, Grandpa Sam had a pair of ponies waiting for me in the stables. I was good in the saddle." And in those few seconds, he was free from the hurt—his and his brothers'—that came from his parents' divorce. Their father had walked away without a backward glance. Same it seemed did their mother. But in the arena, he wasn't missing his mom or his old life. It was just him and his horse. He added, "Over the years, I realized I could be better if I worked harder. Trained more. Dedicated myself. So that's what I did. And I got better." And that hurt faded. "So, I kept pushing."

"Now you're at the top. You made it." She studied him. "What's next? Do you keep pushing?"

"You want to know if I'll ever be satisfied." He rested his elbows on his knees and cradled the wine glass between his palms.

"Will you?" Her voice was faint like the smoke from the candles.

"I don't know," he admitted. "I always had that fire in me for as long as I can remember."

"Had." She shifted on the couch to face him and tucked her bare feet up under her. "That sounds like it's gone."

He scrubbed a palm over his cheek and beard. Finished off his wine. But apparently, he wasn't finished sharing. He said, "I never thought I'd see this day."

"What happened?" She set her arm on the back of the couch. Her fingers sank into the plush blanket draped there.

It would be a simple thing to slide his hand into hers. Even easier to tug—just barely, just enough—to pull her toward him. Into his arms. So, he could hold her and hold back those fears. But he'd always faced things head-on and alone. Until recently. And that had to stop. He might not be in the saddle, but he had to get to who he was.

He leaned back into the cushions behind him, putting her farther out of reach. "Would you believe me if I said I woke up one day and it was just gone?"

Her fingers stilled in the blanket. A shadow of disappointment curved over her face. "If that's the story you want to tell."

He let her down. That was why he was better on his own. Only himself to disappoint. "It's just that I haven't told anyone the truth."

"What truth is that?" She tucked her hair behind her ears as if she wanted to see him better. "That you're not really injured."

He lifted his eyebrows, opened his mouth.

She cut him off and said, "I haven't seen you limp once. Or even wince as if in pain. Not when you climbed into the tractor or jumped the fence or gathered the goats."

"I pulled my hamstring badly several seasons ago. It took me off the circuit for a few weeks while I rehabbed it." He rubbed his hand across his left leg. "Barely bothers me these days."

Her eyebrows pulled together. "Then why tell everyone you reaggravated your injury and couldn't ride?"

"Because I couldn't tell them I hurt Sundancer." Ryan stood, stretched his legs as if he could run from that truth. The flames of the candles swayed from his hasty movements around the coffee table.

"What do you mean?" Elsie's gaze tracked him as he paced.

"Sundancer's injury was my fault." Ryan swung around and faced her. He'd come this far. Might as well give it all up. She couldn't fix it. Or him. "I was on set for a Western action movie. For their horse stunts. It was the last day of filming. And the director decided to reshoot the pinnacle stagecoach chase scene at sunset. It was nothing I haven't done dozens of times before." Ryan stretched his arms over his head then ran his hands through his hair. "But I miscalculated. My boot hooked in the stirrup on my jump from Sundancer to the stagecoach. Not long, but enough to tip Sundancer off-balance. He stumbled and fell while I clung uninjured to the stagecoach and finished the scene."

Elsie unfolded her legs, set her feet on the floor and clasped her hands in her lap.

"The director got the shot he wanted. The filming wrapped. I brought Sundancer home to recover," he explained. "And I haven't been able to get in the saddle since."

"But it was an accident and Sundancer has healed. Maggie told me he was cleared," Elsie argued. "You've been injured in the arena too and still gotten back in the saddle. Still competed."

"This is different," he countered. "It's the first time I hurt a horse."

"Not intentionally," she said gently.

"Does it matter?" he asked then shook his head. "I told myself I was talented and fearless when I was really arrogant and reckless."

"So, you walk away from the life you love as a sort of punishment and penance." She stood up and walked over to him. "What does that prove?"

He didn't know. Knew only he wasn't sure where he belonged anymore. "I should probably go."

"You can't walk home in this weather." She closed the distance between them and held his stare. Her words direct and firm. "And I'm not driving you home in this weather either."

"Elsie." *I'm lost. And when I look at you...*

"Just don't move." She held up her hand, stopping his retreat, then came closer. "When I was a little girl, do you know what I wanted more than anything from my dad?"

Ryan was sinking. In the compassion swirling in her silver-gray eyes. His voice was rough in his own ears. "What was that?"

"This." She wrapped her arms around him. Tightened her hold when his shoulders stiffened. With her cheek pressed against his chest, she explained, "I just wanted someone to hold me and tell me it was going to be okay. That I was going to be okay."

Ryan dropped his chin on her head. Squeezed his eyes closed. Still, he was fighting.

She whispered, "You are going to be okay, my cowboy prince."

And finally, he gave in. Curved his arms around her and drew her as close as he possibly could. Then he held on. Because right there. With her. He started to believe again.

CHAPTER FIFTEEN

"ELSIE." RYAN'S ARMS anchored her against him.

Her reply was part sigh, part hum. Just enough to let him know she'd heard him. Her cheek was pressed to his chest. Right over his heart. The beat matched her own. Steady. Strong. And Elsie held on. To him. To the moment.

His embrace tightened. A gentle squeeze. She felt his exhale. Felt him settle around her. Then he said, "Thanks."

"Anytime." If only that were true. They only had this time. Elsie tipped her head up and met his gaze. She could lose herself in the warmth there. In him. If she wasn't careful. "That's what friends are for, right?" Just like that, as intended, the moment collapsed around her. With one simple word: *friends*.

Ryan released her and stepped back as if retreating behind those invisible friendship barriers.

She wanted to reach out. Capture his hand. Pull him back to her. Cross those boundaries. But that would be reckless. Careless. A risk she couldn't let her heart take. She was only passing through. A visitor like she'd always been. Meant to leave like always. This wasn't her place, even if being in his arms felt so very right. This was for the best. Friends was all they could ever be.

She stuffed her hands into her pockets. "We should probably get to work on those mislabeled honey jars. We've got hundreds of labels to remove."

"We could do that." He rubbed his fingers across his bottom lip and watched her.

"Or there's the new labels to create and order." Elsie hurried into the kitchen where she'd left her laptop on the table. "We also need a new sign for the booth. And the booth layout. We should probably design a flier or brochure. Postcards. Something to give out at the festival that tells people where to find us online to order more honey."

Ryan followed her and leaned his hip against the edge of the kitchen island. "This is sounding a lot like work."

That was good because otherwise she might start to imagine a different sort of evening with Ryan. One that included secrets shared. Hand holding. And hearts falling. "There's still so much to be done before this weekend."

"That can wait." He touched the petal of a gardenia floating in a vase she'd filled with water that morning. "If you don't stop, Elsie, and smell the flowers, you're going to get to New York and fall over from exhaustion."

The thunder rumbled outside. The rain splattered against the windowpanes. LED candles cast pockets of soft, buttery light into the shadows. It was intimate. Private. New York seemed a world away. But her cowboy was within reach. And when she looked at him, she felt everything. She curled her fingers around the back of a kitchen chair. "That's dramatic."

"That's the truth," he countered. "I look around here and do you know what I see?"

Elsie frowned. "Too many cases of honey with incorrect labels." Too many unpacked moving boxes. Too many fix-it projects to count. A house craving a refresh. A home she always...

"I see you," he said and pointed at the gardenia vase as if to back up his point. "I see you up all night. Unpacking boxes. Putting things away. Restoring this house room by room."

He wasn't wrong. That didn't make what she was doing wrong either. The house was quite large. Elsie feared it was too much for her aunt to keep up on her own the past few years after her Uncle Robert passed. She lifted her chin. "I haven't done that much."

"You've unpacked every single moving box upstairs," he countered. "I know how many there were because I helped Bryce unload his moving truck."

That had been months ago. All the boxes made it feel like Bryce and her nieces were still living in a storage unit. Elsie kept silent. She'd spent two full nights tackling the upstairs and transforming each guest room into an inviting refuge. The kind her brother could fill now with family and friends.

"You gave the girls their own suite and transformed it into a cotton-candy-pink princess wonderland," Ryan continued. "I peeked in when I went to Bryce's room to raid his closet."

"The girls love it," Elsie said, her words defensive. She would gladly trade a week of no sleep to see her nieces that excited again. "Their rooms turned out well, I think."

"Their suite is better than anything in the movies," he said.

She smiled. "That's a nice thing to say."

"It's not a compliment." Disapproval worked across his face. "You need to slow down. It's okay to take a break."

"I can't." Resolve was clear in each syllable. "I'm not in town for much longer. I want the girls to feel comfortable here. To feel settled. To feel like this is their..."

"Home," he said simply.

Don't. Don't do that. Don't act as if you get me. Then she'd like him even more. Still her words flowed out, as if she wanted him to understand her. "I want them to love this place as much as I did growing up."

The grand house had been her secret retreat. Every room a new place to explore. An adventure. Full of light. Rich scents. Textures. An escape where she wasn't an inconvenience. Or in the way. Where she was always wanted. "If you would have asked me to show you happiness back then, I would've pointed at this house. I want Autumn and Gemma to have that same feeling."

"And if I asked you to show me happiness now, where would you point?" he asked.

At you. Elsie touched the front of her throat. "I came here to help my family. That's what I'm going to do. You can do that with me or not."

"Fair enough." He straightened away from the counter. "Anything else?"

I'm going to leave. Knowing her family was good. Knowing it was the right decision. Because her own happiness had to be in the city. Waiting for her. New York was proof she was finally living her life. On her own terms. Stepping out of her comfort zone. That was everything to be happy about, wasn't it?

She released the chair and walked into the pantry. "I have a box of unopened vanilla wafers I'm willing to share if you help me peel off labels."

"Those are my favorite."

"I know." *I know a lot about you. But not enough. Could you tell me more? Anything. Something to take with me. Like a souvenir.* Something she could hold on to during the deepest part of the night when she wasn't always so happy. She shook the cookie box lightly. "How about one cookie for every five labels removed?" Or even better. A cookie for a truth.

He ran his fingers through his beard. One corner of his mouth lifted. "This sounds a little bit like bribery."

"Is it working?" She grinned at him.

"I'll help you, Elsie Marie. No cookies necessary." He walked slowly toward her. "I'll help you because I want to. And do you know why that is?"

Elsie's pulse picked up. She managed the smallest shake of her head.

"Because I like seeing you happy." He stopped just out of her reach. An intensity she hadn't seen before swirled in his hazel gaze. "You never asked me what I think of when I think about happiness, Elsie Marie. Do you want to know?"

Awareness spiked. Elsie's mouth dropped open slightly. Words failed her.

"You." His half grin pressed into his cheek. "When I think of happiness, I think of you."

With that he plucked the cookie box from her weak grip and walked out of the kitchen, whistling.

Elsie grabbed the wine bottle they'd opened earlier and rushed after him into the family room. He was already sitting on the couch. The wafer box open and a case of honey on the coffee table, waiting for labels to be removed. She set the wine on the side table and sat beside him. "You can't say things like that."

"Why not?" He popped a cookie into his mouth. "It's the truth."

Elsie reached for the wine bottle, pulled out the cork and splashed wine into her glass. "You can't say it because I don't make you happy."

He ate another cookie and took a honey jar from the box. "That's not the point. I don't need you to make me happy."

Whatever this is, Elsie, it's not enough. We don't make

each other happy. And I want to be happy. You should want that too. Elsie rubbed her forehead.

"It's not so very complicated." Ryan refilled his wine glass then went to work on the honey label. "When I think of you, I feel happy. Just like when you think of this house, you feel happy. It's simple."

He made it sound simple. But nothing was that cut-and-dried in a relationship. Her first marriage proved that. Elsie reached into the box and took out a cookie. "My ex-husband told me I wasn't enough for him anymore."

Ryan paused and lowered his wine glass. His expression and words suddenly grim. "He told you that?"

She appreciated his anger on her behalf. She bit into her cookie as if the sweetness would mellow her words. Then she picked up a honey jar. "He told me that he wanted more from life than what we had." *This can't be all there is. We settled. Now we're stuck, Elsie, and sinking.*

"What did you have?" He lifted the edge of another label.

"Our careers." She took another jar from the box, ripped the label off and reached for another. "Work goals like promotions. Partnership for him. We were both career oriented. Motivated and financially responsible. We aligned that way." At least on paper they'd been compatible. A logical fit. Destined to last for the long haul unlike her parents.

"Sounds like it was all work and no play." He crinkled the incorrect label into a ball and tossed it on the floor with the growing pile.

Or rather it'd been all work, no spark. But her parents had sparked brighter than fireworks on July Fourth and look where that had gotten them. The label came off like a Band-Aid being removed. She started on another. "We had plans for fun eventually."

"When you reached your goals," he said.

"Yeah, then we were supposed to be alright." And they'd have that spark. Feel that magic. Remember why they'd even said "I do" in the first place. The label tore in two, leaving half stuck to the glass. "Finally, we would've made each other happy."

Because wasn't that what love promised? A lifetime of happiness. Yet when it was all stripped away, her ex-husband hadn't been wrong. Neither of them had been happy. Not for a while. So, Elsie would find it on her own.

She rubbed her thumb over the glass, removing the last of the label. "That obviously didn't happen."

"Where is your ex-husband now?" He paused for a cookie break.

"He remarried. They're expecting their first child next month." Her ex-husband hadn't taken long to find the life he wanted. She didn't resent him. Rather, she envied him. One more label gone. "I'm glad he found what he was looking for."

Ryan reached over. His hand settled on her leg. When her gaze met his, he said, "You deserve that too."

The warmth from his touch curved through her. Encouraged more than a flicker of awareness. *I like you.* There was that spark. *Will you warn me before you break my heart, please? That's only fair, isn't it?* Elsie swallowed, willed her pulse to slow and backpedaled into that friend zone. "What I deserve is more vanilla wafers. Hand the box over." She swept her arm toward the pile of discarded labels. "I've done twice as many jars as you."

"I didn't know it was a competition." Amusement flickered across his face. He picked up the cookie box and held it just out of her reach. "What are the terms exactly?"

She snatched it and said, "Most labels removed in an hour, which happens to be bedtime around here. Loser comes back and makes breakfast for everyone tomorrow morning."

"I already promised the girls waffles." He held out his hand for a cookie.

Elsie pressed a wafer into his palm. "When did you do that?"

"When we were building the princess fort and they told me I needed to sleep over in case you got scared during the storm tonight." He tossed the cookie in his mouth and grinned.

Elsie touched her cheek. Glad the dim lighting hid her blush.

"They even told me what room I need to sleep in," he continued. His words casual. "The one right across the hall from yours is apparently the closest to you. I won't have to run far to reach you."

The idea of having him close appealed a little too much. "That's good to know." She cradled the cookie box and considered him. "When you get scared tonight, I'll know where to find you."

"Or, we could leave our doors open and just talk across the hall." He lifted his wine glass and took a sip. "Save ourselves all that unnecessary running around."

She laughed. "Or we could just work through the night." *Sit right here. Together. Like this.*

He shook his head. "We've got one more hour of work. Because the royalty in this house needs their rest. Consider it like a royal decree."

"We should get to it." Elsie sat up and straightened. "What about those terms?"

"Let's make it more interesting," he mused. "Seeing as how you are making me work after normal business hours."

"There's no normal business hours on a farm," she chided then waved at him. "Fine. Let's hear it."

"If I win, I want a day." He watched her over the rim of the wine glass. "If I win, you spend an entire day with me. From sunrise to sunset. No work. All play."

All day with her cowboy. That spark flared. Unstoppable. Unbidden. Not so very unwelcome. She worked the catch out of her words. "Fine, but if I win you take me horseback riding."

His eyes widened. He considered her for a beat then said, "Deal. Start the timer."

Elsie opened the timer on her cell phone, set it for an hour then glanced at him. "Go."

The only sound for the next sixty minutes was the ripping of stickers off glass. Over and over. One jar after another. They were both efficient, fast and focused. Finally, the timer chimed on Elsie's phone, and she called a stop. Stiff from leaning over the coffee table, Elsie stood and stretched her arms over her head, then looked at the discarded piles of labels that appeared equal. "I'll count those to see who won."

"I'll check on the girls." Ryan leaned down in front of the blanket door of the princess fort. His voice dipped into a regal and extremely formal tone. "Cowboy Prince would like to request an audience with Princess Gem and Princess Autumn."

Muffled giggles drifted from the fort. Then Autumn announced, her words equally stiff and starched, "Cowboy Prince, you may enter now."

Elsie chuckled and marveled again at how comfortable Ryan was with the girls. Her cowboy would be a great father one day. She flopped onto the couch, picked up a pile of crumbled labels and told herself it was just a passing observation. The kind one friend makes about another. Nothing that toppled her over those friendship borders, of course. The labels clung to her fingers. Sticky and un-avoidable like her growing feelings for her cowboy.

"Can we play a game, Cowboy Prince? Please." Gemma's blond head peered out of the opening. "Autumn finished all her homework and now our movie is over too."

"Unfortunately, your aunt has overruled me and declared it a school night." Disappointment spread through Ryan's words. "That means we don't have time for a board game."

"But we always read before bed," Autumn chimed in. Hope drifted through her plea. "Can you read to us? Please."

"And use all the different voices like you do," Gemma pleaded. "That's the best part."

There were a lot of parts to her cowboy she was discovering. Hard to declare the best. Elsie tugged off those labels. But her feelings, well, those still stuck.

Ryan glanced over his shoulder. "That okay with you, Elsie?"

No, she wasn't okay. But she would sort that all out in the morning. For now, she had the night to keep her secrets and she had her cowboy. She stood up and smiled. "Only if I get to join you guys too."

The girls cheered.

"Make room," Ryan said. He lifted Gemma, making her squeal with laughter and plopped her down on one of the blankets. Then he scooted carefully inside the fort. Too tall to sit without toppling the fabric ceiling, he stretched out on his back and propped several pillows behind his head.

Elsie squeezed in, surprised the interior was bigger than it appeared. She laid on her side and curled herself around Gemma. Autumn handed a book to Ryan then adjusted herself until her head rested on his shoulder. Ryan read the first line, his deep voice filling the cozy space, blocking out the thunder rolling on outside and captivating his audience.

Elsie fell into the story. And fell a little bit more for her cowboy.

Then promised herself, tomorrow when the sun rose, she would heed those caution signs. Tomorrow in the morning light, when her head was clear, her heart would see it too. That falling for her cowboy was a bad idea.

But for tonight. For right now, she let herself be enchanted.

CHAPTER SIXTEEN

IT WASN'T AN alarm that woke Elsie the following morning. Or even her cowboy with a soft hello and an even softer good-morning kiss. Not that Elsie expected that. Wished perhaps.

No, it was her phone vibrating in her sweatshirt pocket that jarred her awake. She slipped her phone out and blinked at the screen. *Mom.*

She crawled out of the princess tent where she'd spent the night nestled between her nieces under several thick blankets. Her nieces only rolled over into the space she'd left and kept on snoozing. Ryan wasn't on the couch where she'd last seen his silhouette stretched out when she'd woken in the middle of the night. She sighed. Finding her cowboy had to wait.

And those wishes in her heart, well, those had also disappeared. The sun shone through the windows, brightening the room. The view was clear now. Her eyes were open, and her heart was closed. Lifting her phone to her ear, Elsie greeted her mom and frowned at the clock on the mantel. She'd overslept.

Rushing upstairs to change, Elsie listened to her mom detail their trek through the Egyptian pyramids. And noted the door to the guest bedroom across from her room was closed. Cowboy located. When she came out of her bedroom, her phone tucked in her legging pocket, the door across the hall was open yet the room was empty. Elsie dashed downstairs, heard dishes clanking in the kitchen. But had no time to investigate. She woke her nieces and hustled the slow-to-rouse pair back upstairs for showers.

Autumn was dressed for school and downstairs without delay. Gemma requested French braids to match her new friend Madeline. And that required Elsie to watch a how-to video for a quick refresher. When they finally made it downstairs, their plates with waffles and fresh strawberry slices waited on the island. The syrup was still warm. The girls' lunches were packed. And her cowboy was nowhere in sight.

There was little time for disappointment. Teeth needed to be brushed. Backpacks loaded and seat belts buckled. Then it was straight to the elementary school with minutes to spare before the late bell rang. A pit stop at the gas station for diesel to fill the generator and Elsie headed back. In the driveway, she disconnected her phone call with Bryce and spotted Smarty Marty already perched on the top of her moving van like a sentry. Then Ryan rounded the path near the greenhouses and her smile stretched wide.

Her cowboy was still there. Back in his jeans, boots and cowboy hat. Wearing another one of her brother's pullover shirts. The fit snug across his broad shoulders. And all Elsie wanted was to wrap herself back in his embrace. Confirm her theory that the deep forest green color of the shirt complemented his hazel eyes. Not exactly the appropriate greeting for a simple friend.

A flash of caramel behind her cowboy caught her attention. Elsie chuckled. Butter-Belle trailed him like a loyal pet. She couldn't fault the goat. Spending more time with her cowboy was becoming more and more appealing.

Elsie grabbed the baggie of grapes Gemma had left in the cup holder, opened her car door and forced herself to slow down. Lean back into that friend zone where hearts were safe.

"Good news. You're off the hook." Elsie opened the back gate on the Jeep. She grinned at Ryan. "You can go back to being a silent partner." And she could go back to being resistant to her cowboy. Uninterested. And unaffected.

He lifted the portable gas container out. "Is that so?"

"Bryce just called." Elsie shut the gate, offered a grape to Butter-Belle and congratulated herself for not reaching for her cowboy. Nothing to it. "Bryce is being discharged today. The girls and I are going to pick him up when they get out of school. Since Bryce is on limited duty, I figure he can finish removing labels and put on the new ones."

Ryan nodded and walked toward the generators located on the far side of the house. "What about the festival booth?"

"My mom called this morning." When Elsie had still been content to put off facing the day and her misplaced feelings for her cowboy. She touched her sunglasses, fearing she might still be hiding. Yet he was there. And she was delighted. That hardly meant she couldn't stick to the friend zone, right? "They changed their flight out of London. They'll be home tomorrow afternoon. And they couldn't have been more thrilled about the festival."

"Busy morning." He refilled the generator fuel tank.

"Looks like you've been busy too." She gave Butter-Belle more grapes. "Sundancer is already grazing in the pasture. I saw Midnight Rose almost fully out in her paddock. And if I'm not mistaken both the tractor and UTV have been moved."

"I drove out to the bee pasture." Ryan glanced at the sky as if looking for rain. "It'll be a few days before the seeds can be planted. Soil is too wet. Caleb dropped off a load of hay. I used the tractor to load the bales into the stable loft."

"What's left for me to do?" Elsie asked.

"I thought maybe that horseback ride." He tapped the spout of the gas can and replaced the cap on the generator fuel tank. The brim of his cowboy hat shaded his expression. "You won."

She won. Elsie touched her cheek, stalling her frown. She didn't have time for a no work, all play day with him anyway. No reason to be let down. Besides, her family was coming home. That meant she would be on her way soon enough. Spending an entire day with her cowboy—what would that solve? She pressed her fingers against her chest. "You counted the labels then."

"Woke up early. Couldn't sleep. Call it my version of counting sheep." His words were light and playful. But there was a reserve to his movements as if he wasn't quite certain where they stood.

Or perhaps that was only more wishful thinking. Elsie wanting to believe he might be considering more than a friend situation too.

"What do you say?" he asked. "Ready to ride?"

With him. "Definitely."

Half an hour later, Elsie was in the saddle on Sundancer. Without her cowboy. Not exactly what she'd meant last night when she'd made the wager. Nothing for it now. If she clarified, she risked revealing too much. Right now her feelings for her cowboy were private. Her own. She meant them to stay that way. She adjusted her position and loosened her grip on the reins. "What do you want me to do?"

"Just walk around the pasture." Ryan sat on the fence that connected Midnight Rose's paddock to the pasture. Butter-Belle grazed near his boots. "I want to watch his gait walking. Just keep it easy for now. Then we'll move to trotting."

Elsie guided Sundancer into a circle. She'd surprised Ryan earlier when she'd mounted Sundancer without assistance. She'd taken riding lessons years ago, then continued to ride for pleasure in college whenever she could get out of the city. Later, work and marriage had taken her away from the saddle completely. Now she was counting on muscle memory to keep herself properly seated to impress her cowboy.

Four turns later, Ryan nodded as if satisfied with Sundancer's gait. Elsie passed by Ryan and whispered, "Midnight Rose is coming."

Ryan never moved. Kept his focus on Sundancer. The pleasure was there in his words. "Her curiosity is overwhelming her nerves. Don't pay attention to her."

Ryan's current position on the fence was no accident. He had an unobstructed view to the pasture. And Midnight Rose had a full view of him. He was observing Sundancer as much as he was waiting out the mare.

Elsie praised Sundancer softly and expanded to circle more of the pasture. Dozens of turns later, Ryan finally okayed the gelding to trot. Sundancer transitioned easily, seeming more than ready. More than eager. Ryan finally smiled. "It's good to see he's back to himself."

What about you, cowboy? Elsie pulled back her words and slowed Sundancer.

Midnight Rose had finally joined Ryan. He held his lower body completely still. No doubt to keep from startlingly the mare. The only constant was his continuous words of affection and praise for the horse.

Elsie held her breath. Mesmerized by the pair. By his extreme patience. By how he gave the mare his undivided attention. As if he had all the time in the world to sit there. With her. Until she was comfortable. Until she trusted him.

Carefully, he raised one arm. The movement slow. Quiet. For one gentle stroke along her sleek neck. He rewarded her with a carrot. More praise. Time stilled or perhaps it was that Elsie could've sat there and watched the pair all day. There was something extraordinary—and touching—in the simplicity of a horse and a cowboy. Healing each other.

The mare nuzzled his shoulder. And Ryan beamed as if he'd just won the greatest prize. He offered the mare an apple. "Sorry, Midnight Rose, I'm out of treats. You'll have to settle for grass like Butter-Belle."

The mare snorted and shook her beautiful mane. Her thick tail twitched higher. Ryan chuckled. "You're definitely a beauty. And I'm going to be spoiling you something bad, I can already see it."

And Elsie could already see the bond forming between the pair. She nudged Sundancer closer to the fence. "You're really good with horses."

"I like the connection." Ryan watched Midnight Rose extend her head over the fence to graze near Butter-Belle. He grinned. "Don't get me wrong. The thrill of riding a bucking bronc for eight seconds is quite addicting. But this connection, it's special."

"And it's lasting." Like the connection she was beginning to feel with her cowboy.

"Exactly." Ryan braced his hands on the fence and studied her. "There's no pretense. They give so much more than they ever take. If you take care of your horse, they will take care of you."

Could I trust you to take care of my heart? I could take care of yours. Elsie urged Sundancer into a trot around the pasture as if that would prod her thoughts back into line.

When she passed closer to him again, he said, "You ride well." He paused then added, amusement and a touch of impatience in his words, "Let me guess, Josh taught you to ride, didn't he?"

She caught her laughter, but couldn't stop her smile. "Why would you think that?"

"Well, Carter taught you to drive, and Caleb taught you to dance." His words sounded surly. "You learned something from all my brothers. So, it makes sense. Josh is a well-known horse trainer."

"But your brother wasn't a trainer back then." She chuckled then added, "Josh gave me tips, but I took lessons." She slowed Sundancer to a walk in front of him. Then as they moved away, she glanced over her shoulder and called out, "I wanted to impress a cowboy I liked."

Then she urged Sundancer out of talking range for another loop around the pasture. On her return, she checked her grin. Now her cowboy definitely looked surly too.

At her approach, he straightened slowly on the fence. "And was your cowboy impressed?"

Elsie shrugged. Passed him. Then circled Sundancer back around and met Ryan's gaze. She said, "He never asked me to ride that summer. I never got to show him. Then I left for college."

Something shifted over his face. Her breath caught. He eased off the fence. His boots landed softly in the grassy pasture. Her heart thumped in her chest.

He watched her. She watched him. Neither moved. Both waited.

Her pulse raced. Her stomach wobbled.

They'd been circling around this moment for a while. She should've held on to her secrets. She wasn't a risk-taker. Not with her heart. But here. With him. She wanted…

Wanted to know if she could be enough for this cowboy. Even if only for one moment. This one. Because they only had this one.

Finally, he stepped forward. Slow. Easy. As if giving her the opportunity to back out. Elsie exhaled, slow and deep. It was only one small risk. A test of that spark she felt. Surely that wasn't too much. Nothing she couldn't come back from, right?

He was beside her. His focus on her completely. Fully. He said, "I think that's enough for Sundancer today."

But they were far from finished. Her words were breathless. "I can get down myself."

"I'd rather help you." He reached up. His hands settled around her waist.

His touch gentle. Steady. But the choice was hers. Lean in. Lean away. One risk. Her pulse pounded. Her hands fell to his shoulders. One minute she was seated on Sundancer. The next, his arms wound around her waist. He held her closer than the evening before. Impossible. Perfect.

His thumb brushed across her cheek. "Who was the cowboy?"

"You already know." Elsie curved her arms up around his neck. Curled her fingers in his hair touching his collar. Curiosity appeased. Her heart raced faster. Surely, he could feel it too.

He drew her tighter against him. "Why didn't you say anything?"

No backing out. She was where she wanted to be. She whispered, "You never looked my way that last summer."

"But I always saw you." His palms cupped her cheeks. The heat in his gaze skimming over her face was better than a caress. His voice was rough. "Same as I'm seeing you now."

"It was for the best." She searched his gaze.

"Says who?" he asked.

She no longer knew what was best. Knew only she was lost to him. In him. She trailed her fingers over his bearded cheek. "I want to kiss you, but we both know it's a bad idea."

He leaned into her touch. "Does it make it worse to know I want to kiss you too? More than anything I've ever wanted."

Her heart tumbled. She wasn't falling alone. But who would catch them after? "Somehow it makes it better."

"Are you going to kiss me then?" he asked, his words hesitant. Tentative as if he feared her reply.

"I shouldn't." But she wanted to. Despite all the reasons not to. "What about you?"

"I should let you go." He tipped his head toward the gate. "Walk on out of this pasture. And keep on walking."

She stayed anchored in his embrace. "Why don't you?"

"Gran Claire always told me that I never did what I should." That half grin returned. The one she found so appealing. The one she thought of as hers. For her. He added, "Seems I haven't gotten over that flaw quite yet."

"We should both move away." Her words were too breathless to carry any force. Any conviction.

Still, he nodded. His fingers flexed around her back as if he was preparing to let go. He cleared his throat. "Say when."

"On three."

"One." He leaned toward her.

"Two." She met him halfway.

And their lips connected. That spark flamed. And caught. Surrounding them both. He wasn't reluctant. She was far from shy. It was remarkable. Thoroughly perfect. And over entirely too soon.

The kiss slowed. Still her heart beat too fast. Her knees wanted to buckle. Her mind was scattered.

Yet, she wanted another kiss. Just one more.
Elsie opened her eyes. Their gazes collided. Held.
And they both said, "Three."

CHAPTER SEVENTEEN

EVEN THE DEVIL was laughing now. When would Ryan ever learn to walk away?

Ryan released Elsie. Before he kissed her again. Before he got swept up in her completely.

Once was…not ever going to be enough.

Now he knew that with the same certainty that he knew being thrown from a twelve-hundred-pound bucking bronc was going to sting. But a fall from a bronc he would recover from. Something told him there might be no getting over Elsie. If he let himself fall.

He looked at her. Her cheeks flushed. Her silver eyes wide. Her lips parted. Part flustered. Part mystified. As if she was as unbalanced by that kiss as he was. She was adorable and captivating. And everything he could want. If only.

He rubbed the back of his neck, searched for words. How was he supposed to make this right? When everything he wanted to say was wrong.

I don't regret that.

I can't apologize.

Can I kiss you again?

But he had to say something. Anything. He started, "Elsie…"

She bit into her bottom lip and shook her head. Her gaze imploring. "Don't. We can't." Pause. "We knew." Another pause. "We shouldn't."

Ryan closed his mouth. He wanted to pull her back into his arms. Convince her they should. But she was right. He couldn't. She was leaving soon. And his heart had never been up for grabs. Never been on the line. And one world-tilting kiss wouldn't change that. "What now?"

Before she could answer, his phone chimed. The sound crackled between them like a divide.

"You should answer that," she said.

"It can wait." He kept his focus fixed on her.

"At least see who it is," she urged. "It could be someone important."

You're important too. To me. More words that would only make a complicated situation even more so. *You're important, but I can't give you what you deserve.* He sighed and took his phone out of his back pocket. He frowned at the screen. Talk about impeccable timing.

"Who is it?" Elsie prodded.

"My mom," he replied.

"You have to answer her," she said, her voice insistent. "It's your mom."

"It's complicated between us," he admitted. Seemed he had a talent for finding complicated relationships.

"Ryan," she said, resolve in her words. "Answer it."

He pressed the accept button on the screen. Maybe—just maybe—when he finished this conversation, he would have the right words for Elsie. The video call opened, and Ryan greeted his mother. He turned, adjusting the angle of the phone until the sun wasn't blocking his mother's face on the phone screen.

"Fletcher has been texting you all morning, Ryan." His mother skipped over any pleasantries and got straight to the point, as was her style. She continued, "He has a new list of places he wants to show you."

Ryan squeezed his forehead with his other hand.

Unfazed, his mother asked, "Are you free in the next hour?"

He lifted his gaze over the phone and caught sight of Elsie's moving truck in the distance. Well, it looked like he was free for the rest of his life. He said, "Sure. I can meet him."

"Alone?" his mother said, displeasure in her expression.

He wasn't entirely sure he wanted to be alone. But Elsie was moving to New York for the life she wanted. Besides, what did Ryan even know about sticking around? He'd only ever stuck to one thing—the rodeo. Once he was back on the circuit, he'd be on the move again too. Just the way he always preferred it. "I'll be fine."

His mother frowned. "Surely there's someone who can go with you, for both our sakes."

For both their sakes, Ryan hoped this house-hunting endeavor ceased soon. He already had one woman turning his world upside down. At least Elsie had warned him from the start that she was leaving. It wasn't a goodbye he wanted to face. Still, he didn't need his mom coming in only to back out of his life all over again as well.

"Ryan." His mother's sharp voice pulled his attention to her. "Who is that behind you?"

Ryan shifted, realized Elsie and Sundancer were standing in range of the camera lens. "That's Elsie Parks. She is Marlena Doyle's niece. They are our neighbors."

His mother leaned closer to the camera. "And she's a friend of yours?"

Of sorts. The lines were certainly blurred now. He scratched his cheek. "I'm helping her at the farm. Her brother had an accident last week."

"How serious?" The physician Lilian Sloan stepped forward. "Is he okay? Recovering at home?"

"He fell through the greenhouse roof. His ankle suffered the most damage, but Grant already did surgery," Ryan explained. "He's being discharged this afternoon."

At Grant's name, pride washed over his mother's face. "Well, it's fortunate Grant is there. Her brother will no doubt be walking again soon, thanks to your brother." She paused and seemed to check her appearance in the camera then said, "Introduce us, please."

"Mother," Ryan started.

"Ryan," she interrupted then continued patiently, "It may come as a surprise to learn that people do like me. That I have more to offer than a medical prognosis."

He wondered what his mom's prognosis would be for his heart. Lost cause, most likely. He didn't need a medical degree for that. He said, "Hold on." Then lowered the phone and twisted around. "Elsie. She wants to meet you."

Elsie moved beside him. He whispered an apology and then completed the introductions.

To his surprise, his mother was correct. Elsie seemed to like Lilian Sloan almost immediately. At least their conversation flowed easily, as if they understood each other. Within minutes, Elsie had his phone in her grasp and full control of the conversation.

It was both bewildering and fascinating. Ryan had Sundancer's saddle and gear removed before the conversation between the women had even wound down. It was several more minutes before Elsie disconnected. She joined him, reached over to rub Sundancer and grinned. "Your mom is going to help me locate an apartment in New York. Can you believe that?"

There was so much he didn't want to believe. Like Elsie really was leaving. He lifted the saddle and started for the gate. "My mother has lived in New York for decades and she's well-connected. You couldn't ask for a better re-source than her."

Unless of course you wanted to stay here. Then I could show you... Ryan ground his teeth together. There was nothing more to show Elsie. Except that he was as tempo-rary in town as her. His boots sank in the dirt as if testing the ground for roots. But he was too restless. Too much of a cowboy rambler seeking his next adrenaline-fueled ride. And more likely to trip over those roots than plant them. He lengthened his strides, heading for the stable.

Elsie kept pace beside him. "So, in exchange for her help in New York, I'm going to join you for those house showings today."

"You definitely don't have to do that," Ryan managed, even though relief loosened his shoulders.

"It's already decided." Elsie opened the door to the stable for him. "You're stuck with me for a while longer today."

Would you mind being stuck with me for something like, say, forever? He frowned and ducked into the tack room. He was seriously in bad. But not too deep he couldn't still get out intact.

He just had to set things straight between them. En-sure they were both on the same page as it were. How hard could that be?

As it happened, one simple conversation was proving very hard to have. And not through any fault of his own, actu-ally. It was simply a matter of bad timing and no privacy.

Ryan had left Elsie after his mother's video chat to shower and change. Fletcher had picked Ryan up. And Elsie had agreed to meet them in her own car, as she'd planned to collect the girls and head to the hospital for Bryce's discharge afterward. That meant between Fletcher's escort and the multiple video calls to his mother, Ryan had no alone time with Elsie.

Then he'd returned home only to find his entire family preparing to descend on the Doyle farm that evening. Tess thoughtfully prepared dinner for the group to bring over before she and Carter headed to Belleridge to purchase more supplies for the babies' room. His grandfather and uncle made their special dessert. And Grant claimed he wanted to check on his recently discharged patient. Then Caleb decided he was perfectly content eating a meal he didn't have to prepare himself. Worse, his grandfather pressed the butterscotch and rum bread pudding dish in Ryan's hands, ushering him back to his truck before Ryan could come up with an excuse not to attend dinner at the Doyle farm.

Now he was standing on the front porch of Elsie's house with his family, holding a glass casserole dish and realizing that conversation with Elsie was going to have to wait a while longer. He only hoped he could keep his attraction to Elsie in check a few more hours. If his family caught on, there would be nothing but more problems.

Maggie jumped out of her truck and joined them on the porch as Elsie opened the front door.

Maggie's irritation was obvious and directed solely at Ryan. She frowned and said, "Ryan, we were supposed to practice this afternoon."

One more thing he hadn't dealt with yet. The tinfoil crinkled underneath his tense grip.

Elsie stepped in and eased the dish from Ryan's grasp. "Sorry, that was my fault. I promised Lilian when Ryan and I spoke to her that we'd see as many houses as we could today." Then she added, "I also told Lilian's real estate agent, Fletcher, that we had time to look at a few more houses before I checked with Ryan to make sure that was okay with his schedule."

Maggie appeared mollified.

As for Ryan, he appreciated the save. But he couldn't keep hiding. Especially not behind Elsie. Not only was she not going to be there. It just wasn't right. At least he'd had one small victory that afternoon. A short ride on Mischief, his mustang. It was a step.

"Wait." Grant moved beside Ryan and slung his arm over Ryan's shoulders. "Elsie talked to our mother. With you. Today."

Ryan nodded.

"We had a very nice conversation in fact," Elsie stated. "Lilian was very appreciative of our assistance. We even found several places both Ryan and Lilian agreed on."

"Elsie, you're a miracle worker." Grant squeezed Ryan's shoulders then followed Elsie into the house.

Caleb laughed and joined the pair. "I seriously think this might be the first time Ryan has ever agreed with our mother on anything."

Ryan held back, let his grandfather and uncle inside before him and put more distance between him and Elsie. How was it possible she looked even prettier that evening? In another flowy sort of sundress. With her long hair twisted into a casual bun, showcasing her mesmerizing silver-gray eyes. He wanted to pull her into his arms and get lost in her all over again. He feared it was going to be a long night.

Unfortunately, his sister-in-law lingered too. Maggie eyed him and toyed with her wedding ring on her finger. "Rumor has it you didn't come home last night."

Ryan tipped his head back and stared at the white shiplap ceiling over his head. "It's not a rumor, Mags. You and everyone in the family know I was here with Elsie and the girls last night."

"Of course, we know where you *were*." Maggie chuckled. "But I want to know where you *are*."

He dropped his chin and eyed her. "I'm standing right here."

"Don't do that. We've been friends for far too long." She punched his shoulder lightly. "You know exactly what I'm asking."

He also knew he had no good answer. Certainly not one he believed Maggie would buy. They had been friends too long. Traveled too long on the rodeo road together and shared more than one secret with each other over the years. But Maggie was head-over-boots in love with his brother and Grant with her. Couples like that tended to color every situation with love-tinted markers, wanting everyone to have what they shared.

Yet love couldn't be what was between Elsie and him. Because Ryan had only ever committed to things where his success was guaranteed. If he believed, worked hard enough and trusted in himself, that is. But he never trusted love. Not enough to believe in it for himself.

He gripped Maggie's shoulders, turned her around and gently nudged her inside. Then he followed her. "I'm right where I was the last time we discussed this, Mags. Firmly in the friend zone."

That was where he belonged. And if he dwelled on the incredible kiss he'd shared with Elsie that morning for the rest of his days, well, that was his business.

Maggie opened her mouth.

Ryan shook his head. "Let it go, Mags." He certainly was. "Trust me, it's better this way."

And if his heart disagreed, well, that was of no consequence. He couldn't remember the last time he'd ever truly paid his heart any mind anyway.

CHAPTER EIGHTEEN

ELSIE WAS RUNNING out of patience. Not that she wasn't grateful for the delicious meal the Sloan family brought over so she didn't have to cook that evening. Leaving her free to see to her brother's comfort on his first night home from the hospital. Really, she appreciated every one of the Sloans.

However, what she didn't appreciate was not having one moment—not even a minute—alone with her cowboy. There were things that needed to be said. Things she needed to tell him.

That was why she was stalling in the kitchen, trying to catch Ryan's attention through the wide window that looked out over the porch.

Her brother had decided he wanted to eat outside. They'd set him up on one of the cushioned chairs with his ankle propped at the appropriate height on pillows stacked on an end table. Then they'd adjusted the large outdoor table near enough for him to reach his plate. Dinner had been lively and entertaining and animated. Despite Elsie and Ryan being seated at opposite ends of the table. Again.

"Dessert is served." Sam walked into the kitchen and interrupted Elsie's third slow pass in front of the wide window.

Startled, she spun around and took in the two older cowboys.

Sam's grin stretched into his white beard as if he knew

exactly what she was up to. Then he motioned toward the island. "We just came to pick up our bowls and make sure you were joining us too, Elsie."

"We'll help you clean up those dinner dishes before we leave," Roy promised. He scooped a large dollop of whipped cream over a piece of butterscotch bread pudding and handed the bowl to Elsie.

"And we just wanted to thank you while we have you to ourselves for a moment." Sam plunked more whipped cream on his dessert.

"I should be the one thanking you for this meal." And so much more. Elsie passed out spoons.

"Ryan told us it was you who convinced him to prep our dandelion field," Sam admitted. "We sure do appreciate you."

"And the dandelion seed you found us too." Roy took a bite of his bread pudding and grinned around the mouthful. "We'll be planting that soon enough. And just waiting on those dandelions to bloom."

Elsie pictured the wide field of yellow blossoms. Now the pair would have something to remember her by. She knew she wouldn't be forgetting the two cowboys anytime soon. "Well, don't forget to save me some wine from your first batch."

"You can count on that." Sam held his arm out to escort her back to the porch. "We will have a bottle for you ready and waiting for when you come on back home to us."

Back home. The words swirled around Elsie, yet she was afraid to let them settle fully.

Roy held open the door. "And we will share a few glasses together."

"I can't wait," Elsie said and meant it. She was already looking forward to coming back and hadn't even left yet. She slid into her chair and told herself not to make anything of it. Her brother and nieces lived there now. Of course, she would want to return.

"Auntie, where is Marty going to sleep when you leave?" Autumn asked from the other end of the table where she slipped Butter-Belle a grape and gave the goat a quick pat. "Marty sure likes your moving truck a bunch."

The other conversations around the table quieted at Autumn's question. Elsie's spoon stilled in the butter rum sauce pooled around her bowl of butterscotch bread pudding. The sweetness was suddenly too heavy in her mouth. Too cloying in her throat. She reached for her water glass and searched for a conversation detour.

"Maybe you could leave that truck and get a different one," Gemma offered. She plucked a cherry from the top of her ice cream sundae with her fingers. "Then Marty can still sleep on it, and he won't be sad."

"I'm afraid that truck has to come with me," Elsie said gently. Then took another sip of water. Already foreseeing the conversation slipping where she hadn't wanted it to go. Not yet. Not before she talked to her cowboy alone. "It has all my stuff in it."

"You could keep your stuff here." Gemma watched her from her seat beside her sister. Hope lifted her words an octave. "Then you could stay too."

Elsie set her spoon down and kept her gaze on her nieces. "I've got a job and people waiting for me in the city."

Autumn rubbed her nose and frowned. "But we'll be waiting for you here."

"So, you have to come right back," Gemma declared then nodded as if it was all settled.

But nothing was settled. Elsie chanced a glance at Ryan. He sat across from the girls and next to Elsie's brother. He leaned back in his chair as if he'd extended his long legs out under the table. His posture was casual. His fingers tapped a silent beat on the armrest. He never looked her way.

"How about we let Aunt Elsie get to New York and get settled," Bryce suggested then brushed his fingers lightly across Gemma's nose. "Then we can talk about when she can come back to see us."

Gemma wrinkled her nose.

Autumn straightened in her chair and grinned, the way she did when she solved a hard math problem. "How about we go with Auntie when she leaves Monday?"

There it was. That bit she'd wanted to tell Ryan. Before anyone else. She slanted her gaze toward him. He'd gone still. Even his fingers stopped tapping. *Look at me. Please.*

Bryce smoothed his hand over his mouth then smiled at his daughters. His words sympathetic. His expression affectionate. "I'm afraid Monday is a school day."

"And we can't miss school." Gemma jammed her spoon into her ice cream sundae, looking defeated.

Elsie felt a bit defeated herself. "You can come visit me," she suggested. Ryan's gaze collided with hers across the table. *You could too, cowboy.* To what end? Another goodbye. Best to leave whatever it was between them right here in town. She smiled at her nieces. "I would really like to show you the city."

Autumn perked up. "Can we, Dad?"

"Yes, we will certainly plan a trip to visit your aunt this summer," Bryce assured his daughters.

The girls returned to their ice cream bowls with more enthusiasm than before.

"You're leaving Monday." Maggie sat on the porch swing with Grant. Her husband dipped his spoon into Maggie's bowl. Maggie handed Grant her dessert to finish and frowned at Elsie. "That's so soon, Elsie. I was hoping we'd have more time to spend together."

Elsie nodded then explained, "I got a call late this afternoon from my new boss. The Heartscape Foundation lost its venue unexpectedly and my hotel agreed to host their gala. It's in less than three weeks with a guest count of over five hundred. They need my help now." Elsie paused and added, "I already have several video conferences scheduled for tomorrow and Friday."

"Elsie is calm under pressure." Bryce grinned at her. "She's exactly who they need. She'll make the gala a big success."

Elsie appreciated her brother's support.

"Then it's good timing with your aunt and mom returning from their travels tomorrow," Sam mused.

Yet it felt mostly like really bad timing. Still, it was one kiss that Ryan and she had shared. Not a promise exchanged. Not the start of something. They'd both known that. Accepted it. Elsie pushed her bread pudding bowl away and forced herself to smile. "I'm looking forward to hearing about their trip."

"We need to sit down and discuss your budget, Els." Bryce stacked the girls' empty sundae bowls into his bowl. "I've worked out several scenarios to help with your apartment search."

Yet Elsie hadn't worked out one scenario where it worked between her and her cowboy. Elsie collected Sam's and Roy's empty bowls. Caleb gathered the other dessert bowls like a trained waiter and headed toward the sliding glass door. Elsie added, "No business talk tonight, Bryce. You just got home."

"I must say it's good to be out of that hospital bed and outdoors again. Breathing fresh air." Bryce stretched his arms over his head then pressed his palm against his stomach. "But I think I ate enough for the next week."

Murmurs of agreement rolled across the table.

Caleb returned and swiped a hand over his mouth. "Elsie, if you're not going to take advantage of your brother's skills with numbers and finances, can I?"

Elsie laughed and waved toward her brother. "He's all yours."

"How about we play some cards while we chat?" Bryce ran his hand through his hair. "I seem to recall I need to win back the money from the last time we played."

"Deal me in." Caleb rubbed his hands together. "I don't want your wallet to be too heavy. It might slow down your recovery."

Bryce laughed. "Not a chance."

"Count us in too." Maggie stood then grabbed Grant's hand. "We really like beating you guys."

"Don't be counting those winnings before you've collected 'em," Sam said then he pointed to his place mat. "Deal Roy and me in too, Bryce. We've bested all you more than once."

"Tonight won't be much different." Roy chuckled.

"Elsie," Sam said. "You in?"

Elsie looked at Ryan.

Just then Autumn skirted around the table and took hold of Ryan's hand. "Cowboy Prince, can you take us to say good-night to Midnight Rose and Sundancer?"

"We gotta give 'em good-night wishes," Gemma added. "So they have sweet dreams."

"I would love to do that." Fondness softened across Ryan's face. He stood, kept his hand in Autumn's and took hold of Gemma's. Then the trio stepped off the porch and walked away. Butter-Belle trailing after them.

And something twisted in Elsie's chest. Nothing that hurt her. Nothing she couldn't handle. She rolled her lips together then offered the table a small smile. "Just give me a minute." *To work that catch out of my chest*. She added, "I'll go inside and find those playing cards."

Elsie returned and handed the deck of cards to Caleb. She glanced at her empty chair and admitted she was too restless to sit. Too out of sorts to pay attention. Checking to see if her guests needed anything else, she offered an excuse that she wanted to check on Ryan and the girls then retreated before anyone stopped her.

She took her time walking to the stables. Wandered by the greenhouses. Checked on the seedlings. Peeked into the goat pen. Noted Smarty Marty was still out carousing somewhere on the property. The stable door swung open. She heard the girls' giggles before she saw her nieces. They rushed toward her for quick hugs, then decided to go on a hunt for Smarty Marty. Each one certain they knew where Marty was.

And like that, Elsie had what she wanted. Her cowboy alone. All she had to do was open the stable door. Step inside. Yet she hesitated. *Come on, Elsie. City girls are stronger than this*. Elsie pushed her shoulders back and walked into the stable.

The interior was dim. The sun minutes away from setting completely. She made her way toward Sundancer's stall. Ryan's quiet murmurs drew her to Midnight Rose's stall instead. She stopped and held her breath. Not wanting to interrupt the pair.

Midnight Rose's dark head was bent, resting against Ryan's shoulder. His hands rubbed her elegant neck. And Elsie captured the image in her mind. She knew when she thought of the pair, this was the moment she would always remember.

Seconds passed. Minutes. It seemed the bond between cowboy and horse only strengthened. Right before her eyes.

Midnight Rose's ear twitched. The horse's head lifted.

Ryan twisted and looked right at Elsie. Caught, Elsie stilled and offered him a small smile. "Sorry. I was checking on the girls."

Ryan nodded then gave the Arabian one more rub and more whispered words. Then he walked to the stall door.

Elsie watched him. "What did you tell her?"

The corner of his mouth twitched. His expression secretive. His gaze unreadable. "I told her that she's going to be okay."

The same words Elsie had given him last night.

He stepped out and slid the stall door closed. "I also told her I'm going to be okay too."

"You sound like you believe that?" Elsie strolled beside him toward the main door.

"I rode today. Bareback." He held the door open for her. "Just for pleasure. Nothing formal. Nothing fast."

But he'd gotten back on a horse. Elsie liked to think she had some small part in that. That maybe she left some small lasting impression on her cowboy. She smiled. "This is good news."

"I found myself inspired recently." He seemed amused. His shoulders relaxed. His words rolled out easily. "It felt right. Better than that actually. I can't remember the last time I rode for fun. For the pure joy of riding."

He was finding his way back to where he belonged. She could see the joy in his gaze and the relief in his expression. He even stood a little straighter as if he'd found that footing he'd been missing. He'd be practicing soon enough. She'd bet on it. After that, back to the circuit full-time. "I'm really glad for you, Ryan."

"Thanks." He sobered, tucked his hands into the back pockets of his jeans and moved toward the house. "So, Monday is the day then."

His steps were slow. The pace unrushed. Easy for her to keep up. "I wanted to tell you earlier. Several times."

He nodded then said, "It sounds like you're needed. They'll be lucky to have you on their team."

Enough. Enough with the polite. Enough with the courteous. Elsie turned, stepped right in front of him. Stopped him completely. Her words dropped like a challenge. "I'm not sorry we kissed this morning."

"Is that so?" He crossed his arms over his chest and rubbed his cheek.

She notched her chin higher. Like a dare. "Yes."

"That's good to know." He stepped around her and continued on toward the house.

Elsie jumped and grabbed his arm, turning him back to face her. "That's all you have to say?" That can't be all. One kiss. Nothing more. *You're leaving, Els. Of course, there isn't more. Get it together.*

"Elsie Marie." His sigh was wrapped around her name like a ribbon. His gaze trailed over her face. One corner of his mouth finally lifted but barely enough to dent his cheek. "Elsie Marie, I'm not sorry for any time I've gotten to spend with you. And I'm especially not sorry about our kiss."

Her breath escaped. The breath she hadn't realized she'd been holding. Behind her, she heard voices and laughter on the back porch. Still, she searched his gaze. For what, she wasn't certain. His words should be more than enough. Yet a tremor passed through her smile. "Then we are okay?"

"Yeah." He eased around her again. "We're okay."

CHAPTER NINETEEN

ELSIE TOLD HERSELF she was still okay four days later. Despite not a single run-in with her cowboy. Or even a fly-by sighting of the man. Even though he'd been around the farm. That she knew thanks to her family's reports.

Aunt Marlena had a lovely visit with him in the stables the morning after her return from overseas. Bryce talked hive management with him just yesterday. Gemma and Autumn fed the goats lettuce with him before school both days. And even Elsie's mom ran into him on her morning nature walk. *Two days in a row.*

Her cowboy had certainly been around. He just hadn't been around Elsie. At least not close enough for her to test out exactly how okay she was.

I'm fine. She was fine. Nothing wrong with reminding herself that a couple dozen times a day.

Besides, she'd been busy herself. Mostly on video conference calls with her new team at the ritzy hotel. Organizing the last-minute charity gala for the Heartscape Foundation and getting familiar with the other upcoming events already on the schedule. The workload would be far from light. But she was ready for the challenge. Welcomed it like always because she was fine. *I'm fine.*

Good, really. It was better not to see Ryan again anyway. This way she would leave with bruises on her heart, not broken pieces. And some day in the future, when she thought of him, she'd even feel happy. That was enough.

Elsie straightened the postcards then the bottles of honey on the display she'd created that morning when she'd set up the Sweet House of Bees booth at It's Blooming Spring. That had been hours ago. Lunch had passed and dinner was approaching and still, she manned the booth.

Her mother and aunt had floated in and out with Autumn and Gemma throughout the day. But they'd left to bring the worn-out girls home for the night. Noticing her mom and aunt both looked equally weary, Elsie had told them to stay home too. Promised them that she was perfectly fine closing up the booth herself. As it was, the crowd was thinning as the first of several live bands scheduled to play that night had taken the stage.

Elsie greeted a cheerful couple and handed the wife a honey sample. Then she spotted a familiar foursome approaching the booth and her smile widened. She waved to the Baker sisters and the older cowboy duo accompanying them.

Sam Sloan worked his way into the booth and gave her a hearty hug. Then he leaned away, his hands still resting on her shoulders. His gaze twinkling, he asked, "You know what day it is, Elsie?"

"Saturday," Elsie said. The others piled into the booth and surrounded Sam.

"Do you know what Saturdays are good for?" Gayle asked. The lively retiree had traded her usual denim-colored overalls for a pair of poppy-red ones. Underneath she wore a cream-colored shirt with flowers embroidered down both sleeves. Her eyebrows spiked higher, revealing her matching pink-red eyeshadow.

Elsie shook her head.

"Dates." Breezy smoothed her fingers through her short hair as if fixing herself for said dates. Then she leaned forward, set her hand on the side of her mouth and whispered loudly, "And we have it on good authority that you and Ryan already have a Saturday date night scheduled."

"Well, that was just…" A silly thing with her nieces. Ryan hadn't been serious. Elsie touched her ponytail then the back of her neck. Then finally tucked her hands into the pockets of the yellow apron Aunt Marlena had made with the words: *It's a bee thing.* "Who told you about that?"

"The most reliable sources in the Doyle household," Roy chimed in then fluffed his salt-and-pepper curls. "It was Gemma and Autumn, of course. When we shared cotton candy and funnel cakes with them at lunch today."

"My nieces are wonderful, but I'm not sure they're the most reliable of sources." Elsie winced. Although they'd been correct. Tonight was Ryan's and her supposed date night.

"Don't worry about not being dressed in your fancy date clothes," Breezy assured her and linked her arm around Elsie's. "The best dates are the ones that are spur-of-the-moment. Everyone acts more like themselves. More natural and genuine instead of stuffy and reserved."

"Isn't that the truth." Gayle nodded and grinned as if remembering her own spontaneous date nights.

Not that anyone would ever consider the Baker sisters standoffish or unfriendly. They were more dynamic and persuasive. And for two petite older women, decidedly determined. Like right now. Breezy guided Elsie out of the booth with a single-minded precision. That didn't break until Elsie found herself standing right in Ryan's path.

He was there. Her cowboy. She was fine. Better than that. She couldn't stop looking at him. Clean jeans. Polished boots. Pressed button-down sky blue Paisley-print shirt. Cowboy hat. *Where have you been? I missed you.* Elsie swallowed, her throat suddenly dry. *But I'm fine.*

"Well, it seems to me that your date has arrived, Elsie."

Delight circled around Breezy's bright announcement before she released the bow holding Elsie's apron around her neck.

"What about the booth?" *What about my heart? The one I wasn't going to break.* Elsie caught the apron, but Breezy snatched it out of her grip.

"We've got it covered," Sam called out and appeared at Elsie's other side. "We're going to take turns manning the booth for the evening."

"That way we can sneak over and dance a quickstep or two," Breezy confided and patted Elsie's arm. "Then we'll come back and let the others have a turn on the dance floor too."

"But you two take all the turns around the dance floor that you like." Gayle spread her arms and completed an intricate series of dance steps weaving between Ryan and Elsie. Then the spry retiree grinned wide at Elsie. "I've found the dance floor is one of the best places to get swept off your feet."

But Elsie didn't want to be swept off her feet. She wanted her feet on the ground. Firmly. And solidly. She watched Ryan. Surely, he wasn't interested in a date. With her. Where could that lead?

"A commitment is a commitment," Sam said with pride and determination. "You gave your word to take Elsie on a Saturday night date, Ryan. Gran Claire would be sorely disappointed if you broke your word. Same as I will be."

Ryan held out his hand toward Elsie, his smile compassionate. "I really don't think they're going to let this alone."

Elsie dropped her hand in his. And, too late, discovered her error. Their hands fit. In just that right way. No readjusting. No awkward finger maneuvering. Just a simple slide and joining as if their fingers were always meant to link. Just that way. The way she'd always been searching for. *Let go.*

Ryan's grip tightened as if he felt it too. And Elsie allowed him to lead her away. Her hand in his. As if she never meant to let go.

"Are you hungry?" he asked, breaking the silence between them. "We can eat. Or dance if you want."

"Dance," she said. Then there would be no words. Nothing revealed she might later regret. Nothing said she would want to take back.

He nodded and guided her out onto the dance floor. The music was upbeat. The steps quick. He danced as well as his brother Caleb. Partnered her like no one ever had. And Elsie escaped into the moment. Twirling. Laughing. Matching him step for step. Beat for beat.

Then the music slowed.

He didn't release her. Simply brought her into his embrace and said, "Elsie."

"Let's not." She reached up, touched his cheek. "Can we just dance?" *Can you hold me? Just for now. Then I can pretend you'll be holding on to me forever.*

He pulled her in closer. Close enough she tucked her cheek against his chest. Close enough she felt the beat of his heart. And pretended her own wasn't breaking.

Pretended she really was fine after all.

CHAPTER TWENTY

TAILLIGHTS. THAT WAS the last Ryan thought he'd see of Elsie.

They had danced until the last set the evening before. Then they'd closed up the festival booth together with his uncle and grandfather. Afterward, he'd walked Elsie to her car. Then he'd waited in the parking lot, watching her taillights disappear down the road. The last he'd heard from her had been a text, letting him know she'd arrived home safely. His reply: a thumbs-up emoji.

And that was where it was supposed to end with Elsie Marie Parks. A thumbs-up emoji. Proof they were okay. Just like he'd told her they were the other night at the stables.

They'd both known there couldn't ever be more between them. One kiss. One moment. One goodbye. And they were both okay.

Or so he'd assumed.

Never would he have imagined that his girl from the city would be the one to get him back in the saddle and riding no-holds-barred into the night.

But he was in the Sloan stables at that very moment, saddling his mustang, Mischief. Trying not to panic. Trying not to worry. Trying not to let his fear override every bit of common sense. *I'm okay. She's okay. They're okay. Repeat.*

"We're going to find them." That from his younger

brother. Caleb worked quickly and efficiently to saddle Whiskey Moon in the neighboring stall.

Ryan forced himself to slow down. No sense rushing only to find himself sliding out of the saddle later when he galloped across Sloan land. And he would be galloping. And not slowing until he found Elsie and her nieces.

Less than fifteen minutes ago, Bryce had called Ryan. Worry and desperation thick in his voice. Elsie had taken the girls out on one last UTV ride around the property after dinner, but the trio hadn't returned. It was now more than an hour past sunset. More than four hours since they'd left the house. And the night was settling in faster and deeper.

Carter and Grandpa Sam had already jumped into a UTV and left. Grant and Maggie were en route from their house to the Doyle property. While Uncle Roy stayed behind with a concerned and very pregnant Tess. Ryan and Caleb had determined they could cover more ground on horseback.

There had been nothing to consider. Nothing to hesitate about. Ryan had to get to Elsie. Had to know she was safe. Unharmed. He had to hold her. Check her over for himself. And that meant getting in the saddle and riding harder than he ever had before.

Ryan led Mischief out of the stable, mounted and curved his fingers around the reins. Steady. Focus. *Please be okay.*

He reined in his worry. His fear for her and the girls. It was time to ride. Just ride.

With that, Ryan urged Mischief into a run with the barest pressure of his knees and settled into the saddle. Rode with one purpose: Elsie. Caleb rode beside him, his palomino quarter horse keeping pace. At the property line dividing Sloan and Doyle land, the brothers slowed, nodded to each other and rode in separate directions as they'd agreed on earlier. With the plan to send up a flare when one of them located Elsie and the girls.

And the search began.

WHAT HAD SHE been thinking? That she'd driven a tractor. Plowed a field. And that suddenly qualified her for UTV exploration on open land she wasn't the least bit familiar with? *You're a fool, Elsie.* And a lost one at that. Not exactly the memory she'd wanted to leave her nieces with. *Hey, it's Auntie Elsie. The one who got you lost in the woods that night with no supplies. That was fun, right?*

Elsie grimaced and dug through the toolbox in the bed of the stalled UTV. Roy Sloan hadn't been wrong at the mud pit last week. The toolbox was woefully understocked. She dropped into the driver's seat and looked at her nieces. "Well, we've got a flashlight and a tire jack."

Autumn propped her feet on the front passenger seat and wrapped her arms around her raised knees. "But we don't have a flat tire."

Good thing that. There wasn't a spare tire anywhere. She passed the flashlight to Gemma in the back seat and said, "You're in charge of our light, Gemma." And hoped being in control would keep her niece's fear from getting the best of her.

Gemma straightened and her shoulders went back. Her face relaxed as her distress receded. Relief eased through Elsie.

"Auntie," Autumn said, her voice low as if she didn't want to disturb the night. "How lost are we?"

"Not so lost they won't find us." Elsie stretched as much optimism through her words as she could muster. But the truth was she couldn't exactly tell how lost they were.

They'd been headed to the waterwheel barn. But a wrong turn put them on the opposite side of the stream.

After the mud pit fiasco, Elsie was leery about driving into the water to cross it. So, they had searched for a bridge. Never found one and instead ended up losing sight of the stream when the woods swallowed them. Then the UTV died. Just stopped running. No warning. No heads-up. Her phone battery had less than ten percent left and worse, no signal. Now Elsie wasn't sure what to do next. Or which way was home. *Can't read your way out of this one, Els.*

"But Dad can't find us." Gemma leaned between the two front seats. "Dad can't walk or ride a horse."

"And Grandma's eyes are bad in the dark. That's what she always tells us," Autumn added then flung her arm out. "And Aunt Marlena's arches hurt from walking all over Egypt and back."

Panic washed out any lightness Elsie might've found in Autumn's pitiful declarations. Worse, Autumn wasn't wrong. It wasn't the strongest of search teams for certain. Still Elsie held out hope. It was all she had. Her nieces were too precious. "They'll get help."

"Cowboy Prince," Gemma declared and lifted the flashlight like a baton. "He'll come get us. Right, Auntie?"

If ever she needed her cowboy, it was now.

"What if he doesn't see us?" Autumn hunkered down in her seat. "It's getting awful dark out here."

I see you. I've always seen you, Elsie. That's what Ryan had claimed. Well, Elsie was starting to see now too. Even more clearly. That she didn't belong here. How many people did she have to put in danger to realize that? First Sam and Roy at the mud pit. Now her nieces. If she'd had any doubts—any second thoughts—about leaving last night, those were gone now.

After all, she hadn't required one cowboy rescue in all her years living in the city. Out here in the country, she couldn't claim the same. She reached over and took Autumn's hand in hers. "We are going to be fine."

"Because we are together." Gemma hopped out of the UTV and squeezed into the seat with her older sister. "Dad always tells us that we're stronger together."

Yet Elsie wasn't feeling quite so strong right now. She was worried she was something she'd never wanted to be—an inconvenience. Because of her, people were most likely out in the woods when they should be at home, safe with their families. One more reason she was better off alone. Even if she'd forgotten that this past week.

"I hope Cowboy Prince hurries." Autumn hugged Gemma. "We didn't get to tell Sundancer and Midnight Rose good-night. I hope they are okay."

Okay. That was how Elsie had ended the previous night with her cowboy. Ryan had hugged her outside her car last evening. Then he'd framed her face in his hands. His touch impossibly gentle. Impossibly tender. While she'd held on to him, finding it almost impossible to let go.

When their gazes had connected, he had said simply, "Okay."

And Elsie had swallowed everything she didn't want to say, like *Goodbye.* Everything she couldn't say, like *Come with me.* She'd nodded and managed a heartfelt "Okay" in return.

Then she'd climbed into her car, driven away and refused to look back. With her heart bruised, not in pieces. Small victory there.

Now she needed Ryan again. Elsie pressed her palm against that ache in her chest and concentrated on her nieces. "You know what? I think we should sing."

"We don't have any music." Autumn frowned.

"That's okay." Elsie tapped a beat on her leg. "I'm thinking if someone can't see us, then they might hear us." And if they were all belting out the words to their favorite songs, there would be no space for the worry.

"Cowboy Prince has good ears," Gemma confessed. "He heard me sneaking my broccoli to Butter-Belle at dinner one time."

There were a lot of things her cowboy hadn't heard from Elsie. But what good would sharing her feelings do if she wasn't sticking around? Or worse, what if she walked away from her career, left her life behind and instead bet it all on love? What happened when he realized she wasn't the life he wanted? When he gave up her love and her. After she'd lost her whole heart to him. Who would she be then?

Thanks, but no thanks. Not a risk she could take. That was a heartbreak she just might not get over. Besides, she hardly had a track record for success when it came to love. No, she was better off betting it all on her career and life in New York, not on love and her cowboy.

"Still, we should sing super loud," Autumn decided. "Just in case Cowboy Prince is far away."

How far away would be far enough for the pain in her chest to dull? Elsie looked at her nieces. "What song do we all know?"

"'Happy birthday,'" Gemma shouted.

"Good one." Elsie launched them into the birthday song. Followed by "The ABC Song," half a dozen nursery rhymes.

Until Autumn found her inspiration. "Christmas songs. We all know those."

"Those are my favorite." Gemma swayed in the passenger seat with her sister.

And they were off. Decking the halls. Rockin' round the Christmas tree. And dashing through the snow.

Elsie lifted her voice above her worry. And hoped for one last cowboy rescue.

CHAPTER TWENTY-ONE

ALMOST AN HOUR into the search, Elsie and the girls still hadn't been located.

The wheelhouse had turned up empty. Not even a sign they'd been there. Ryan had been convinced that was where Elsie would've gone.

He slowed Mischief. Searched the night sky for the green laser rescue flares that his family carried. Nothing. He checked his cell phone. No signal. He angled his flashlight toward the ground. Scanning for tracks—for anything really.

That was when he heard it. The first chorus of "Jingle Bells." He knew those off-key voices. Relief flooded him. He might have dropped to his knees if he wasn't seated atop Mischief. As it was, he dropped forward and hugged the reliable, loyal mustang. Then he stilled and listened. Got his bearings and followed the direction of the carolers. It was the sweetest off pitch rendition he'd ever heard.

When he was close enough to see the parked UTV and the shadowy figures huddled inside, he joined in with the carolers. Dismounted, continued his approach and his harmonizing.

It only took the first line of the chorus. Four words. Then silence from the UTV. Then a mad scramble. A shout for Cowboy Prince. Pounding footsteps. Two small figures careening into him. And he held his ground, waiting for the third.

Elsie never hesitated. Stepped straight into his arms. Buried her face against his chest then shuddered. Full body and powerful. So much so he tremored in turn. Then he pulled the trio even closer. Tethered them all together within his embrace. Grounded himself.

They're okay. They're okay. They're okay.

It was several minutes and several deep breaths all around before anyone spoke. Then they surrounded him in a half circle and talked all at once. As if getting the story out faster got rid of all their pent-up fear.

A drive. Sunset. Wrong turn. Another wrong turn. The stream. Too deep. No gas. Stalled. Lost. No signal. Flashlight. Tire thing. Together. Strong. And singing. Finally, Gemma cheered and exclaimed, "Then you found us, Cowboy Prince!"

Ryan decided to leave the retelling at that for now. He'd get the details filled in later. "And I'm glad I found you. How about we tell the others?"

"Others?" Elsie asked, worry skimmed across her pale face.

"Everyone is looking for you," he replied. "You have a lot of people who care about you guys."

"I caused a lot of trouble for everyone." Elsie rubbed her forehead. She looked weary and miserable.

And much too far away. Before Ryan could pull Elsie back into his arms and reassure her, Autumn captured his hand and tugged.

Distress filling her face, Autumn said, "The phone doesn't work out here, Cowboy Prince."

"We don't need a phone. I have something better." Ryan lifted Autumn into his arms and squeezed her gently. "Want to see?" At her nod, Ryan walked over to Mischief and opened the saddlebag. He took out two handheld laser flares and gave one to Autumn. "We're going to shine these green beams into the sky. And then they will use the light to locate us. Watch."

Gemma and Autumn both finally grinned, equally fascinated by the green laser beams extending toward the stars. Ryan positioned the flares on the UTV and patiently answered their questions about how the lasers worked. Then he gathered the trio back into the UTV. Gemma ran first to sit with him. Autumn sat with Elsie in the passenger seat. And Ryan skimmed his gaze over each one. Told himself again that they were all okay. It was all he needed. It was enough. For now.

"What should we do while we wait?" He flipped on the UTV headlights. One more signal for his family.

Gemma pointed at the sky. "We can wish on falling stars."

"We have to watch the stars, Gem." Autumn yawned loudly. "We can't look away or we might miss it."

"I'm watching." Gemma yawned too then burrowed into Ryan, flattening his shirt until it was comfortable under her cheek. Settled against him, she mused, "Auntie, you should watch for a shooting star too. Then you can wish to stay with us forever."

Elsie looked at Ryan. Her eyes shimmered from the tears pooled there. But her will was strong enough not to allow the escape of a single one.

And just then Ryan was certain Elsie would not be making that wish. Not tonight. Still, he reached over and linked his fingers with Elsie's. As if all he had to do was hold on tight enough.

Elsie didn't pull away. She kept her hand in his and buried her head in Autumn's hair.

Her skin was cold inside his. Her grip steady, if not distant. And Ryan knew. Knew to his already chilled core. This goodbye was going to hurt. He ached already.

His family arrived before a shooting star was spotted. Before wishes could be made. That was fitting. Ryan's heart wanted one wish. His head recognized the folly. Good thing, he'd never been a fool for love.

He loaded a sleepy Gemma, then an exhausted Autumn into the back of his family's UTV. Then covered the pair with the blankets Tess had tossed in back at their house. Carter and Sam left with the girls, eager to get them to their anxious dad. Meanwhile, Caleb refilled the gas tank on the stalled UTV and checked it over.

Minutes later, Caleb dropped the empty gas can into the UTV bed. His gaze passed from Ryan to Elsie and back, then he said, "The UTV is good to go. Started right up. I can take Mischief with me, and you can drive Elsie back to her place."

Elsie turned toward Ryan. Her gaze unreadable and her expression reserved. "Ryan, could we…"

No. Don't ask me. Please. He held his breath. Held her gaze. Willed her not to ask. Anything but that.

"Could we ride Mischief?" Her words were faint, but all too clear in the crisp evening air. "Could we take that ride together? I'm not ready…"

Her words fell away. He wasn't ready. Not to hold her in his arms one last time. Not to say goodbye again. He was already sinking. Already knew where this was leading. It was there in everything she wasn't saying. Ryan glanced at his brother, seeking a save.

But Caleb shook his head slightly then eased back and offered, "We can get the UTV tomorrow. No one is going to bother it out here tonight."

Tears pooled in her eyes again. Her whisper was as fragile as she looked. "Then we can ride together."

Together. All he wanted. All he couldn't have. Ryan

squeezed his eyes closed briefly, then nodded. "Caleb, you take the lead."

His brother looked all too relieved. Caleb was in his saddle and walking toward the trail before Ryan guided Elsie onto Mischief. Ryan swung up behind Elsie. Wound his arms around her, took the reins and urged Mischief forward.

"Thanks for coming for us." Elsie's soft words broke the silence.

I will always come for you whenever you need me. "I'm glad everyone is..." *Okay.* He lost his voice. Cleared his throat then managed, "I'm just glad everyone is safe."

"And you're back in the saddle." She shifted and glanced over her shoulder at him. Concern was there in her face and words. "How does it feel?"

But he didn't want her to worry about him. He wanted her to... He pressed mute on that thought and gathered her closer. Then he whispered in her ear, "It feels like home." *You feel like home.*

She kept her head pressed against his. Her words were just above a murmur. "Then perhaps I wasn't too much of an inconvenience after all."

"You were never that." *Not to me.*

She settled back against him as if she no longer wanted to resist. He did the only thing he could. Tucked her fully against his chest. Held her as close as he could. And wondered how exactly he was supposed to let her go.

This was why he always left his emotions alone. This was everything he hadn't ever wanted to feel. He willed his heart to remain detached. Put his feelings on lockdown. Then maybe the fallout wouldn't be more than he could handle. Then perhaps he would be okay.

Too soon, the lights at her family's house flickered through the trees. Too soon, they'd walked the horses into the driveway. Too soon, Caleb dismounted, led the horses away and left Elsie alone with Ryan on the front porch.

And it was too late. Too late for Elsie to ask Ryan to keep on riding. To nowhere. To anywhere. *Just take me with you.*

Elsie lingered under the dim porch light in front of the double doors.

Ryan held back near the top stair. His fingers curved around the handrail as if he needed an anchor. "What time are you leaving tomorrow?"

"Before sunrise." She cleared her throat. Twisted her hands together in front of her, keeping herself from reaching for him and anchoring them together. "I'm hoping to make it to St. Louis. I made a hotel reservation for the night there."

"Sounds like you have it all planned out then." He stepped down to the next stair, farther away from her.

Elsie clenched her hands tighter. Looked away. They'd both known she was leaving. They'd both known this was all they'd have. But her heart hadn't listened. Now she hurt. And she had only herself to blame. "You know I can't stay."

He stilled. His fingers tightened on the rail. Then he countered, "Can't or won't?"

"Both," she said and leaned into the facts. The logic that would smother the splintering of her heart. "I don't fit in here any more than you fit in the city."

"You don't know that." He lifted his gaze toward the sky as if searching for a star to wish on. Perhaps to wish that things were different between them.

But they were beyond wishes. Beyond whispers inside hearts. *Stick to the facts. Now isn't the time to follow your heart.* She watched him. "If I asked you to leave all this behind, I'd be asking you to leave a part of yourself behind too. I won't—I can't—do that."

A muscle tensed along his jawline. His lips pressed together. He offered no argument. No denial. He knew the same truths.

Time for more. Time to face what they had known along. She lifted her chin, ignored that ache in her chest, like the first crack in her heart. "And I don't belong here." *Even if in your arms everything felt right. As if for the first time, I found where I belonged.*

"Are you making that determination because of tonight?" He paused and studied her. "Even experienced trail guides get lost. It happens. It's not a good reason to leave."

But you haven't given me a reason to stay. "I should've known to check the gas tank. To pack better supplies. I should've been more prepared. I know better." *I knew better than to fall for you. But I fell anyway.*

"You will be next time," he offered.

There would be no next time. It was time to walk away. When all she was leaving behind was a piece of her heart. A sliver. Surely, she wouldn't miss that. Surely, she would recover. "I'm better in the city. It's where I belong. Same as you belong on the circuit."

"Seems like you have it all figured out for the both of us." He remained still. Contained. Out of her reach.

Where she wanted him. Why was she hurting so much? She pressed her palm against her chest. "How many cowboy rescues do you have to make before you admit I'm right?"

"That's just an excuse." He shook his head and wiped the back of his hand over his mouth. But his frown remained. "You're just scared to stay here and take a real risk."

He meant her heart. He wanted her to risk it all. For him. But she wasn't falling alone. He would have to risk it all too. *Give me your heart, cowboy.* She charged, "What about you, cowboy? You're scared too."

He brushed his fingers over his bottom lip. "Is that so?"

"Yeah." She never backed down. Hearts were on the line. Hers. His. She said, "You're scared to commit to something outside the arena."

His gaze widened and flared.

Her words had hit their mark. Little satisfaction there. No victory.

"What do you want, Elsie? Do you want me to ask you to stay?" He moved back up the stairs toward her. "Fine. Elsie, stay here. Stay. Don't go to New York. Is that what you want me to tell you?"

No. Don't do it. Don't open your heart, Els. Turn around. Walk away. But she was already charging down that path, following her heart. At warp speed. "I want you to tell me that you love me."

"Love you." He scrubbed his palms over his face. Then settled his gaze on her. Steady. Direct. Unflinching. "I've always loved you, Elsie Marie."

No. Not like this. His words challenged. His confession was filled with impatience. More like a warning than an ardent declaration.

If he loved her then she would be soaring through the sky. Touching the stars. Never wanting to come down. Not falling. Not tumbling without a net, without someone to catch her. Completely alone.

No, this couldn't be love. It was heartfelt. But in all the worst possible ways. It hurt too much. She hurt too much.

"I love you, Elsie, but I can't ask you to stay." His words were resigned and composed. Same as he was. "Because this place isn't what you want. It's never been what you wanted."

That ache expanded inside her. Her throat tightened.

He gave her no reprieve. "All I've ever wanted for you, Elsie, is to be happy." He retreated. Back down the stairs. Away from her. "So, go, Elsie. Head to that big city and be happy. Not for anyone but yourself."

"Don't do that." *Don't shut me out. Ask me to love you. Let me love you.* She swept that scratch from her words. "What about you?"

"Don't worry about me." A ghost of a smile filtered across his face. There and gone. "I've got my horses and rodeo. What more could a cowboy like me need?"

Love. My love. She crossed her arms over her chest and refused to sway. Then she searched his face for more than indifference. A dent in his composure. Saw something there in his narrowed gaze. A faint flicker that gave him away. "It's not love that scares you, is it?"

"I already told you how I feel about you." He met her stare. Again, so steady. So very stoic.

But his words were cavalier. Almost careless. And so not freeing. For either of them. They felt more like a trap. Like a weight on her chest. He loved her, but who cared? He looked far from moved by his declaration. Far from love struck. Far from enchanted. He loved her but it wasn't enough. Not for her. And her own heart broke a little bit more.

"You love me." She shrugged. Three easy words. Simple to toss out there. Like flower seeds in a field. "But you're scared to commit to something outside the arena." *Or someone.* And what was his love if she didn't have her cowboy too? Same as that flower seed without water. Nothing special.

"I've got a career I'm dedicated to." He swiped his hat off, tapped it against his leg. "Obligations. People counting on me. Same as you."

"You're allowed to be happy outside of the arena too. That doesn't make you any less of a cowboy," she said. "You can be more than a bronc rider. It's not all or nothing."

"You're happy outside the city too," he countered.

But for how long? She wasn't happy now. Far from it. "But this was always temporary."

"It doesn't have to be." His cowboy hat rested against his leg. His words as always were earnest and for a moment he wasn't quite so withdrawn. "You could choose to stay."

"What if I stayed? Gave up everything." *For you. Would you give me everything in return?* She wanted his love and more. She wanted him to stand by her. Never give her up. No matter what. And she wanted to love him the same. *All or nothing, cowboy.* She continued, "And when you decide I'm not the life you want? What will I have then?"

"I can't promise, but I can..." he started.

"You're right. You can't promise." She stopped him and shook her head. She couldn't take the risk. No matter how much her heart begged her to. No matter how much she ached now. "And I don't trust love. I won't. Not enough for both of us."

"Then we know where we stand." He smashed his cowboy hat on his head.

Apart. Alone. Like they both preferred. Like they both wanted. She ached all over. The pain pressed on her. Love wanted to lay her low. But still she fought it. She swallowed her tears and held herself together. "City streets never were good for horses or cowboys."

His eyebrows flexed. Up. Down. He nodded slowly as if absorbing her words. Then he was back to impassive. Back to contained. Unreachable. "Then I guess there really isn't anything left to say, is there?"

"Only goodbye, cowboy." She barely kept herself from choking on her words.

He stiffened and considered her. She met his stare. Clamped her jaw together to stop the tremor. Still the quiver in her chin. He had her heart. He would not get her tears too.

Finally, he touched the brim of his hat and said, "Goodbye, Elsie."

Then he turned and left. Simple as that. As if there was nothing to it. And nothing more he cared to say. Simple as that, he let her go.

Yet Elsie stood there. On that porch. Under that dim light.

Watched her cowboy walk away. And held her chin high.

Watched her cowboy mount his horse. And kept herself standing tall.

Watched her cowboy ride away and never look back.

Not her cowboy. Not anymore. Just a cowboy.

And still she stood there. Waited for the last piece of her heart to fall. Right there on that front porch. Where she intended to leave it. No good could come from dragging it with her.

She'd known better than to follow her heart. Known better than to believe in love.

Finally, she went inside. Climbed up the stairs and collapsed face-first on her bed. And cried. Long and hard and from the deepest parts of her.

She cried for the scare she'd caused her nieces that night. For the family she was leaving in the morning. For the friends she would miss. For the goats she'd come to adore. And the horses too.

Her tears kept falling. And she kept finding reasons

for each one. Because girls from the city knew better than to cry over cowboys. Especially cowboys who loved with limits.

CHAPTER TWENTY-TWO

EIGHTY-FOUR. RYAN NEEDED to score eighty-four to win the saddle bronc event at Rodeo Rides for A Cause.

It was time to do just that. Win.

Ryan exhaled. Beneath his legs, Midnight Star Catcher shifted. The black-and-white paint was more than anxious to leave the chute. More than eager to make Ryan work for every single one of those points. More than willing to buck Ryan right out of the standings.

Ryan relaxed in the saddle. Let everything around him fall away. The sold-out crowd in the Belleridge arena. The noise. His own thoughts.

He had eight seconds. Just him and a horse. No more time to think. Only react. One jump. Then the next. Eight seconds to forget. To ride in the moment. Adrenaline sparked along his nerves. Welcome and addicting. It was all he ever wanted to feel.

Ryan adjusted his grip around the thick braided rein. Lifted his head. Gave the okay.

The gate opened.

Midnight Star Catcher launched out of the chute. Jumped high. Kicked fast. Bucked harder. His cowboy hat hit the dirt. Another midair kick. Ryan held on. Found his center. Found his rhythm. Kept his seat. One powerful horse. One determined cowboy. A clash of wills that somehow synchronized. Against all odds.

Eight seconds. And it was finished.

Ryan accepted an assist from his brother Caleb. One of two pickup riders in the arena. His boots landed in the dirt. And his score flashed on the screen. Eighty-five.

Cheers erupted around the arena. A win for the hometown cowboy. He caught his breath. Felt that adrenaline recede. Struggled to hold on to it. Just a few more seconds. It'd been a reprieve. But it was over. Ryan swiped his cowboy hat from the ground, waved to the excited crowd and headed out of the competition area.

His family surrounded him. Laughter. More cheers. Congratulations. Ryan soaked in every word. Clung to each heartfelt job well done. Yet a part of him felt eerily hollow inside. More hugs. More embraces. A kiss on the cheek from Breezy. Then Gayle Baker. But the void remained. Firm handshakes. Squeezes on the shoulder. Nothing filled him completely.

But he had won. Doing what he loved. What he'd always loved. For the people he loved. The horses he loved. That was supposed to be enough. More than enough.

Ryan smiled wider. Accepted more congratulations. Convinced himself it was just the aftereffects of an adrenaline rush. That he would get to his true happy soon enough. Surely after the team roping event.

An hour later, Ryan checked the saddle on Tango one last time and mounted the muscular horse. The gelding belonged to Maggie's older sister and former team roping partner and had helped the sisters become a top women's roping team. Now Ryan was counting on the talented quarter horse to help him win again.

"It's you and me, cowboy." Maggie mounted Lady Dasher and eyed Ryan. Her smile bright. "Don't forget what I taught you this past week. I won't be satisfied with second. We're here to win."

"Got it." Ryan guided the horse into the header roping box. Exhaled. Steadied himself in the saddle.

Maggie moved into the second box on the other side of the chute holding the steer.

One more ride. One more chance to win. Only this time with Maggie—his family and his friend. What could be better?

Less than ten seconds later, Ryan and Maggie clocked the fastest time. Ryan had another first-place finish. Another win. But that happy place seemed even further out of reach. Good thing Ryan was a master at masking his true feelings. Same as he had for the past week.

Once again, he smiled through the cheers from the crowd. The congratulations from friends and peers. The hugs and pats on the back from his family.

He was back. At the top of his riding game again. That was something to celebrate. He supposed he had Elsie to thank for that. It seemed a broken heart saved his career.

Ever since he'd walked away from Elsie that night, he had doubled down on just about everything else in his life. From practicing for the rodeo to repairing the old wheelhouse barn to working with the horses at the sanctuary. Even clearing land for the new stable barn and seeding the dandelion pasture. He'd stayed later. Pushed harder. Right into exhaustion. Whatever it took to numb the pain of losing Elsie.

And he'd discovered two important things:

Physical pain had nothing on heartache.

And Elsie was wrong. It was all or nothing.

He had to give his all to keep from feeling like he had nothing without Elsie.

But she was back in the city where she wanted to be. He would soon be back on the road to the next rodeo. Everything was as it should be. As it'd always been. Soon enough his heart would fall back in line too. All he had to do was wait it out. Good thing he was a patient man.

"We missed you in the hospitality tent tonight." Maggie leaned against the stall door in the stables at the Belleridge arena. "It was quite the celebration in there."

"I was getting Tango and Lady Dasher ready for their victory ride home." Ryan ran his hand over Tango's sleek neck and avoided looking at Maggie. The problem with having a best friend turned sister-in-law was that she saw too much and wasn't afraid to call him on it. But he wasn't ready to talk. Same as he hadn't been ready all week. And might not ever be.

"Grant is pulling the truck and trailer around now," Maggie offered.

Ryan nodded then kept his words light and upbeat, and the conversation away from himself. "I'm thinking I should take up roping too, Mags. We could tear it up on the circuit together."

"I might take you up on that." Maggie slid the stall door open for him. "But for now, I'm afraid I need to give you a nine-month rain check on your offer."

Nine months. Ryan paused and glanced at his sister-in-law. Her eyes sparkled. Her smile was looking hard to contain. Ryan said, "Mags, are you pregnant?"

"Yes." Maggie tossed herself into his arms. Her joy overflowed into her words and her expression. "I'm pregnant. Grant and I are having a baby. A baby," she marveled, then pressed her palms against her mouth and caught her squeal inside her hands. She rushed on, "But you can't tell anyone, Ryan."

"Wait." Ryan's own grin spread wide. Watching Maggie, he was starting to feel a sense of that happiness himself. He decided to hold on to it a bit longer. He said, "I'm the first one to know?"

Maggie nodded and bit her bottom lip. But her bright smile couldn't be contained. A pregnant Maggie took happiness to a whole other level. "Grant and I are going to tell everyone tomorrow night at the house party to celebrate the rodeo."

"But I know first," Ryan clarified. "Before my entire family."

Maggie's eyebrows pulled together. She pushed on his shoulder playfully. "Don't make me regret telling you."

Too late for that. Ryan waggled his eyebrows at her. "You know what this means, right, Mags?"

Maggie set her hands on her hips and eyed him.

"It means I'm the favorite uncle of course." Ryan spread his arms wide then patted his palm against his chest.

"The baby isn't even here." Maggie shook her head. But there was amusement in her words. "You can't claim favorite uncle status yet."

"I just did." Ryan stepped beside Maggie and dropped his arm around her shoulders. "It's fate, Mags. If favorite uncle was meant to be Caleb or Carter or Josh, you would've told them first."

Maggie jabbed her elbow into his ribs. "I'm beginning to wonder why I told you."

He squeezed her tighter. "Because I'm your favorite too."

"What about Grant?" she countered. "My husband."

"Well, besides Grant," Ryan qualified. Then he gave her a quick side hug and said, "Seriously, Mags, I'm thrilled for you and my brother."

"I'm kind of thrilled myself." She lifted her hands and pressed her fingers against her cheeks. "And, I admit, I'm a little bit terrified too. I'm going to be a mom, Ryan."

"One of the best ones out there," he said, believing it

and wanting to assure her of it too. "And you'll have lots of help from us."

"Speaking of letting family help," Maggie started then glanced up at him. There was concern in her gaze, understanding in her words. "We're here for you too. I'm here for you, Ryan."

"I know." Ryan dropped his arm and stuffed his hands into his back pockets. "I'm good though, Mags."

"You're not, despite how many times you say it." She stopped and faced him. "We can all see it. You're in pain, Ryan. You can't keep pushing yourself like this. This pace you've set. It's not sustainable."

But it had to be. All he had to do was outlast his heartbreak. He rubbed his chest then grinned at Maggie. "Look at you, Mags. You're already acting like a mom. I knew you were going to be good at it."

Maggie frowned at him. "I'm serious, Ryan."

So was he. Being a cowboy on the rodeo was all he knew. Now all he had. He had to make it count. Had to make walking away from the best person in his life count. "I just won twice this weekend. First place, Mags. That means something must be working right."

"But you're not happy," Maggie stressed.

"Of course, I am," he declared, perhaps with a little too much intensity if Maggie's raised eyebrows were any indication. Still, he kept on rolling with it and added, "The sanctuary is getting that new stable. Fully funded. Five more retired rodeo horses will have their forever home. That's fulfilling. That's everything to me."

"But that's not everything, Ryan." She stepped closer to him and set her palm over his heart. "You're not happy in here. That matters."

But Elsie and Ryan had gotten exactly what they wanted. That was something to be happy about, even if his heart hurt a little. But it was nothing he couldn't manage. On his own, like he always had. "I'm alright, Mags."

Maggie studied him then shook her head. "I hope my child isn't as stubborn as you Sloans."

"Good luck with that." Ryan laughed. "Grant's middle name should've been stubborn."

Maggie chuckled.

"Speaking of names, you do know Ryan works for both a boy and girl name, don't you?" Ryan started walking again. "It also makes for a strong middle name. Like for instance Samuel Ryan Sloan or James Ryan Sloan. Or Olivia Ryan Sloan or even Elizabeth Ryan Sloan."

"Those actually aren't bad suggestions." Maggie walked beside him.

"I know, right?" Ryan grinned at her some more. "Leave it to Uncle Ryan. I've got a barrel full of suggestions."

"Why do you have all these name ideas?" Maggie slanted her gaze toward him and frowned. "You already pitched these names to Tess and Carter for their twins."

"Can you blame me? They are good solid names," he countered. "I need to hedge my bets. Have a namesake niece or nephew. Now I've got three chances to get my name in the conversation."

"Or you could keep these names and use them for your own kids," she suggested quietly.

Ryan barely had time to dodge that hit. It struck right inside his chest where his heart used to be and knocked him slightly off-balance. He managed, "I'm proud to be a favorite uncle, Mags. That's enough for me." He spotted Grant climbing out of their truck with the horse trailer attached. Saved. And just in time. He jogged over to greet his brother and said, "Well, if it isn't the dad-to-be."

Grant hugged Ryan then wrapped an arm around Maggie and tucked her in close. Grant said, "You told him."

"Of course, Maggie told me," Ryan said. "And now I know I really am your favorite brother."

Grant frowned at Maggie. "He's not going to let this go."

"And to think I know a full twenty-four hours before the rest of the family." Ryan wedged himself between the pair and linked their arms with his. "Come on, you two parents-to-be. We can discuss baby names while we load up the horses."

And Ryan could keep pretending he really was alright.

ONE WEEK AFTER she left Three Springs, Elsie spent her Sunday night ironing. For the second night in a row. Last night, she'd spent her Saturday evening with takeout from the nearby Thai restaurant and a stack of work blouses. Tonight, it was takeout from the local deli and a stack of work pants. Her entire business wardrobe would soon be pressed and wrinkle-free and ready to wear. She would be all set for the many weeks ahead.

She hung a pair of navy suit pants in the closet and stubbed her toe on her farm boots. The ones she hadn't put on in over a week. There'd been no reason. The same ones she meant to pack away but hadn't yet.

Rubbing her toe, she considered the boots. When she'd been in Three Springs, she hadn't picked up an iron once. She'd cooked every meal. And loved every minute of it. Of course, she had. It was only temporary. Like a vacation. A reprieve from her normal, everyday routine. Sure, there had been stress, but it was nothing she had to take on fully. She'd only been a stand-in for the short term. What wasn't there to like about that?

Sure, life in Three Springs seemed enticing. More than a little appealing. Even now. She supposed it always would until she had to live it full-time. Then there would be stresses and burdens she couldn't begin to imagine. And that life would be less than charming.

But in Three Springs, she wouldn't be alone. Like she was now.

Elsie sighed and glanced around the clean but sparsely furnished studio apartment. The short-term rental was her temporary living quarters until she found a place she could afford. Boxes were stacked to the ceiling, filling the already cramped space. She made a mental note to follow up with the real estate agent Lilian Sloan had recommended. She needed to pick up her house hunt. Surely once she was settled into her own place, unpacked, and put her own spin on the decorating, then it would be better. Then she would start feeling like she was home.

The tape on one of Autumn's pictures Elsie had hung around the apartment came loose. The drawing of Sundancer and Midnight Rose drifted to the floor behind the couch. Elsie set her iron on standby on the ironing board and went in search of the picture. It wasn't like she didn't have others. The girls' drawings filled the walls and even stuck to the outsides of her moving boxes. Elsie picked a different drawing to stare at each night and fall asleep too. Wishing for those fun dreams Gemma claimed she'd find. And hoping she'd wake up in the morning happy.

Unfortunately, her nights were restless. She was awake more than she dreamed. And the morning sunlight only seemed to highlight her discontent. Still, she was undaunted. Her heartache might have followed her to New York. She accepted that. But surely, she didn't have to hurt all day and all night. Not because of a cowboy.

She located the picture and stuck it to the lampshade. Within sight of her pillow. Telling herself tonight she would find that good night's sleep. That cowboy would become a memory. Not someone she couldn't get over. Not someone she didn't want to get over.

The video app on her tablet lit up the screen. Elsie grinned. Just the distraction she needed. She grabbed a blanket, propped the tablet on a pillow on her lap and accepted the video chat. Her nieces' adorable faces filled the screen. Their bubbly greetings filled her heart.

Quick enough, they launched into a detailed retelling of the past two days since their last video chat on Friday evening, when the girls and Bryce had called to tell her that they'd found Smarty Marty in her bedroom, bleating so loud he'd woken everyone up. Gemma was convinced the goat was looking for Elsie. And all Elsie wondered was if a certain cowboy was looking for her. The same way she'd been searching for him on the city streets.

The girls quickly shifted the conversation from their Midnight Rose and Sundancer update to their weekend. Elsie steeled herself and anchored her smile in place. She knew what was coming.

"We got to sit in the front row at the rodeo, Auntie," Autumn said cheerfully. "'Cause Ms. Maggie got us special seats. 'Cause she runs the rodeo. Did you know that?"

Elsie smiled and nodded. She'd been texting with Maggie and Tess on the daily since her arrival in New York. And if she was honest, she felt even closer to the two women now. She'd also been talking more with her brother. Sending him articles on beekeeping and best honey producing practices from her research in the evenings. Even more they'd been sharing with each other, getting to know each other better and Elsie liked to think becoming friends too.

"The rodeo was so fun," Gemma added, stretching out every word into multiple syllables. "Did you see Cowboy Prince win?"

Only several dozen times. Her brother had opened a video chat during the different rodeo events. Elsie had watched live for Vivian's barrel race, Ryan's saddle bronc ride and finally Maggie and Ryan's team roping. Then Bryce had emailed the video of Ryan competing to Elsie. And she couldn't stop watching him. She'd been terrified, anxious, excited and in awe. Then incredibly relieved when Ryan had gotten off the magnificent black-and-white paint without getting thrown or injured.

She'd wanted to be there. Wanted to check Ryan over herself. As it was, she'd made Maggie and Bryce and Sam assure her Ryan was in fact fine. Then she'd asked them all not to say anything to Ryan. She was just a friend concerned about another friend after all. Still, she wasn't entirely sure who she was trying to convince—them or herself. And feared that she hadn't fooled anyone, including herself.

"Guess what, Auntie? Ms. Maggie says I can rope like her one day." Gemma wiggled her way farther onto the video screen. "And I can race barrels like Ms. Vivian too. They're going to teach me how to ride fast like them. They told Dad I'm not too young to learn."

Elsie concentrated on her nieces. "I think you will be very good at whatever you decide to do, Gemma. And Ms. Maggie and Ms. Vivian will be excellent teachers." Elsie watched Autumn chewing on her bottom lip. "What about you, Autumn? Did you pick your rodeo event too?"

"Cowboy Prince took me riding with him on Mischief last week," Autumn said and nibbled on her bottom lip a bit more. "Cowboy Prince told me that I don't have to compete in the rodeo if I don't want to. I can love horses all the same and ride them whenever I want."

A sigh swirled through Elsie at Ryan's kindness and awareness. He understood Autumn's reserve and her nature then offered her something of her own. Elsie smiled. "Cowboy Prince is right, Autumn. Horses need your love and attention and care. They'll be better for it."

Autumn smiled wide then peered into the camera lens. Her face filling the screen. "Auntie, are you sick?"

"No, I'm fine," she said. Or she would be. In time. With a decent night's sleep. One she intended to get that very evening.

Autumn scratched her nose and leaned away again. "But you're all wrapped up in that blanket."

"It's just a little chilly in my apartment," she hedged.

"That's the blanket Cowboy Prince got you," Autumn announced. Her eyes widened and her smile grew. "I remember 'cause I found the bag by the door that night after dinner. The night you and Caleb danced. Remember? That was so fun."

Elsie nodded and curled her fingers around the blanket. She remembered more than she wanted to. Remembered too much. Like dancing with Ryan. Laughing with Ryan. Kissing Ryan.

"And then we used that blanket in our princess fort when Cowboy Prince stayed over," Gemma added, seeming as thrilled to see the blanket as her sister. "It's so soft and warm and cuddly."

It was all that. And if it still smelled faintly of Cowboy Prince, well, that was for Elsie to know.

"Cowboy Prince is back from the stables." Autumn lifted her face out of the camera view. Then she leaned back in, "Gotta go, Auntie. Cowboy Prince is showing us how to make proper s'mores now."

Good-nights and air kisses exchanged. The video call disconnected. And silence filled the studio apartment in the high-rise building once more.

Elsie buried herself in the plush blanket, drawing it

up around her face. Told herself she never really liked s'mores anyway. She always burned the marshmallow to something past blackened. The melted chocolate made her fingers too sticky and she ultimately had more of a mess than a delicious dessert.

No, she never much liked s'mores. But unfortunately, she still liked her cowboy. More than she should.

CHAPTER TWENTY-THREE

It was midweek and Ryan hadn't slowed for the past ten days. Not since he'd accepted his belt buckle at Rodeo Rides for A Cause. He'd spent last week working at the wheelhouse barn and the sanctuary. With his demo of an old storage barn on-site and land prep done, the new stable barn build was ahead of schedule. Then he'd collected one more belt buckle that past weekend in Tulsa, Oklahoma and took second place in Dodge City, Kansas one day later.

And no matter how many miles he traveled or how well he competed or how hard he worked, that heartache stuck to him like a persistent shadow. So, he did what any sensible cowboy could. He kept moving. Kept forging ahead. Certain the pain would call it quits soon. It had to, right?

Now he was back home, touring more properties for his mother. And sticking to his Keep Busy motto. He walked through the single-story house and panned his video camera on his phone around the family room. "Just to recap. The cottage sits on just under four acres. The barn is small, but relatively new. It could house three horses and maybe a pony. No more." He turned in a slow circle. "The kitchen could hold our entire family if the weather was in our favor and the back porch could be used too for additional seating."

"Ryan." His mother's voice was crisp yet thoughtful on the speaker. "Is this house for you or me?"

Ryan stilled then flipped the phone toward himself,

putting him in the camera view and allowing himself to see his mother.

"This property sounds more suited to your needs," his mother said, touched the pearl earring she always wore and tilted her head. "Are you asking my opinion?"

"Maybe," he hedged and dropped onto a stool at the island. The property was staged for a sale. There he propped the phone up against a cookbook holder. "I don't know."

"But you're looking for your own place," his mother pressed.

"I can't live with Tess and Carter forever." He linked his fingers together on the cool countertop. "They will need the bedrooms if they have more kids."

"That may be so, but let's look at this particular home you're in right now a bit closer." She lifted her fingers and tapped against them in a precise count. "First. You've already outgrown the stables there and you've yet to move in. What with Mischief, Sundancer and Midnight Rose needing stalls. I doubt you'll be able to turn down another mare or gelding in need in the future."

Ryan worked to keep his mouth closed and not gape wide-open. Still, surprise shifted through him and was hard to contain. His mother knew his horse's names. Knew also his affinity for rescuing the animals.

"Second. That house, while quaint, is just that… Quaint," his mother continued. "There's no office. Where will you go to discuss contracts with your sponsors and deal with the business of bronc riding? And what about your workout equipment? I suppose you could put it in the garage, but that's hardly ideal."

Now his mouth did drop open. Just a parting of his lips.

"Lastly there's the location." His mother shook her head slightly. Her precision-cut hair swayed across her jawline.

"It's on the other side of Belleridge. Not exactly close to your brothers or grandfather."

Ryan lifted his arm and rubbed the back of his neck. It was rare he'd found himself dumbfounded. But he was. Right then. Right there. On a video chat with his mother of all people.

His mother's eyebrow twitched. One side of her mouth ticked up. "I seem to have surprised you."

"Caught me off guard," he admitted.

"Well, I like to think I know some useful things about my own sons," she added then motioned to the screen. "Now, tell me. What is it about this particular place that appeals to you?"

He wasn't exactly certain. He just knew he needed to find a place of his own. Ryan scratched his cheek. "It is priced well. Affordable."

"If it's money that is the issue—" she started.

"It's not the money," he interrupted. Not exactly.

He'd invested a portion of his rodeo earnings from his first cash payout years ago. At Bryce's direction. As he'd won more, he'd invested more, always with Bryce's wise and watchful guidance. His investments performed well— again, thanks to Bryce—and he'd had the funds to invest in Carter's distillery, then recently in Josh's equestrian rehabilitation center and Bryce's Sweet House of Bees. He'd been thrilled to help his family and friends. Yet never gave much thought to how he would fund his own future. Until now.

He ran his hands over his jeans and looked at his mother. "It's about proving I can commit to something outside the arena."

"Then you should commit to Elsie," his mother said, direct and on point as was her style. "Don't buy a house that isn't suitable just to prove a point."

Commit to Elsie. Ryan stretched his legs out. His boot tapped on the tile floor. "This isn't about Elsie."

"Isn't it?" his mother asked. "I've spent a good deal of time with Elsie the past few weeks. She's as miserable as you are."

"I'm not miserable," he argued. He just wasn't happy. At all. Not like he'd been with Elsie. "This was supposed to be about a house."

"Things are never what they seem." His mother chuckled then considered him, her voice pensive. "You and I are not so very different."

They were also nothing alike. Ryan braced his elbows on the countertop and stared into the screen. "How is that exactly?"

"We're both considering a complete change of lifestyle," she explained then leaned toward the camera as if imparting a sage secret. "We're both terrified of what that means. And even more terrified we'll get it wrong and fail. We're comfortable doing the things we know we're good at."

He wanted to deny her claims. Tell her that she was entirely wrong. Completely mistaken. That she did not in fact know him at all. Instead, he tugged at the hair covering his cheek. Even hidden behind a thick beard, his mother saw him. Understood him. It was nothing he would have ever foreseen. "I don't intend to leave the circuit."

"But you intend to live outside of it too," she countered. "Just as I intend to live outside the operating room."

Ryan swiped his hat off and dropped it on the countertop. Nothing seemed to be fitting right. Or sounding right. He eyed his mother. "You're seriously leaving New York and your practice?"

"I believe the term is retiring," she said. A faint smile creased her lips and disappeared. "I'm still getting used to the word myself. I won't be practicing. I will be guest lecturing at the college, speaking on panels and consulting with peers when asked. But I will be retired."

"It's all you've ever done," he said. All she'd ever known. *How* she was known. Dr. Lilian Sloan, renowned heart surgeon. Same as him. He was a cowboy. Only ever known as a bronc rider.

"I've come to realize my medical career isn't my entire identity," she said. Her face softened. "I'd like to believe there is more to me than a medical degree. And it's time I find out what that is."

It's not all or nothing, Ryan. He reached for his hat, pressed it on his head. At his core he was a cowboy, but was there more to him? Elsie seemed to believe so, but did he? Suddenly restless, Ryan stood and said, "Okay, Mother, I think we should find you a home, so you at least have a place to start your new journey."

"What about you?" she asked.

"You're right," he said and reached for his phone on the countertop. "This place won't suit either of us."

"Then let's continue our search, shall we?" His mother smiled. "And, Ryan, thank you for being part of my journey. I hope I can return the favor one day."

SEVERAL HOURS LATER, Ryan added more two-by-fours to his growing stack inside the wheelhouse barn. He'd already repaired two of the walls and practically rebuilt the entire workbench. The safety violations were dwindling with every repair. With luck and a bit more renovation, the barn would be safe for his grandfather and uncle to produce their dandelion wine in the summer.

The door creaked open, and his grandfather stood in the doorway. "Thought I might find you here."

"How'd you know where I was?" Ryan brushed his

hands on his jeans. He hadn't told anyone what he was doing. He'd wanted to surprise his grandfather and uncle.

"You can sneak around behind your brothers' backs." Grandpa Sam smiled and stepped inside. "But your grandmother taught me how to pay attention to you boys years ago. I've not forgotten, even if I get around a bit slower these days."

"Gran Claire was certainly watchful." Ryan checked to make sure the floor was clear where his grandfather was stepping then added, "She never did miss much."

"But I think she fretted over you the most." Sam stopped beside the workbench and ran his hand over the newly sanded top.

"Me?" Ryan said.

"You were always comforting your younger brothers." Sam leaned against the workbench and considered Ryan. "But you never let your gran fuss over you. She always worried about that. She worried you weren't getting enough of her care and attention."

"I never felt like that." Not once. He always welcomed Gran Claire's embraces. Always felt stronger after one of her warm hugs. Reassured and loved too. He'd felt something similar recently with someone else. *Elsie*. Ryan adjusted several two-by-fours, rebalanced the stack and his thoughts. "If anything, I felt like I got more hugs from Gran Claire than anyone else."

"That's because you stopped her fussing at hugs." Grandpa Sam chuckled. "No matter what it was, your gran would give you a hug then you'd proclaim you were fine. Even when you were sick. Broke your arm. Fell off a horse too many times to count. You had a one hug limit, then you always told her not to worry about you."

"You both had five young boys to look after," Ryan said. "You already had too much to worry about."

"But that was for us to decide where we wanted to put our worries." Grandpa Sam watched him. A knowing gleam in his gaze. "When you love someone the way your gran loved you, the worrying and the fussing are all part of the package."

Ryan knew something about that kind of worry. He'd worried about Elsie. And wanted to fuss over her. Take care of her, not because she couldn't take care of herself. But because he...

"You're fussing and worrying about this old barn because you love your uncle and me," Grandpa Sam continued as if he already knew what Ryan was fighting. "Same as we love you."

"I just want it to be safe." Ryan paced around the barn, picked up an old nail and tossed it into the debris pile in the corner. "I want to make sure you're okay."

"We appreciate that." Grandpa Sam braced his arms on the workbench as if more than content to watch Ryan pace circles around the barn all day. He added, "But I'm here to make sure my grandson is okay."

"I'm fine." Ryan completed another circle. Picked up another nail.

Grandpa Sam held his silence but kept his vigil.

"Or, I will be." Ryan stopped and faced his grandfather then qualified, "I want to be. I'm trying to be."

"What's the problem?" Grandpa Sam asked.

"I wished to be a real cowboy all those years ago," Ryan blurted. As if somehow in this barn, with his grandpa, the past still mattered. Maybe it was talk of his Gran Claire. Maybe it was needing someone else to understand. Maybe he needed to understand. Whatever it was, Ryan spilled those secrets he'd kept locked away. "After you taught me to ride that summer and I fell in love with the rodeo. Then the next summer, Mom left us here and never came back. And my wildest wish came true."

"And you thought the bad stuff was your fault." Grandpa Sam smoothed his fingers through his white beard. Wisdom and compassion in his gaze. "The divorce. Your mom leaving you and your brothers. You blamed yourself because you wanted the rodeo, horses, being here so badly."

Ryan nodded. "Ever since, I wanted to prove it wasn't the wrong wish. That I truly belonged here." Ryan speared his arms to the side. "I had to be fine for my brothers. For you and Gran. I had to look after you all and I couldn't do that if I wasn't fine. And to be that I had to be the best cowboy I knew how."

"Now you are the best bronc rider and an even better brother and grandson." Grandpa Sam waited a beat and said quietly, "Isn't it about time you let yourself off the hook?"

Ryan lowered his arms. "I don't know how."

"I imagine if your Gran Claire was here now, she'd tell you it's simple." A small smile curved across his grandpa's face.

Ryan waited.

"Your gran would tell you that you can start by letting someone look after you," Grandpa Sam said, his eyebrows lifted toward his head as if he wanted to make sure Ryan was paying attention. "And then your gran would tell you to let someone love you."

Love him. That meant letting someone in. Completely. Fully. Trusting his heart to another. It meant more than words. It meant showing up. Proving it. "And if I'm going to let someone love me, it's only fair to love them fully in return." No half measures. *All or nothing.*

"Now you're catching on." Grandpa Sam grinned then pointed out the window. "Those dandelions out there will start to sprout soon. They'll go from seed to seedling to a plant to a flower. And eventually they'll become wine. We're on a similar path of growth that includes our successes and our failures. It's what your uncle and I like to call the journey of a life well spent. Falling in love is a blip, but staying in love, well, that's the reward of a life well spent. A journey worth taking."

But was he ready for that journey? Ryan stepped next to his grandfather and stared out the window at the dandelion field.

"You've always been in for only eight seconds," Grandpa Sam mused beside him. "Maybe it's time to try something that'll last a bit longer. Like a lifetime perhaps."

That meant committing to Elsie. Ryan's words sounded wry. "That seems to be the theme today. Mom told me something similar this morning."

"Then what's the problem?" Grandpa Sam asked.

Ryan channeled his mother and kept it right to the point. "I seem to have a bit of a commitment problem when it comes to things outside the arena."

"I don't believe that's true." His grandpa shifted to face him. "You've never wavered on your commitment to this family."

"That's family, Grandpa. There's nothing to waver about," he said. "I was talking about my track record with relationships. I'm not known for sticking around long."

"That's not a problem. It just means you weren't willing to commit to the wrong person." His grandpa set his hand on Ryan's shoulder and drew Ryan's attention to him. "But when your heart knows, Ryan, there's nothing to fear. And that's when you'll want to stick."

Ryan flattened his palms on the workbench top. "How do I know Elsie is the right one?"

"Listen to your heart." Grandpa Sam squeezed his shoulder. "It didn't steer you wrong before. It won't now either."

What was in his heart? Ryan stilled, quieted his mind inside the old barn with his grandfather beside him. And beyond the pain and hurt he discovered love. A whole bunch of love for one woman. Elsie. So much love he hurt from not knowing what to do with it.

He was in love with Elsie.

He drew a deep breath, feeling freer than he had in weeks. Lighter, yet stronger. He knew what he wanted. He wanted to take that journey. He wanted to prove he could love Elsie for a lifetime. And that would be a life well spent.

"I know what I need to do," Ryan said then pulled out his phone.

His grandpa grinned wide. "And your family is here for you. Whatever you need."

Ryan tapped a name on his contact list, set the phone to his ear. His mother answered on the second ring. He offered a quick greeting then got right to the heart of things. "Mom, it turns out I could use that favor after all."

CHAPTER TWENTY-FOUR

It was Friday and Elsie had officially completed her first full week on-site at her new job. With the drive from Texas to New York last week, she'd hoped her early days in her office would be a quiet chance to get settled. But it had been one meeting after another. Coordinating with her staff and cross-checking last-minute details for the weekend's events at the hotel, including a high-profile gala.

Elsie picked up the embossed invitation for the Heartscape Foundation's Annual Charity Gala. The one her boss had delivered not ten minutes earlier at the request of Dr. Lilian Sloan. Elsie was expected to attend as the personal guest of Lilian's. Turned out Dr. Sloan sat on the Heartscape Foundation's board and was partially responsible for the foundation reaching out to Elsie's hotel when the nonprofit lost their original venue.

Elsie's boss was more than grateful for the event and the exposure for the hotel. Elsie was to attend the ball and not worry about staffing. Her boss assured her all would be covered for the evening. All Elsie needed to do was enjoy herself.

Looked like Elsie would be going to a gala tomorrow night. If only she was feeling more excited. She appreciated the invitation. Yet feared seeing Lilian again would only make her think of Lilian's son even more. And Elsie wasn't sure she could think of Ryan much more than she already did. And here she was supposed to be moving on.

Her cell phone vibrated on her desk. Elsie glanced at the screen, saw her brother's contact picture and quickly answered. Setting the call on speaker, she said, "Bryce. You're calling early. Is everything okay? Are the girls okay?"

"Everyone is fine. We're all really good. My ankle is getting stronger every day according to my physical therapist," Bryce assured her then added, "I wanted to talk to you before I picked up the girls from school. If you haven't noticed I can hardly get a word in when they're on the phone with you."

Elsie chuckled and relaxed into her office chair. "Yes, they have a lot to fill me in on. And I must admit I don't mind."

"They miss you," Bryce said. "I do too."

"Thanks. I feel the same." Elsie stared out her second-floor office window at the busy street below. "I've already been looking at my calendar to see when I can slip in a weekend trip." *Home.* She left that out. New York was her home now.

"That would be wonderful." Bryce's words came out in an excited, somewhat nervous rush. "If you could perhaps come around the end of May that would be very helpful."

"What's happening at the end of May?" Elsie flipped open her calendar notebook on her desk.

"I'll be moving into my new office in Belleridge the last week of the month," Bryce said. Then he paused but his words tumbled out. "Because of my official open date for Parks Investment Services the first day of June."

Elsie straightened in her chair and stared at her phone. "What? Did you say Parks Investment Services?"

"Yes." There was a scratch across the speaker then her brother's voice strengthened. "It's what I called to talk to you about."

"I'm listening," Elsie said.

"The short version is I'm not a farmer, Elsie," Bryce said, his words matter-of-fact if not slightly sarcastic.

Elsie slapped her hand over her mouth to catch her burst of laughter. She managed a muffled, "Okay," then a more clear, "Go on."

"It's fine if you laugh," Bryce said, not sounding the least bit offended. "I've learned to laugh at myself quite a bit since we moved here. I've also learned to face some hard truths about myself."

"Like the fact that you're not a farmer," Elsie supplied.

"Like the fact that I'm really good at numbers, money and planning for the future," Bryce explained. "But the everyday things trip me up. The marketing, the customer service, the actual selling of the honey. Not to mention the grocery runs, the elementary school homework and the girls needing their dad."

Elsie sobered. With certainty, she said, "You're a really good dad, Bryce. One of the best. Never doubt that."

"I want to be," Bryce said, his words sincere and heartfelt. "I want to be the dad you never had, Els. The one you deserved."

Elsie squeezed her eyes closed. Still, she felt the tears pooling behind her eyelids. "You already are that dad, Bryce."

"Well, I need to go back to what I'm good at, Els, so I can continue to be that dad for my daughters. The farm, the bees, the house. It's all more than I can handle while trying to be present for the girls too. I want to do this right."

"You are," Elsie assured him. "You will."

"Thanks," Bryce said. "Believe it or not, I already have clients lined up from the rodeo and the hospital for my financial planning services."

"I believe it," Elsie said, pleased for her brother. "I'm

excited for you, Bryce. But can I ask what will happen to the house?" Their aunt and mom had already booked three more monthlong trips for later in the year. And last she'd spoken to the travel-bug-bitten pair, they were already discussing next year's vacation itinerary as well.

"That's the other thing I wanted to talk to you about," Bryce said. His words picked up speed as if he wanted to get everything out in one breath. "You made this place more of a home than I ever could, Els. You've always loved it. I think you should come back and manage it."

"Me?" Elsie gaped at her phone even though her brother couldn't see her. "Manage a farm? Did you forget that I'm your sister, Bryce? Neither one of us are farm grown."

"It doesn't have to stay a working farm." Bryce's amusement was clear over the speaker. "The house is too large already. You could turn it into a real venue for all sorts of events and still have plenty of private space for yourself. No reason you can't start your own business too."

Her own business. Surely, she couldn't do that, could she? Elsie rubbed her forehead then set her palm flat on the desk as if things were starting to tumble too fast around her.

"Aunt Marlena and I talked about using the greenhouses as a venue for weddings and such," Bryce continued. "Did you see the pictures of the charity gala Aunt Marlena hosted there last Christmas?"

Elsie nodded. Set her other palm on her desk. Told herself to slow down and not to get ahead of herself. This was just an idea being tossed out. Bantered about. Not a viable, actual solution. Elsie managing Doyle Farm. Full-time. And as a proper business too. The idea was impractical, but very tempting. She said, "Yeah. The greenhouses looked spectacular for that Christmas ball."

"And now with Three Springs hosting more rodeos and

events in their local arena, there are more people coming to town and venue space needed," Bryce explained. "And the closest halls and ballrooms are in Belleridge. There isn't anything in Three Springs."

"I didn't know that," Elsie said and told herself to stay objective.

"Look, I've run some numbers," Bryce continued. He slipped into his professional, business tone. "Just preliminaries if you want to see them. The other way I figure it is if Aunt Marlena and me decide to sell the place, we could use the information to entice a potential buyer. Additional income streams are often appealing to certain buyers. This could certainly help with a sale."

Sell the farm. Elsie tensed her fingers on the desk, fought the slow roll of her stomach. That idea did not sit well. Not even a little bit. She said, "Send me what you've put together and I'll review it."

"Really, Els?" Bryce said, hope in his tone.

"I'll look it over, but I'm not saying I'll do it," Elsie countered.

"But you'll think about it," Bryce said. "At the very least consider it."

"That I will agree to." She was already thinking about it. Already turning it over in her mind. And it wasn't objections she was coming up with.

"While you are considering things, can we please talk about you considering how you might work things out with Ryan?" her brother asked.

Elsie stilled. "What do you mean?"

"Come on, Els," Bryce said. His words were not impassive. And far from indifferent. "You're my sister. Ryan is one of my best friends. It's obvious there's something between you two."

"There was something." Elsie rubbed her chest then

added, "That's past tense in case our phone connection was bad."

"Are you sure about that?" Bryce challenged.

"I'm sure we don't have a future," Elsie said.

"But how do you feel about Ryan?" Bryce asked, seeming intent to keep pressing her. "Do you still love him?"

Elsie closed her eyes, but her words still slipped out before she could catch them. "Yeah, I do."

"Then it's not so past tense," Bryce argued.

"But Bryce, I've got one failed marriage," Elsie argued right back. "Where I got love entirely wrong. Then there's Mom and Dad. And what about you? We aren't exactly lucky in love in our family."

"Luck has nothing to do with it, Els," Bryce countered. "Love. Marriage. It takes two to make it work. And two people can't put their careers before their marriage and expect it to last."

That was what Elsie and her first husband had done. Careers first until they were ready to focus on the marriage portion. But they'd waited too long and there wasn't much left to work on. "But what about that spark Mom always talks about?" Like the one she felt with Ryan. "The one Mom claimed burned out too fast."

"I suspect it's not about the strength of the spark, Els," her brother said, his words pensive. "But instead, it's about actively choosing to keep that spark lit. Choosing love first. Always."

Choosing love. Always. Elsie closed her mouth and rolled her lips together.

"And if one person doesn't want to put love first, how can it work?" There was a pause then her brother continued, "Sometimes love is about letting go. When, sadly, you know your love won't ever be what the other person truly needs."

Her brother was talking about his ex-wife. The one he'd loved and let go for her happiness. Elsie was hesitant. "Bryce, how do you know when to let go?"

"When you both stop wanting to fight for love and your partnership," he said quietly.

Elsie squeezed her eyes closed.

"But, Elsie." Her brother's voice was strong across the speaker. He added, "You have to fight for love first."

She'd fought. Hadn't she? *No.* Not exactly. She had walked away from Ryan. Driven away. Fled to New York. She hadn't wanted to take a risk on love. Hadn't wanted to stay and fight for what Ryan and she might be. She'd been out before she'd ever been in. But she loved Ryan.

I love him. But she hadn't given love or him a chance. She hadn't given them a chance. *I love him.*

Everything inside her suddenly settled as if falling into place. She loved Ryan. She wasn't tumbling. Or hurting. Or running. She was ready. To love.

Elsie snapped her eyes open and picked up her phone. "Bryce."

"I'm still here," her brother said.

"Send me those numbers for the farm today," she said, an urgency to her words.

"Does this mean..." her brother started.

"It means I've made my choice, Bryce," she said, her smile drifting into her words.

She was going all in on love. It was time to win her cowboy and his heart.

CHAPTER TWENTY-FIVE

A PILE OF dresses lay on Elsie's bed. Several more were draped over the back of the love seat couch. A longer black satin gown hung on the open bathroom door. Panic about what to wear to the charity gala that evening had driven Elsie out of bed too early for a Saturday morning. Within minutes of waking, she had most of her closet strewn across her bed. And not long after that, she had more than one open moving box as she'd attempted to locate the co-ordinating heels for her formal outfits.

For the past hour, she'd been trying on and discarding one gown after another. Finally, she'd given up, propped her tablet on the short kitchen counter and dialed for help. Now Tess and Maggie were on video chat, considering and eliminating one dress after another.

Elsie twirled in front of the camera then stopped and set her hands on her hips. "What about this one?"

"That dress is nice." Tess sipped a cup of tea.

Beside her, Maggie frowned and shrugged. "But that's all it is. Nice. There's no flash or sparkle or anything memorable about it."

"But it's formal," Elsie argued and trailed her fingers over the nondescript deep navy sheath gown that lacked a bold plunging neckline. Or a daring open back. Or even a shimmery sheen. She added, "In my defense, I'm usually working at these events too. So, my outfits need to do double duty. It's not easy to clear buffets or help my people in a princess ball gown."

"That's it, Elsie." Maggie lifted her hands, pointed at the screen and smiled wide. "You should wear a princess ball gown tonight."

Elsie scanned her dresses. "I definitely don't own one of those."

"Time to go shopping." Tess smoothed her hands over her very pregnant stomach and sighed. "I wish I was there. I love a good shopping day. I want one after these babies arrive. Ladies, promise me."

Maggie and Elsie both laughed. Elsie walked closer to the camera, leaned in then said, "Tess, we promise to take you on a full day of pampering and shopping after the babies are born."

"Wonderful." Tess picked up her cup and fiddled with the tea bag. "Now back to you, Elsie. I'm afraid you need a new gown for tonight."

Elsie's shoulders drooped. Her frown followed. "I was worried you were going to say that."

"It's fine." Maggie waved her phone at the screen. "I've already been looking up dress stores near you ever since you put on that not quite salmon, but not really orange dress earlier."

Tess laughed. "Definitely don't wear that one, Els."

"I already explained that. The dress was part of my putting-color-back-into-my-wardrobe phase," Elsie said, but she couldn't quite stop her own laughter from spilling free. She reached out and touched the not quite silky, not quite satiny fabric and shook her head. "Although I'm not sure why I chose to start that color change with this dress."

"Well, there's nothing wrong with classic, bold colors," Tess said and grinned. "Besides, Elsie, it's you that brings the color to everything, not the gown."

"That's a very kind thing to say," Elsie said.

"It happens to be true." Tess toasted her with her teacup. "And remember, if you can't name the color immediately, maybe it's not the dress for you."

"Good advice." Elsie dropped an oversize sweatshirt over her head and let her dull strapless gown slide to the floor in a puddle. Much like her enthusiasm. But her mind wasn't on shopping and ball gowns and galas. It was on winning back her cowboy.

"We can't be there, but we can guide you." Maggie paused then grinned a satisfied grin. "There. I just sent you the addresses to three highly rated boutiques close to you."

"Call us when you've narrowed down your options," Tess ordered. "We will be here on standby and can help you decide."

Elsie pulled the black sheath gown with cap sleeves off the bathroom door and held it up in front of herself for one last shot. She asked, "Are you certain this won't work?"

"No." Maggie shook her head. "Sorry, Els. It looks like a bridesmaid gown."

Because it was. She'd worn the dress years ago for a former college roommate's wedding. Elsie shoved it back into her closet.

"You're going to a black-tie event as a personal guest of Dr. Lilian Sloan, Elsie," Tess said, her expression thoughtful, her words firm. "You've got to level up, Els."

"What if I made up an excuse," Elsie offered. She hadn't told her two friends about her plans yet. She was still working out the details with her brother. And she could use the evening to finish finalizing her strategy before she presented it to them for their input. She already knew winning back Ryan was going to be a team effort.

Alarm filled both women's faces.

"You have to go, Els." Maggie shook her head. "You can't bow out on Lilian."

"Right, she's your mother-in-law." Elsie nodded. "And Lilian has been really kind to me since I arrived." She reached for her purse. "Looks like I'm going shopping."

Maggie and Tess cheered, wished her luck then ordered her to text as soon as she had options for them to consider. With that, Elsie tied her running shoes, checked her phone for the first boutique's address and headed out.

Two hours and a dozen dress samples later, Elsie twirled around in an elegant sequined royal blue gown. The hemline swept just so across the floor. Her tablet was propped on the dressing room chair.

"Do you feel like a princess?" Maggie asked. "You certainly look like one from our view."

"Yeah, I kind of do," Elsie admitted and propped her hands lightly in the pockets on the skirt. She couldn't quite believe she'd found a dress in her size that fit so perfectly. As if it was meant for her. She said, "That sounds silly, doesn't it?"

"No. It's perfect," Tess gushed. "And everyone deserves to feel like a princess, Elsie, especially you."

"Well, your compliments make me feel like royalty," Elsie said then smiled into the camera. "I think this is the one."

"Now, find yourself a pair of fancy slippers and head to the ball," Maggie said. Enthusiasm stretched across her face. "Who knows? You might even meet your prince tonight."

Her prince. He was back in Texas. Elsie held on to her smile and said, "I'll stick to feeling like a princess tonight and attending that gala."

"Whatever you wish." Maggie waved her hand as if she held a magic wand. "It's your night. Just have fun."

"Don't forget to send lots of pictures," Tess ordered. "So I can feel like I'm at that ball with you."

Elsie thanked her friends and disconnected. She'd head to the ball and, like a fairy-tale princess, skip out early. After all, she still had a cowboy, not a prince, to win.

RYAN SLIPPED HIS arms into a black tuxedo jacket and walked over to the full-length mirror in the guest bedroom at his mother's penthouse flat in New York City. He stared at his feet. Dress shoes were polished and gleaming. The tuxedo pants pressed perfectly. The waistcoat vest buttoned. The silver cuff links his grandfather had surprised him with were in place and secure. He adjusted the silk lapels of the formal jacket. Then finally looked at his face.

Gone was the thick beard. Gone was the shaggy hair that had touched his collar. The wavy strands were cut and styled, not smashed and flattened on his head from his cowboy hat. Gone was the cowboy.

Ryan inhaled. Exhaled. Considered the tuxedo again. Not bad, he decided. And if it helped him convince Elsie to let him love her forever, well, he might consider wearing it all the time.

He turned around, felt the stiff insole of the dress shoes cut into his foot. Then amended that thought about all the time. He'd wear the fancy tuxedo but with cowboy boots. After all, he could be polished up, but he'd always be a cowboy.

He picked up a black slender necktie from the bed and left the bedroom. He stopped in the doorway and took in his mother standing at the floor-to-ceiling corner windows across the flat. She wore a floor-length black gown with brilliant white lace and sequin embroidery on the top that extended down her arms. She looked elegant, attractive, and yet there was a shadow of loneliness wrapped around her. Nothing obvious, but perhaps he saw it because he'd felt the same too without Elsie.

He looked at his mom and decided then he'd do whatever it took to find her a home near Three Springs. Perhaps then she too might find a way out of that shadow of loneliness. He walked farther into the room and cleared his throat.

His mother spun around from the windows and gasped softly.

Ryan held up the ends of his slim black silk tie. "I need some help with this and then I think I'm ready."

His mother smiled affectionately and walked over. Her movements graceful and effortless even in her formal attire. She said, "I'm surprised your grandfather or grandmother didn't teach you how to properly tie a tie."

"They tried." Ryan touched his cheek. Surprised when he felt skin and not his beard. That would take getting used to. He added, "But I never paid much attention. Never thought I'd have to put one on."

"You wore a tie for Maggie and Grant's wedding." His mother eyed him.

"Only for the ceremony and photographs. And Grant tied it for me." Ryan grinned. His family always stepped in to help him, but they weren't there now with him in New York. It was surreal that his mother was. And she never once hesitated to assist him. She'd jumped right in and offered a few tips of her own. He cleared his throat again. "Thanks."

"I'm not an expert like your brother and grandfather, but it'll do." She adjusted the knot then smoothed her palm over the tie. Her gaze was tender, her words warm. "I wouldn't have believed it was possible for you to be any more handsome than you already were."

Ryan took her hand and squeezed her fingers. "When

I said thanks, I meant for all this. For everything you're doing for me."

"Thank me after you win back Elsie." His mother tipped her chin and regarded him. "Otherwise, I won't feel quite so good, and you might not feel quite so grateful."

Ryan didn't release her hand. Instead, he tucked her arm around his and said, "Whatever happens tonight, I appreciate this and you, Mother."

"That's quite lovely to hear." She reached up and touched the corner of her eye. "I'm delighted you asked me. Now, shall we get to that gala?"

"I can't think of any place I'd rather be," he said, certainty in his words.

Wherever Elsie was, he wanted to be.

CHAPTER TWENTY-SIX

ELSIE SMOOTHED HER hands over the sparkling skirts of her gown and took in the crowded ballroom. One circuit. That was her plan. She'd complete one full circuit of the ballroom. Greet guests, check on her staff then make a quick exit. She needed every minute for her win-back-her-cowboy strategy. Hearts were at stake. And she wanted it to be foolproof. That wouldn't happen at a gala.

Even if she did feel slightly like a princess. And the chandeliers sparkling over the dance floor made her want to indulge in a waltz. With a prince. That she still needed to win back first.

Elsie navigated to the far end of the ballroom away from the dance floor. There the buffet tables were arranged and the food presented exactly to her specifications. She was more than pleased with how the event turned out, especially given the tight timeline. She greeted one of the catering staff then moved in to shift empty appetizer dishes around.

"I was told you would have enough staff here tonight," a familiar voice said behind Elsie. The woman added, a hint of amusement in her words, "I was also assured that you wouldn't need to work."

Elsie brushed her hands together and turned around to greet Lilian Sloan. "I was just checking with my staff quickly."

"You were working, dear." Lilian chuckled and waved

her hand lightly in the air. "I won't tell anyone, but tonight can't be all work and no play. There's little joy in that."

But if she was working then she wasn't dwelling on a certain cowboy. Her host's son, in fact. Wondering where he was. What he was doing. Was he thinking about her too? She had already spent the car ride over trying to decide which rodeo he was competing in that weekend. She'd narrowed it down to possibly Santa Fe, New Mexico or Colorado Springs perhaps.

"Come with me, dear." Lilian wrapped her arm gently around Elsie's and guided her effortlessly back into the crowd. "There are some people I'd like you to meet."

Lilian stayed by Elsie's side the entire time and completed one introduction after another. Each one thoughtful and insightful about the guests. The chair of the foundation's board was an accomplished CEO, but an even more talented violinist. The director of the cardiac unit at the local hospital was a forerunner on cardiac advancement, but also a trivia expert. And on the introductions went. Soon Elsie had a champagne glass pressed into her hand and she was looking forward to meeting the next person to discover their unexpected talent. There didn't seem to be a person Lilian Sloan wasn't acquainted with. It was impressive, even more so was her poise and elegance.

Elsie sipped her champagne and enjoyed a lively debate about the latest superhero movie from several of Lilian's colleagues.

"Oh, if it isn't Elsie *please-dance-with-me* Marie Parks," a male voice drawled behind her.

Elsie lowered her champagne flute without taking a sip. Her heart suddenly raced. Her palms suddenly felt damp. She very carefully, very delicately turned around on her brand-new three-inch strappy heels.

Let it be him. Please.

Her gaze collided first with a tuxedoed chest. Her breath caught.

Please. Let it be him.

She lifted her chin. And gaped. Mouth wide-open. Eyes even wider.

Her cowboy was there. He was there.

Only her cowboy looked like he had stepped out of the pages of a men's fashion magazine. Picture-perfect. Impeccable. Handsome. Her gaze traveled all over him, yet she couldn't seem to stop staring. Finally, she swallowed and found her voice. "Ryan." She blinked at him, barely held back from reaching up and touching his smooth cheek. "You look more like a prince than a cowboy."

"That was the plan." One corner of his mouth hitched up into his cheek, revealing a dimple. "I wanted to show you I can fit into your world, if there's room."

Room. Elsie wasn't certain there was enough room to breathe. Her cowboy was there. Within reach. And how had she forgotten he had dimples? *Dimples.* Once again, she found herself speechless.

"Elsie Marie, may I have this dance?" he asked, clearly not struggling for words. "In truth, I want your first dance. Your last dance. And every single one in between, but we have time for all that." He held out his arm, opened his hand. Then he leaned closer. "By the way, you look absolutely stunning. I would've gotten to you sooner, but I had to catch my breath first."

That's what she needed to do. Catch her breath. Everything seemed to be happening so fast. She eyed her champagne flute, wondering what to do with it.

Lilian eased the crystal glass from Elsie's grip and smiled warmly at her. "It's time to find the joy portion of your evening, my dear."

With that, Elsie set her hand in Ryan's. And finally

found her anchor. Found her center. She linked her fingers with his. Found her reason.

He led her to the dance floor, turned to face her and drew her into his arms.

"Ryan. What are you doing here?" She braced her hands on his shoulders and held herself back to look into his eyes. "Not that I'm not thrilled." And stunned. Delighted. And nervous. Anxious. All those feelings Ryan stirred inside her came rushing back through her.

"I promise to explain." He curved his arms around her waist. His touch gentle, yet secure. "But can I please have this dance? I missed you, Elsie."

His confession softened her. The affection in his gaze melted through her.

Elsie moved fully into his embrace. Close enough to feel his heartbeat under her cheek. At the end of the song, Elsie held on to him and said, "Now it's my turn. Dance with me, cowboy, and let me hold on to you."

"Whatever you want." He tucked her even closer into his embrace then added, "This is your night."

It was a dream come true. But too soon the song drew to a close. And Elsie knew dreams ended and dreamers woke, even princesses. She walked with him off the dance floor toward the wall of windows where the music and crowd were muted. Where it seemed like it was only her and only him. Elsie eyed him. "Ryan, what rodeo is here this weekend? I didn't see one even close to here."

"I was supposed to ride in Santa Fe this weekend." He rubbed his cheek then pulled his hand away as if surprised at the lack of a beard. "But I pulled out."

"Why?" Her gaze drifted over him. "Are you injured? I saw you ride last weekend. It was clean. You weren't thrown on either day."

"You watched me?" He grinned at her and leaned closer. "Elsie Marie, are you following me?"

"I've been following Maggie and Vivian on the circuit," she said. And checking up on him every chance she got. In truth, she'd seen every single one of his rides more than once. There was something fascinating about watching her cowboy compete. The strength. The determination. The dedication. It was all a part of him.

"To be fair, it seems I'm following you now." He tucked his hands behind his back and watched her.

She did the same. Clutched her hands behind her back. But she really wanted to reach for him. Pull him back to her. But he was holding himself away. "What do you mean?" she asked.

"I'm here for you, Elsie Marie." He motioned toward the crowded ballroom. "I'm here to prove I can fit into your world."

Elsie's throat tightened. Was he giving everything up for her? "But what about the rodeo?"

"You're more important to me." He stepped closer to her and held her gaze if not her hand. "What we have is more important to me. I don't want to lose you, Elsie. I want to be wherever you are, whether it's New York or the North Pole."

Elsie searched his gaze and saw only sincerity on his face. Heard only honesty in his words. "What are you saying?"

"What I should've told you the night before you left." He wound one arm around her waist. His hand connected with hers and linked. "I love you, Elsie Marie Parks. I want to share a life with you. Put down roots. Have a family. I want all of it with you."

"Ryan," she said. "Are you sure?"

"That I want a life outside the arena with you." He pressed their joined hands on his chest. "With all my heart."

Tears swelled in Elsie's eyes. For this man who'd given her his heart. For the love she had for him. For the gift he was. "I love you, Ryan Sloan."

He pressed his forehead against hers. His eyes closed briefly then he focused again on her. There was a sheen in his gaze. "I won't ever get tired of hearing those words."

"I love you," she said again. Felt him sigh. Felt his heartbeat steady and strong under their joined hands. She straightened and curved her other arm up around his neck. "Will you be happy here?"

"I'll be happy with you," he said, confidence in his words and resolve in his expression. "And if that's here then I'll make it work. I want to make us work, Elsie."

So did she. Very much. She chose them. She chose love. She asked, "What if I told you there's this other place I'm considering?"

"Yes," he said, without hesitation. Without pausing.

She laughed and squeezed him tight. "You haven't heard anything about it yet."

"Will you be there?" he asked.

She nodded.

He pulled her into his embrace. Lifted one shoulder and said, "Then that's all that matters."

Oh, how she loved her cowboy. She brushed her fingers against the back of his neck and considered him. "Let me tell you about it anyway."

He pressed his lips against hers. Gentle. Tender. Perfectly. Then he grinned and said, "Sorry, I'm listening. I've just been wanting to do that since I saw you."

She framed his face in her hands and leaned in for a longer kiss. One filled with love. One that promised lifetimes.

That joined two hearts. Slowly she pulled back and smiled at him. "I've been wanting to do that since I saw you."

His quiet laughter shook his shoulders. "I love you, Elsie Marie Parks."

She pressed her hand on his chest, held him in place. "I can't think when you kiss me. And I want to tell you about this place."

He shifted, pressed a kiss to her cheek. "Absolutely."

She took a deep breath and dived in. "There's land. Quite a bit. That we'd need to tend together. Are you okay with that?"

He nodded.

"And a stable that needs updating if we decide on more horses," she continued and held his gaze. "Hives that need looking after."

He shifted slightly. Suddenly alert. His focus fixed on her.

Oh, she had his full attention now. She added, "And there's a rather large house. It needs work too. And it has rooms that need to be filled."

"Filled," he said, his voice low.

"With family and friends." She lifted one shoulder, tried to sound indifferent, but failed. "Kids, one day. It's a house that wants to be a home. That's when it's happiest."

His gaze lit. His slow drawl stretched out. "Is that so?"

"Yeah," she said. "So, what do you say, cowboy? Do you want to build a home with me there?"

"Every day," he promised and held her impossibly close. "Every day I choose you, Elsie Marie."

She smiled at him. Felt love swell inside her. Finally knew where her happy was. It wasn't a place. It was what she shared with him. It was the life they would build together. She kissed him and said, "And I choose you, my cowboy prince."

Today. Tomorrow. Always.

EPILOGUE

One Month Later

"Do YOU HAVE the ring?" Caleb turned from the window in the wheelhouse barn where he was keeping watch for Elsie and her nieces.

Ryan patted the front pocket in his jeans. "It's in my pocket."

"Well, pull it out," Caleb ordered and closed the distance between them. He motioned to Ryan. "We have to see it. You have to know you have it."

Ryan glanced around the barn, filled with his family and Elsie's. Everyone looked at him expectantly. Several even nodded as if to encourage him to display the ring. He obliged, slipped the ring box carefully from his pocket and opened it.

"Put it away," Caleb said, looking suddenly worried. "You don't want to drop it."

"And whatever you do, do *not* drop it in the stream either." That from Grant.

"I won't drop it," Ryan said then tucked the box back into his pocket.

"Do you know what you're going to say?" Maggie stood in the shelter of Grant's arms and smiled at him.

"I imagine I'll say..." Ryan started.

"Don't." Caleb cut him off then added, "Don't tell us. Save it for Elsie."

Ryan eyed his younger brother. Watched Caleb pace around the barn, weaving in and around the others. He looked restless and nervous. But that should be Ryan. He was the one proposing. He set his hands on his hips and stepped in front of his younger brother's path. "Caleb. What is wrong with you?"

"This is about Elsie." Caleb tugged at his wavy hair. "Elsie is like my little sister, Ryan. I taught her to dance. This has to be perfect."

No pressure there. Ryan eyed his sibling.

"I taught her to drive," Carter offered from his post near the ladder to the loft. "It does need to be perfect."

Not his big brother too.

"I shared my books with her." Grant grinned. "And it really needs to be perfect."

Of course, Grant would join in. If only his other brother Josh was there, he could add to it. Ryan took it all in stride. His brothers would watch over Elsie like their own sister. That was more than enough. Once again, he was grateful for his family.

"And she really is my baby sister." Bryce turned around from the window and eyed Ryan. "So, they're right. It has to be perfect. It's one of those important life moments she'll remember and talk about."

He would too. And if it wasn't perfect, they'd talk about that as well. Hopefully laugh about it and keep as one of many memories they'd gather in their life together.

"Don't be nervous, big brother." Caleb dropped his hand on Ryan's shoulder. "Then you will drop the ring in the water."

Ryan seemed to be the calmest one in the barn. He had Elsie's heart. And Elsie had his. There was nothing to be nervous about. Nothing to second-guess. Nothing to question. He knew what he wanted. Who he wanted. For the first time, he knew the future he wanted. He said, "I'm not going to mess this up. I promise. Elsie is my everything."

"Don't tell us." Caleb squeezed Ryan's shoulder. "Save it for Elsie."

Ryan saw his mom press a tissue to her eyes then hand another tissue to Elsie's mom and one to Marlena. Grandpa Sam and Uncle Roy joined the three women.

"I had a great plan to tell Elsie, but you all wanted in." Ryan eyed his brother.

"We had to make sure it was perfect for Elsie." Caleb shrugged and walked back to the window to stand beside Bryce.

Ryan had talked to Bryce, Elsie's mom and her aunt about his intentions and asked their permission to marry Elsie. He would swear he hadn't made it to his truck when they'd called his family and told them. He'd arrived home to find his family waiting for him with ideas and suggestions for his proposal.

Fortunately, Ryan already had a plan, and the two families were more than willing to help him with the proposal. Of course, that hadn't stopped any one of them from offering advice and tweaks to make it better. More special. Perfect, as it were.

"Okay, it's time. Elsie and the girls are in the dandelion field." Bryce motioned to the door. "Get to the bridge, Ryan. And don't drop the ring."

Finally. Ryan eased out of the barn. He heard Autumn, Gemma and Elsie laughing and talking in the dandelion field next to the barn. He snuck around the corner of the barn and headed for the new bridge spanning the stream. Quickly and quietly.

Although he would've liked to shout his love for Elsie

to the fields. He didn't care how it looked. He wanted the world to know he loved one woman. Cherished one woman. He'd tell everyone and anyone who wanted to know. But first, he wanted to tell Elsie. Because when he cut through all the noise only one person mattered. *Elsie*.

Ryan waited in the center of the new bridge and rested his arms on the railing. The wheel spun slowly behind him. The water splashed and trickled over the rocks and along the stream bed. The sun was out. The sky that perfect blue. And the winds were more breezy for once. Finally, he watched Elsie round the corner. Gemma and Autumn waved to him before slipping inside the barn together.

And Ryan's day was suddenly perfect.

Elsie slowed and paused. She shielded her eyes from the sun. Then her grin spread wide. Her excitement filled the warm air. And she ran. Straight to him. Right into his arms.

"Where did this bridge come from?" she asked and caught her breath. "It's like artwork."

"I built it," Ryan said. "With a lot of help from our families. It joins our families' lands together."

"That's lovely." She ran her hand over the smooth railing. "I'm going to want to spend a lot of time out here with you."

"I'm counting on it," he said.

"Wait. What are you doing here? I got so distracted by this bridge." She framed his face, checked him over as if worried something was wrong. "You're supposed to be in Arizona competing."

"It's next weekend," he said.

"No." She shook her head. "I have it in my calendar for this weekend."

He captured her hands in his before she could pull out her phone and check. "You had it in your calendar for this weekend because that's what I told you."

Her eyebrows pulled together. "Why would you…" Her voice dropped away when he dropped to one knee. "Ryan."

"It's not easy to surprise you," he said. "You know all our calendars better than we do."

"That's so I can look after everyone better," she said.

"And we all appreciate it," he said and squeezed her hands. "Now I want to look after you and your heart, Elsie Marie."

She bit into her bottom lip. Her chin quivered. Tears filled her eyes. Her words sounded water soaked. "You already do."

"But I want it all, Elsie." He held her gaze. "The kids. The family. The roots."

Those tears spilled free.

"And that all starts with you becoming my wife." He reached into his pocket and pulled out the ring box. Opening it, he said, "Elsie Marie, will you marry me?"

Her reply was part laugh, part sob. She was in his arms before he could slide the ring on her finger. He dropped back onto the bridge and cradled her on his lap. Then poured all the love in his heart into their kiss.

The kiss slowed, but their love only strengthened. Right there on that bridge that connected two families. Joined two hearts.

"I think I was supposed to wait for you to put the ring on my finger." Elsie twisted in his lap and held out her hand. "I'm ready now."

Ryan slid the diamond ring onto her finger and heard

her small gasp. Then she whispered, "It looks like something for a princess."

He lifted her hand, pressed a kiss to her fingers and smiled. "A city princess for a cowboy prince. Sounds perfect to me."

* * * * *

WESTERN

Rugged men looking for love...

Available Next Month

The Maverick's Thirty-Day Marriage Rochelle Alers
A Cowboy For The Twins Melinda Curtis

Fortune's Lone Star Twins Teri Wilson
Her Temporary Cowboy Tanya Agler

LOVE INSPIRED

Safe Haven Ranch Louise M. Gouge
A Cowgirl's Homecoming Julia Ruth

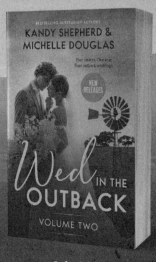

Subscribe and fall in love with a Mills & Boon series today!

You'll be among the first to read stories delivered to your door monthly and enjoy great savings.

WE SIMPLY LOVE ROMANCE

MILLS & BOON

JOIN US

Sign up to our newsletter to stay up to date with...

- Exclusive member discount codes
- Competitions
- New release book information
- All the latest news on your favourite authors

Plus...
get $10 off your first order.
What's not to love?

Sign up at **millsandboon.com.au/newsletter**